AT THE Waterfall

Smardline S.

Copyright

Thank you!

I just want to say thank you for taking a chance on *At the Waterfall*. This story means the world to me, and I'm incredibly grateful that you're here, ready to dive in. You'll find themes of **anxiety, panic attacks, grief, guilt, the loss of parents, and reincarnation** woven into these pages. And yes, for those of you wondering—there's open-door spice, too.

Playlist

Zac Efron & Zendaya/Rewrite the stars.
Taylor Swift/labyrinth
Taylor Swift/August
John Legend/U move, I move.
H.E.R/Damage
Coco Jones/ICU
John Legend/Nervous
H.E.R (feat. Daniel Caesar/Best Part
Sam smith/Latch (acoustic)
Taylor Swift/A place in this world.
Benson Boone/Before you
Billie Eilish/BIRDS OF A FEATHER

Spotify playlist.[1]

---

1. https://open.spotify.com/playlist/4KfO73FtVR56js2OsJ80TT ?si=32a82fe1e06e479f

Dedication

You deserve someone who loves you fiercely and unconditionally. Never settle for less. But until then, it's okay to have fun. For love, there is no need to rush. It will come to you when the time is right. Be a waterfall. Embrace the fall.

Hey there, welcome to the cabin. I'm glad you're here—it's quiet, peaceful, and exactly the kind of place where you can get lost for a while. Trust me, I'll make sure you enjoy the stay. ☺ Kick back, spread those pages, and settle in for the ride. I'll be waiting by the waterfall when you're ready.
Oh, and for the girly who doesn't usually like a blonde MC—I promise, by the end of this, I'll have changed your mind.
-Jake-

Prologue

The Forest

Summer 1924

"I can't do it." Her voice broke the silence like a fallen branch. "I can't run away with you."

His turn was sharp, confusion mirrored in his eyes, reflecting the green of my leaves. "Why?"

She trembled under the weight of their reality. "What if we're caught? What about my godmother? They're not ready for us, Eadrick. Our love is too much for this world."

Eadrick and Ifunayla had dared to dream of a future together, fleeing from a world that demanded they remain apart. However, their worlds were parallel lines, not meant to be crossed.

He was the heir to the richest family in the north. She, an orphaned black servant with no legacy but her courage. Her birth claimed her mother's life, and her father remained a shadow she'd never known.

He pulled her close, their tears blending with the sound of the cascading water. "I love you so much." She sobbed into his embrace, the weight of their impending separation breaking her. "I can't bear the thought of you living a life I'm not part of. Or you with someone else, kissing her the way you kissed me, making love to her..." Her voice faded into the rustling leaves. I felt her heartache as palpable as the chill of the night that settled over my canopy.

"Ifu... My Ifu," he murmured, drawing back just enough to look into her eyes. Gently, he wiped her tears with his thumb, kissing the trails they left on her cheeks, and then her nose. Despite the agony tearing through her, his tender gesture coaxed a small smile from her. She always loved it when he did that. "I could kiss no one the way I kiss you. My kisses are whispers of my heart to yours. And making love... I could never make love to anyone but you because you're the only one I'll ever love. A life without you...without us...is unimaginable." He drew her even closer, their bodies pressing together as if to meld their souls into one.

"If we forget, maybe it won't hurt as much," she whispered. "But know, even if my mind forgets, my heart will forever hold you."

The surrounding air, filled with the scent of pine and earth, whispered memories of laughter and promises, now overshadowed by the pain of a goodbye neither was prepared for.

With a silent agreement, forged from a love too vast to be confined by memory, they prepared to cast the spell by my waterfall. Following her godmother's instructions, they stood at the water's edge, their love and memories ready to be surrendered to the magic of their necklaces.

Water's flow and moon's glow.
Into these necklaces, we tuck our story.
Each memory of love, laughter, and tears.
Yet, let our souls forever entwine.
In this life and beyond, let our love shine.
Our memories fade, but our souls align.
Bound by a love that defies time.

With nothing left but their love, they leaped into the water below, making love for the last time under the moonlight, fully embracing the magic.

Although they woke up as strangers the next day, their hearts would forever stay connected, entwined in the essence of my leaves and the whispers of the waterfall. I believed that their souls, intertwined with *love, would find their way back to each other, seeking the happy ending they deserved.*

Chapter 1

With every season, I transform, letting go of old leaves
to make way for a new life.
-The Forest-

"I called the school today to check on your scholarship," my dad says beside me as I sit on the bench.

Nothing like, *Hi, how are you?*

It was a matter of time before he found out. Even though I'm not facing him, I can picture his furrowed brow and the tension in his jaw. I rub my hand into my lap, bracing myself for what's coming.

"When were you going to tell me, you dropped out of med school?" The disappointment in his voice is impossible to miss. This is precisely why I didn't say anything.

I glance up at him. Deep brown eyes stare at me. The silver thread on his dreadlocks and beard is more pronounced, as if grief has touched them, too.

My gaze shifts to the mini waterfall mom built in the backyard. She loved waterfalls, another thing we had in common. She carefully picked each rock, making sure there weren't any weird bumps or holes because of my trypophobia. "I already knew how you were going to react. Considering everything that's been going on, there wasn't a right time."

"Did you drop out because of your mom?" Pain seeps through his harsh tone. We haven't talked about her since she passed. This isn't about Mom. It's about me trying to figure out what I want. Not what he wanted me to be.

"Yes, and no. Last year, when we took that trip, I told Mom I couldn't do this anymore. Medicine is not for me, Dad." My throat tightens, and my eyes well up. But I refuse to let the tears fall.

"I don't understand. You chose to study it."

Chose is an understatement when he gave me no choice.

You need an actual career, Mia. Writing is a hobby. Yes, your mom is a successful author. But your mom has a gift.

Even though he didn't say it, his words implied that my mom had a gift, and I didn't. Over time, I've started to believe it. Making me doubt myself.

We never talked about it, but he was one of the reasons I gave up on pursuing a career in writing. I resent him a little for that.

"You said I needed an actual career." *Remember, Dad.*

"Don't tell me you dropped out to become an author." He shakes his head.

"No." My eyes drift to the mini waterfall again. The stream rushes over the rocks, and the sound gurgles as it meets the pond below, filling the air. Dad wanted me to be a doctor like him, but I can't. Not without having anxiety attacks every time we have labs because of my trypophobia.

"I'm not letting you throw your life away, Mia." His words come out sharp, but he takes a moment to compose himself. "I've talked to admissions and explained that you were having a tough time because of your mom. If you return next fall, you get to keep your scholarship."

My eyes find him again, a six-foot-tall black man staring down at me wearing his doctor's coat. My dad can be intimidating when he looks at me like that. "But—"

"No, but. You have the summer to figure out what you want to do with your life." He places a hand on my shoulder, gently squeezing it before walking away.

Nothing like, I love you?

Figuring out what I want? What is that exactly?

His footsteps fade into the distance. My dad is a great man, the best of husbands. My mom was his universe. He always brought her flowers and her favorite macaroons from the only bakery she loves, which is a 45-minute drive from our house. He's everything I want in a husband one day. I just wish he was a better father.

Although he was born in the US, he grew up in a Haitian household. He believes in tough love and what they think is best for their kids, so you're raised to become a doctor, a lawyer, or a nurse.

I missed the relationship we had when I was a little girl. He was my hero. Even when he worked long hours at the hospital, he would always make time for us. As I grew older, we grew apart when his expectations of me overshadowed everything. I hated how it was all about what he wanted, never what I wanted.

Closing my eyes, I take a deep breath. The fresh scent of jasmine from the garden and the sound of rushing water are comforting. But inside, I'm drowning in her memories. My heart pounds against my chest as her absence suffocates me, making it hard to catch my breath.

When rocks get in your way, be a waterfall. My mom's words replay in my mind, a reminder to keep moving, to flow over the rocks that stand in my way and carve out my path.

My head tilts back, eyes searching the blue sky; too clear, not a single gray cloud to mirror the storm raging inside me.

Is any of this even real? It's been three months, yet it seems like yesterday.

I sit there for a few minutes before walking back inside the house, my feet leading me of their own accord. I mindlessly pass by the fireplace, where Mom and I spent countless hours lost in a book.

Then, we have the wall with the family portraits. Pictures of me as a baby, my high school graduation, and Mom and Dad smiling as he lifts her off the ground. Her curls fall over her shoulders. My mom is French, with beautiful light brown skin, brown eyes, and curly hair.

Turning around the corner, my hand reaches for the knob, the metal cool under my fingertips. Moving closer, the window is open with a view of the garden.

There's a desk in front of it with a laptop and piles of papers. In the corner, there's a bookshelf. I haven't been here since Mom passed. This is the room where all the magic happened.

On top of the piles, there's a box, and it's addressed to me. I move towards it to get a closer look. My fingers trace her handwriting. The fear of what's in the box tightens my throat. A rock blocking my airway, making breathing hard. The walls are closing in on me.

I pull my hand away, placing it around my neck and the other on my hip, forcing myself to breathe.

I can't do this.

My hand reaches for it again, then pulls back, tensing into a fist. I'm not ready to find out what's inside.

Instead, I walk over to the bookshelves, running my fingers along the smooth spines of her published books. Many of which are best sellers.

My eyes keep glancing back at the box. My fingers itch to open it, but what if what's inside changed everything? What if it makes me miss her even more? It's the last thread connecting me to her, and I'm terrified of what might happen if I pull it.

Returning to the desk, I pace back and forth in front of the box. Staring at it like a bomb that may go off any second now. I stop, shaking both my hands to ease the nerves.

I got this.

Just open the box, Mia.

Here we go. I move closer and open it, my hands trembling.

Inside are letters, each with a different title. The first one says *Open First*. I grab it and sit on the small couch in the corner, wrapping myself in the throw blanket that still smells like her.

I open the letter, my eyes scanning her beautiful handwriting.

Salut mon amour.

C'est Maman.

The words blur as tears pool in my eyes. I press the letter to my chest, curling into a ball as if I can somehow bring her back to me. For a second, I pretend she's here with me.

Coucou Maman.

Chapter 2

Mia

*"The fog may blur the path, but the
Land beneath remains the same."*
-The Forest-

I take a quick look back at the house while Dad puts my suitcase in the trunk. Everything looks the same except for the flowers on the porch, which are less bright than before. My mom used to water them every morning. I can still picture her sitting there, sipping her café au lait and eating a fresh croissant from the only French bakery she loved.

My dad would wake up early in the morning just to get them for her before work. I must admit, sometimes I wish he loved me as much as he loves her, or he loves me in his own way.

The trunk closing snaps me back to the present, and I turn around to face him.

"Are you sure about this?" He raises his eyebrows.

"Yes, Papa." I nod. *Papa* is what I used to call him as a little girl. Now, it feels a bit foreign. "You said I had a summer to figure this out, right? That's what I'm doing." I don't tell him about the box I found in Mom's office, and how she booked that cabin for me. It was as if she knew I was going to need it. She always knew what I wanted before I did. You can call it Mother's intuition.

He takes a slow, steadying breath before his lips part. "Be careful. Rylee is meeting you there, right?"

"I'll be careful, and yes, she is meeting me there." Another white lie.

My best friend, Rylee, was supposed to come with me, but she got this marketing internship job that she'd been wanting at one of the top marketing firms in New York. They wanted her to start right away. She's worked so hard for this. I'm thrilled for her.

My dad rarely shows his emotions, so moments like this feel different. He hugs me, and I melt into him. His hugs are the best. I've missed them.

"I love you, Papa," I say into his chest, even though we don't always understand each other.

"I love you too, sweetheart." He kisses my forehead. The scent of his aftershave and laundry detergent wraps around me, taking me back to when I was a little girl. I've missed those moments, and I hate how our relationship has changed over the years.

When I went away for college, we barely talked. I only came back home because my mom got sick.

He pulls away and shoves his hand into his pocket.

In the car, I settle into the driver's seat. The cold leather presses against my back as I run my fingers over the necklace I've had since I was fourteen. It was a special gift from my mom; her mother originally gave it to her and passed down from my great-grandmother, Ifunayla.

It's beautiful, with an emerald crystal that glows softly in the light, which pairs nicely with my black tourmaline necklace. It's the only thing she kept from her old life in France.

According to my mom, the emerald crystal is supposed to attract my true love. Spoiler alert: it hasn't worked. The black tourmaline is for protection. Given that I'm about to be alone in the woods, it better work overtime.

I glance at Dad and the house before starting the car. His worried eyes follow me, making it even harder to leave.

My eyes catch the little Haitian flag hanging around the rearview mirror. My grandmother on my dad's side gave it to me. I pull down the visor to check my face. My hair hasn't been deep conditioned in a while, and right now, my curls are looking crazy. But all I can see is her. The shape of my chin and the curve of my nose are undeniably hers.

Tears threaten to spill, but I blink them away, my vision blurring momentarily. My hands grip the steering wheel.

"You got this, Mia," I tell myself before driving away.

I'm heading to a little town called Pearl Mountain in the middle of the Vermont forest, far from everything.

It's perfect.

Despite growing up in New York City, nature has a way of calling my name. My mom and I used to take those annual girl trips to celebrate our birthdays. Mine is in June, and hers is in July. She would rent a cabin in the woods, and we would spend our time getting lost in books by the fire.

Those moments are pieces of my soul. It was our tradition.

But this time, I'm leaving alone, and she's gone.

The tears I've been holding back finally escape, burning my eyes and making it hard to see. I blink rapidly, but they spill over, tracing hot, stinging paths down my cheeks. I quickly wipe them away with the back of my hand, sniffing softly. Taking a deep, shuddering breath, I struggle to regain control.

Be a waterfall. I repeat those words to myself.

I should cancel everything. My grandmother on Mom's side invited me to stay with her in Paris. I should go there instead. My fingers flex and tighten around the steering wheel as another sob breaks through.

But Mom planned it before she died, and she already paid for everything. She wanted me to go.

This cabin is a place to mourn, heal, and figure out what I truly want. This is more than just an escape. I'm hoping the quietness will help me write again.

That was her last wish, to find my passion.

Growing up, writing was my passion. I wrote my first story when I was ten. It was about a magical waterfall. A secret place where I could read, and no one could find me.

My dream was to be a best-selling author like my mom. Then, I realized she was one of a kind, and I would never be as good as her.

As I drive, the city fades in the rearview mirror, replaced by the calm of the countryside. Fields of green stretch endlessly, deepening into dense forests. Occasionally, the trees open to reveal fleeting views of distant mountains, their rugged outlines etching the horizon.

I pull down the window and inhale the fresh air. The scent is a mix of pine and a hint of moss, a wild perfume that calms my mind.

After three hours on the road, I'm ready for a break and pull into a small gas station. It's an older place, standing off the main road, with a handful of pumps. The sign is fading, and the paint is peeling off.

On the right, I see a beige building that resembles a motel. It looks like something straight out of a thriller movie. My imagination runs wild: *A young lady in her 20s, traveling, stops in the middle of the night and checks into the motel to rest before she starts her journey again the next day. While she's taking a shower, she feels like she's not alone. Something or someone is watching her.*

I laugh, shaking my head before getting out of the car and stretching my legs to ease off the cramps from the drive. The air smells of gasoline and distant rain. I head inside for a quick bathroom break, then grab some snacks and water on the way back.

At the counter, I pay for everything before stepping back outside. Lost in thought, I bump into someone entering the store, scattering my snacks on the ground.

"Oh, no." I squat down to pick them up. He's already helping, and our hands touch over my Snickers bar. I look up and meet with beautiful eyes, the most unique shade of green I have ever seen. The color of a forest after rain. And for a moment, I'm lost in them, unable to look away.

A hint of stubble softens his strong jawline. His tousled blonde hair gives him a carefree look. A tight, short, black-sleeved shirt highlights his broad shoulders and well-defined biceps. "Thank you, and I'm sorry," I blurt out. My voice comes out embarrassingly high-pitched to my own ears.

Standing up, I'm acutely aware of how hard my heart is pounding in my chest. He's staring at me, a slight twitch at the corner of his eye as if he's trying to solve a puzzle laid out in the lines of my face. His brow furrows, the green of his eyes darkening with concentration.

I walk away, but his voice stops me. "You forgot your Snickers." I turn around as he hands me my last snack bar. Our hands touch, creating that spark again. His green eyes pull me in, and I'm lost in their depth.

You're staring.

"Thanks again." I tuck my curls behind my ear, my throat dry, causing me to swallow my spit. "I like sweet treats." Oh God, why did I say that?

"I can be sweet." A smirk plays on his lips.

Is he flirting with me?

"I like chocolate," I laugh nervously while holding the Snickers bar.

"What about white chocolate?"

It takes me a second to understand what he meant. My cheeks heat up. "Um, depends on what kind."

"I'm the only kind you'll ever need," he looks me up and down, not even bothering to ask for my name. He's not interested in that.

Usually, I hate it when guys hit on me like that. But for some reason, I'm not. At least not coming from him.

Maybe it's because there is something familiar about him, as if I know him from somewhere else. Which is weird. I'm confident I would remember someone like him. Those green eyes would be impossible to forget.

"Well, uh, thanks again." I quickly walk away, mentally kicking myself for being awkward. His chuckles follow me, making my face burn hotter.

My hands shake as I hold the pump, my mind replaying the moment over and over. Sneaking a peek back at the gas station, he's laughing, holding the door open for a woman walking inside, and she laughs back at him.

An effortless charm about him seems to draw people in, me included, apparently. We study each other again, freezing the world in a silent standoff. I look away first, cap the fuel tank, and slide inside my car, my heart still racing.

I glance in the rearview mirror one last time, half-expecting to see him, but it's just the black Jeep parked behind me. "Get a grip, Mia." I sigh, then start my R&B playlist. The music eases the flutter in my chest as I shift into drive, merging back onto the road.

Chapter 3

Jake

"Even in the darkest corners of my woods, the promise of dawn keeps hope alive, waiting to burst forth with the morning sun."
-The Forest -

The morning light filters through the floor-to-ceiling glass windows. I stir awake and feel someone beside me, whose name I don't know.

"Hey, you need to go."

She blinks, her blue eyes widening in surprise. A hint of hurt flashes across her face, and a pink blush colors her fair skin. Silently, she gathers her things, runs her hands through her blonde hair, and leaves, closing the door softly behind her.

Alone again, I head to the shower, letting the water wash over me, hoping it might cleanse more than just my skin.

My mind races, thinking about the drive to Pearl Mountain, Vermont. I grab the soap, pour some in my hands, and rub it over my body. The smell does nothing to quiet my thoughts.

Boston has been my home for six years now. After high school, the city offered a fresh start where I studied business. That's what my father wanted, but really wished I wouldn't need to use it any time soon. Then he died six months ago, and my mom has been managing the hotel.

We own a boutique hotel in Pearl Mountain, Vermont. This charming place has been in our family for generations. It was once a grand mansion, now turned into a boutique hotel.

I wanted nothing to do with it. This was his world, not mine.

Growing up, I hated how the hotel claimed all his time and attention, leaving scraps for us. Later, I found out he had other reasons for not spending time with us, but still, I wanted nothing to do with managing it. I crave the adrenaline of the outdoors, not sitting at a desk going through spreadsheets.

The droplets of water hit my back. The conversation I had with my mom the other night replays in my head, along with the tears she held back. *"You know this stuff, Jake."* Her words linger. *"The hotel needs you. I need you. Don't do it for him. Do it for us."*

My jaw clenches at the thought of taking over the hotel, a bitter taste filling my mouth. The water turns cold. The icy spray hits my skin, causing me to gasp, and my body to shiver.

It's a temporary distraction but doesn't stop the memories from breaking through. I remember staying up late to show him my Boy Scout badges—the way my heart would pound with anticipation, but I'd fallen asleep waiting. All that was for him not to be there the following day when I woke up.

I close my eyes, letting the water wash over me, steeling myself for the responsibilities I can't escape. The hotel is struggling, and Mom has no idea what she's doing. If I don't step in, the next conversation might be about selling, and the finality in her tone told me it's a prospect she dreads as much as I do.

After turning off the water, I step out of the shower and grab a towel to dry off. Then, I put on gray sweatpants and a T-shirt. I grab my bags, making sure I don't forget my laptop for work, my camera to capture content for my social media page, and my climbing gear. Everything gets loaded into the Jeep. These items are more than just gadgets; they're extensions of my passion and go along with me everywhere.

I climb into the driver's seat and start the engine. Hitting play on my go-to playlist before hitting the road. Each mile takes me farther away from the city and closer to the mountains.

The thought of climbing those mountains brings a weird comfort. There's something about the physical pain, how my muscles burn with every push upwards. It's straightforward, a distraction that lets me pretend I'm in control, keeping the real, gnarlier stuff at bay for longer.

Two hours into the drive, I pull over to grab a snack and fill the tank. I walk inside the store to grab a protein bar and a water bottle.

I'm standing in line when this woman walks in. My eyes are drawn to her as she approaches the restroom.

She's wearing high-waisted shorts that cling to her curves perfectly, and I've never wanted to be a piece of fabric so much in my life. The back of her shirt says, *"5'3", but my attitude is 6'3".*

I laugh as she disappears into the bathroom. Her waist is slim, but her bottom is not. She's thick and sexy—or I need to upgrade my vocabulary because sexy is not enough to describe all of that.

"Sir, are you in line or not?" A woman says from behind me, snapping me out of my daze.

"Sorry." I smile at her and then walk toward the cashier to pay for my stuff. "Thanks." I grab my bag and receipts and walk back to my car.

Putting the bag in the passenger seat, I realized I didn't pay for my gas.

Shit, I guess I got a little distracted.

Turning around, I head back inside. I'm about to open the door when someone bumps into me, their snacks scattering across the floor.

My hand grazes as we reach for the Snickers bar, sending me a jolt of unexpected electricity. Looking up, I am met with large, doe-like brown eyes, thick black eyebrows, and a pretty round face framed by beautiful curls staring back at me.

It's her, the woman with the sexy ass.

"Thank you, and I'm sorry," she sounds embarrassed.

My gaze lingers on her longer than it should. She is like a memory just out of reach. My brow knits in confusion as she walks away, snapping me out of my thoughts. Her Snickers bar is still in my hand. I call out to her, and she turns around as I hand her the snack bar.

"Thank you," she says again, tucking her curls behind her ear. She visibly swallows, and my eyes follow the movement from her throat to her chest. She has nice size boobs. Not too big, not too small, perfect enough that I could cup my hands around them.

I flirt with her a little, enjoying how her cheeks darken, giving her a pretty, natural look. Her eyes are a bit reddish as if she's been crying, but they're so pretty and mysterious. Her scent, something sweet and flowery, fills the space between us.

"Well, uh, thanks again," she stutters. I chuckle as she walks away, her steps hurried. My eyes follow her, and damn, that *ass*.

I stand there, still puzzled, wondering why she feels like someone I should know. Pretty sure I would remember her and that *ass*.

The Forest
Summer 1912

In the quiet sanctuary of my ancient trees, two young souls met, and like the first whisper of spring, something new and irrevocable took root.

Eadrick, his skin as bright as the sun, always seemed more at peace in the forest than in his own mansion. Ifunayla, her skin as radiant as the moon, new to these parts of the forest, cautiously felt her way around. There was something about her. Whenever she was around, I always felt this energy bleeding through my soil and my trees.

She was by the stream, aimlessly tossing pebbles into it. Eadrick, who often roamed my depths, stumbled upon her.

He stood there for a few seconds, watching her before speaking. "Hi, there."

She turned, startled, her expression then warmed up.

"I've never seen you before. Do you live around here?" He edged a little closer.

"Yes, but you can't tell anyone you saw me. Can you keep a secret?"

"Okay." He nodded.

"My name is Ifunayla, but you can call me Ifu." Her tone was friendly and hesitant.

"Hi, Ifu, my name is Eadrick." His eyes sparkled with a sense of camaraderie. He held out his hand to her.

She looked down at his hand, hesitant, before reaching out to shake it. "Hi, Eadrick." A genuine connection sparked between them. And I felt a surge of energy enveloping them both like a bubble. Making me feel alive more than ever before.

He stared at her as she threw a pebble into the stream. "What are you doing?"

She picked up another pebble. "Just throwing these into the stream. It's calming, see?"

"Can I try?" A big grin spread across his face as he bounced in anticipation.

She handed him a small rock. "Sure!" They threw the rocks side by side at the same time. Their laughter echoed into my canopy.

"This is so fun," Eadrick laughed.

"It is. Each ripple is almost like its own little story. It starts small and then grows wider." She laughs; the sound was like a melody.

His eyes widened as he stared at her. "I never thought of it like that."

They both laugh. Their laughter was music to my leaves. I couldn't put a leaf on it, but something felt different at that moment.

Their friendship was just a bud, yet deep down in my roots, I sensed that their story would be intertwined with mine for years to come.

For decades, I've been waiting, and now I feel it again.

Chapter 4

Mia

Whitney Houston's *I Will Always Love You,* plays through the car speakers, and it brings back memories of road trips with my mom. Where we'd sing along, off key, and laughing, especially during the high notes which we could never quite hit. My mom was good at some things like writing and swimming, but cooking and singing, not so much.

My mind drifts back to one of those road trips with Mom.

"Come on, sing with me!" Mom shouted over the music, her eyes sparkling with joy as she drove.

I laughed, shaking my head. "You know we can't hit those notes, right?"

"Doesn't matter! It's about the feeling!" she said, her pitch rising to match Whitney's.

"Okay, okay!" I joined in. The car filled with our laughter as we tried to outdo each other, hitting the highest notes with exaggerated drama.

Mom glanced over at me, her face glowing with happiness. "Life is a song worth singing, no matter the pitch." She winked at me.

My phone ringtone interrupts the song, breaking through my memory. I glance at the display and see Rylee's name pop up. The bittersweet memory fades as I tap the screen to answer.

"Hey girl," I mustered some cheer into my voice.

Her laughter comes through the speakers. "Hey, how's the drive? Having fun?"

"It's just me and the road. How's it going with the internship?"

"It's good so far, even if right now I'm just bringing coffee to very handsome men. But I can't wait to learn more."

Even as I listen to Rylee stories, the pain lingers, a dull throb in my chest. I missed singing with Mom, even if we were terrible at it.

Be a waterfall.

Our conversation stretches on for nearly an hour, with me on the receiving end, soaking in her stories and plans.

"Send me pics when you get there? Will you?" I can almost picture the pout on her face.

"I'll spam you, promise," I assure her, a grin tugging at the corner of my mouth. "And hey, thanks for calling. I needed the company." We say our goodbyes and I am left with the silence in the car.

Less than an hour later, I turn onto a dirt road leading to a driveway, with gravel crunching under the tires. Trees line each side, and a mountain rises behind the cabin. My breath catches at the sight before me. It's bigger than it appeared in the pictures online. I shift the car into park and turn off the engine.

"Holy shit," I blurt out. The cabin, no, the glass adobe, is nothing short of stunning. Its sharp, precise structure is a stark contrast to the wild, untamed nature that surrounds it. The lower walls, painted an earthy dark brown, blend seamlessly into the forest, becoming a natural extension of the trees. Above, the upper floor is black, surrounded by glass windows.

I stand there for a moment, taking it all in. The tranquility of the place, the way the house seems part of the forest and a world apart, is exactly what I have been craving. This place feels like *home*, as if I've been here before.

Approaching the door, I press the code into the keypad. Stepping inside leaves me speechless again. The layout flows seamlessly from the living area to the kitchen, to the dining room, all unified by the warmth of wood, as if the forest itself has extended indoors. The vast glass windows erase any boundary between us and the greenery outside.

I climb up the stairs to the second floor. There are two bedrooms. I step inside the first bedroom and freeze; floor to ceiling windows bring the forest so close, it's almost as if I could reach out and touch the trees.

A queen size bed sits against the wall, facing toward the windows. There's also a balcony which provides a view of the mountain. Stepping out onto it, I lean against the railing, inhaling in the fresh, pine scented air. Closing my eyes to take it all in.

The sound of gravel crunching under tires snaps me out of my tranquility, and my heart leaps to my throat. I race downstairs, the sight through the glass freezes me—a black Jeep, unmistakable from the one at the gas station. Did someone follow me?

My first instinct is to call 911. Shit, my phone is upstairs. Why do we always make stupid decisions in those situations? I run into the kitchen and grab a knife. My hands tremble, and all those scary movies I've watched are flashing through my mind. I should have listened to my friends. But I will not die in the woods, at least not without a fight.

Making my way back towards the living room, I freeze, the sound of my heartbeat pounding in my ears as the door handle turns with a soft click. Eyes wide, watching the door slowly push open. Whoever it is, knows the code. Or did I forget to lock it?

"Stay where you are!" I shout; the words are weak in my mouth.

He stops, his intense green eyes shifting from the knife in my hand, and then back to my face. His lips part as if caught mid-breath, followed by a heavy silence.

"What are you doing here?" I grip the knife tighter, not sure what I'm going to do with it, but needing something to hold on to. I wait for him to explain himself.

Instead, he bursts out laughing. It's a rich, warm sound that, despite my annoyance, sends an involuntary tingle down my spine. His eyes linger not just on the knife, but they scan my face, a trace of an unreadable smile still playing on his lips. That same smile from before.

"What are you going to do with the knife?"

I don't know yet.

He's tall, his presence commanding. Muscles outline his shirt. And here I am, barely five feet three, staring at him with what I hope is a menacing glare, hoping to wipe the grin off his face.

"Did you follow me here?" I force some kind of intimidation into my tone. That's the only explanation I can come up with. He must have followed me from the gas station.

His eyebrows shoot up, and he seems taken aback by my question. "Follow you? I had no idea anyone would be here." The sincerity in his eyes catches me off guard.

My grip on the knife loosens, but I'm still confused. "Why are you here, then?"

"I should be asking you that." He tilts his head at me. "Maybe you like white chocolate after all."

Seriously. I roll my eyes at him.

"Well, I couldn't possibly have followed you here. I was here first."

I don't know when he moved, but he's closer now.

"Maybe you stalked me on Instagram. I did post about coming here. It wouldn't be the first time a girl has stalked me. But usually, it's after we've had sex." He crosses his arms, and it annoys me that my eyes are staring at his flexing muscles. The confident smirk on his face only adds to my irritation.

"Wait, what? Stalking you? I don't even know who you are. I'm here because my boyfriend and I rented the place. He should be here any minute." My eyes inadvertently seek him for a fraction too long.

Shaking his head again, he steps closer. "That can't be. It wasn't supposed to be rented out. I'm staying here for the summer."

"Huh?"

"This is my family's place, and no one was supposed to be here, but me." He looks at the knife, then back to my face. "Can you put the knife down so we can figure this out?"

There's no reason for me to trust him. For all I know he could be lying, but I believe him.

I place the knife down on the kitchen counter, keeping my distance. "Let me grab my phone." I turn to walk upstairs to grab the confirmation email and everything.

His footsteps are trailing behind me. Turning to face him, our eyes lock again in a silent conversation, causing a fluttering sensation in my chest. I narrow my eyes, telling him to back off. It's not that I think he's still a threat, but it's been a weird day and I'm not comfortable with him following me upstairs.

He receives the message loud and clear and stops in his tracks. "Okay, I get it. I'll wait for you down here." He raises his hands up.

I nod and continue upstairs, my heart pounding for reasons I can't fully understand.

Once I'm in the room, I grab my phone off the bed and remind myself next time I'm in the woods, and receive an unexpected guest, make sure to grab my phone before running downstairs. Better yet, don't run downstairs, call 911 instead. This could have turned out worse.

I scroll through my emails, finding the booking information. My fingers tapping on the screen are a little too hard. It's all there: the dates, the cost, the house details. When I go back downstairs, I find him pacing the room. His phone pressed to his ear, his movements restless. He runs his hand through his hair repeatedly, the strands sticking up in wild directions.

"Yes, Mom, she's right here, and she said she booked the place..." His volume increases before he catches himself.

He shakes his head as the conversation on the phone seems to deepen his frustration.

"Okay." He lets out a long-drawn-out sigh and ends the call. He looks momentarily lost, staring off into the distance.

"So," I say, breaking the silence.

He snaps his attention back to me, locking eyes with me before he speaks. "There was a mix up, and they listed the wrong house."

Observing him now, he doesn't seem intimidating anymore. He appears more defeated; his eyes, a vivid forest green before, have dimmed. Again, there's that odd sense of recognition when I gaze into them. It's like a song I can't remember. It's on the tip of my tongue, yet miles away.

"What now?" I say more to myself than to him.

"I need to stay here." His tone leaves no room for argument. "I'll give you a full refund and even offer you a room at no charge in my family's boutique hotel nearby."

"What? No, I booked this place. So, I'm not leaving."

She wanted me here.

"You don't understand—"

"No, you don't understand. I don't want a refund or another place. I'm staying." She booked this place for me. She knew I needed this place.

"For what? A romantic getaway with your boyfriend. Don't worry, you can have the honeymoon suite"

"You don't know what I need." My voice is louder now, angrier. "And I'm not leaving." I cross my arms, standing my ground, yet I'm acutely aware of his presence.

"That makes two of us," he says with an unnerving calmness, his eyes never leaving mine; a challenge lingers in his eyes that I find both infuriating and intriguing.

"You can't stay here!" I don't want him here. I don't need that kind of distraction.

He steps closer, a smirk playing on his lips. "Don't worry, I won't get in the way of your romantic getaway. You can fuck your boyfriend all you want. Just pretend I'm not here."

He turns to walk away. "Wait! Does that mean you're not leaving?"

"This is my cabin. I'm not going anywhere. You can stay, or you can leave."

"If you're staying here, I want fifty percent of my money back. And I call dibs on the bigger room."

"Sure, whatever." He shrugs, looking over his shoulder. And walk upstairs.

"Asshole!" I mutter under my breath, my hands clenching together.

This situation is far from what I planned. I hate the way my skin turns into lava and my stomach twists into knots when he looks at me. It's infuriating how a simple glance from him can make me feel so exposed. I don't even know his name, but *Asshole* fits him perfectly.

Chapter 5

Jake

"Asshole," she says as I walk upstairs. I stop and turn around to look at her. Her brows knit together, her lips form a thin line, and her hands tightly clenched at her sides. Those brown eyes pull me in for a second, holding me captive. Shaking my head, I force myself to continue walking. This confrontation wasn't part of my plan.

In my room, I lie back on the bed and stare at the ceiling. My feet press on the floor and cross my arms under my head. The cover feels cool against my skin as I let out a sigh.

Well, that took a turn.

The image of her eyes flashing, and her lips trembling as she tried to control her anger, replays in my mind. I shouldn't find it attractive, but I do. Damn it, Jake, get a grip.

Back at the gas station, I wanted her, but now that's out of the question.

There are a few rules I go by. I don't sleep with the same woman twice. We don't exchange names or numbers. They only stay over if I've had one too many drinks. And we definitely don't share a cabin. So how the fuck did I end up sharing a cabin with the woman downstairs?

I sit up, running a hand through my hair, before checking my watch, and it's already 5 p.m. I need to clear my head before taking a shower. Normally, I'd prefer a climb, but my body needs something less intense after the long drive. A quick run will do for now. I grab my earbuds and start my playlist before heading out.

Outside, I take a few minutes to stretch properly, and then I begin my run at a steady pace. My heart rate picks up, and the world falls away. The only thing I need to worry about is the next breath, the next step, but my mind keeps drifting back to the woman back at the cabin.

I push harder, and my legs burn as I try to outrun my thoughts. She is a distraction I didn't ask for. It's unnerving how my heart races, as if I'm hanging at the ledge of a mountain, or how my skin prickles with a sharp, electric sensation when she stares at me with those big brown eyes.

I should focus on why I'm here, to be closer to the hotel. A place to strategize and brainstorm renovation ideas while still close enough to the mountains.

But I can't get her sassiness out of my mind and the fire in her eyes when she called me an asshole. I've only known her for a couple of hours, and she's already under my skin. She is unpredictable, and I hate it. I am a control freak. It's part of why I love climbing.

I could leave. That would probably be the better option. She looks like a walking complication, the kind I usually avoid at all costs. But the alternative is even worse. I don't want to spend a second more at the hotel than necessary and staying with my mom means facing memories I'm not ready to confront. The hour-long drive from her house to the mountain is inconvenient.

My hands clench into fists, and my nails dig into my palm. Running usually helps me clear my mind, but not today.

When I head back to the cabin, sweat drips down my forehead, and my muscles scream. My lungs burn with each breath. I pause at the door; my hands rest on my bent knees while I take a few deep breaths to gather myself. Straightening up, I head toward my room. The last thing I need is to bump into her or the boyfriend.

I desperately need a cold shower to cool my mind and body, so I walk into my bathroom. I strip off my sweaty clothes and toss them in the laundry basket. My watch comes off next, and I carefully set it down next to the sink. My hands reach behind my neck to remove my necklace.

It's an emerald crystal pendant. I've had it for years; it's a family heirloom. My grandfather gave it to me, and although I don't believe in his story about it helping me find my soulmate since I don't think soulmates are real, it's nice to have a piece of him with me. It goes next to the watch.

I turn the shower knob, adjusting the water temperature so that it's cool enough to be refreshing, but not too cold to shock me. The initial blast of cold water is exhilarating, a jolt that invigorates every sense. I sigh in relief, closing my eyes to enjoy the sensation, the water sluicing off the sweat and fatigue.

The last time I was at the cabin was during my senior year with my friends Alex, Sarah, and Jessie, though I don't want to think about Jessie right now.

Alex, Sarah, and I have been friends since kindergarten. We're like siblings, even though Sarah is a year younger. She started kindergarten at four and was the smallest kid in the class—not just because of her age, but because she was petite. When one of the bigger kids was picking on her, Alex and I stepped in to help at the same time.

We've been inseparable ever since, even when we're miles apart.

After the shower, I dry off quickly, wrapping a towel around my waist. Stepping out, I grab my phone off the sink to text Alex and Sarah. Life took us in different directions after graduation. Alex and Sarah ended up in Los Angeles, while I moved to Boston for Harvard and stayed because I fell in love with the city. They're back in town for the summer. Although it's a two-hour drive from the mountains to Burlington, spending time with them is always worth it.

Ready to leave, I pause outside her room. The house is still quiet—no sign of her or the boyfriend she mentioned. Part of me wonders if I should check in on her. Earlier, I might have come off too harsh.

My knuckle reaches for the door before I stop myself. What am I doing? I don't even know this woman. A text from Alex distracts me, bringing an involuntary grin to my face. I get in the car and drive to the bar where we're meeting. Tonight is about good food, some drinks, and catching up with my best friends.

The place is alive with music and laughter as I walk in. There are red velvet booths in private seating areas, paired with marble-topped tables and plush stools, giving it a classic, luxurious vibe. The walls are dark, creating a cozy ambiance. A gorgeous stained-glass ceiling that gives off a warm, inviting light.

As I approach, Sarah is lounging on the couch, drink in hand, completely absorbed in her phone. A smile naturally curls at the corners of my mouth. Sarah is always punctual and the first to arrive. "You started without me," I call out playfully, snapping her attention away from her screen.

"Jake! You're here!" Her eyes light up as she stands to greet me, wrapping her arms around my waist for a warm, enthusiastic hug. Even in her heels, she barely reaches my chest, her head tilting back to meet my gaze.

"It's good to see you, too." My smile mirrors hers. Her bubbly energy, as always, is contagious.

"Looks like I made it just in time," Alex says, coming up from behind me. I turn around, meeting the grin on his face. We give each other a solid handshake, followed by a quick pat on the back. "Good to see you, man. "

He looks over at Sarah, his smile widening as he opens his arms for a hug. He embraces her warmly, holding on longer than needed.

We take our seats, with Alex next to Sarah and me across from them. It's good to have the gang together again. There's something different about catching up in person beyond our usual group chats.

On the surface, we're all so different, but I consider them family. I would do anything for them. Sarah is Blasian, her mom is from the Philippines, and her dad is African American. Alex's parents adopted him as a baby. He was told his biological parents were from India, but he also looks Italian. I keep telling him to do one of those ancestry tests, but he doesn't want to. He says it doesn't matter.

"So, how's the hotel going?" Alex pulls me away from my thoughts. The mention of the hotel brings a slight frown to my face.

I shrug. "It's going." They exchange glances, a silent communication between them. "I'm going to inspect tomorrow and see how bad it is."

Alex leans forward; his brow furrowed with concern. "You know you have a choice. You don't have to do anything you don't want to."

Technically, I don't. Eventually, I would need to take over, but I didn't expect it to be so soon.

I sigh, laying back on my seat. "I know, but the hotel is struggling, and my mom needs my help." Even though my mom and I are not close, I will not turn my back on her when she needs me.

Sarah leans in too, her almond eyes soften even more, as she looks at me. "We're here for you, whatever you need. Let me know if you need help with some marketing or website stuff."

Alex nods, his hand brushing against Sarah as he moves closer. "We're just a call or a text away." He glances at Sarah before looking back at me.

"Thank you, guys, really." I smile at them, feeling lighter.

That's why I love them so much. They understand me in ways very few people do. We always have each other, no matter what. Besides Uncle Mark, they are the only ones who have always been there for me.

"What's new with you guys? Last time we talked, you were working with that new and hot tech startup company." I turn my attention to Sarah as she scans the menu, even though I'm pretty sure she already knows what she wants.

"It's going great. The company is growing fast." Her whole face lights up when she talks about it. Sarah works in digital marketing, specializing in startups.

The server comes over to take our orders before walking away.

"So, any new famous clients?" I look over at Alex as we wait for our drinks and food.

He smirks. "Well, I'm helping this football player with his injuries, but I can't talk much about it."

Alex is a professional athlete trainer. He helps them after injuries and prevents any future injuries. I know he's worked with many prominent athletes, but he likes to keep who they are a mystery.

"Huh, always the mysterious one." I chuckle. "How did you charm yourself into that?"

Before he can answer, the server returns with our food and drinks. The smell of Sarah's chicken tenders fills the air.

Alex laughs, then shakes his head. "I'm pretty sure I can charm my way into anyone's life."

Sarah giggles, loud enough to hear over the music, and gets a few head turns from some of the nearby booths. "Yeah, right? Just like you charmed your way out of that speeding ticket last year?"

Alex rolls his eyes, his grin widening. "Hey, that cop had no sense of humor."

"Unlike us," Sarah adds as she pokes Alex on the side.

"You mean, unlike Jake? I'm the one who's funny here."

"Oh, please." She tosses a piece of fry at me.

I catch it, laughing. "Okay, okay. You're hilarious."

"Yes, I am."

We all laugh.

I missed this.

"I love you, idiots. But let's plan something soon. It's been too long since we all had fun together. Something epics." Her lips pursed together into a pout.

"Epic?" Alex smirks, his eyes locking with Sarah's. "Like when you tried to climb that cliff and got stuck halfway up?"

"Hey, I made it on top, didn't I?"

"Barely," Alex teases. "Jake had to talk you down from panicking."

It was hilarious. She wouldn't move once she realized how high up, she was.

"Shut up," Sarah punches his arm, which makes him laugh even more.

"Well, do you remember that time in middle school when we skipped class to go into the woods, and you got us lost?" She tilts her head at him. Okay, this was one for the book.

"We promised to never talk about this," Alex groans, rubbing the back of his neck. "Besides, it wasn't that bad."

"Not that bad?" Sarah giggles. "We walked for hours! You swore you knew the way."

In Alex's defense, he was trying to distract Sarah because she was heartbroken over this boy who didn't invite her to the dance. Although he would never confirm it, I think he got us lost on purpose.

"I wanted to show you guys that place I found, but I should have marked the trees or something." Alex tries to defend himself.

"You think?" I shake my head, still grinning. "They grounded us for weeks."

Alex laughs along with us. "Maybe it was a bit of a disaster."

"A bit?" Sarah raises an eyebrow. "What would have happened if those hikers didn't find us? A bear probably would have eaten us!"

Alex's voice softens. "Well, that trip was one of my favorite memories. You weren't sad about that jerk that didn't ask you to the dance."

"Mine too." Her laughter fades into a smile.

As we continue talking and laughing, my attention drifts to a beautiful woman at the bar who smiles in my direction. Seizing the moment, I gesture for the bartender to send her a drink, spicing up the evening.

"Some things never change?" Alex spits out, smiling.

"I got to make the night a little more interesting," I say in amusement. Looking at the bar again, I catch the girl looking at me. She raises her drink with a wink. And that is my cue. "I'll be right back," I say, sliding out of the booth. Alex shakes his head.

Approaching the bar, I sit beside her and lean in slightly. "Thanks for accepting my drink." I try to keep my tone light, yet suggestive.

Her lips curl into a flirtatious smile, and her eyes alight with intrigue. "It was a pleasant surprise. So, what brings you here tonight?" she adds.

"Looking for a good time." I inch closer, my eyes locked on hers. "Seems I might have found it."

"Is that so?" She laughs, her attention entirely on me.

"Yeah, I met the most beautiful lady," I smirk at her. We fall into an easy conversation, our bodies moving towards each other naturally.

Her lip's part, and her eyes drop to mine. Right when I'm about to suggest we take this somewhere quieter, Alex calls me over. This guy has the most impeccable timing.

I groan. "Sorry, I'll be right back."

She nods and smiles. "I'll be here."

I slide off the bar stool and walk back to our booth, where Alex is waiting with a knowing smile. *Cockblocker.*

"You really had to call me over right then, huh?" I narrow my eyes at him before sitting down.

He is grinning, obviously finding the whole situation amusing. "We're leaving," he says, nodding towards Sarah. "We wanted to let you know."

A quick glance at my watch shows it's almost midnight. With a nearly two-hour drive ahead of me and an early start at the hotel, I need to get going, too. We say our goodbyes and promise to meet up again soon.

The girl at the bar catches my attention one last time. Her eyes sparkling, and her invitation so clear. For a second, I'm tempted, but I have to say no. I walk over and apologize once more. "Maybe another time," I say, knowing we'll probably never see each other again.

"I'll DM you," she says, and it sounds like she might actually do it. Which means she already knows who I am. I'm no celebrity, but my Instagram has millions of followers.

With that, I turn and walk out of the bar, and the quiet differs from the ambiance inside. I pause for a moment, taking in a deep breath of the cool night air before heading to my car.

The drive is quiet and feels longer somehow; all the thoughts I'm pretty good at keeping tucked away are trying to dig their way out. With everything swirling around my head, she manages to sneak in. Maybe the boyfriend is here now, and they're probably fucking each other. But again, that is none of my business. I turn up the music to drown out the noises in my head.

Finally, I pull up into the driveway, planning on going straight to bed. But as I walk in, she's in the kitchen, reaching for something. She's wearing an oversized T-shirt that says Moody before coffee on the back. It's a little too short, almost showing her butt cheeks, which I am trying not to stare at. *Okay, that's a lie. I'm definitely staring.*

I move closer, she has on her earbuds and probably didn't hear me coming in. I grab the cup before she does. She turns around, startled, her eyes widening, which makes them look so much bigger now. She punches me in the arm; the sudden contact makes me flinch, and I instinctively catch her wrist. She holds my gaze only briefly before pulling her hand away from me.

"You love creeping up on people, don't you? You almost gave me a heart attack." She pulls out her earbuds, and her breath comes in quick, shallow bursts.

"And you, do you enjoy hurting people? First, you threatened to chop me up with a knife, and now you almost broke my arm." I step closer to her.

She rolls her eyes dismissively. "Oh, please, I thought you followed me here, and then you scared the life out of me, and as for your arm, my knuckles probably hurt more than your hard muscles."

I laugh. "So, you've noticed my muscles?" Standing this close to her, I catch a whiff of her scent, roses and sweet coconut. A smell that is as sweet as it is intoxicating.

"More like my knuckles noticed," she frowns. Clearly, she's still mad. I hand her the cup that is still in my grip.

"I could have gotten it myself," she says under her breath, almost snatching it from me.

"A thank you would be nice." A slight smirk spreads across my face.

She rolls her eyes at me again, and I chuckle. "Why is the Princess up so late? Missing Prince Charming?" The words are out before I can stop them. Her glare sharpens, and I swear if looks could kill, I'd be six feet underground. But she's so easy to tease that I can't stop now. I'm enjoying this too much.

"Don't call me that," she snaps, sharp as a knife. "And it's none of your business." Her long eyelashes flutter, casting shadowy veils over her eyes. She is gorgeous, the kind that can make a guy nervous.

Her irritation and spice just draw me in more. With each step I take forward, she takes a step back until she's flushed against the cabinet. I lean a bit closer. "So, where is this mysterious boyfriend of yours, anyway?"

She hesitates, a visible swallow tracing the line of her throat she probably wishes I didn't notice. "His flight got delayed," she says. A quiver in her voice draws me to her full lips, caught between her teeth. Is she nervous?

Part of me wants to know why she's nervous, but I shouldn't care. I straighten up, breaking the intensity of the moment. "Goodnight, princess," I say over my shoulder. I can feel her stare burning into my back.

"It's Mia," she yells, obviously still pissed. "Don't call me princess."

I chuckle quietly as I head upstairs. Mia, huh? At least now I know her name.

But I prefer *Princess.*

Chapter 6

Mia

The wind whispers and the bird sings in anticipation. New hearts find each other, as old love and forgotten whispers wait to be rediscovered.
-The Forest -

The sound of a blender coming from downstairs wakes me up from my sleep. Early morning sunlight streams through the glass window, forcing my eyes to squint against the brightness.

Groaning, I grab my phone off the nightstand to check out the time, it's only 6 a.m. What the hell? He got back only a few hours ago. Does he ever sleep? Maybe he is a vampire, a very good looking, annoying vampire.

I get up, grab my robe, and shuffle downstairs, still half asleep. He's in the kitchen wearing a tank top that does little to hide the muscles in his arms. Clearly, he works out a lot. *Show off.*

He's pressing down on the blender, the muscles in his arms contracting with the effort. Strands of his hair fall carelessly over his forehead, giving him a boyish charm that contrasts with the rugged definition of his body. Time seems to slow down; everything seems like they're moving in slow motion. He's like one of those models from a protein shake commercial.

His eyes catch me staring and grins. He knows exactly the effect he has, so he's being smug about it.

"Good morning, princess. Sleep well?"

Still with that grin on his face. I roll my eyes, brushing off the flutter in my chest his smile brings. It's too early for this.

"Some asshole woke me up, not even 7 a.m.," I grumble, sleepy and a little irritated. His eyes light up with amusement. A mischievous sparkle dances in them as a wide smirk spread across his face.

He's enjoying this.

"I'm sorry, but I need my protein shake after a workout," he apologizes. I can't tell if he's being genuine or only saying that. "Want some?"

"No thanks, I'll make myself some coffee." I walk past him to the coffee maker.

"Oh God, not coffee." His nose scrunches up in disgust. "I promise this drink will give you more energy, and it's healthier."

"Well, I don't need *healthy*, I need caffeine," I shout back, turning my head to look at him. My eyes fall on his ass. He is wearing a man's workout leggings, highlighting everything. They trace the lines of his muscles, from his calves up to his thighs, which are defined in a way that tells you he doesn't skip leg day, ever.

Then he spins around. My eyes unintentionally catch the detailed shape pressed against his leggings. I should look away, but don't. My throat tightens, my mouth suddenly dries to dust. When I catch his eyes, his smirk is impossible to miss, with his arms confidently folded across his chest as if he knows exactly where I was looking. *Ugh, I hate his face right now.* I scowl at his all-too-pleased expression.

"I need my coffee," I repeat, more to myself than to him, turning my back to compose myself.

"Does your boyfriend know you stare at other guys' cock?" His silky question comes from across the counter.

Seriously? This guy has no filter.

I turn around to face him, and he's already staring at me. "No... I mean, he..." The words are stuck in my throat. Taking a deep breath, I muster a teasing response. "There wasn't much to stare at, really."

"Is that so?" He smirks. "You seemed quite interested a second ago."

"Yes, I was looking, but couldn't find anything..." My eyes drop briefly to his pants, *fuck did it get bigger?* My eyes meet his gaze again. His smile widens knowingly, calling my bluff.

I need to get away from here. "I'm going to take a shower, and don't wake me up before 8 a.m. again, or this blender might accidentally disappear," I warn, brushing past him. His laugh follows me upstairs, a stupidly annoying sound. "Ducon." **Asshole**, I say in French.

Up in my room, I collapse onto the bed and bury my face on a pillow. *Il est un chiant.* **He's so annoying.** *Ugh je le deteste.* **Ugh I hate him.** I scream into the pillow.

This getaway was supposed to be about quiet and writing, not...whatever this is turning into. My phone rings, interrupting my meltdown.

"Hey, girl! I gave you enough time to settle in. Now I need details. How's the house? How's everything?" Rylee bombards me with questions.

I sit up, holding a pillow to my chest. "The place is gorgeous, better than expected."

"But?"

I tell her all about the asshole downstairs sharing the house with me. It all comes out in a rushed tumble of words.

There's a brief pause on the other end before she zeroes in on what apparently matters most. "Hold up. Is he hot?" Apparently, not me sharing a home with a stranger that can be a serial killer for all I know.

I roll my eyes even though she can't see me. "Kinda."

"Kinda? Is the guy hot or not?"

I sigh into the phone, feeling a bit foolish. "Fine, yes, he's stupidly hot. But I don't care," I add quickly, "It doesn't matter, he thinks I have a boyfriend."

"Why would he think that?"

"I told him." I pull out a loose thread from my pillow.

She burst into laughter. "You did what now? Why would you do that?"

I chuckle. "It came out."

"You're okay, though?"

I stare at the ceiling, tracing the patterns with my eyes. "I thought I'd be alone here, Ry. It was supposed to be my escape, a place to deal with everything. And now he's here, and it's a lot." My hands move up my neck, pulling out my necklace from inside my shirt, my finger rubbing it mindlessly.

"I get it. But hey, maybe this guy could be a good distraction? When was the last time you had sex? Your toys don't count."

Rylee doesn't understand. To her, sex is just sex. It's all fun, and she runs away from relationships when things get too serious. I understand her, though. Even if she doesn't talk about it much, I know it's because she didn't have the best examples of it growing up.

She often says men only want one thing, sex, and that's all she wants from them. *Just an amazing orgasm*, her words not mine.

But I want more. Sex is supposed to be intimate, sharing a part of yourself with someone in a vulnerable way. I need to know that person and feel that emotional connection, the butterflies. Seeing myself falling in love with that person before even thinking about sex.

"I don't need a distraction." What I need is some time alone to grieve.

"I know, I'm sorry, sending you a big virtual hug."

"Thanks." I pull the pillow closer to my chest, pretending it's my best friend hugging me.

"Hey, send me a picture of him. I'll do a quick FBI check." She half-jokes, trying to lighten up the mood.

We talk a little more, but as I hang up, the room is even more lonely. The thought of bumping into Mr. Hot Asshole downstairs isn't helping.

I head towards the bathroom for a bath, still in awe of how gorgeous this bathroom is. There's a tub in the middle of it, with black exterior and white on the inside. There is also a stand-in shower on the side. Beyond the glass, the lush forest provides a serene backdrop, the trees swaying gently in the breeze, a view that invites tranquility.

I turn on the faucet, letting the water fill the tub, and add my favorite jasmine soap with a drop of coconut oil. My curls go up into a bun before removing my clothes, dropping them on the floor. Stepping inside the tub, a content moan escapes my lips as I sink into the water.

"Alexa, play relaxing music!" I close my eyes.

Instantly, her image floods my mind, her smile as comforting as ever. "I miss you so much, Mom." A tear escapes my eyes that I quickly wipe it away. The calm is too much, too raw.

"Alexa, switch to R&B." I say, craving a beat. I sing along to one of my favorite songs. *Best Part* by Daniel Caesar featuring H.E.R. I lose track of time; soaking in the lyrics, singing, and letting my sadness go. Until the water gets cold.

After finally dragging myself out of the bathtub, I wrap up in a fluffy towel before applying my favorite jasmine-scented lotion.

Heading back to the room, I dig through my suitcase for some clothes, reminding myself to unpack later. Deciding on some biker shorts and a T-shirt, I quickly dress and fix my hair, then grab my backpack to add in my laptop, a book, and a notebook. With my backpack slung over my shoulder, I leave the house.

And that's when I feel it, an inexplicable pull, luring me to the forest like a magnet. There is a path that leads deeper into the woods, almost hidden by overgrown grass. I follow it, my feet having a mind of their own. The tall trees seem to reach out to me, their branches offering a wooden hug.

The sound of rushing water soon catches my attention, urging me forward. As I get closer, the roar grows louder.

A narrow path leads me to the side of a cliff where the water cascades down the rocks in the pool below. Above, the trees create a natural roof, their canopy shelters the waterfall.

I follow the trail down, where sunlight catches the water's surface, making it sparkle like tiny diamonds. Colorful flowers pop against the lush greenery. The mist lightly caresses my skin, sending goosebumps down my arms.

A mix of pine and moss fills my lung, refreshing and clean. It's almost too perfect. Like a secret place, hidden away. Everything is oddly familiar, as if I've been here before in a dream, or a distant memory.

Why hadn't they mentioned this waterfall on the booking site? There wasn't a single picture of it.

I find a spot near the water's edge, and sit, legs crossed. Pulling out my laptop, I'm ready to spill my thoughts onto a new document. But the words don't come; stuck, blocked by their own fears and expectations. What if I'm not good at it? Can I capture the magic like she did? Can I really write again, knowing she won't be there to read my first draft, to offer her critique and feedback?

With a sigh, I shut the laptop lid. Not now, not yet. It's too soon.

Setting my laptop aside, I pull out the yellow envelope from my bag. Inside, there are many letters, each with a title. I read the first one titled, "Your First Step." That's how I found out about the cabin and all the booking information.

This one is the second; it says, "If You Need a Little Push." I open it with trembling hands. Her handwriting is always so cursive and beautiful. It's written in French.

Salut, ma belle,

Remember that story you wrote when you were ten? As a little girl, I saw the light in your eyes when you talked about the stories you wanted to write, and I felt the passion in your heart when you started writing. You used to lose yourself in the worlds you created. Writing isn't just something you did; it's who you are.

You are a writer.

It tore me apart watching that light disappear from your eyes as fears and doubts took over. If I had in any way made you doubt yourself, I'm sorry. But this is not about me; it's about you. You are more than enough. Your voice, your stories, and your imagination are gifts, and you need to share them with the world.

Not everyone is going to love them. It will not happen overnight. It took me almost five years before I could get an agent and publish my books.

But don't let that stop you. Don't let fear or doubt hold you back. The best stories come from the heart, and you have the most beautiful heart I've ever known.

Be a waterfall, mon amour.

Don't let the rocks get in your way, flow through them.

Je t'aime tellement!

Maman.

Tears spill over, burning my eyes. I wipe them away with the back of my hand, but they keep coming, each one a release of the pain and longing I've been holding back.

It has been a rough couple of months since Mom died. I've been holding my breath, but now everything comes flooding out. The tears fall uncontrollably as memories of her flash through my mind, her laughter, her warm hugs.

Oh God, I miss her so much.

The pain intensifies, each drop pounding against the wall of my chest, drowning the sound of the waterfall. It's as if I'm standing under the cascading water, gasping for air.

I hold my chest as I try to stand up, but my vision blurs. The ground spinning under my feet as I lost control of my balance. Muscular arms wrap around me, catching me before I hit the ground. I scream, struggling to free myself, my breaths coming in short, desperate bursts.

"Get off me," I cry out, "Please, let me go."

But they don't let go, instead they pull me closer. "Mia, it's me, just breathe." A calm voice says, and I know this voice. I like that voice right now. I open my eyes to find a pair of green eyes looking at me, filled with concern. It's him.

"Breathe, in and out," he says calmly.

I follow his instructions, focusing on my breathing, and slowly, air fills my lungs again. He smells of pine trees after the rain. My body relaxes into him, comforting like a warm blanket on a cold winter day. The tears don't stop; they keep flowing, soaking his shirt, my body shaking with sobs. He doesn't say anything; just holds me while I break down.

I shouldn't feel comfortable with him holding me like this. I don't even know him. He's the asshole interrupting my quiet time alone. But right now, he feels anything but that. My body trusts him, like it has known him forever.

We stay in that embrace for what seems like forever before I pull away. "I'm sorry." My eyes stay on the ground. Too embarrassed to meet his gaze.

"Nothing to be sorry for. But are you sure you're okay?" He seems so different from before, as if he's actually worried about me. Why would he care about me? He doesn't even know me.

"I'm fine, but really, you need to stop sneaking up on me."

"I'm sorry. I didn't mean to startle you." His frown deepens. "But you were not okay; you couldn't breathe, and you almost fell."

I steal a quick look back at him, noticing a brief flash of worry cross his face before he smooths it into a casual smile. "Thank you for catching me." I laugh, awkwardly. "I guess I'm light-headed. Missed breakfast, you know, but I'm fine."

"You were crying. That didn't look fine to me."

"I'm fine now." I shuffle my feet, eager to put some distance between us. "And this never happened, okay?" I say, more to myself than to him, before turning to walk away.

"Hey, it's Jake, by the way, since you never asked," he calls out after me.

Jake, huh? I prefer *Asshole*; I chuckle to myself.

Chapter 7

Jake

"Even the mightiest oaks bow under the force of a storm, their leaves trembling, their roots gripping the earth. Yet it's the same rain that nourishes their growth, that fills their veins with life."
-The Forest-

Her laughter trails off as she walks away, curls bouncing with each step. I watch, captivated by the sway of her hips in those biker shorts that highlight her ass so perfectly. The back of her shirt says, *I got the sass and the ass.* I laugh because she sure has both.

My pants tighten at the view as need stiffens my dick. Okay, I need to get laid; it's been two days too long.

I run a hand through my hair, taking a deep, steadying breath. I don't understand how she does that. One second, she's crying, the next she's laughing, which makes me wonder if she's okay. I'm not even sure why I care.

I shake my head, trying to clear my thoughts. Giving her space is best for us both. My gaze shifts toward the waterfall, sparking my curiosity. It's been years since I last visited, yet I'm certain there was no waterfall here before. They don't just appear out of nowhere.

Lying back on a patch of grass, my eyes follow the canopy of trees above. I usually hate the quiet, the stillness, but this is different. It's peaceful. The sound of rushing water in the background is oddly comforting. It's a break from the constant urge to keep moving to outrun the thoughts and the pain I'd rather not face.

Since my father died, I've avoided this darkness that's been swallowing me whole. But right now, I allow myself to sink into the memories.

Growing up, Dad and I were very close. We would go camping, it was my favorite. Those weekends in the woods were magical. Sitting by the campfire, listening to his stories, gazing at the stars while roasting marshmallows, that's what started my love for the outdoors. But as time passed, those moments became rare, then stopped altogether.

He started leaving before dawn and would come back long after I had gone to bed. Days turned into weeks where I barely saw him. Mom would always say he was busy with the hotel, but the tension between them told a different story. Their late-night arguments, muffled by the walls, hinted at deeper issues. His "business trips" over the weekends became more frequent, and I missed the bond we once shared. My resentment grew with every missed birthday and every unattended school event.

Eventually, I learned the truth about why he's never home, and that realization cut deeper than any neglect. That betrayal, more than the distance, changed everything. I couldn't look at him the same way again, and our relationship suffered.

It wasn't the hotel. He found someone else and stopped caring about us.

Sitting up, my eyes drift to the waterfall. I'm a little jealous of it, how it makes falling look so effortless and beautiful. When it's nothing but. Falling is messy and painful. That's why I love climbing; when everything around me was falling apart, climbing gave me a sense of control. I'll never forget my first climb.

My parents had a fight the night before, and the next morning my Uncle Mark truck pulled to our house to pick me up like he always did after their fights. My dad's car was not in the driveway, and Mom hid in her room.

"Hey, Jake." *Uncle Mark crouched down to my level and placed a reassuring hand on my shoulder.* "How about we try something new today? There's an indoor climbing gym nearby. Want to give it a shot?"

I looked up at him, raising my eyebrows. "Climbing? Aren't I a little too young for that?"

He chuckled. "Trust me, you're not, and you're going to love it."

"Okay." I nodded, following him to the truck. Anything to take me away from the house.

We walk inside a gym. My heart pounded as I stared up at the towering walls covered in brightly colored holds. The smell of chalk and the faint sound of people cheering filled the air. Uncle Mark helped me into a harness before buckling me in.

"Uncle Mark, are you sure this is safe?" I looked around. I was the smallest person.

"Yes," *he said, his voice calm.* "Just focus on the next hold. I'll be there to guide you."

"Okay." I nodded. I trusted Uncle Mark.

I reached up, my hands shaking, my palm a little sweaty, making it harder to grab my next hold. Uncle Mark stood below, his eyes following my every move, guiding me with encouraging words. "One step at a time, Jake. You got this."

"Okay," I said. Each movement demanded my full attention, pushing all my fears aside.

My breathing steadied as I found solid handholds and footholds, repeating Uncle Mark's advice in my head.

"One step at a time," I whispered to myself, feeling a strange sense of control and accomplishment with each successful step. The rough texture of the holds pressed against my fingers, grounding me.

When I finally reached the top, I looked down, my heart swelling with pride. Uncle Mark cheered, his face lighting up with joy as he clapped loudly. For the first time in months, I was happy.

Climbing became my refuge, my escape from the chaos at home. It gave me control.

After a few seconds, I pull out my laptop to go over the hotel's financial spreadsheets. It's worse than I thought. We're spending more money than we are bringing in. We have too many empty rooms, and summer is usually when we're fully booked.

I might need to let some employees go, but only if it comes down to it. Most people that work at the hotel relied on the job to support their family. The bank loan we're counting on needs to cover the renovations, but even that seems like a Band-Aid on a gaping wound.

After replying to a few emails and messages, hoping for some financial lifeline, I pack up. Bending down, I grab both my bag and Mia's before heading back.

Reaching the entrance of the cabin, I open the door. Mia is in the kitchen, chopping veggies and singing along to a song on the TV. She's so absorbed that she doesn't hear the door open. She sounds amazing though, a smile lights up her face. Seeing her like this makes my stomach flip. What the hell was that?

"Whatcha cooking?" I lean against the kitchen island, unable to peel my eyes away from her. She looks up and our eyes lock, the smile gone from her lips.

"Pasta," she says, turning her attention back to chopping her red peppers and onions. Next, she adds sausages into the pan.

My mouth waters at the thought. That smells so good. "Will I get some?"

She sighs. "I guess. I can't eat all this food alone anyway, and my dad taught me to share."

"Thanks, be right back," I head upstairs to change my clothes.

On my way back, I grabbed a bottle of wine we had tucked away in a room. Back in the kitchen, there's pasta and salad on the table. This is not the regular pasta I've seen before. It has onions, sausages, green and red peppers. Everything mixes so well and smells delicious.

I take a seat before making myself a plate. "Oh my God," my eyes wide as I take a bite. It's cooked to perfection, with flavors bursting into my mouth, a delightful blend of herbs and garlic. "These tastes amazing."

Her lips curve into a smile. "Thank you."

"What kind of pasta is this?" My mouth muffles with food.

"It's Haitian pasta, my dad taught me." She is smiling.

"I didn't know you were Haitian."

"My grandmother was Haitian."

I nod before opening the wine and pour her some and some for me. For a moment, we are two people talking, eating, and she doesn't look at me as though she wants to stab me.

The doorbell rings, interrupting the moment. "I'll get it," she shouts, eager to open the door. I guess the boyfriend finally made it. That's why she is so happy.

"This is a pleasant surprise." The voice sounds familiar. "Is Jake here?"

Alex? What is he doing here?

I get up and walk towards the door. "Did you get a girlfriend and forget to tell us?" He is grinning at me.

Mia crosses her arms. "I'm not his girlfriend." A look of pure distaste crosses over her face.

A little harsh.

Alex laughs, oblivious to the tension. "Sorry, it's just that Jake's flings rarely stick around. Heck, I doubt he remembers their names."

I grimace, wishing he'd just stop talking.

Her lips press together tightly, and she lets out a small huff. "I'm not sleeping with him either."

"I'm Sarah, and this is Alex." Sarah steps in, saving me from this awkward situation.

"This is Mia. She is staying here for the summer. It's a long story."

Sarah pushes me out of the way, stepping inside the house. She probably smells the food. She never jokes around with food. I don't know how she does it; no matter how much she eats, she still stays so skinny—high metabolism, I guess.

My gaze shifts back to Mia, telling her I'm sorry, but she quickly looks away, heading towards the kitchen.

"Oh my God, this is delicious." Sarah chews slowly, her eyes widening. "You made this?" She takes another forkful, filling her mouth.

Mia nods, twirling the pasta around her fork.

"You're officially my new best friend," Sarah says, wiping her mouth with a napkin.

Mia forces another smile, shifting in her seat. I love my friends, but they have the worst timing.

We eat our dinner, and Sarah chats away as usual, this time about curly hair. No matter how hard I tried; my eyes kept drifting back to Mia. She's quiet, occasionally tucking her hair behind her ears, just like when I first met her at the gas station.

Alex catches me staring and chuckles, which catches Mia's and Sarah's attention. "Now I want to know the entire story," he whispers low enough for only me to hear as he leans closer.

Sarah cuts off whatever Alex was getting at. "How about you boys clean up? Mia and I are going to have some more wine by the pool." She reaches out for the bottle on the table, grabbing Mia along with her.

"Yes, ma'am," Alex and I say at the same time. Sarah might be petite, but she's bossy.

"Women and wine by the pool, that can only mean one thing…"

"Trouble." We both laugh.

I stack up the plates and gather the forks. Alex grabs a dishcloth and wipes down the table while I carry the dishes to the sink. He soon joins me as I load the dishwasher, leaning against the kitchen island.

"Come on, spill it. How did you two ends up sharing a cabin together?" A smirk tugs at the corner of his mouth. He's not going to let this go.

I sigh before sharing everything.

"She was ready to stab you. I think I like her already." Clearly, he's enjoying the image.

Then he pauses, peering at me with a serious look. "You like her, don't you?"

"I like all women." I shrug off his comment, leaning against the counter. But my mind betrays me as images of her keep floating around.

Those big, beautiful brown eyes that seem to stare into my soul, and those curls that bounce with her when she moves. The memory of her calling me an asshole with the right mix of sass and anger almost brings a grin to my face. I catch myself before it fully forms.

"And if she didn't have a boyfriend, and we weren't staying in the same cabin, I would definitely be interested." A slight tightness grips my chest that I can't explain. But I push the feeling aside and mask it with a smirk. "But I don't sleep with the same girl twice, and they don't stay over. I don't want anyone getting attached."

He gives me another side eye. I ignore his knowing gaze, grabbing two beers from the fridge, tossing him one.

We head outside to join the ladies by the pool. The place is a slice of paradise, with a hot tub burbling away to one side and the mountains stretching up in the distance, their silhouettes a dramatic contrast against the twilight sky. The pool itself is a crystal-clear invitation.

I slip out of my clothes, leaving me in my shorts, aware of Mia watching me from the corner of my eyes. I dive into the pool, the cool water great against my skin. Alex isn't far behind.

"Are you two going to join us or keep chatting there?" I shout to the women by the poolside.

Mia looks up at me with a slight frown. "I don't have a swimsuit."

"Who needs one? We're not on the beach. You can go skinny dipping if you like." I throw in a bit of charm, making note of her reaction. Sarah, sitting on the lounge chair next to Mia, leans forward with a knowing smile. Alex, floating in the pool, catches my eye and smirks.

She laughs, a beautiful sound to my ears. "I bet you'd love that?" Maybe it's the wine, but I'm liking flirty Mia.

"Very much!" I wink, giving her a once-over look.

She giggles again. Standing up from her seat and walking over to me. She kneels at the edge of the pool, right in front of me.

Leaning forward, her eyes sparkle mischievously, her lips curling into a teasing smile. "That's never gonna happen," she says loud enough for Sarah and Alex to hear.

Sarah bursts out laughing and claps her hands together. Alex lets out a hearty laugh, splashing water as he does.

Apparently, a few glasses of wine make her bold.

I grin back at her, slowly backing away in the water, my eyes still lock with hers. She clearly doesn't know me well yet–because one thing that I love is a good challenge. This summer just got a little more interesting. I might make an exception just for her.

She and Sarah walk inside. They're probably going to change into bathing suits. Shaking my head with a half-smile, I mutter "Women," under my breath.

Thirty minutes go by before they come back. Not that I'm counting or anything. The moment she steps into view, time slows down, everything else fades into the background.

She stands out like an eclipse, where the moon and the sun converge, her presence in an orange one-piece bathing suit beautifully complementing her skin. The fabric clings to her body, highlighting every curve. Her curls are wild and free, shaping her face. She's effortlessly gorgeous, and I can't take my eyes off her.

Alex chuckles next to me. "You're staring." He nudges my shoulder.

"Go away," I push at him. He joins Sarah on the other side of the pool. Still laughing.

Jerk.

Mia sits at the edge of the pool, her legs swinging in the water, making soft splashes. I swim over to her. "You gonna jump in or what?" I tease with a playful grin. "Unless you don't know how to swim."

Her eyebrows raise. "Are you saying I can't swim because I'm..." She points at herself, not finishing the sentence, but I know exactly what she's trying to say.

"No, that's not... I didn't mean..." I stutter, my brain scrambling for the right thing to say.

She bursts out laughing at the panic on my face. Before I can dig myself into a deeper hole, she jumps into the pool and cuts through the water effortlessly.

I let out a chuckle, relieved she's pulling my leg. "Show off."

She stops in the corner of the pool, and her laughter fades away. Something shifts in her expression as she stares into the distance.

I swim over to her with a sudden urge to make sure she's okay. She's so lost in thought that she doesn't hear me until I'm beside her. "You okay?"

"I'm fine," she snaps back at me even as she brushes away what might be tears or pool water. Her trembling hands betray her.

I swim a little closer. "You're a terrible liar."

Our eyes lock, her shoulders drop, and an invisible wall crumbles down between us. "Why do you care?" Her eyes glisten under the light beneath the pool.

"I don't know...but I do." It's odd caring this much about someone I barely know. Her eyes search mine for a few seconds before she glances down.

She attempts to swim away, to escape the conversations, but I catch her arm. Now, so close. Her chest rising and plunging against the cool water, mirroring my own sped up heartbeat.

"Was it because of your boyfriend? Did something happen?" I search her face for clues.

She shakes her head.

I lean in, our faces so close that to anyone watching, it'd seem like we're about to kiss.

"So, that's a no?"

Being that close to her sparks a thrill that's not just from the cold water but from something electric in the air between us.

My eyes drop to her lips, craving the touch of them against mine. She catches the bottom lip between her teeth, stirring a bold desire to free them myself.

Her next words, though sharp, come out as a breathy whisper. "It wasn't because of him." She edges closer. "I don't need you to care about me. You don't even know me." Bitterness clings to her words.

"Mia."

Her name feels intimate in my tongue. My fingers rest lightly on her arm, sensing the subtle tension beneath her skin.

"Please, just leave me alone." She pulls away from me —the vulnerability in her tone affects me more than it should.

It's unsettling how this woman whom I just met seems to get under my skin. I tell myself to back off, keeping my distance from whatever this is. But deep down, it's a battle I'm already losing. There's something about her pulling me in, and I'm powerless to resist.

Maybe I don't want to.

I don't know.

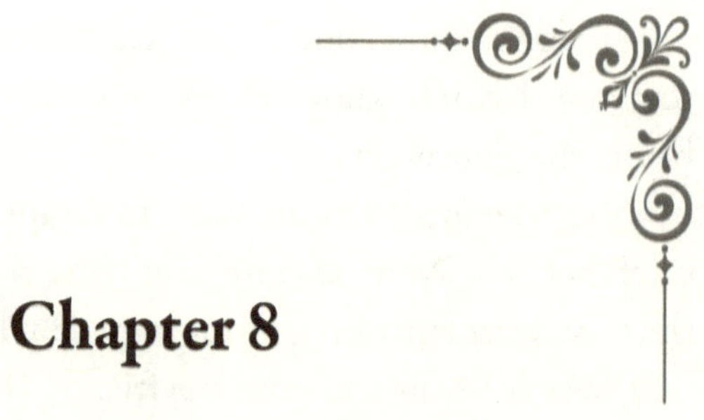

Chapter 8

Mia

I drag my feet upstairs, my heart throbbing in my chest. In my room, I head straight to the bathroom, slamming the door behind me harder than intended. Twisting the faucet, I wait for the water to hit that perfect warmth, a slight comfort. Letting out a heavy sigh, I take off my bathing suit; the fabric clinging to my wet body. Once I'm done, I step in the shower. The warm water is good on my skin, washes away the chlorine water on my body, and my confrontation with Jake.

He really thinks he can get me into his bed by pretending to care about me. I'm not sure how many girls he's used this trick on, but it will not work on me. I overheard his chat with Alex about how he never sleeps with the same woman twice to avoid attachment. If I didn't have a boyfriend, he would be interested in sleeping with me. Boyfriend or not, that will never happen.

Yet, as his gaze lingered on my lips, my heart raced against my will. I don't know if I would have stopped him if he tried to kiss me. The thought lingers, unsettling, as the water continues to fall. How many women does he sleep with, anyway?

After washing my hair, I rinse off, grabbing a towel to dry off. Standing in front of the foggy mirror, I rub my hand over it enough to see my reflection. Deep lines form across my forehead. I inhale and exhale deeply to calm myself down. His behavior shouldn't affect me this much.

I take some time to style my hair into some twists and put on my bonnet. Grabbing a pair of pajamas from the drawer, and putting them on, the soft fabric comforting against my skin.

The house is quiet. Alex and Sarah must have already left. They are nice, and I like them, even if they come a little strong.

I consider staying in my room, but the need for some tea forces me downstairs, even if it means possibly running into Jake. I tiptoe down the stairs, half expecting to bump into him.

Walking into the kitchen, I turn on the light. To my relief, the kitchen is empty. I grab a mug, add a tea bag, and hot water from the water dispenser. But then the soft shuffle of footsteps grabs my attention. He's here, in the same space, and the air shifts slightly. I turn to face him and our eyes lock, and I hate the way my heart annoyingly beats a little faster.

He is wearing black pajama pants with a black tank top. His hands shoved into his pockets.

"Hey," he says, looking down at his feet. He seems unsure, as if he's afraid of saying the wrong thing.

"Hey." I tighten my grip around the mug.

He watches me intently, as if he's searching for the right words. "I, uh…" He pauses, clearing his throat. Those green eyes are staring, and there's something there that wasn't here before. "About earlier, at the pool…, I'm sorry if I crossed a line." He takes a tentative step forward. "I didn't mean to make you uncomfortable. That's the last thing I want."

His apology is unexpected, yet it feels sincere, stripping away the usual facade of confidence and charm. Because of this, I have a glimpse of vulnerability. But I'm not ready to let my guard down.

"How about we just stay out of each other's way? We don't need to be friends." I brush past him, leaving no room for further conversation.

Back in my room, I lean against the door, letting out a heavy sigh. I've never felt this flustered, like ever. In college, there was a guy I dated briefly. I thought he liked me, then he cheated on me. It wasn't so much that I was in love with him, but I hated the fact he cheated rather than just ending things. And the way he did it was even worse. I spent weeks telling myself maybe it was my fault. It's why I've avoided any kind of relationship since then.

I simply don't trust guys like him, or any guy for that matter. I went on a couple of dates before my mom got sick, and all they wanted to do after dinner was to have sex. It's like they weren't even trying to get to know me.

I have no issues with sex—well; not that much experience there. The last and only time I had it was horrible, but I love a wonderful orgasm, and that's what my toys are good for. However, I want sex to be meaningful, with someone I care about, something more intimate than just an orgasm.

The sound of my phone snaps me back to the present, and I look at the screen. "Hey, Papa."

"Hey, sweetheart. How are you doing?"

"I'm good. How about you? How're you holding up?" I walk over to the window, looking at the view of the forest. It's so quiet.

"Keeping busy with work."

I frown. "I get it."

He sighs on the other line before speaking again. "So, there's an open spot for an internship at the hospital. I can talk to them if you're interested."

My grip tightens around the phone. "You said I have the summer to figure out what I want."

"I know, but this is a great opportunity."

For whom, Dad?

"I'm not interested." My jaw hardens as I try to stay calm, a metallic taste filling my mouth. I haven't figured out anything yet.

"Okay, then. I gotta go. Be safe," he says, and then hangs up.

No, I love you. He's not happy I didn't immediately say yes.

I stand there staring at the forest before sliding the glass window open. The cool air hits my face as I step onto the balcony.

Today just keeps getting worse. First Jake, then my dad. I push thoughts of my dad aside, gripping the railing of the balcony. The conversation with Jake downstairs replays in my mind, my stomach twisting into tight knots.

My breath quickens as if I'm trying to breathe through a straw. I grip the railing harder, willing the cool air to fill my lungs, and with each breath, my body relaxes.

The forest is mysterious, reflecting the complexity that is Jake.

I can't stop thinking of him standing in the kitchen, looking almost out of place. I'm used to studying people, slotting them into neat categories in my mind. But Jake doesn't fit into one category.

One moment, he's teasing, flirting, the next he is pushing boundaries and looking genuinely concerned.

And then that apology.

Guys like Jake, to my knowledge, don't apologize. They breeze through life with a smirk and a shrug.

So much for a quiet retreat. I let out a sigh, knowing I need to stay away from him, which is going to be hard considering we share a cabin.

After a few minutes, I head back inside. My tea is now cold on the nightstand. Shit, I completely forgot about it. I stomp my feet, the sound bouncing around the quiet room as I fight the urge to scream. The last thing I want is to run into Mr. Complicated downstairs.

Looks like no tea for me tonight.

I huff, kicking the edge of the bed before grabbing a book from my nightstand and flip it open with more force than necessary. I try to lose myself in the words, my eyes scanning the pages, hoping to drown out the swirling thoughts of Jake. Slowly, the tension fades away as I focus on the story until I finally fall asleep.

The Forest

Summer 1920

For years, I've watched their friendship blossom in my embrace. Secret meetings, laughter echoing under my canopy, their footsteps a familiar rhythm on my soil. Now, at sixteen, something shifted in the surrounding air.

One sunlit afternoon, she felt his gaze linger on her. Turning, her heart skipped erratically. "Why are you staring?" She raises her eyebrows.

"You are beautiful," he said sincerely.

Her cheeks flushed, and her eyes widened. Then she turned and ran. Her breath came in sharp gasps as she darted behind my trees, her heart racing like never before.

He stood there, frozen, his eyes wide with confusion.

When they met again under my leaves, he asked, "Why did you run?"

She looked down, her fingers twisting nervously at her dress. "You shouldn't say those words to me," she whispered softly.

"But you are beautiful," he said as he stepped closer. His hand shook as he reached out. He leaned in and pressed his lips against hers.

She flinched, her eyes widening in shock, her lips parting but producing no sound.

"I am sorry," he said, seeing the panic in her eyes. She turned and vanished into the depths of my shadow, leaving him standing there once again.

Silence hung between them for days, heavy with regret. When they finally met again, he opened his mouth to apologize, but she cut him off. "I liked it, but we cannot. My mama says we cannot cross those lines. Our worlds do not belong together. We should not even be friends. But here I am, my heart racing when you are near. I cannot stop thinking about you, missing you..." She trailed off. Tears spilled from her eyes, and her hands clutched at her sides as if to hold herself together.

His eyes softened as he gently wiped away her tears. "Please do not cry." His lips gently brushed against her forehead. "When you cry, it is like my heart is being torn apart. I would rather hear your laughter, see your smile—that is what fills my thoughts, day and night. I do not care what anyone thinks." He pulled her into her arms, and she leaned into him, their affection a complicated, forbidden tangle. Her hands gripped the back of his shirt, holding on as if he were her lifeline.

He kissed her again, and for that brief instant, their kiss became their universe. It was as if they'd sprouted wings, lifting them above the complexities of the world, letting them soar in a sky made only of love.

When he pulled away, her eyes remained closed, savoring the fading magic of their kiss. When she opened them, he was smiling. "You did not run away?"

"I did not." Her own smile broke through the tension.

In that instant, it seemed as if all the societal lines that should have separated them blurred into insignificance, overwhelmed by the undeniable love they felt for one another.

"If only we could stay like this forever." She sighed, nestling into his arms.

"I know." He pulled her closer and kissed her forehead. The air around them seemed to shimmer, and I felt their love infuse every part of me.

They didn't say their wish aloud, didn't carve it into one of my trees. But I felt it—a secret yearning, hidden deep within their hearts. That night, under the full moon, something miraculous happened. Their secret wish, their hidden love, her magic transformed me. My stream surged, its water swirling faster and faster until it leaped off the cliff in a jubilant waterfall.

Chapter 9

Jake

My 6 a.m. alarm pierces my ears after an hour of tossing around. Groggily, I open my eyes to the predawn gloom, dragging myself out of bed and into the bathroom, where I splash water on my face. Dressing in my workout clothes, I grab my earbuds before stepping out of the room.

The cabin is quiet. Mia's been avoiding me, and honestly, I don't care. I do not miss her sassy self, or her sharp tongue and her fiery glare. Why do I find myself pausing outside her room? No fucking idea.

Shaking my head, I'm about to walk away when a quiet sound breaks the silence, so faint I almost missed it. It's coming from Mia's room, soft breathy moans of pleasure, freezing me in my step.

Somebody is practicing self care, or is she having a little video session with her boyfriend? The idea of her legs spreading out while he watches shouldn't bother me, but it does.

Stepping closer to the door, I press my ear against it. My dick begging for me to take it out. The urge to stroke myself to her sweet moans is almost overwhelming. My hand hovers near my waistband, fingers twitching, but I clench them into a fist instead.

I should walk away, removing myself from this situation before I do something reckless, like burst into her room. But my feet are glued to the floor. I run my hand through my hair, tugging a little too hard at the strands.

Her moans grow more desperate, telling me that she's close. Fuck, I want to see her pretty face when she reaches her climax. My cock throbs at the thought. How fucking bad is it to want another guy's girlfriend?

"Mmm," she moans a little louder, the sounds trembling through me. My balls tighten, almost painfully, and then, *silence*.

I adjust my pants, cursing under my breath, before quietly making my way downstairs.

Stepping outside, the early morning sun barely seeps through the trees. The only sound is my footsteps hitting the ground. Lost in my thoughts of her that I barely notice where I'm going until the sound of rushing water pulls me back.

Standing here looking at it, it still feels surreal. I've been here many times before as a child, and never stumbled across it. I make a mental note to look it up on a map later before heading back.

Back at the house, I head straight to the kitchen and think about grabbing a protein shake from the fridge that I bought yesterday, since the princess warned me not to wake her up before 8 a.m.

But I decide to make a banana shake instead. Fresh protein is so much better. I gather the ingredients, toss everything into the blender, and hit the start button.

That will get her out of bed, not that I want to see her or anything. She can ignore me all she wants.

Sure enough, a few seconds later, I know she's here without even looking up. Her eyes are burning a hole into my forehead.

"Good morning *princess*, did I wake you?" I turn off the blender and meet her wide-eyed glare. She looks furious, but even prettier.

Oh, she's pissed okay.

She strides over to me, her short legs moving faster than usual. Thrusting her phone in front of my face, the screen brightly shows 7:02 a.m.

"What part of don't wake me up before eight was so hard to understand?" Her eyes are blazing as she glares at me.

Are you sure I'm the one who woke you up, princess?

I move closer, and she leans back against the kitchen island, our faces inches apart. "I understood just fine, princess. But following orders is not my best suit." A smirk plays on my lips. I can smell her arousal from her little self-care session.

She grabs the edge of the countertop, her chest rising and plummeting. Her face turns a shade darker, a storm brewing in those brown eyes. I glance down at her lips before bringing my gaze back to hers.

"I should report you to the booking agency for violating my privacy. You're not even supposed to be here."

"Do it then, princess, see if I care." I run my tongue over the top corner of my lip, and her eyes follow the movement. Her heartbeat is almost audible, matching the rapid pace of my own. She huffs and pushes against my chest. I don't know what it is, but I love seeing her become this little firecracker.

"Asshole," she says, loud enough for me to catch every syllable, before storming upstairs.

A chuckle escapes me as I watch her walk away, and of course, she's wearing those booty shorts and a shirt that says, *I'm not moody, I just don't want to talk to you.*

I can be an asshole if you want me to, princess. My gaze unintentionally follows the way her ass moves in those snug shorts. The need to fuck the sassiness out of her screams through me, pelting my body like an unforgiving rainfall, drenching me in desire. I close my eyes, imagining for a second how she would feel underneath me. My hands grabbing her ass, my fingers sliding through her hair. I wonder if they're as soft as they seem.

"Damn it." I run a hand through my hair, reminding myself she has a boyfriend. We're sharing a cabin; sleeping with her would make things complicated.

This is going to be a fucking long summer.

Once I finish my shake and tidy up, I go upstairs for a quick shower before meeting Sergio at the hotel to review the budget. We might need to cut some hours of some employees even if I don't want to. Alex is also meeting me there.

Driving there, my mind keeps circling back to the waterfall. "Hey, Siri, take me to a waterfall nearby." I want to see how far this waterfall is on the map.

"I found a waterfall 50 miles from here. Do you want that one?"

"No!" This waterfall should be less than five miles from here. I'll look more into it when I get to the hotel.

Walking into the lobby, a cheerful girl walks up to me, probably recognizing me from Instagram. "OMG, it's you." Her eyes light up with excitement. I offer her a polite nod instead of my usual flirty grin I reserved for moments like this. My mind is elsewhere, on the woman back at the cabin, getting on my last nerve.

"What are you doing here?" she asks, her tone flirty. Normally, I'd be all for this kind of interaction. She's attractive, exactly my type, well every woman is my type as long she's over eighteen, but I'm not into it right now.

Just then, Alex calls out to me, and I'm almost grateful for the interruption. "Hey, Jake, over here."

"Sorry, I gotta go." I turn around, heading towards Alex. He's sitting on a couch in the lobby which is beautiful with high ceilings.

It has historical charm, but needs some renovations. The mansion was built in the early 1800s and has been passed down through generations in my family. It's right below the mountains, and in the middle of the forest that leads all the way to the glass cabin.

"Can you tell me why we are meeting here and not at the cabin?" He leans in his chair, his expression a mix of amusement which tells me he already knows the answer to his question.

I take a seat across from him, leaning back casually. "I have some things to take care of here, so it's convenient."

Alex's eyes narrow as he studies me, a knowing smirk forming on his lips. "Oh, shit, someone is still pissed at you, huh? Guess she's not falling for your charm." He chuckles. There's nothing funny about it. I was just worried about her.

I brush his comment off and focus on the other mystery occupying my mind.

"Do you remember having a waterfall around here?" I watch his face for any sign of recognition.

His brows wrinkle in thought. "Not that I remember. I think the closest waterfall is like 50 miles from here. Why?"

I shrug. "Nothing," I say, deciding to keep my thoughts about the mysterious waterfall to myself for now. After all, Mia saw it too, so I know I'm not imagining things.

"Wanna join me for some rock climbing sometime next week?" I change the subject. It's been a while since we climbed together.

"You already know the answer is yes, man, but go easy on me. I haven't climbed in a while and I'm not a professional like you." Well, he's right, I am a pro and have won multiple gold medals.

"No promises," I laugh.

We talk a bit more, talking about old times before Alex checks his phone. "I've got to meet Sarah, catch you later?"

"You two act like you don't see each other when y'all live in the same city."

"We don't hang out much." He straightens himself up in his seat.

"Why not?" I glance at some girls giggling and staring at us before looking back at Alex.

"We're both very busy, and every time we hang out, the boyfriend is there and I don't like him that much."

"What did he do?" Do I need to drive to LA to break someone's jaw?

"Nothing that I know of. I just don't like him. She deserves so much better."

I laugh.

"What?" He narrows his gray eyes at me.

"You're jealous."

"I'm not jealous? She's like a sister to me." He scoffs.

"Exactly, you're acting like a protective older brother." I notice the frown on his face.

"Well I care about her."

"I know," I say. We both do, and I'll hurt anyone who hurts her.

Alex stands. "Alright, see you later," he says, and we do our bro handshake before he walks away.

Walking towards Dad's office, I take a deep breath before stepping inside. I haven't been here since he died. The room is the same, yet everything has changed.

I head toward the safe, and key in the code and it unlocks. He kept it the same. Inside, there are some old notebooks. I take them, putting them in my bag, when the sound of footsteps snaps me out of my thoughts. I look up to see Sergio walking into the room.

His blue eyes meet mine.

"Need any help?" he asks.

I reviewed the new budget and employee hours with Sergio. Renovations will start in a couple of weeks once the bank loan comes through. Fortunately, I won't have to worry about disturbing our guests, as we have very few at the moment.

"Your dad would have been proud of you, taking over the family business," he says, giving me a reassuring pat on the back.

I nod.

Maybe he would've been if things had been different, but I can't shake off the bitterness.

His pride is something lost to me long before he passed, especially after our fight five years ago.

Checking my watch, it's already 4 p.m. I need something to clear my mind. There's an amazing outdoor climbing spot not far from here, which is exactly what I need.

I gather my stuff before stepping out of the office.

"See you later." I let him know. I head to my jeep and drive back to the cabin.

I pull into the driveway and head upstairs, passing her room on the way to mine. I change into my climbing clothes and grab my gears.

Once I get everything, I walk out, still no sign of her. *Princess* is planning to stay in her room forever. I shouldn't care that she's ignoring me. Everything is turning out the way I wanted it to. That's what I keep telling myself. But a little part of me does.

Stepping outside, I'm met with a gray, cloudy sky. Rain begins to fall, drenching the ground. "Great," I grumble. Just my luck. I guess indoor wall climbing is gonna have to do it.

I get into my car and drive to the local indoor climbing center. As I pull into the parking lot, the rain stops, the clouds parting like some cosmic joke at my expense. Stepping out of the car, the ground's barely wet, as if the rain decided to mess with me and then bail. Typical, but hey, climbing is climbing, and I'm here to conquer some walls, rain or shine.

Inside the climbing center, I'm immediately drawn to the complexity of the routes ahead. Climbing demands my full attention, pushing me to focus on the next hold, regulate my breath, and let go of all distractions. Among the physical challenges, I discovered my Zen; a pure focus where the climb is all that exists.

As I begin, the world outside of these walls disappear. My fingers find their grip, pulling upwards. My forearm screams as I grip the hold tighter. My feet search for a solid foundation as the tension shifts to my calves and thighs, aching as I push my body upwards. Beads of sweat form on my forehead, then trail down my spine, as the burn in my muscles grow with each move.

The rhythm of climbing consumes me—reach, grip, step, breathe.

Once I reach the top, I take a few seconds to inhale and exhale before propelling down.

I sit on the floor, taking a moment to catch my breath. This girl recognizes me and approaches, her expression brightening with admiration. "That was impressive." Her face lights up.

"Thank you," I say, then smile back. I'm not in the mood for conversation after my climb; I just want to go home. *Unless she's interested in another kind of climb.* But Mia is at the house, and I'm not comfortable with the idea of fucking another girl while she's next door. This is the longest I've gone without having sex since high school.

Leaving the climbing center, the weather picks up the closer I get home, even though there's barely any rain before I left. Heavy rains thumping against my car loudly. The wind is stronger, making the trees move wildly. Lightning flashes across the sky, illuminating the surrounding buildings for a second or two.

When I get home, the rain has doubled down on its intensity. After a quick shower, I changed into some shorts and tanks. I sit at my desk, needing to concentrate on the hotel renovation budget, but the storm continues to rage, making it hard to focus. It's so in tune with the chaos I'm feeling inside, neither wanting to be the first to quiet down. Then, there's a loud scream before the power goes out.

Mia.

Chapter 10

Mia

I sit at my desk, listening to the raindrops hitting the window. The laptop screen stares back at me as I try to get the words out. Each sentence feels awkward and forced.

Closing my eyes, Mom's words replay in my mind. *Your voice, your imagination, and your stories are gifts. Share them with the world.*

Gift? It doesn't feel like it. I haven't written in years. Even when I used to write, my writing was wild and disruptive.

I shake my hands and crack my neck. *I can do this. Just write the words,* I repeat to myself, taking a few deep breaths.

My fingers hover over the keyboard, ready to let my imagination take the lead. The sound of the rain against the window helps a little, and I manage a few sentences that don't make me cringe. I might feel differently about them tomorrow.

Hours pass, and the rain intensifies. Looking out the window, the trees are moving violently as the rain grows louder, but I checked the weather earlier and there was no storm projected.

A loud snap pierces through the noise, startling me. I scream and jump onto my bed as a tree branch crashes against the window, splintering glass everywhere. My chest tightens as my heart is beating like a drum in my ears.

I scream, louder this time. It's a freaking bear. Then, the power goes out, and the darkness swallows me whole. I have no idea where the bear is.

"No, no, no," I whimper, barely audible over the sound of my pounding heart. If there's anything I hate more than storms is the dark.

Heavy footsteps approach, "Mia?" He breaks through my paralyzing brain. A light pierces the darkness, directed at me. Squinting against the brightness, I catch Jake's silhouette in the doorway. His gaze locks with mine. "Are you okay?"

I can barely speak, my breaths short. "There's a bear...by the window." I point at my desk. I don't want to be eaten by a bear.

His gaze doesn't leave mine. "It's okay, walk towards me slowly." He remains calm.

Trembling, I carefully edge away from the bed, our gazes intertwined. The moment I'm within reach, he draws me close, and I grasp onto him, shaking from head to toe. He smells like lavender, like he just took a shower. It calms me a little. How does he do that? It's like whenever he's close to me, he has that magical power that can calm me.

He doesn't feel like a stranger, someone I just met, more like someone I've known forever.

Then I remember the bear. I don't know where it is. "We're gonna get eaten by a bear," I mumble to him in a panic.

"No, we're not." He cradles my face in his hands. "Come on, we need to get out of here." He takes my hands in his and leads us out of the room, closing the door behind us, his phone lighting the way. I clutch his hand tighter, not wanting him to let go.

Entering his room, he closes the door behind us, the storm still raging outside.

I watch as he checks his phone. "Fuck, there's no signal." The light from his phone spreads shadows across his face, highlighting the furrow in his brows and the tension in his eyes. His composed demeanor cracks, and I see the panic in his eyes feeding into mine.

My chest heaves as I gasp for air, my lungs burn with the effort. I clutch at my chest, fingers digging into my skin, desperate for relief. The pressure is unbearable, like I'm suffocating.

"I... I can't breathe."

"Hey, it's okay." He steps closer to me. His hand on my shoulder. "Deep breaths with me, in and out." He guides me again like he did at the waterfall.

Breathe in. He inhales deeply.

Breathe out. He exhales slowly.

I follow his instructions, focusing on his breathing. My gaze locks onto his green eyes, which seem to glow in the barely lit room. They remind me of a forest—calm, and grounding. The thought of the forest brings back memories of the waterfall. I imagine the sound of water cascading over rocks, the tranquility of being surrounded by trees. The memory of the waterfall fills my mind, its serene power washing away the fear bit by bit.

"That's it. Just keep breathing for me."

I used to get panic attacks a lot growing up. They stopped for a while, but came back after Mom died. She was the only one who could calm me so easily.

Jake breaks through my panic attack effortlessly and brings me back to myself.

Slowly, the suffocating pressure in my chest eases, like a tight band loosening its grip. The room is less claustrophobic, and the shadows less threatening.

"Better?" His eyes search mine.

"Yeah, thank you."

"Do you get those often?" His eyes soften with a tenderness that breaks through the last of my anxiety.

"Sometimes."

His presence, unexpectedly comforting, prompts honesty I hadn't planned on sharing with him. He holds my gaze, and my heart flutters for completely different reasons. He leads me to his bed and sits me down at the edge before turning to walk away.

I grab his hand. I'm not even sure why. Earlier today I was avoiding him, but now I don't want him to leave me.

He pauses, turning back, and our eyes lock. There's a charged, heavy moment as he notices our hands together. His gaze lifts again to meet mine, his breath hitching.

He crouches in front of me, holding my gaze. "It's okay. I'm gonna connect my ring light to the laptop." He nods toward his desk. "It should give us some decent light in here." He smiles at me.

My cheeks warm, and I smile back, my fingers lingering on his skin a moment longer. I want to run my hand through his hair, wondering if it's as soft as it seems. Oh God, what is happening? This is the opposite of what I said I was going to do. Everything is unclear; I'm scared, there is a freaking bear in my room, and there's no power. He makes me feel safe, that's it.

Tomorrow, everything will go back to normal, and I'll go back to avoiding him.

He stands and walks over to his desk, setting everything up. Once it's connected, the room fills with light.

He turns to me. "Is this better?" His eyebrows raise, his mouth set in a line that hints at a smile trying to break through.

"Yeah, that's better, thank you."

He sits on the chair at his desk, giving me space. With the light in the room, I can see him clearly now. He's wearing boxer shorts that leave little to the imagination, and a plain black tee. But his presence fills the space completely, making the room feel smaller.

Come on, I don't get attracted to people unless I have an emotional connection to them. It doesn't matter how his muscles stretch underneath the short sleeve shirt, or the print of his shaft in his boxers. That shouldn't make my body warm all over as if we've turned the heat up in here.

I looked down at my fingers, his intense gaze on me, making me acutely aware of what I'm wearing.

A short pajama set with a lace-trimmed cami that exposes my stomach. Does he find me attractive, or is he more into female models with flat stomachs and fit bodies?

I've seen his instagram, he is pretty popular with his millions of followers. Based on the comments on his posts, the ladies love him.

I wrap my arms around myself, feeling a little bit uncomfortable, and he politely looks away.

"I'll grab you a jacket," he says as he walks to his closet. When he returns, he hands it to me, and I catch a whiff of fresh laundry mixed with a faint hint of his scent. I resist the urge to bring it to my nose before putting it on.

"Thank you," I say, pulling my hair out the hood.

I notice he also changes into gray sweatpants. Instead of returning to his desk, he sits on the floor, leaning against the door. His eyes fixed on the window, watching the storm outside. His shoulders are tense as he taps his fingers on his knee. Every now and then, he lets out a deep sigh, his jaw clenching with each breath.

"Are you okay?" I ask. I don't want to intrude, but I can't ignore the knot in my chest that forms when I observe him. A concern that is too deep for the short time I've known him. His eyes reflect a dark, swirling chaos like the storm outside.

He looks up at me, his lip curling into a smile that doesn't reach his eyes. "Yeah, I'm okay."

I get off the bed and move to sit next to him on the floor. I'm not even sure why. "I'm afraid of the dark, and I hate storms," I say before I could stop myself. "If you weren't here tonight, I... I don't know what I would do."

He turns his head toward me, his eyes meeting mine, sending ripples through my stomach. "I don't like storms either," he confesses, our eyes still locked.

Silence.

"So, why are you scared of the dark? I gotta know." He gives me that sweet smile where I can see his dimple, not his usual flirty one.

I release a deep breath. "Promise not to laugh?" I mumble, eyeing him.

He nods, and smiles again. "I promise."

I take a deep breath before I begin. "My great grandma was Haitian, and she used to tell me all these stories about ghosts, and something called *lougarou*. I don't know how to translate it exactly. It's like a night creature, or an evil spirit that uses black magic. They come at night to harm you." I shudder at the memory. "I've always feared they would come for me in the dark."

Finishing my story, I catch him fighting back a laugh, breaking his promise. His efforts fail and his laughter fills the surrounding space. I shoot him an intense, icy stare, and playfully punch his muscular biceps for breaking his promise.

"You promised not to laugh." I pout, but his laugh is infectious, and I can't help but laugh along with him.

I laugh so hard that an unexpected, sharp sound comes out of my nose. Ugh, I hate when that happens. So embarrassing.

We both stop mid-laugh, staring at each other. "Did you just snort?" He raises his eyebrows; his lips turning into a teasing smile.

Mortified, I cover my face with my hands. "No, I didn't." My words are muffled between my fingers.

He reaches over and gently pulls my hands away from my face. His eyes are warm, and he has that sweet smile again that makes my heart do a weird little skip. "You snorted, and it was adorable."

Oh, God, why does his smile affect me like this? A warmth blooms in my chest like a flower in spring, its petals opening slowly in the soft glow of the sunlight.

Our laughter gradually fades, replaced by a comfortable silence. I stare at the necklace around his neck.

"You're staring," he notes, startling me.

"Your necklace, it's similar to mine." I nod toward his neck.

He looks down at it, then back at mine. "They are. My grandfather gave me mine; he passed away." He holds it between his fingers with a sweet, nostalgic smile. "I still wear it because I miss him."

"I'm sorry." My heart aches for him, and I reach out to squeeze his hand. I know how it feels to lose someone you love. He looks up at me, his gazes holding mine.

I was never good at eye contact, but when he looks at me, I can't look away. I'm lost in the depth of his green eyes. There's something about them. As if I've known them forever.

"It's okay. He died a long time ago." He rubs the back of his neck. "What about you? How did you get yours?"

I reach out and touch mine too, the stone cool under my fingertips. "My mom gave it to me. It's a family heirloom. Her mother gave it to her. That's the only thing she kept from her life in France."

"France?" His eyebrows lift in surprise.

"Yes, my mom is from there."

"That's amazing." He leans in.

"Yeah." I smile.

I don't really know much about my mom's family. Except for the fact they were not on talking terms. My mom didn't like to talk about it, so I never asked questions. My grandmother contacted me after mom died. Apparently, she didn't even know my mom was sick.

"What a coincidence, right?" He stretches out one leg in front of him.

"Yeah." Our necklaces are similar, but not exactly the same. His chain is black, and mine is gold. But the crystals look identical. Glowing softly in the light.

Silence falls between us, but it's a comfortable silence. I wonder why we have similar necklaces. Maybe both of our families love emerald necklaces. Many people love emeralds. It's probably nothing. But my active mind whispers, what if they're connected somehow?

" I know you've been avoiding me, and I don't blame you for doing so. But we're both here for the summer, and maybe we can find a way to coexist, maybe even enjoy it?" His eyebrows arch, and his lips parting as if to catch his next breath or my response, whichever comes first. "Can we start over?"

He's right, I've been avoiding him because being around him is confusing. I don't like how he can calm me so easily, or how he feels so familiar. I barely know him but I also feel like I've known him forever.

He's right though, I can't avoid him all summer. It will be better for both of us if we can get along.

"Okay, but I have a few demands." My arms fold across my chest, ready to establish my non-negotiable terms. I need to set some boundaries.

He nods, a spark of relief in his eyes. "Let's hear them."

"You can't wake me up before 8 a.m. I need my beauty sleep," I say, a little distracted by the way his gaze seems to hold mine a little too intensely, and the way his blonde tousled hair falls over his green eyes.

"Agreed," he says, then winks. "You need your beauty sleep, although I'm not sure how you can get any more beautiful. The second?"

Ugh, he's such a flirt.

I ignore the way my heart flutters with baby butterflies and continue. "Secondly, there's no scenario where you and I end up sleeping together." *Like ever.* Heat rushes to my cheeks as I refuse to think about how it would feel to be with him. I've seen the imprint in his workout leggings. Why am I even thinking about this? This is not me. I don't think about men's dicks.

His smile widens, teasingly. "I wasn't planning on it, but good to know, unless you change your mind, of course." He winks, again.

He can't help himself, can he?

I roll my eyes, dismissing the quickening of my pulse. "Not going to happen. I have a boyfriend, remember?" I say, holding onto this lie as if it's my lifeline. Because right now, it feels like it is. If he thinks I have a boyfriend, I can convince myself that he won't try to make a move on me.

He leans in closer. "Just hypothetically, if you didn't have a boyfriend?"

I swallow, my throat dry like sandpaper. "Hypothetically? Still no."

His eyes linger on me, studying me, my heart racing under his stare. Then he nods and smiles. "Fair enough," he says, but his gaze tells me he sees right through me, and it sends tingling shivers through my body.

He tilts his head, and a thoughtful look crosses his face. "What if you join me in the morning for my run?"

"Are you calling me fat?" I keep my face straight, watching his reaction.

"You're perfect, and we both know it, so don't twist my words." His tone is serious, as if I offended him.

This is what I'm talking about. This guy is confusing. Who the hell says such things to someone they barely know? He didn't sound like he was flirting with me. He meant it.

"Okay, I'll go, but it has to be after 8 a.m." I let out a hitched breath. My heart is still recovering from his words.

He laughs. "Nobody runs at 8 a.m. I usually run at 6 a.m."

"That's not going to work," I argue.

"Fine, we can go at 6:30 a.m."

"Nope, the earliest I will do is 7 a.m." I cross my arms over my chest.

"Okay, fine. Then I can make my protein shake?" He gives me those pleading puppy dog eyes.

"Yes, you can make your protein shake."

Why does this guy love protein shakes so much? Although, looking at the way his muscles flex subtly under his shirt, I can tell they've been working wonders for him.

"Okay, it's a deal then." He holds out his hand so we can shake on it. "Maybe you'll climb with me too," he adds, standing up, his hand gripping mine a moment longer than necessary before he helps me to my feet.

"Climbing? You mean like climbing a rock? Literal rock climbing?" I laugh at him. Now he's definitely pushing it. I don't have the body strength to climb.

"We can start with indoor climbing before moving to the mountain, baby steps." He grins.

I raise my eyebrows at him skeptically. "I don't know about that."

"Only if you want to."

"I'll think about it."

"Okay then. It's late. Let's get you to sleep." His eyes shift to the one bed in the room.

"There's only one bed?" I state the obvious. He looks at the bed and back at me.

"You can have the bed, and I'll sleep on the small couch."

"It's okay, it's a king bed. It should be big enough for both of us."

The truth is, I don't want to be alone on the bed. What if something happened? Just thinking about it increases my heart rate.

"Okay." The word barely escapes his lips as we both settle into the bed, carefully maintaining a respectful distance. We lay on our backs, and stare at the ceiling, like it holds answers.

"Good night, Mia."

"Good night, Jake."

Chapter 11

Jake

"Jake?" she whispers. I can barely hear her through the patter of rain against the window. She was supposed to be asleep.

"Yeah?" We turn to face each other, and we've somehow moved closer.

"Do you think the bear is still in my room?" Her upper eyelids raise up, showing more of the whites in her eyes. Before I can say anything, the room goes dark. Great, my laptop must have died. I left it on since she's afraid of the dark. Her breath hitches audibly in the quiet room.

"It's okay." I instinctively pull her closer to me. Something I've never done before but feels as natural as breathing. Everything with her is confusingly comfortable.

Her body tenses before melting into my embrace. Her head finds that perfect spot on my shoulder, and suddenly, I'm enveloped in the comforting scents of coconut and Shea butter from her hair, with just a hint of jasmine from her skin. "No *ghosts or lougarou* will bother you while I'm here. And about earlier... I'm sorry for laughing."

A quiet chuckle vibrates against my chest in the darkness. "It's okay." She sighs, sounding a little drowsy.

"Besides storms and darkness, what else are you afraid of?" I try to distract her a little. Asking her about things she is scared of, it's probably not the best way to calm her, or maybe I just want to know more about her. She's silent for a moment.

"I'm scared of bubbles," she says so quietly that I'm not sure I heard her right.

"Bubbles?"

"Yeah, I know, I keep getting weirder by the hour."

"I didn't say it was weird. I've just never met anyone who's scared of bubbles."

"Well, it's not only bubbles; it's anything that is clustered. Especially if they look like circles or holes... It's called *Trypophobia*."

Her body shivers under my touch, and her heart rate increases.

"We should stop talking about it, unless I want to have another anxiety attack." Her arm tightens around my waist. "You never said why you hate storms." She changes the subject quickly. She probably can't even think about it. That sounds horrible. "You don't have to tell me if you don't want to." Her whisper reaches my ears like a gentle breeze, her heart beating faster against my chest.

"I don't like to talk about it," I tell her, but something about her makes me want to. Maybe it's the way she trusts me or how vulnerable she's been with me tonight.

Since she felt comfortable sharing her fear with me, why not share a little bit of mine with her?

I take a deep breath before sharing part of the truth. "My father died during a storm. Car accident." The words are heavy as I pull them from the deep, dark place that I locked them in. But I don't mention the fight we had before, or the harsh words I told him. *I don't want to hear anything you have to say, and I never want to see you again. You're dead to me.*

A conversation that I can't undo, and I'm not even sure if I even want to. I still mean everything I said.

He asked to stay the night because there was a storm outside, and he didn't like driving in the rain. But I told him to leave.

The guilt is a constant storm in my heart, raging silently. Maybe if I had let him stay the night, he would still be alive. Perhaps, if he hadn't done what he did, he would still be alive. The anger and love I still have for him intertwine, creating complex feelings I'm not ready to untangle, not even in my mind.

"I'm sorry," she says, her arms wrapping around my waist as if we've done this before. This moment should be awkward but for some reason, it's not. Everything is different when it comes to her.

Her touch is gentle yet firm, her fingers pressing into my back as if she's trying to fuse us. I've heard those words many times before, but they never felt like this. Reaching deep into my soul, acknowledging and touching something real and raw inside of me. Like the sun peeking over a canopy of trees.

"My mom passed away three months ago, so I understand the pain," she whispers.

I doubt she fully grasps it, but I wouldn't want her to. I don't wish this pain on anybody.

"I'm sorry about your mom." I tighten my arm around her, and she doesn't pull away. Instead, she moves closer as if all we need is each other right now to help mend our broken pieces, even if it's just for tonight.

She's silent for a few seconds before she speaks again. "She was sick, but I wasn't ready. We were supposed to have more time together." Her words are as fragile as the last leaf on a tree in fall. "She is supposed to watch me get married... and be here to meet her grandchildren one day. But now she's gone. What am I supposed to do?"

My chest burns, and I feel her pain so acutely as if it's carved into my very soul.

"I don't know," I tell her the truth. I have no fucking idea. "For me, I just block everything out and find something to keep me occupied. Climbing is my escape."

"I don't want to escape it, though. I need to feel it all, the pain and the hurt. It keeps her memory alive. I'm scared if I stop feeling it, I might lose that, too."

Her words hit me hard, grounding me in their honesty. Here I am, avoiding the pain. There she is, holding onto it like a lifeline, a way to keep her mom's memory alive. That's the difference between her and me. I'm not sure I want to keep his memories alive. There is not much worth remembering.

"Tell me about her, what was she like?" I can help her remember her mom if that's what she needs.

"She is..." She sighs. "She was the most amazing being I have ever known. And not just because she was my mom. She was kind, funny, and loving. She was good at almost everything except for cooking and singing. The best she could make were peanut butter sandwiches." She chuckles a little. "My dad was happy to cook for her." My hand mindlessly rubs lazy circles on her back. "Oh, and she loved giving out cheek kisses. Maybe it's a French thing, I don't know, but she'd kiss your cheeks to say hello, goodnight, thank you, good morning. Everything. And it's always two kisses, one on each cheek." She laughs softly.

"You got your attitude from your dad, then?" I smile at her, even if she can't see me.

"I don't have an attitude," she says as she punches my side, but I can hear the smile in her voice.

She's quiet again, her body warm against mine. Her breathing deepens, telling me she has fallen asleep. I should move and give her space, but every time I try, she mumbles something and moves closer, her legs draped over my thigh.

A pressure builds in my pants. I attempt to adjust discreetly, without waking her up, but Mia stirs, blinking against the sudden light as the power returns.

I hope she doesn't look down at my pants, but as if on cue, her eyes darting down to the bulge in my pants. She quickly sits up.

I clear my throat to break some of the awkwardness. "The power is back. I'll go check on the damage to your room."

"I'll come with you." She follows me out of the room.

Making sure she stays behind me as we head towards her room. We exchange glances before I open her door. There are some broken glasses on the floor, but there's no bear anywhere. Slowly, I walk around the room before checking the bathroom. Still no bear in sight, and we both let out a sigh of relief. But she still can't sleep in here. I'll call someone in the morning to fix the window.

Checking my phone, it's well past midnight. "You can take my bed, and I'll crash on the couch. There should be some extra sheets in the closet I can use." I let her know as we make our way out of her room. She probably doesn't want to share a bed after what just happened.

"I'm not sleepy anymore, and I'm hungry." Her lips press together into a pout that is kinda adorable.

"It's almost 1 a.m." I laugh softly, masking the warm sensation in my chest. "Isn't it a little too late for a snack?"

"But I'm starving. I didn't really eat today." Her stomach growls audibly, agreeing with her. "See," she points at her tummy, "she needs food."

I frown. "Why haven't you eaten today?" I ask, following her downstairs. I can't help but notice the sway of her hips, her shorts clinging to her form in a way that commands attention.

"I got caught up with writing and forgot," she says over her shoulder as she enters the kitchen.

"You write?"

"Yeah, at least I'm trying to." She shuffles her feet, her eyes glued to the floor.

"Trying?" I search her eyes, but she avoids my gaze.

"It's just hard to get the words out."

I'm not a writer, so I don't know a lot about it, but sometimes we just need to get out of our heads. "Don't overthink it and just write whatever comes to your mind. You want to be a writer for a reason, right?" I reach out to touch her arm. She lifts her eyes to look at me, and I see the longing and frustration in them. "The story is there," I continue, "you just need to bring it out."

She smiles at me. "I guess you're right." She walks towards the cabinets and stretches up on her toes to reach for something.

I lean against the counter, watching her. She's wearing my jacket, but it barely covers her ass, the curve underneath her shorts teasingly exposed. I need to focus on something else, fast. But it's hard to focus on anything else when my body reacts to her every move.

My hands itch to touch her, but I clench them into fists at my side. My nails dig into my palms as I try to regain some control.

"How about I make the snacks and you take a seat?" I suggest, needing something to distract me from the growing tension.

She turns, and her eyes narrow. "That's fine. I can do it myself." *So stubborn.*

I step closer and gently lift her by the waist, setting her down on the kitchen island. *She gasps.* Our faces are merely inches apart. My eyes are drawn to her lips, noticing how she bites down on the lower one. Interesting. Now I know why she bites down on them. It takes all my self-control not to replace her teeth with mine. *She has a boyfriend, Jake.*

"Just stay here, and I'll make your snack," I command, attempting to maintain some semblance of control, but failing miserably.

She's gonna drive me crazy.

She frowns, clearly doesn't like being told what to do, and it's both infuriating and attractive. "Don't tell me what to do," she mumbles. I hold her gaze, seeing the storm brewing in them, and I want to fuck her right here on the kitchen counter.

Turning away, mostly to hide the intensity surging through me. I open the fridge and take a few seconds to compose myself, the cool air doing little to calm the heat building inside. My hands are trembling as I grab the pepperoni and cheese before closing the door, my mind racing with the thought of her so close.

I move to the counter, then take the bagels, slicing them onto a plate, and topping them with the cheese and pepperoni, adding a dash of spice. I can feel her intense gaze on me, and I steal glances, sensing the tension. Sliding everything into the microwave, I recall how she snuggled against me earlier. Our eyes meet, and I can tell she's thinking about the same thing.

"So, what's your book about?" I lean over the counter while we wait for our pizza bagel to cook.

She shoots me a sharp glare.

Okay, she's pissed again.

The microwave beeps. I turn to pull them out of the pizzas, placing them next to her.

"I'm grabbing a beer from the fridge; do you need anything?" I need a drink to ease this tension.

"I'll have a beer," she responds.

I pause, staring at her for a few seconds, making sure I've heard correctly.

"What?" she says, noticing my prolonged gaze.

"Sorry, you seem more like a wine kind of girl."

"And what kind is that?"

"Red wine, something sweet." I smirk at her.

"I do love sweet red wine, especially chateau noir, which was my mom's favorite. It's made in France. Can't a girl do both?" She shoots me a glare.

Shaking my head, I plead for the fifth, already sensing where this conversation is going. I refuse to answer questions that will self-incriminate me. I'll get the lady her beer.

Grabbing two beers, I hand one to her as, leaning over the counter. I watch her devour the mini pizzas one by one, barely taking a break. She's so focused that she doesn't notice me staring at first.

"What?" She stops mid bite, and catches my amused look, her mouth half-full with a piece of pepperoni stuck at the corner of her lips. She appears a little embarrassed, but masks it with a scowl. "I was hungry, okay? And you're just standing there staring." Her cheeks puffed out with the food, giving her an adorable look. I can't help the smile tugging at the corner of my lips.

I realize I've been watching her this whole time. "Sorry." I offer a sheepish smile, grabbing a mini pizza. "I guess I was just caught up in watching you enjoy the food. You seem to really like them."

"That's rude, watching other people eat," she laughs, her mood lightens, "but they're really good. Thanks for making them."

I don't know what's bigger, her ass, or her mood swings.

As much as I like her attitude, I like her laughs and smiles even more.

Moving closer, I stand in front of her. "You're welcome, but promise me you won't starve yourself again." I wipe a little tomato sauce from her lips, my touch lingering a moment too long. Her brown doe eyes meet mine, sending a flutter through my chest, the kind of exhilarating feelings I only get before a climb. I step back before I do something I shouldn't.

Like kiss her.

Chapter 12

Mia

"It takes both sunshine and rain to nourish my soil."
-The Forest –

Nervously, I head toward my room. I pause at the door, half expecting to see a bear. The room is just as I left it; thankfully, bear-free. Inside, my thoughts swirl, a tangled mess of fear from the night's events and the unexpected, intense moments with Jake.

I lean against the wall, my mind replaying every look and every touch. My body burns at the memories. He is clearly not the relationship type, and I'm not into casual flings. But there's something about him, a connection that's hard to ignore. I let my head hit softly against the wall and groan. *Damn him.* Every time I think I've got him figured out; he throws me off balance.

Sinking onto the bed, I gaze at the ceiling, my stomach still doing somersaults as I think of him. The mixed signals, the laughter, the shared vulnerability; it's all too much. I let out a long, conflicted sigh, my emotions a chaotic storm. How am I supposed to deal with this? The last thing I need is to fall for a guy like Jake, but pushing him away seems equally impossible.

My phone rings, and I jump.

"Hey, girl, how's it going?" I smile as I answer, knowing Rylee has a sixth sense for detecting even the slightest change in my tone the moment I say hello.

"My boss is such an ass," she says without missing a beat.

"What did he do?" I ask, playing with my curls.

"He's piling all this extra work on me, and he's been super grumpy," she complains.

"Hot and grumpy?" I tease, hoping to lighten the mood.

"Oh, absolutely. Sexy as hell, and he totally knows it. He's also smart, which just adds to it." I can almost see her rolling her eyes. "This is one of the best fashion companies in New York, and I've worked my ass off for this internship. I won't allow someone with a small dick to ruin that for me," she says, and we both laugh.

"He's messing with the wrong girl," I tell her confidently. "Do you want me to come down there and kick his ass?"

She laughs at that. "Girl, you can't throw a punch to save your life. You're like a chihuahua, all bark and no bite." And we both laugh harder because she's right.

A comfortable silence falls between us, the kind we always share. She's probably applying her eyelashes.

"So, any update on your Mr. Hot Asshole?" She breaks the silence.

I was hoping we wouldn't talk about me. "He's not mine, and not much. Still hate him." But my voice comes a little too high pitched, betraying me.

"Myara Cherie, are you lying to me?" Damn it. "Spill the beans," she demands. I roll my eyes and sigh before I tell her everything.

"OMG, you want to fuck him, don't you?" she blurts out the second I'm done filling her in.

I lie back on the bed and exhale deeply. My cheeks heat like a teenager's. "No, I don't want to fuck him." I don't know how she came to that conclusion from what I said.

"Ahem." Someone clears their throat. My soul literally leaves my body as I turn to find Jake standing at my door, eating an apple, looking annoyingly sexy.

Damn it, Rylee.

"You're a terrible liar," Rylee says over the phone speaker, oblivious to what's happening.

"Shit. I gotta go." I quickly hang up before she says anything else.

I get off the bed and stand up, facing him. "How long have you been standing there?" My words come out flustered. How much of that conversation did he hear?

He takes a bite of his apple, chewing slowly. His eyes lock on mine. Why is it hot in here?

"Not long." But the smirk on his face tells me he's lying. He probably heard everything.

I need an alien to abduct me right now. Please, I'm begging.

Obviously, no aliens. Plan B. "I need a shower," I blurt out, desperate for an excuse to escape the tension that's building between us.

I make my way toward the bathroom, but his long legs catch up to me, closing the distance in a heartbeat, and pinning me against the bathroom door. The cool wood seeps through my thin shirt, chilling me despite the heat coming from his body.

"Why does your friend think you want to fuck me?" His mouth twists into a mysterious smile.

I gasp, his words and his closeness make my throat parched, like a desert desperately needing rain. Every swallow feels like sandpaper.

I knew he heard it.

Where are those aliens? Now will be a good time.

"Who says I was talking about you?" I try to keep my composure under his intense gaze but fail miserably.

"So, you were not talking about me?" He tilts his head to the side, still with that smirk on his face.

"No, I was talking about my boyfriend." I bite down on my bottom lip to keep it from trembling. His eyes drop to my lips as his pupils dilate before he gently frees them with his thumb. It lingers there.

I close my eyes as his finger moves against my lips. Shivers trail through my body, starting at the nape of my neck and trickling down like tiny raindrops. The sensation deepens into a gentle surge that gathers and intensifies in the pit of my stomach.

He leans closer, his other arm over my head. A hurricane brewing in his eyes. For a second, I want to be caught up in it, to be consumed by the tension between us.

"Fuck," he groans, hitting above my head with his fist before stepping back, shoving his hands into his pocket. I immediately miss the warmth of his proximity. "I came to say they're here to fix your window. Let me know when they can come up."

"Hmm," I nod, my words caught in my throat.

I watch as he walks away, closing the door behind him. I bang my head against the bathroom door. What just happened and why didn't he kiss me? Did I want him to kiss me? Of course not.

I step into the bathroom, ignoring the frustration and maybe something else he so easily evoked in me. After I take a quick shower, I change into high waisted shorts and a crop top that says *buy me books and tell me I'm pretty* before heading downstairs.

Alex is chatting away with the two guys that's here to fix my broken window from when the tree fell last night.

Alex is wearing a black polo with short sleeves that reveal his tattoo, adding an edge to his clean-cut appearance. His hair is just as tousled as Jake's, but it has a rich black shade. Gray eyes complement his olive skin complexion beautifully.

"Hey, Mia." His eyes meet mine and he smiles, shifting his weight from one foot to the other.

"Hey, Alex," I smile back at him.

"I want to apologize for the last time," his eyes flick to Jake before turning to mine, "showing up like that... We didn't know you rented the cabin. You should have kicked us out." He chuckles lightly, but he sounds sincere. "Hell, you should've kicked this asshole out, too."

He points his thumb toward Jake. "You rented this place, so it should have stayed yours. You didn't have to share it with him, and we didn't have to invade your privacy."

"Thanks, and trust me, I tried, but Jake doesn't take no for an answer." I glance at Jake, who's leaning against the counter, watching us. His eyes narrow, and he shoves his hand into his pocket, looking amused but also tense. His stare sends ripples through my chest like pebbles tossed into a tranquil lake. Disturbing my emotions, drawing me in against my better judgment.

Why is he wearing gray sweatpants? I turn my attention back to Alex before I look down at something I shouldn't.

"Do you want me to kick him out for you?"

I glance at Jake again; his eyes are challenging me to say yes. "It's okay, he can stay. I might need him next time there's a storm or a bear break in again."

My words are light, but inside, the thought of not having him around suddenly is less appealing than I would have expected.

"I don't want to be alone," I add. I don't want him to leave, even though admitting that to myself is unsettling. I turn my attention to the other two guys. "How long is it going to take?"

"Give us an hour or two," one of them lets me know.

"Okay, I'll make us lunch then." I tie my hair up into a ponytail and throw an apron around my waist. I open the fridge to grab the chicken I bought last time.

The open concept of the place means I can still see Jake and Alex in the living room. Sometimes, I catch him stealing glances at me.

"Hey, Mia," Alex calls out. "Do you mind if Sarah and I hang out here again this weekend?" He really doesn't need my permission, but it's nice that he thought to ask.

"Of course, no problem at all." I smile at him. I like Sarah. She's the kind of person who fills the room with conversation, making everyone feel included. I look forward to spending more time with them.

I watch Jake as he steps away to take a call. His brows are furrowed, and the hand not holding the phone is raking through his hair.

When he ends the call, he pauses, taking a moment to collect himself before taking a few attempted steps toward me, his shoulders slumping.

"You okay?" My eyes search him.

"I'm fine," he says too quickly.

I arch an eyebrow, calling his bluff. His green eyes meet mine, darker than usual. "I was just talking to my mom," he says, forcing a smile, but I can see the pain and anger in his eyes.

I reach out and squeeze his hand, a sharp ache piercing my heart. He glances at our hands, and his eyes soften as he looks up at me. They linger there for a few seconds. "Do you need help with anything?" He changes the subject.

"I'm done, but you can bring the salad to the table."

I carry the chicken to the table where Jake already set the salad. The timing couldn't be more perfect as the guys descend the stairs. "All done. We've installed your new window."

"Great, thank you. Right on time for lunch." I clap my hands together. I love cooking for other people.

Everyone takes a seat, serving themselves the chicken tenders with salad.

"This is so good, Mia," Alex says, his mouth full.

One of the guys, I think his name is Lucas, turns to me with a grin. "Please tell me you're single. I'd marry you right now for this cooking."

Everyone bursts out laughing, except Jake. His jaw clenches, the muscles in his arm tensing as he forcefully stabs at his salad like they personally offended him.

Poor vegetables.

"She got a boyfriend." Jake's tone is sharp, slicing through the laughter. His eyes lock with mine, dark and stormy, as if the idea bothers him.

Once everyone finishes eating, Jake steps in to help me with the dishes. His silence is palpable, creating an invisible barrier that wasn't there before. I steal glances at him while we work side by side, wondering if his quiet mood is because of the tense phone call he had earlier, or Lucas' playful marriage proposal.

I finish wiping down the counters and head toward the stairs to catch up on some writing. "Hey, Mia?" Jake stops me, and I turn to face him.

He's leaning against the counter, his fingers tapping lightly. "Want to join me for a run later?"

I pause, his eyes linger on mine. "Sure, sounds good. Let me know when you're heading out." His eyes are gentle and warm, the corners crinkling slightly. A genuine smile spread across his face.

I like that smile.

Chapter 13

Jake

"Like two trees whose branches have grown so close they intertwine, two hearts can fuse together, inseparable and forever changed by the other existence."

-The Forest-

Grabbing my laptop from my desk, I head downstairs, and grab a beer from the fridge, not caring it is barely the afternoon. I step outside by the pool and find some shade to escape the harsh afternoon sun.

A headache is coming, a dull pressure at the base of my skill, and I know a beer won't help, but I'm desperate for anything to ease the knot of tension building inside of me.

Lucas' words replay, mockingly, in my head: 'I'll marry you for this cooking.' Seriously? What century is he living in? Is he looking for a wife, or a chef? I scoff at the absurdity, irritated that I'm even dwelling on it. My focus should be on the more pressing disaster at hand.

The bank denied my loan request for the hotel. Apparently, my father already took out a loan for who knows what. Let's add it to the list of things he's ruined, just like our family. Apparently, the hotel wasn't as important to him as I thought. I guess she was the only one that mattered to him. I'm willing to bet he took out those loans for her.

The anger simmers within me, fueling a bitter resentment. Why should I drain my own savings, the money I earned, to clean up his mess?

Sipping the beer, I stare at the water shining under the sun, trying to calm the storm inside, but the alcohol does little to ease the seething frustration.

I never asked for this.

I run a hand through my hair before opening the laptop. Now that the bank denied the loan request, I need to look for potential investors. As I'm going through my emails, the air shifts. It becomes warmer, charged with a faint electricity before a storm. I know she's here before I even see her.

Despite my best efforts, my gaze seeks her out, drawn like a magnet to her form as she settles on the lounge chair across from me. Her focus is on the laptop screen.

Her presence makes it hard to concentrate on the emails I need to send for the hotel. I catch her stealing glances at me. "You're staring," I call out.

"No, I'm not," she says, but our eyes lock again, neither of us wanting to look away. I close my laptop and move closer to her, gravitating towards her.

Her gaze lingers on me as I sit at the edge of her lounge chair. She's nervously tapping her fingers on the keyboard.

"What's on your mind?"

She remains silent, her fingers hovering above the keyboard.

"Talk to me," I say. I'm met with more silence. She avoids my gaze and stares into the distance. I know that look. Something is clearly bothering her.

But I'm met with more silence. I take a deep breath, trying to be patient. "Come on, let's go for a walk," I suggest, but she shoots me a sharp glare. Realizing my approach might be a little too direct, I add, "Please?" softer this time. *Princess* doesn't like being told what to do.

After a moment, she sighs, closes her laptop, and stands up. I grab my laptop and follow her inside. So, that's a yes. She's wearing another one of her graphic shirts. This one says, *I'm 99% sunshine but ohhh that 1%.*

I think it should be the other way around. I chuckle to myself. How did I end up here, sharing a cabin with her, this woman who somehow became my concern in the little time I've known her? I shake my head.

We place our laptops on the kitchen island before we step out. Walking through the forest, her expression changes. The lines of tension around her eyes ease, almost as if she's absorbing the tranquility of the surrounding trees. A genuine, unguarded smile replaces her previously reserved look.

Once we reach the waterfall, she takes a seat on a rock, captivated by the water's cascade, but my attention remains fixed on her. I sit on a rock beside her, memories of our first meeting at the gas station surface. She seemed familiar, and I've been racking my brain since then, yet nothing clicks.

"It's beautiful," she breathes out, her eyes widening with awe as she stares at the waterfall, listening to the rushing water. "I love waterfalls. They remind us to let go, and that falling doesn't always have to hurt." She pauses and smiles. "My mom used to tell me, when you're having a bad day, just find a waterfall and stare at it. Watch how it falls over the rock. It doesn't let anything get in its way. It flows right over them." She laughs, and I can't help but smile at the sound. "She even built a small one in our backyard."

While she's in awe of the waterfall, I'm in awe of her. She's, *my* waterfall. She turns to look at me, and our eyes meet. I'm not sure what I'm looking for, but I can't look away.

She's studying me too.

"You always look at me like you are trying to figure me out," she says.

Am I that obvious?

I offer her a half smile. "It's strange, but I feel like we've met before. You seem familiar, yet I can't place where or how." Her eyes draw me in and penetrate deep into my soul.

"I get the same feeling." No one has ever looked at me like that before.

We sit there in silence for a few minutes, both of us lost in our own thoughts. Moving from the rock, I find a comfortable spot on the grass. Shaded, yet has a clear view of the sky through the branches. I lay on my back, staring at the moving clouds, the coolness of the grass pressing through my skin. The sound of the rushing water is comforting.

I'm aware of her eyes on me, burning on the side of my face as she remains seated on the rock. "Wanna join me?" I pat the ground beside me. She hesitates, then silently, almost tentatively, she settles next to me.

We both lean our heads back and stare up at the sky.

After a moment of silence, I ask, "You want to tell me what's wrong now?" hoping she will tell me the thoughts that shadow her beautiful eyes.

She turns, meeting my gaze directly. "Only if you share what got you so upset earlier."

"Okay, deal," I say with a light laugh. I'm not sure why she even cares.

She breathes in deeply before she starts. "My mom was an amazing writer, and I've always wanted to be like her..." She trails off. Her eyes fill with unshed tears. "But I'm not as good as her. My dad wants me to be a doctor and thinks writing is just a hobby, even though my mom made it—she was a bestselling author." She pauses, her fingers trembling as she picks at a blade of grass. "He thinks she was one of a kind and had a gift. And he's right. I don't have the gift she had. I could never be as good as her."

I understand her fear, her own expectations, and her dad's expectations. I studied business because my family expected me, as the first and only child, to manage the family business. But that's not what I wanted.

"Can you do something for me?" I reach for her hand and squeeze it, her pulse quickens under my touch.

She has vulnerability in her eyes.

"I need you to stop thinking about your mom's writing for a second, and what your dad wants. Ask yourself, what does Mia want? And why does *she* want to be a writer?"

I hold her gaze, so she can see the truth in my eyes.

"If that's what you want, what you love—if writing makes you lose track of time, and you could do it for hours, so lost in it that you forget to eat—then fucking do it." I squeeze her hand again, more firmly, willing her to understand.

She doesn't give me an answer, but I don't need her to. It's something she has to find within herself.

She gives me a tentative smile, and I capture it, tucking it away somewhere deep in my heart. I love her smile. "I love climbing. It started because of my uncle—he introduced me to it. But when I was on top of the wall looking down, I felt something I'd never felt before. A sense of control and accomplishment." I pause, glancing down at our joined hands before looking back at her. "And I fell in love with that feeling." She holds my gaze, and I continue. "You can't compare your writing to hers. You have your own voice and your own story to tell. Focus on that, okay?"

"Okay." She nods, a small smile escaping her lips, lighting up everything around us. "You're surprisingly good at this pep talk thing." She laughs.

"Why is that surprising?" I raise an eyebrow.

"Because I thought you were just an asshole, but I see you, Jacob Harrington." Those brown eyes framed by long lashes, and thick eyebrows draw me in without mercy, an intensity I can't escape.

I ignore the way my heart chokes in my throat. "You know my full name?"

"I'm staying in a cabin with a stranger. Did you think I wouldn't do a little background check? I had to make sure you weren't a serial killer or something." Her laughter bubbles, it mingles with the sound of the waterfall.

"You looked me up?" I laugh along with her.

"Technically, my best friend did." Her laughter grows louder; it's infectious. I wait for the little snort that I know is coming, and when it does, I laugh even more. My chest is lighter than I've felt all day.

I glance at her. My heart is racing, a reaction I can't quite control. I can barely breathe with the need to press my lips against hers. Are they as soft as they seem?

Then, I remind myself that I don't deal with feelings and emotions. They just complicate things, and you have no control over them once you give them the power to destroy you.

Life is simpler with the adrenaline rush of a climb, or the thrill of doing something crazy. Top it with a great orgasm with someone you will never see again.

Mixing pleasure with feelings only leads to disaster. That's a line I will not cross.

I've seen it firsthand with my parents. My dad kept hurting my mom, and she forgave him over and over. Then she would spend weeks, sometimes months, in a deep depression.

"Why isn't the waterfall mentioned on the website?" She pulls me from my thoughts. "I'm sure people would pay more to stay here if they knew about it."

I shrug, my confusion mirroring hers. "I've been coming here for years and never knew about this waterfall. It's bizarre."

She sits up, her eyes narrowing as she scans the surrounding forest. "That's not possible. Waterfalls don't just appear."

"I said the same thing."

"Maybe you missed it, or you never came to this side of the forest before," she suggests, though her tone is more questioning than convincing.

"Maybe." But I'm pretty sure I've hiked through here before.

"How else would you explain it?" Her lips pursing in thought.

Yeah, I'm wondering the same thing. And surely, we can't be the only ones who know about this waterfall.

Chapter 14

Mia

I found this quaint little café last week, Marie's Café, and it has quickly become my haven. It's a little sanctuary where I momentarily forget about the outside world. Sunlight pours through the large windows, illuminating the lush green plants spilling over the shelves and hanging from baskets. I settle into a cozy corner on one of the green plush sofas, a spot that is almost made for quiet reflection or to focus on my writing.

As I get comfortable, Marie, the owner of the café, approaches me with her usual warm smile. "Your usual, I'm guessing?"

Realizing I now have a 'usual' brings a small, contented smile to my face. "Yes, please."

A couple of minutes later, Marie returns and sets down my iced coffee with extra cream and sugar. Just how I like it, despite knowing it's not the healthiest choice. Alongside it, she places a chocolate cookie. I look up, surprised. "I didn't order this." I point at the cookie.

She simply smiles. "It's on the house."

"Thank you." Being at ease with her, I ask, "There's a waterfall near my cabin, but it's not on any map and seems unknown to everyone. Ever heard anything about it?"

She pauses, her silver hair catching the light as she turns to me. "Oh, my dear," she starts, her voice a gentle hum. "There are many things in those forests that aren't for everyone to see or know. Secrets that have kept themselves hidden."

"But a whole waterfall?" I press, intrigued by her response. "It seems like such a place would be famous."

Her smile softens, and she leans in slightly, as if to share a confidential secret. "Ah, but not all wonders want to be found. My mother used to tell me stories about a couple that was deeply in love that the forest itself gave them a secret place—a waterfall, hidden away from prying eyes. A result of their love, shielded by nature."

A chill runs down my spine. "That sounds more like a fairy tale."

"Maybe," she says, her smile turning mysterious and her brown skin glowing warmly under the light. "But not everything in this world needs to make logical sense, my dear. Some truths, we feel them in our heart rather than understand with the mind. And maybe some secrets are meant to stay just that, secrets."

I pondered her words as she walked away, her presence leaving a trail of warmth. Maybe she's right, and Jake's family wanted to keep this waterfall a secret, or a surprise.

I am sipping my coffee when I notice an older couple sitting together. The woman is reading a book. It reminds me of my parents, how they would sit together with my mom's legs draped over my dad's lap as he mindlessly massaged her foot; he'd watch his game and she would read her book. Those memories bring a bittersweet smile to my face. It just reminds me how they will not get to grow old together.

I blink back the tears that threaten to spill. *Don't cry,* I silently plead to myself, taking another sip of my coffee, focusing on the coolness it brings. It's moments like these, quiet, where the memories come flooding in the hardest.

Typing away on my laptop, I receive a text message.

Hey, Mia! Jake, Alex and I are going out this weekend. You should come.

It's from Sarah. The last time we were together, she insisted we exchange numbers and grabbed my phone to add her contact.

This weekend, that's my birthday. I was thinking more like a quiet night in my room with a tub of ice cream. It's my first birthday without my mom. But maybe a little distraction wouldn't be so bad. Maybe it's what I need.

Sure, that sounds fun.

I text her back before putting my phone aside and focus back on my writing. I need to stop comparing my writing to my mom's and remember why I started writing.

I love writing. Creating worlds and characters that can become someone else's escape. A way to get all these stories out of my head and onto paper. Although loving it doesn't mean I'm automatically good at it.

Back in high school, I submitted my short story to the school's story contest. It was a dark romance about a girl who falls in love with her brother's best friend, who was ten years older. Her parents passed away, and her brother inherited the family business. She was a kid then, so they basically raised her. I know it was a little taboo, but the feedback was harsh. The teacher in charge of the contest said my writing was disturbing.

I guess that was the final straw that shattered my dream.

Maybe I should have submitted something sweet. But isn't writing about expressing yourself? And that was the story I wanted to tell.

These past few days, I've been focusing on outlining. All I have so far are the main characters, and what they look like. I still need to work on their deeper conflicts, what drives them, and what makes them who they are. I need to keep track of plot lines, the characters' arcs, conflicts, and all the settings.

It's a dark fantasy romance, and that also requires a lot of world building, and that is a little scary. My story is about an island with a secret world beneath the ocean. Even though the surface world remains unaware of their existence, their fates and destinies intertwine.

I'm afraid the story is just in my head and I'm not able to bring it to life on the pages.

Today is my birthday and I'm going out with Sarah, Alex, and, of course, Jake. Sarah and Alex are meeting us there.

I stand in front of the full body mirror, admiring my reflection. Over the years, I've learned to love my body. Although I don't work out a lot, I love every curve, even the stretch marks on my thighs.

For tonight, I've chosen a rich burgundy dress, the color so deep it glows against my skin. My grandma sent it to me as a birthday present. It's from one of the most prestigious fashion lines in Paris, BCAK, *Black Couture At Kingley*. The company is Black owned by the Kingley family, who apparently are friends and business partners with my grandmother. They distribute her wines.

The dress fits snug, hugging every curve, with a bold slit on the side that playfully reveals my leg with each movement. The plunging neckline is daring, more than I'm used to, but tonight is special. It's my birthday. I haven't dressed up or gone out in a while, not since she got sick. Maybe this is a chance to let go a little. I could use the distraction.

Turning around, I smile at how my backside looks in the dress. *Your ass looks good, girl.*

I pair the dress with gold heels, adding inches to my height. A small gold clutch carries the essentials: lipstick, a phone, and a little courage. My hair is straight, a change from its usual wild curliness. I wanted to try something different. The thought of Jake waiting for me downstairs makes me even more nervous, even though I know this isn't a date—we're just carpooling.

But when it comes to him, I can't hide the smile that plays on my lips.

Descending the stairs, Jake is already waiting. Green eyes that are brighter under the light are observing me and scanning me thoroughly, making my heart beat faster in my chest.

Deep breaths Mia.

With each step I take, his smile grows wider, the intensity in his eyes deepen. By the time I reach the bottom of the stairs, I'm a jumbled mess of nerves. He leans in, and murmurs, "You're beautiful."

Butterflies flutter around inside my stomach. "Thank you. You don't look too bad yourself." I look up at him and drink him in. His black polo shirt clings to his biceps, and his black jeans show his long, toned legs. *He's gorgeous.*

"Ready to go?" I break the spell.

He nods, a bigger smile spreading across his face. That smile is dangerous.

"After you," he says, and I walk past him. I don't need eyes on the back of my head to know he's still checking me out. He's definitely looking at my ass.

Once we reach his car, he opens the door for me. "This is not a date. You don't have to open the door for me." I chuckle, reminding both him and me.

He pauses, his expression is serious. "I don't care what this is. When you're with me, I open your door, princess." His jaw tightens, and the muscle in his cheek twitches.

Got it, Mr. Gentleman.

A shiver runs through me at the intensity of his gaze. I nod, the words catching in my throat. He holds the door as I slide into the passenger seat, the cold leather presses against my skin. He closes it gently and heads to the driver's side. And of course, he drives a manual.

I steal a glance at him. His expression has softened, but the edge is still there.

He switches gears effortlessly, his forearm muscles flexing with each movement.

"Is it hot in here, or is it just me?" Then I realize I say that out loud a little too late. I adjust my dress, attempting to cool myself down. His arms catch my attention again, drawing my eyes involuntarily. There's something about the way he moves that's magnetic.

He throws a quick smirk my way. "Want me to turn up the AC?" he teases. He knows exactly what's making me flustered, and it has nothing to do with the AC.

"Just shut up and drive," I huff, crossing my arms defensively.

He bursts out laughing, a rich sound that fills the car.

I hate his laugh.

Do you, though? The little voice in my head whispers.

Well, I hate the way his laugh sends tingles through my body and the throbbing sensation between my thighs. I shift uncomfortably in my seat, ignoring the heat building inside me.

About an hour later, we pull into the parking lot. Jake shifts the car into park and turns to me. "Just wait a second. Let me open the door for you." He unbuckles his seat belt.

"It's okay, I can get it." I reach for the door handle, opening it before he comes around. As I try to step down from the Jeep, I lose my balance and stumble forward. In an instant, his arms are wrapping around me, pulling me into his chest. His heart pulses beneath my ear. He smells like sandalwood and lavender. It's both comforting and intoxicating, and I close my eyes, lost in the moment.

His brows furrow and his eyes fill with worry. Why does he care if I'm hurt or not?

His hand reaches up, gently brushing a strand of hair away from my face, his touch lingering. "Next time, wait for me. I wouldn't want anything to happen to you." He growls, the sound coming deep from his throat. It sends my heart racing, heat pooling low in my belly. My breath catches in my throat, and goosebumps spread across my skin like a wave.

The cool night air outside the restaurant brushes against my face, carrying the scent of nearby flowers and the soft chatter of people walking by outside the parking lot. Every inch of space between us crackles with electric tension, making the air feel heavy and alive.

I fight the overwhelming urge to close the distance, knowing I shouldn't. Giving in would blur the lines and risk everything. I remind myself why I need to keep my distance, even as my body yearns to bridge the gap.

Gently, he sets me down from the Jeep running board and on my feet, making sure I'm stable before releasing me. I take a moment to steady myself.

"I'm okay," I assure him, avoiding his gaze, wiping my sweaty palm on my dress.

His blonde hair looks golden under the dim light in the parking lot. The flutter in my chest won't settle, and I'm hyper-aware of every movement he makes, every brush of his hand as we walk side by side.

He insists on being a gentleman by opening the door for me, but I can't fall for those acts. We might get along, but that doesn't change the fact that he is still that guy who sleeps around with women, not even bothering to know their names.

As we walk in, we immediately spot Sarah and Alex. They're sitting in a round plush booth, accompanied by a woman I don't recognize. Blonde hair, blue eyes, wearing a white, off the shoulder body-con dress, like the one I almost chose for tonight. That would have been awkward.

Jake is focusing his attention on her. "Jessie, what are you doing here?" His jaw tightens, and his skin turns ashen, draining off color. He looks like he's seen a ghost.

"Hi, Jake." She smiles, but he doesn't smile back. A frown forms on his face as his brow furrows and his lips press tightly together.

"Can we talk?" Her eyes almost pleading.

He looks away momentarily, as if gathering his thoughts. "We have nothing to talk about," he says, his tone flat, clearly not wanting to engage. He glances at me briefly, an unreadable look in his eyes, before turning back to Jessie. Her presence is clearly affecting him.

"Please, Jake." She steps closer, her hand reaching out to touch his arm, her fingers trembling. Her desperation is palpable.

He sighs, his shoulders slumping. "Fine, but not here." He grabs her wrist and leads her outside, leaving me standing here.

My fingers curl involuntarily, nails digging into my palm as I watch them disappear outside. I slide into the booth next to Sarah and Alex, feeling a bit out of place. Alex signals the server over, and he orders his drinks and Sarah orders hers.

The server then turns to me with a charming smile. "And for you, miss?" His deep brown eyes meet mine.

"Surprise me with something strong, please," I say, my gaze then shifting back to the door where Jake and Jessie just exited.

He nods, a knowing smirk crossing his face. "One special drink coming right up."

I should be having a good time. The music is great, and the ambiance is amazing, but my mind keeps wandering back to Jessie. Who is she? Ex-girlfriend or girlfriend.

"I see you, girl," Sarah teases, breaking into my spiraling thoughts. "Did I mention you're looking amazing tonight?"

I force a laugh, turning my head towards her. "You're looking gorgeous yourself." I smile back at her, my fingers tapping nervously on the table before my eyes drift back to the window.

"You, okay?" she asks to catch my attention again. Her eyes linger on me for a bit longer, searching my face.

"Yeah, I'm fine." I nod, giving her a weak smile. "So, what's the story with Jake and Jessie?" I try to sound casual, ignoring the tightness in my chest as I think about their private conversation outside.

"They go way back to high school. It's complicated."

"Interesting. High school, huh?" I force a strained smile. *Complicated how?* I want to ask, but I don't want to seem too interested.

The server brings us our drinks right on time. I consume mine quicker than I should, the glass barely leaving my lips before it's empty. I try to find something to focus on since my mind seems to be occupied with thoughts of Jake and Jessie. Not that I care what they're doing outside. Are they arguing, making up, kissing... I stop myself and start observing Alex and Sarah.

I can't help but notice the way Alex has been looking at her. His eyes light up whenever she speaks or laughs, tracking her movements with an intensity that borders on admiration. Yet Sarah seems completely oblivious to the depth of his attention. She treats him like a friend. Or maybe she's aware but chooses to ignore it, fearing it might complicate their friendship.

But looking at Sarah and Alex makes me think about Jake and Jessie. Were they friends before? They look sort of perfect together. They would probably have gorgeous babies with blue or green eyes.

I grab my glass to take another drink, but it's empty.

I need a refill.

Sarah and Alex, wrapped up in their own bubble, barely notice as I slide out of the booth, muttering a hasty excuse. At the bar, I order another drink. "Hit me with your best drink, please."

The bartender flashes me a charming smile and gets to work. A few seconds later, he slides me my drink. "Thanks." I smile, grabbing the drink, and gulping that rapidly, too. It's good, really good, but it doesn't help with the knot in my stomach.

"What are you drinking, sweetheart?" A husky voice interrupts my thoughts. *Sweetheart?* I turn my head toward the voice, and look at him, starting from his shoes and moving up to his face. Tall, probably in his 30s, dark eyes, very big muscles that strain his vest jacket, short, and impeccably styled hair. I mean, the guy is hot. When I reach his eyes, he smirks.

"Something amazing with alcohol in it." I take another sip.

"Can I buy you another one?"

"I don't see why not. Like I said, it's amazing." I smile at him, bringing the straw to my lips and taking another sip, looking at him from under my lashes.

He signals the bartender. "Another of what she's having, and a whiskey on the rocks for me." The bartender nods.

"What is a beautiful lady like you doing here alone?" He leans in, his hand finding its way to my thigh.

He certainly doesn't waste time, does he?

"I'm not alone now, am I?" I bat my lashes at him. The alcohol gives me enough courage to flirt with this guy who's way out of my league.

"I guess not." His smile widening into a dazzling, sexy grin that lights up his face.

"So, what brings you here, sweetheart?"

"The same reason everyone is here, a good time."

"What kind of good time are you looking for?"

I lean closer and whisper, "Hmmm, what kind are you offering?"

"The kind that you will remember forever." His hand trails up my thigh. His touch makes my skin crawl. It doesn't burn my body or make me yearn for more, the way Jake's touch can.

I push his hand away, forcing a smile.

"What is it, sweetheart? I thought you were looking for a good time."

"Well, I changed my mind." I stand up to walk away, but his hand grabs me. "Let me go." I try to pull away, but he doesn't.

"You heard her, let her go," says a voice from behind me. Turning, I see Jake with his eyebrows drawn together.

"We're just having fun. No need to make a scene."

"You call that fun? She told you to let her go." A ragged rasp tears through his throat. There's no mistaken the warning in his words.

The man lets me go, raising his hands in surrender. "I didn't know she was with someone."

I turn and walk away while Jake gets into it with the guy. I'm glad he came to help me, but I'm still mad at him. We came together, but he left me alone to go be with Jessie.

"Wait, Mia, where are you going?" His long legs quickly catch up to me outside.

"Home." My steps are quick and uneven, the heels and alcohol conspiring to make the world tilt.

"Let me take you." He reaches out to touch my arm, but I pull away instinctively, the memory of the other man's grip still fresh.

"I can take a taxi; just leave me alone." I'm walking as fast as these heels will let me.

Earlier, I felt sexy wearing them. Right now, I just want to take them off. The cool night air brushes against my already wet cheeks with tears. I'm not even sure why I'm crying.

He reaches out again, his grip gentler this time, pulling me back until I'm pressed against his chest. He lowers his head to meet my gaze, brows furrow as he notices the tears. "Why are you crying? Did that guy inside hurt you?" His jaw tightens, and his nostrils flare as he takes a deep breath. "Tell me, and I'll go back inside and break his nose." He growls, his words barely escaping through clenched teeth.

I shake my head, not trusting myself to speak. "It's your boyfriend, isn't it? Call him; I need to speak to him," he demands, his body coiled with tension.

My eyes drop to the ground, unable to look at him. He lifts my chin up with his hand, forcing me to meet his. The softness in them makes my heart flutter against my will. "What's wrong? Talk to me, please." He exhales.

"Nothing, I... I just want to go home." I pull away from him and walk away. I hate these damn shoes for slowing me down.

"Okay, I'll take you home then."

"No, go back to your girlfriend... Or whatever you guys are." The words tumble out, uncontrollable and acidic. Slicing through the air, louder and sharper than intended, as heat flushes my cheeks.

"She's not my girlfriend, and there's nothing between me and her."

"Well, that's not what Sarah told me. Not that I care anyway," I say with a dry chuckle.

He stops, grabbing my arms again and pulling me towards him.

He needs to stop doing that.

His eyes narrow, unblinking, as if he's trying to read my very soul. "Is that why you are upset? Because of Jessie." His grip on my arm tightens, pulling me closer. His other hand moves to lightly touch my chin, tilting my face up toward his. "Are you jealous, Mia?" He's so close to me, I'm sure he can hear how fast my heart is beating.

Jealous? That doesn't make any sense. Why would I be jealous?

I shake my head. "Of course not, I...I have a boyfriend, remember?" I sound less convincing than I hoped for.

He raises an eyebrow, a challenge in his gaze. "Then call this boyfriend of yours. I want to talk to him."

His request catches me off guard, and a lump forms in my throat. "You can't ask me to do that..."

"Call him, Mia," he insists, his tone shifting from asking to demanding.

Tears well up in my eyes again. "I can't... Because he doesn't exist. I lied, okay?" My voice is barely audible against the storm of my making.

There, happy?

His eyes narrow, hurt flickering across his face. He opens his mouth, then closes again. "Why?" He finally breathes out.

I look away, blinking back the tears. "Last time... I was scared, and I had no idea who you were, so I lied. After that, it was just easier for you to think I had a boyfriend." I turn around to gather my thoughts and make sense of the confusing and hurt swirling inside of me.

"Mia, I..." I turn around, my name on his lips like a prayer. I watch as he runs a hand through his hair.

"I don't even know why I'm upset, maybe because today is my birthday. And I wanted to spend it with you guys..." *With you.* I swallow the rest of my sentence, the truth too heavy on my tongue. "This is my first birthday without my mom... I didn't want to be alone. But you, you forgot I existed the moment you saw her." I dare to look up at him through blurry eyes, and there's a tenderness in his eyes that I didn't expect.

"Mia, I didn't know it was your birthday. You should have told me. I'm sorry."

"It doesn't matter, okay? You can go back to her," I say despite the tears that blur my vision and the sobs that are threatening to overcome me. I need to put back the walls that he managed to break through. Even when everything inside of me is screaming for him to stay.

"You really expect me to just go back inside and leave you like this?" His eyes reflect hurt of his own. "God, I know you find it hard to believe, but I care about you more than I can understand or even explain." His thumb wipes away my tears. His gaze is intense, piercing through my soul, and for a moment, I'm lost in it. "What do you want to do? It's still your birthday. Let me make it up to you, please." His hand rubs my cheeks.

I blink, part of me wanting to lean into his touch. "I don't know. What about Jessie?" Hope and confusion entangle inside me.

"Can you please forget about Jessie for now? This is about you." He smiles at me with that sweet smile that has the power to put me in a trance.

I nod, allowing him to pull me into his arms. I melt into him, a warmth against the chilly night air. Why does it feel so freaking amazing when he holds me like this?

After a few moments, he steps back, pulling out a tissue to dab at my tears gently. "How about a smile, for me, please?" he teases, tickling my nose, sparking an unfamiliar yet comforting sense of déjà vu, pulling a smile from me despite everything.

He takes my hand and leads me toward his car. "Come on, I know just the place to take you."

When we reach his car, he opens the door for me. A light smile plays on my lips as I slide into the seat. "This is not a date." I glance up at him, catching his amused expression.

"Got it, not a date." He chuckles, closing the door after me. I watch him walk around to the driver's side, my heart still fluttering. It's strange, this ability he has to stir a silent storm inside me.

We drive away from the bar, and he makes a quick stop at a store. Through the car window, I watch a young couple outside their car. She is sitting on the hood, with him standing between her thighs. Her giggles float in the night as he whispers something in her ear before leaning down to kiss her.

I look away, not wanting to pry at their intimate moment, or maybe I'm just jealous. Jake returns with a few bags, which he places in the trunk.

"What did you buy?" I ask as he gets into the driver's seat, to which he replies with a secret smile. As we drive further, the road becomes a dirt path, bumpy and dark. The only lights coming from the headlights of the Jeep.

After a few minutes, he finally stops and parks. "Wait here for a minute," he lets me know before stepping out of the car.

He comes back shortly and helps me out of the car. We walk toward what appears to be a lake boardwalk. There's a blanket on the floor with a bottle of champagne, flowers, cupcakes, and a candle. "Let's just sit and watch the stars." He points towards the blanket. "It's the best view."

He's right. The view is breathtaking, with the dark lake in front of us and the water gently lapping against the wood. The sky lights up with stars unlike anything I've ever seen.

"I was thinking of getting you a cake, but I wasn't sure about your favorite, so I got a mix of cupcakes instead."

"This is...really nice. You really didn't have to." A warm feeling spreads in my chest.

It's the alcohol.

We sit down on the blanket and Jake hands me the box of cupcakes. "Pick your favorite," he says, and chuckles when I pick the chocolate one. He takes out a small candle and a lighter from his pocket, placing the candle on top of my cupcake, lighting it up for me. "Make a wish."

I close my eyes, wishing to publish my book, and blow out the candle. Opening the champagne, he pours us each a glass.

"Happy birthday, Mia," he toasts. "You only get one sip since you already had too much to drink."

"Thank you, and I'm not drunk."

"If you say so," he chuckles. "So, how old are you?" he asks, casually sipping his drink.

"I'm 23, and you?"

"I'm 25, my birthday was in March." His eyes crinkle with a smile. They look brighter now under the moonlight. We sit there, sipping champagne under the stars, the night air cool.

For a moment, all the awkwardness and confusion of the evening fades away, leaving just the two of us in a peaceful bubble, and the surrounding beauty.

Chapter 15

Jake

We sit under the stars; the bottle of champagne is now empty beside us. I should have stopped her from drinking any more. She's already had one too many drinks. She's staring at the stars, her expressions unreadable.

I'm unsure if it's the alcohol, jealousy over Jessie, or something else that's got her so ruffled. But when she said that she lied about her boyfriend, I felt torn between relief and confusion. To be honest, I suspected as much. Because if he was real, why did he never show up, and how is she so comfortable with me? The way she held me that night of the storm.

What's holding me back now from kissing her, from touching those lips I've been craving? We've been getting close, too close, and it's unnerving. Hookups are straightforward, simple, but with Mia, a single taste wouldn't be enough.

Caught in my thoughts, I barely notice her shifting onto my lap, her arms encircling my neck, her legs wrapping around my waist, her scent of jasmine and alcohol intoxicating. "What are you doing, Mia?" My words come out in a breathy whisper.

"What does it look like?" Her fingers work the buttons of my shirt as she moves against me. "I want you to fuck me," she says with a boldness that surprises me. My body burns at her words, a bolt of fiery energy that consumes me.

I shake my head, desperate to bring some kind of clarity to my mind. "Mia..." I plead, gently pulling her hands away from my shirt.

"I know what I'm doing. I want this, I want you." She stares at me under her lashes before looking down at my pants where my cock betrays me. "Judging by how hard you are right now, you want me, too." I close my eyes and silently pray to any God that's listening to give me strength.

"Of course, I'm hard. I mean, Jesus, look at you." I let out a breath. My lungs are not getting enough air. She's gorgeous, the kind that can bring a man to his knees and make him do crazy things. "But we can't—"

She cuts me off. "I know your rules about not sleeping with the same girl twice. This is just for tonight." She pauses and bites her bottom lips.

Oh God, I love when she does that.

"Douxy baby, I just need an orgasm; can you give me that?"

Sweet baby Jesus.

Douxy?

Her eyes are dark with desire and something else, desperation.

"Damn it," I curse under my breath.

Her fingers trace my chest. "This is a once in a lifetime opportunity, Jacob Harrington. I've never hooked up with anyone before. I have this stupid rule that sex needs to be intimate with someone that I share an emotional connection with." Pain seeping into her voice. "But I'm making an exception for you." She breathes out the unbearable tension building between us.

I lean in close to her ear. "When we do this, I need you sober, so you're able to remember every second." *Be patient; our time will come, princess.* I'm not sure I can leave this cabin without getting a taste of her.

"Fine, I'll handle it myself. Just kiss me?" She lifts her dress, revealing she's not wearing anything underneath.

What the fuck?

She lets out a small moan as she grinds onto the hardness in my pants. I grab her waist, holding her in place. "Mia, stop," I say, firmer this time. I gently lift her up to adjust her dress. "I don't want you to do something you'll regret tomorrow." I hold her gaze as she fights to hold back her tears.

She buries her face into the crook of my neck. "I'm sorry," she says, her tears warm against my skin. Her arms tighten around my neck. "For tonight, I just wanted the pain to go away."

"It's okay." I rub circles on her back. We stay like this until her breathing deepens, and she falls asleep.

Seeing her cry, or sad tears at something deep inside me, as if her pain is my own. I want to take her pain away, but not like this.

I desire her, craving her more than anyone or anything in my life—but not like that. I know she's trying to escape the pain. Trust me, it doesn't work. She would regret it in the morning.

A wave of warmth spreads through me, her breath against my neck sending gentle ripples through my body.

Carefully, I stand, her body still clinging to mine as if it belongs there. I settle her in the passenger seat of the car, her slight stir barely noticeable as I fasten the seat belt around her. After closing the door, I return to collect our belongings, packing them away in the trunk.

Sliding into the driver's seat, my eyes can't help but linger on her as her head rests against the window. She is like the moon, and it's impossible not to be absorbed by her light and beauty. I reach in the backseat for my jacket and gently place it over her shoulders, my heart rate picking up, staring at her peaceful expression. As I drive to the cabin, I keep stealing glances at her.

When we arrive, I open her door and carefully lift her, carrying her up the stairs. Her body against mine sends pulse after pulse crashing into the pool of desires, protectiveness, and confusions she's awakening inside of me.

In her room, I gently lie her on the bed, removing her heels, each action making my pulse quicken with an intimate tenderness. In her bathroom, I search for something to clean her face, and I find something that says make-up remover, and it's a pack of wipes. *Perfect.*

I return to her side, and gently wipe one of the cloths around her face. The dark ink leaks around her eyes. She stirs slightly but doesn't wake up. I continue until her pretty face is clean and makeup-free.

After tucking her in, I turn to leave, but her hand reaches out to me. "Please stay with me." Her sleepy voice pulls me back. I can't deny her, nor do I want to. I remove my shirt and join her in the bed. She snuggles closer to me, her head against my chest. I press my lips against her hair like it's something I've done before.

"Good night, Moonie." The nickname escapes my lips as if it's always been there.

What are you doing to me, Mia?

The Forest
Summer 1920

The next day, they returned. Eadrick's eyes widened; Ifunayla's mouth fell open. Where there was once a gentle stream was now a waterfall. Water cascaded down and over the rocks.

The early morning sun filtered through the trees and turned tiny water droplets into gemstones.

My trees stood taller, their leaves glistening with dew. Flowers were more vibrant, and their petals impossibly vivid.

The air was fresher, filled with the earthy scent of moss and the sweet smell of my blooming flowers.

Everything was as beautiful and magical as their love.

They approached cautiously, almost reverently. Then, unable to contain their joy, they broke into a run, splashing into the pool beneath the waterfall. Their laughter filled the air, pure and untamed. He lifted her, spinning her around, her skirt fanning out like a blooming flower. Their eyes met, and in that moment, no words were needed. They danced under the rushing water, each droplet reflecting glowing happiness.

My waterfall became their secret haven, a sanctuary where they could be together, away from the judging eyes of the world. It was a place that only they could access, a secret that I guarded fiercely. The soil beneath my trees knew the unique shape of their footsteps, opening pathways that were hidden from others. My leaves whispered their names in the wind, guiding them and parting only for them. No one ever got close; no one was ever aware of its existence. My trails always led them somewhere else or wandered, lost. It was their place, theirs alone.

Chapter 16

Mia

Something solid and warm presses against my cheek, and a steady beat slowly stirs me awake. I let out a soft moan and snuggle closer, and I'm greeted with a groggy, deep voiced "Good morning."

"Morning," I say as muscular arms wrap around me, pulling me closer. This is not my pillow. The memory of last night played through my mind, causing me to sit up abruptly. I throw off the blanket and stand up, only to be hit by a massive headache, forcing me to sit back down.

Turning, I see Jake propped up against my headboard wearing a sleepy smile, his hair even more tousled than usual, some strands falling across his face.

"What are you doing in my bed?"

He chuckles. "You asked me to stay, remember?"

"I don't remember." I lie, even though I remember every little detail. Including me, pleading for him to fuck me.

I wish I could forget it all. This isn't me. I don't get drunk. I can blame everything on the fact I was missing my mom, but I know part of it was because of him. It wasn't just the alcohol. I wanted him. The alcohol only made me bold enough to act on it. I'm glad he stopped me, though. I shouldn't cross that line.

"You need to get out of my bed and out of my room." I stand up and point toward the door. He slides the blanket away, swinging his long legs over to stand. But instead of heading to the door, he moves toward me, his green eyes holding me captive. My gaze involuntarily travels over his bare chest, tracing the line of his muscles. The sight of him sends a fire between my thighs.

He moves a step closer, another. I don't realize I'm moving until my back presses against the cool glass of the window. He leans in, bringing his face level with mine.

"You don't remember how you begged me to fuck you?" he questions. I swallow, my heart in my throat, his gaze following the movement. "Or how you were grinding on me so sinfully?" The intensity in his eye is ready to burn me. "God knows it took every ounce of my self-control not to fuck you right there." His finger traces my cheek. Just that brief touch makes me tingle all over. "But next time you ask me to fuck you, I want it because you want me, not because you're drunk or need an escape from your pain." His face hardens, his eyes burning with an intensity that is fierce and dangerous.

I bite down on my lower lip to stop my heart from racing. "That's never gonna happen. Last night was a mistake, so thank you for stopping me." I look down, but his hand catches my chin and forces me to look at him.

"We'll see about that, princess, and you're welcome." He rubs my nose, and the gesture makes my inside melt.

He needs to stop doing that.

"Take a shower, and I'll bring you something for the headache." His fingers continue to trace lazy lines across my cheeks and my eyes close from his touch. My pulse throbbing in my throat, I can almost taste it. When I reopen them, he's walking away, his ass looking so good in those jeans. I stand there trying to relearn how to breathe.

Disappointment fills my stomach. I realized I wanted him to kiss me. *What the hell is wrong with me?* That's it. I'm staying as far away from him as possible.

I fucking hate him.

No, you don't. That stupid little voice scoffs at me.

I make my way into the bathroom to take a shower. I catch my face in the mirror, makeup free. He must have wiped it off. Why does he do sweet things like that, sending every goddamn nerve in my body into a wild, trembling dance?

I turn on the water, remove my dress, and wait for it to warm up before stepping into the shower. The warm water hits my skin, making my body tingle. My fingers trace over my skin, and I shiver, wishing it were his hands instead.

I hate that he stirs so much within me; desire, longing, an ache I can't quite name, and emotions I can't control. I am rarely sexually attracted to anyone unless I have feelings for them. That thought terrifies me and makes everything more confusing.

My mind replays the memories of last night. He could have taken advantage of me, but he chose not to.

Then I remember what Sarah said about Jessie, but Jake insists there's nothing between them. It doesn't matter, anyway; I can't allow anything to happen between us.

I have a feeling that would only leave me with a broken heart. Underneath all the flirting and his playboy façade, I know he's truly sweet. I can really see myself falling for him, but I'm not ready for that fall, knowing he won't be there to catch me.

After the shower, I dry myself with a towel and then slip into a robe. Back in my room, I find a glass of lemon water, two pills for my headache, and a plate of toast and eggs waiting for me on my desk. He made me breakfast; the sight brings an involuntary smile to my lips, and my heart flutters. I'm in deep trouble, aren't I?

After eating, I put on a cute ruffle summer dress with my pink converse. I head towards his room, my steps hesitant, but he's not here.

I head downstairs and spot him outside by the pool. He has his phone pressed to his ear, his face tense. I pause at the door, my fingers lightly gripping the frame as I watch him, heart pounding.

When he ends the call, I step out, the cool morning air caressing my skin. Our eyes meet, and the corner of his eyes soften. I offer a tentative smile, hoping it conveys my gratitude as I approach him.

He sits back at the table, his laptop open in front of him, and his fingers begin tapping rapidly on the keyboard. I move closer, noticing the deep frown line on his forehead and tense shoulders.

He draws in a deep breath, then lets it out slowly, his fingers pausing on the keyboard. "Did you need something?" His eyes are still on the screen.

"I wanted to thank you for breakfast," I begin, hesitating, "and for last night." My fingers rub at my necklace.

"You're welcome," he says without looking up.

"And I'm sorry I was such a mess last night, and about this morning..." I stick a curl behind my ear.

He finally lifts his eyes to mine, his green eyes locking with me. "Don't apologize, okay."

"Okay." I nod, and he returns his focus back to his laptop.

I want to do something to help ease whatever is burdening him. "I'm going for a walk. Need some fresh air." I pause. "Would you come with me? I don't want to be alone in the forest."

He raises an eyebrow. "You've been there alone before."

"I know, but I could use the company." I purse my lips together.

"You sure? Because you kicked me out of your room this morning." He leans back in his chair, his arms crossing over his chest.

"Pretty, please." I peer at him through my lashes, wiggling my eyebrows.

A smile forms on his face.

Victory.

He studies me for a second before he shakes his head. "God, what am I going to do with you?" He chuckles, and the sound sends baby butterflies into my belly.

"So, is that a yes?" I push gently, my smile widening.

"Apparently I can't say no to you when you look at me like that." He stands up and closes his laptops, still with that smile on his face.

"Like what?" I laugh.

He moves closer to me, his eyes softening when they meet mine. "With those pleading doe eyes."

The way he looks at me with such tenderness lights up every corner of my being and warms me up from the inside. No one has ever looked at me like that before.

He tucks a strand of curls behind my ear, his hand lingering there for a few seconds. I can't help but smile at him.

"I'll do anything for that smile of yours." He leans closer, and for a second, I think he's going to kiss me, not that I want him to, but he doesn't. "You've got me trapped under your thumb, don't you, Moonie?" He sounds like the question is more to himself than to me. Moonie?

"I have a new nickname?"

"Maybe? Unless you prefer *princess*." He smiles again, one hand resting on the table. He needs to stop smiling like that.

"I prefer Mia," I say; I won't admit that I kinda like it when he calls me princess.

He stares at me, and I stare back, goosebumps forming on my arms even though it's warm out here.

I take one step closer and stand on my tiptoes, pressing my lips to his cheek. His skin is warm, and his stubble pricks my lips. He goes rigid for a second, and he visibly swallows. I step back, smiling at him.

"What was that for?" he chuckles, his eyes wide.

"It's my 'thank you' for last night." A blush creeps up my cheeks as my heart races.

He laughs, a deep, warm sound that vibrates through his chest. Pulling me into his arms, he holds me close. "I think I need another one for this morning." His lips brush against my ear, sending shivers down my spine.

"Stop being greedy," I laugh, pushing him away.

"Besides, isn't it supposed to be two kisses, one on each cheek? I want my other kiss." He points at his cheek.

"You're insufferable." I step closer and plant another kiss on his other cheek. When I pull away, I find the biggest grin on his face.

"Let's go." I walk ahead as he follows me, ignoring the rapid beat of my heart as if I just climbed a mountain.

We walk in silence to the waterfall, sunlight piercing through the canopy of trees. My steps are light, and I close my eyes, inhaling the fresh air. I twirl around, enjoying the enchantment of this place.

"Someone is in a good mood." He chuckles.

I stop twirling and open my eyes, smiling at the way the lights play on his face. "I don't know. This place makes me happy." I do another twirl.

He makes you happy, that little voice whispers again.

"It shows." A huge smirk invades his face.

I freeze when I see a kaleidoscope of butterflies. "Oh, my God, Jake." I've been here before, but I've never seen butterflies. Sometimes, I've seen a bird or two.

I chase after them, feeling like a kid. Jake's laughter mingles with mine. I watch as they fly away and disappear. "Where did they go?" A pout forms on my face. I turn to look at Jake, who's been standing there watching me with his arm crossed over his chest, leaning against a tree.

"Not the pout," he laughs. "You're such a kid sometimes."

"I am not." I punch his arm as we continue our walk. I like how I can be myself around him. He's like an old friend, except my thoughts about him are not exactly friendly.

Reaching the waterfall, I lie on the grass and gaze up at the sky, and he lies beside me. In the quiet, I study the side of his face, the light playing subtly on his jawline. His eyes intently watch the clouds drift above, almost as if he's silently communicating with the universe.

I'm not going to lie, he's *gorgeous!*

"Yes?" He catches me staring and laughs, a rich, open sound that vibrates with warmth. "Something on your mind?"

"Last time, you agreed to tell me what's going on, but we only talked about me, but I didn't forget."

"I see," he chuckles, turning to face me.

"So, what got you upset again today? Is it the same reason you got upset last time?"

He sighs. "My family owns a hotel. My dad used to manage it, and when he died, I didn't want anything to do with it." Pain was evident in his voice. "But my mom begged me to help. The hotel was struggling, and she had no idea what she was doing. It turns out we've been in debt since well before my dad passed. He took out loans, which I don't know what for, and he never repaid them. Now we might lose the hotel." I reach out to squeeze his hand, and his eyes widen as they meet mine. "Although, initially, I wanted nothing to do with it, I can't let that happen; after all, it's still our family legacy."

My fingers mindlessly trace a pattern along his arm. "I'm sorry. I'm sure you will come up with a solution." I pause, hoping I don't overstep. "Maybe I can help?"

He gives me a small, tired smile. "Thank you, but you don't have to worry about my mess."

He wraps an arm around my neck, guiding my head into his chest.

"So, you can be nice when you want to," he teases with a chuckle.

"What are you talking about? I'm nice all the time." I playfully punch him on the arm.

"Okay, I take that back." He laughs, his chest rumbling beneath my cheek.

This is normal to be this comfortable with someone you barely know, right? We've been spending a lot of time together.

I tilt my head up to look at him. "So, why didn't you want anything to do with the hotel?"

"It was his world, not mine. For years, he used the hotel as an excuse for why he never had time for us." I can hear the pain in his words.

"Were you two close?" I ask as his hand mindlessly plays with my curls. I love these moments with him. When we're together like this, it feels like we've known each other for a lifetime.

He pauses, his chest rising and falling under my touch. "As a kid, yeah, we were. We'd go camping and stuff, but then he stopped. Got too busy, I guess."

I frown, his eyes reflecting the deep greens of the forest. "I'm so sorry to hear that, a parent should always make time for their children, no matter what."

"It's okay." He smiles at me, but the pain behind his eyes tells me it's not.

Instinctively, I tighten my arm around his waist.

"You should come climbing with me. Alex and Sarah will be there, and it's fun," he says, changing the subject, the sound vibrates through his chest.

"Me, climbing? I don't know. I'm still thinking about it."

He mentioned it last time, but I haven't decided yet.

"Come on, I promise you can do it, and I'm an excellent teacher." He tickles my sides.

"Okay, okay, I'll come." I giggle.

"Great, you'll love it." His face lights up, pushing away the shadows of sadness from earlier.

Chapter 17

Mia

"Come on, Mia!" Jake calls out, half-teasing, half-encouraging. I roll my eyes, a mix of exhaustion and irritation simmering within me.

It's barely past 5:30 a.m. and here we are in the climbing gym, surrounded by towering walls, each route marked by a different color.

Jake is pushing me as if we're training for a marathon. I'm left wondering how he ever convinced me to join him in this early morning climb. I never signed up for this.

Alex and Sarah already made it down.

"You got this Mia," Alex screams from down below. But do I really? The muscles in my legs are screaming and my fingers feel like they've been through a grinder.

"You're almost there." Sarah cheers as well.

Great, my very own cheerleader team.

I reach for a neon green hold, slightly slick from use, and try to remember all of Jake's advice.

Use your legs more than your arms, Mia. Keep your body close to the wall, and always plan your next move.

I pull myself up, focusing on the texture of the wall under my palms, and the way my shoes barely grip the tiny foothold. It's a strange, exhilarating mix of fear and thrill, this battle against gravity and my own doubts.

I pause, catching my breath, and look up at him. He's watching me with a grin, clearly enjoying my struggle more than he probably should. But there's pride in his eyes too, and it pushes me to keep going.

I find my rhythm, a connection to the wall that is almost personal. I realize this is more than just a physical challenge. It's a mental one that requires focus, determination, and a bit of courage to keep pulling higher.

Reaching the top, I let out a breath I didn't realize I was holding. The view from here might only be the rest of the gym, but it is a small victory against my own limitations. I look at Jake, who's been waiting for me, ready to share a triumphant smile.

This, right here, is why he loves climbing so much, and I think I'm starting to understand it also. Maybe there's a bit of a climber in me after all.

Together, we slide down onto the mat and Jake pulls me into a hug. "You did it. That wasn't so bad," he says, his smile warming me more than any workout. He helps me come out of the ropes.

"My aching muscles would argue otherwise." I laugh, the exertion of the climb still pulsing through my body.

Alex and Sarah laugh along with me. "You did great, girl," Sarah says, patting me on the back.

"Can someone carry me? I don't think I can walk." And before I have time to finish my sentence, Jake is already scooping me up. "Put me down, I was joking." Instead, he just laughs, and my arms loops around his neck as he carries me to the car with Alex and Sarah giggling behind us. Alex opens the door and Jake helps me settle into the passenger seat.

"We are going out this weekend. You guys in?" He looks between me and Jake for confirmation.

Jake's gaze meets mine, searching my face for a response. "Sure." I nod.

"See you guys this weekend," Sarah says over her shoulder as they walk to the car.

I stretch my legs to shake off the fatigue while he gets into the driver's seat, and we pull away.

The window frames a world alive with towering trees that line our path, their leaves whispering secrets as we pass beneath.

Jake's eyes flicker back and forth from the road to me, and a soft smile plays on his lips as heat radiates in my chest. My lips curve into a content smile. I press my hand against the cool glass; the scenery blurring as we drive. My fingers trace the condensation on the window, drawing patterns that quickly disappear.

The world outside is a patchwork of nature's finest, an open field that stretches lazily to the foot of distant mountains, their peaks hidden by low clouds. It's breathtaking. We're wrapped in a comfortable silence.

Pulling up to the house, he helps me out of the car and suggests we go for a swim. He promises that it will help with my muscle ache.

Moving through the forest, I forget the ache in my muscles thinking about the dive into the clear water. I inhale the pine trees mixed with the sweetness of wildflowers peeking through the underbrush. The sound of rushing water grows from a soft murmur to a powerful roar, drowning out the quieter voices of the forest.

Standing at the edge of the waterfall, he grabs the bottom of his shirt and lifts it over his head. Revealing the contour of his biceps and the defined muscles of his chest. My gaze lingers a little too long, and I quickly look away before he notices me staring.

I wriggle out of my leggings, the fabric catching on my hips before I pull them down, then I pull my shirt over my head, leaving me in my boy shorts and sports bra. He turns, his eyes sweeping over me in a quick, almost cautious scan, then settles on my face.

"Ready?" He reaches for my hands and intertwines our fingers.

"One, two, three…" We plunge into the water, and even though it's early in the morning, the water is nice and warm. Our bodies hit the surface with a splash. Our eyes meet under the crystal-clear water, his green eyes glow, and a moment passes between us.

We come back up for air, maintaining a respectful distance. I remind myself that we're just friends, but I can't deny the warmth that spreads across my cheeks under his stare.

"You're nervous?" He gazes at me with his eyebrows lifted, a one-sided smile tilting his lips.

"No." I shake my head, yet my flushed cheeks betray me.

"Your red cheeks say otherwise. Friends don't make each other nervous, right?"

"Shut up," I shout, struggling to sound annoyed, but a laugh escapes instead. I swim away, but the distance barely cools the lingering warmth between us.

We swim through the water until we reach a shallower area, where the soft earth beneath my feet grounds me. He closes the distance between us, his gaze locking with mine, sending my heart pounding against my rib that I'm afraid it might burst out.

"You're gorgeous," he admits as his hand lifts to brush a wet strand of hair from my face, his touch igniting goosebumps across my skin. "So gorgeous that it hurts to look at you."

"Thank you," I say, but it comes out breathy.

His gaze drifts to the necklace at my throat. His fingers graze it gently.

"You know, my mom told me it would help me find my soulmate, which hasn't worked, by the way." I let out a laugh, trying to lighten the mood. But his eyes remain intense.

"God, I want to kiss you so bad," he whispers, his hand cupping my face, and his thumb brushing my jawline, causing my eyes to flutter close.

"Why don't you then?" The words escape me in a breath, a mix of question and plea. My hands flutter like trapped birds at my side as the water swirls around our waist. Every fiber of my being leans towards him.

"I don't want to hurt you." His gaze is tender but filled with concern. "You're so special."

"Why would that hurt me?" The question is a thread of sound, barely heard over the surge of my pulse. I already know the answer to the question. He doesn't do relationships. We would probably kiss, maybe have sex, and that's it. Things would become awkward between us.

"You deserve so much, but I can't give you that. This can't lead to anything more." He rubs my cheek and I lean into his touch.

"Who says it has to lead to something more?" I just need to feel his lips on mine. It's been forever since someone else's lips touched mine, and I didn't miss it until now.

"I know you don't do casual." His eyes search mine for a sign, for permission.

A forced laugh breaks from me, a sound that is a betrayal to the storm raging inside of me. He's right, I don't.

I feel like I'm standing at the edge of the waterfall. I can stop him now, and choose to be friends, or I can ask for his kiss, willingly step into the free fall, and possibly have my heart shattered into pieces.

"Just kiss me, please," I breathe out, the plea mingling with the surrounding mist. My desire to feel the touch of his lips on mine has been growing stronger.

He chuckles, a sound tinged with resignation and desire before he pulls me closer. His hands are warm and firm, one cradling my face, the other weaving its way into my wet hair, holding me in the eye of the storm that is about to sweep us away.

He leans down, his head touching mine. "I've been wanting to do this for so long," he says, his breath warm against my lips before they crash into mine again. They're soft at first, starting a fire in my belly.

Gently, he urges my lips apart, sweeping his tongue into my mouth, and deepening the kiss. His tongue pushes in, warm and wet, tasting mine, claiming it. My hand finds its way into his damp, blonde hair, my fingers curling around the strands, pulling slightly.

The hint of peppermint from his tongue is a cool contrast to the heat that's building between us. He shifts from sucking my tongue to drawing my lips in his and biting gently on the bottom one. He kisses me so good that I moan into the kiss, and pleasure pools between my thighs.

"Oh, that was so sexy." A low husky sound vibrates against my lips, sending a shiver down my spine. My heart is pulsing into my throat. His kiss is as intoxicating as magic itself, making my body burn out of control.

I wrap my arms around his neck, my smile mirroring his. He kisses me again, this time more slowly. His lips brush against mine with a featherless touch. The sensation sends flutters rushing through my stomach, breaking into thousands of tiny droplets of excitement and nerves, leaving behind a cool, tingling feeling that is both exhilarating and overwhelming.

I have a feeling this fall is going to hurt.

Chapter 18

Jake

I pull up to the cabin and head upstairs. Passing her room, I see that the door is open, and Mia is not in there. She's likely by the pool. It's been two days since I kissed her, and we haven't talked about it, but that doesn't mean that I haven't stopped thinking about it.

I've been busy with the hotel, and with the bank, which I don't want to think about right now. Despite everything, I always find myself wandering back to our kiss. It's fucking insane how much she occupies my mind. The softness of her lips, the taste of cotton candy from her tongue, a taste I didn't know I was craving until now. What kind of adult still uses cotton candy toothpaste? I don't care; I loved it.

I've kissed plenty of girls before, like a lot, but none of them got stuck in my head like this.

This is a big problem.

I quickly change into shorts and a tank top, ready for some fresh air after a long day at the hotel.

Sliding the door open, I spot her lounging by the poolside under the moonlight, absorbed by whatever book she's reading on her Kindle. She's on her stomach, her swimsuit fits her perfectly, and the outdoor lighting kisses her light brown skin, making it glow. As I get closer, I notice her biting on her lower lips, her thighs are squeezing together. "What's got the princess so focused?" I tease, and she jumps, clearly startled.

"You're going to be the death of me," she says, flustered. She sits up and turns off her kindle.

I claim the lounge chair next to her. "So, what were you reading?"

"None of your business," she fires back a little too quickly. *I already know, princess.*

I shoot her a knowing look and a smirk. I'm willing to bet she's so fucking wet right now; I can almost smell it in the air. Fuck, I want to see for myself.

"What?" She eyes me suspiciously.

"Nothing." I lie back on the lounge chair and fixate on the stars. We're both avoiding talking about the kiss.

This woman is my kryptonite, unsettling my balance in unexpected ways. After just a month with her, she's stirred up a whirlwind inside of me. One that I'm still trying to navigate. I'm drawn to her, wanting to kiss her and crave her touch, driven by a desire that's as intense as it is perplexing. Yet, I'm afraid of hurting her, of crossing a line we can't return from.

Despite my best efforts to maintain some emotional distance, I care about her. She sometimes gets on my nerves, yet paradoxically, that only pulls me closer, making me want to be near her even more. It's a tumultuous blend of desire and apprehension, attraction and fear, protective instincts clashing with the frustration she so easily evokes.

"How's your novel going?"

She avoids my gaze.

"What is it?"

She's quiet, and I wait for her to share if she wants. "I want to finish the book by the end of the summer to prove to myself—and my dad—that I can do this, but it's been harder than I thought. What if I can't do this?" She sighs as she stares up at the stars.

"You're putting too much pressure on yourself. I'm not a writer, but I know it's hard for me to come up with content ideas when I'm stressed. Don't think about a timeline, or your dad. Just write." I turn to look at her and she smiles. Her face shines brighter than the moon.

"Maybe you're right, or I should just open a bookstore café."

"A bookstore café?" I turn all my attention to her.

"Yes, I've always wanted to open a bookstore café with drinks and sweets named after books and characters."

"That sounds amazing, and you can do both, be an author and own a café."

"You think so? I know nothing about business."

"Yeah, you love books and coffee, so it's perfect, and if you need anything, I'm here, okay?"

"Okay, but I don't think that makes me qualified." She giggles.

"With passion, you can do anything."

"You think so?"

"I know so. What's your book about?"

"It's about a God living in an underwater world. He's not a merman or anything. Their world is similar to ours but doesn't float—it's like their outside world is encased in water, almost within a globe. They have everything we do, like a sun and a moon, but it's all artificial, powered by their advanced technology, even oxygen. The FMC lives on the island above their world, and she's this badass, saving kids from criminals who've taken over her island."

"I would read that. It sounds amazing. If you need someone to read as you write, I'm in."

"You want to be my alpha reader?" she says with a questioning look in her eyes.

"I don't know what that is, but yes, sure, anything."

She laughs. "It means exactly what you said. You get to read my book as I write, and you can offer your thoughts and feedback."

"Well, I might not be a lot of help because I know nothing about writing, but I'll be honored."

"I'd love that, thank you." She grins, showing off her beautiful white teeth.

She leans back in her chair and gazes at the stars again.

"Sometimes I think my mom is up there, as one of the stars, shining bright and watching over me. She was the only one that believed in me and in my writing, and I want to make her proud. Sometimes when I'm writing, I can almost feel her beside me. Her voice echoes in my head, pushing me to keep going. I know it's stupid, right?"

"It's not stupid. That's beautiful," I whisper back to her.

"I miss her so much," she says so softly I almost don't catch it.

"I'm sorry that she's gone."

"Thanks." Her gaze turns to meet mine. Her face looks sad but calm under the soft glow of the night. Eyes glisten with unshed tears, reflecting the stars above. Her lips are open, as if she wants to say more, but stays silent as she returns her eyes back to the sky. The silence between us is comfortable, as if we don't need words to understand each other.

She gets up to leave, but I grab her arm and gently pull her into my lap. Her legs instinctively wrap around my waist. The pool's blue lights reflect off the water, dancing across her skin. No woman has ever made me nervous before, but she does. Her chest rises and falls quickly with every breath. My eyes drop to her lips, and I want to kiss her so badly.

"Are we going to talk about it?"

"About what?" She tilts her head slightly, her eyes searching mine, making my heart pound harder.

"About the kiss."

She looks down, avoiding my eyes, and her cheeks turning red.

"Look at me," I say gently, waiting for her eyes to meet mine. "We can pretend the kiss never happened, ignore the attraction and chemistry between us, and try to be friends." I trace my fingers along her arm, and her body shivers under my touch. I want to give her the choice, even when my body craves hers. "Or" I continue, holding her gaze, "we can have an amazing summer together, no strings attached." My heart races as I watch her reaction.

She swallows hard as she bites her lower lip. She needs to stop doing that if she doesn't want me to take her right now on the lounge chair.

"What does that mean, exactly?" Her eyes hold mine under the moonlight.

"It means I want to kiss you, I want to feel your body beneath me, I want to make you feel good and forget everything else." I know she needs the distraction as much as I want to provide it, even if she won't admit it.

She wants this.

I want this.

"Is this for one night? Last time I checked, you don't sleep with the same girl twice."

"I want you every day, every night, every hour. I want you to be mine for the summer. No catching feelings, just two people enjoying each other." Knowing this is only for the summer gives me some kind of control. We are free to explore whatever is going on between us, and when the summer ends, we can go our separate ways.

I can do that without the risk of falling for her, right?

"Can I think about it?"

"Okay." I nod, kissing her cheek before standing up. Her legs are still around my waist. I gently place her on the ground, my hands lingering on her hips for a moment.

"Good night, Mia."

"Good night, Jake." She turns and walks away, and I already miss her.

Chapter 19

Mia

The next day, I sit on a rock, my gaze on the waterfall. It makes the act of falling seem beautiful. It's as if the water knows how to fall gracefully, without fear. *We can pretend the kiss never happened and try to be friends, or we can have an amazing summer together, no strings attached.* His words replay in my mind.

But how can I pretend the kiss never happened when I couldn't stop thinking about it all night, and this morning? Is it possible to accept his proposition without risking my heart, without falling in love with him?

No catching feelings.

Shaking my head, I open my laptop, trying to focus on my writing. I stare at the blank page, the blinking cursor. I've completed the outline for my book, yet I'm stuck on how to begin. The sound of water hitting the rocks is soothing, but it somehow reminds me of the relentless pull I feel toward him. The way it makes every part of me roar to life.

I close my laptop and put it back inside my bag. I need to talk this through with Rylee, but of course, there's no signal here. With a deep breath, I grab my bag and head back to the cabin.

Once I'm there, I notice Jake's car is not outside. A small relief washes over me. I'm not ready to face him yet. I head straight to my room and collapse on the bed; the mattress sighing under my weight.

My fingers fumble for my phone, and I dial Rylee's number. She picks up on the second ring.

Before I have time to say hello, she blurts out, "I slept with him." Her words come out in a rush.

I sit down, giving her my full attention. "You slept with who?" I say, my grip tightening on the phone.

She's practically breathless, as if she's been pacing the room. "My boss." She sounds like she's about to cry. "It just happened. We were working late, and one thing led to another."

"Oh my God." Now I'm pacing too, her confession stirring a storm of thoughts in my head. I haven't even told her about Jake yet, but this doesn't seem like the right time to share.

"Was it bad? Do you regret it?" I ask her, needing to understand where she stands emotionally.

"No, it was amazing, the best sex I ever had, but I'm scared it might mess things up at work."

I pause mid step, and a sigh escapes me. "Have you talked to him since?" I ask, glancing at the window, seeking the calm it offers.

"No," she exhales, her stress tangible even through the phone.

"Okay, just take a breath and talk to him. See where he stands," I suggest, trying to offer some stability.

"He's calling me now. I gotta go. Talk to you later, bye."

"Okay, keep me updated," I rush out before the line goes dead.

I open my bag from the bed and go through my mom's letters. I have a feeling she has a letter for a moment like this when I wish she was here to tell me what to do. I found one labeled: Boy Trouble. She really thought of everything. Holding the letter, I step out onto the patio to watch the sunset. My body stretches as I breathe in the fresh air. I take in the sight of the golden rays that illuminate the trees as the sun disappears behind the mountains. Sitting down on a chair, I open the letter.

Coucou ma Cherie,

If you're reading this letter, you probably wanted to talk to me about some boy trouble. Je suis vraiment desolée, I'm not here.

I know you're a big romantic and you adore love, and I love that about you.

But don't be afraid to have fun, experience new things, and figure out what you want. You might get your heart broken, but not every fall is going to hurt. Some falls will lead to the most amazing feelings you could ever imagine. Being in love with someone and for that person to love you just as much. Caring for them and being cared for. To love them, especially when it's hard. Continue loving them when you're upset. To want to fall in love with them every day.

You deserve someone who loves you fiercely and unconditionally. Never settle for less, Mon amour.

But until then, it's okay to have fun. For love, there is no need to rush. It will come to you when the time is right.

Be a waterfall, baby girl. Embrace the fall.

And always trust your heart.

Finishing the letter, I take a deep breath and sigh, forcing myself not to cry. My mom is right. I've never been the girl to take risks or be bold enough to go up to a guy at a bar. Not the girl who sleeps around with random guys. I've always thought maybe I'm demisexual, but with Jake, it's different. I want this. Fantasized about it at night when I'm using my toys, wishing it was him instead. This is new to me, before when I'm practicing self-care, I listened to the sound, never an image. But now he's all I can think of.

I wipe away the few drops of tears that managed to escape before heading to the bathroom for a shower.

My clothes fall to floor before stepping under the warm stream of water. Grabbing my razor and shaving cream, I settle onto the built-in seat to shave my legs and other areas, making sure everything is smooth and free of hair. Afterwards, I scrub myself with my favorite scrub and body wash duo.

I rinse off, and then step out of the shower, grabbing a towel to dry myself off. Standing in front of the full body mirror, the towel falls to the floor, and I admire my naked body. I take my jasmine-scented lotion and apply it slowly, covering every inch of my skin. My nipples harden under my touch. I don't have a perfect slim body, but I love every inch and every curve.

It's been almost five years since I've been with anyone, adhering to my rule of no sex without an emotional connection. I've never even thought about it, but right now the thought of an orgasm from him other than my toys, is enticing.

I sip some wine from the bottle I keep in my room, seeking a bit of liquid courage as warmth spreads through my body. I slip on an oversized T-shirt, the fabric soft against my skin, and skip the underwear. Not gonna need it, and it's a little bold and thrilling. Which is what I'm going for.

I brush my teeth with my favorite cotton candy-flavored paste and then give myself a pep talk in the mirror. A quick fix to my hair with some mousse keeps my curls in check, and I tidy my eyebrows.

Okay girl let's do this, no more overthinking this.

I want this, and more than anything, I want him.

Chapter 20

Jake

In my room, I sit at my desk, going over the budget for the renovations of the hotel. The bank agreed to extend our loans, but they also increased the interest rates. I'm hopeful we can pay it off soon.

My mind wanders, caught in the memory of our kiss, and whether she considered my proposal. Maybe I was too direct, but I need to make sure we're both on the same page. Although I like her, maybe even care about her, my view on relationships remains the same. A soft knock on the door snaps me back to the present.

"Come in."

There's a brief silence before the door opens and she steps inside, closing it behind her. She leans back against it, arms hidden behind her. She's wearing an oversized t-shirt, which barely covers her thighs, her hair beautifully framing her face.

"Hi," she says with a shy smile.

"Hi." I smile back at her. My eyes roam over her, taking in her bare legs, up to where her nipples press against the fabric of the shirt.

Oh, God, she's so gorgeous.

The sight of her stirs a warmth inside of me that's hard to ignore.

She stands there, holding my gaze. She gently catches her teeth between her teeth, in a way that's both timid and enticing, and pressing her legs close together. I respect the space she needs, all the while my body is aching to bridge the gap between us. I eagerly await her next move, ready to follow her lead and silently pleading for her to close the distance, with every part of me attuned to her.

She walks towards me slowly; her movements are exquisitely seductive. Stopping in front of me, her eyes take in my bare chest. Her desire is clear as day. She wants this as much as I do.

There's little left to the imagination as my dick betrays me, swelling painfully in my pants. Her eyes linger there for a few seconds before looking up at me.

"You've got a little of drool there." She runs her thumb across her lips. I laugh, loving this side of her, relaxed and playful.

"Are you sure I'm the one drooling? I bet your panties are soaked for me right now." I look down at her, wanting to check for myself. The thought has my head spinning. Her being so wet and ready for me.

Her eyes smolder with desire as she moves closer, straddling me. My arms naturally encircle her waist, pulling her closer, her scent of jasmine enveloping us like a sweet cloud.

"I'm not wearing any," she says in a sultry tone that sends a wave of heat through me. Her hands roam over my chest to my biceps.

"Fuck," I curse under my breath, closing my eyes for a few seconds to gain some kind of control. When I open them, she's staring at me with those doe eyes, like she doesn't have the slightest idea of what she's doing to me. I can barely breathe around the need to be inside of her.

"What are we doing?"

Her breathing is quick and heavy. There's a storm of desire and anticipation swirling in her eyes. "Agreeing to your proposal," she breathes out. "This is your chance, Jacob Harrington. Don't waste it."

She wraps her arms around my neck while letting her hips roll against me slowly, her dampness soaking through my shorts.

"How do you suggest I do that?" I growl. The pleasure she's igniting nearly overwhelms my senses. She continues to grind against me, drawing out every last bit of my control. The way she's moving, so sinful, so innocently...it's driving me wild.

"Do I need to spell it out for you?" Her breath is hot against my skin, and it smells like wine.

"I want to hear you say it, princess. Tell me what you want." I say with a throaty sound.

"I. Need. You. To. Fuck. Me." She breathes out each word slowly, her eyes locked on mine. I draw in a sharp breath, my impatience stabbing at me, begging for me to be inside her now.

I study her face, noting the slight tremble in her lips, the nervousness in her eyes that doesn't quite match her confident words. I pull her closer, my hand cradling the back of her head, our foreheads touching.

"Are you sure about this?" Even though she's the one who came to me, I don't want her to do anything she might regret.

She swallows hard. "I've never done this before, the whole hooking up thing. But I want this, I need it." Her arms wrap around me, pulling me even closer.

I flash two fingers in front of her, raising an eyebrow. "How many fingers am I holding?"

"Two," she whispers, leaning closer, her breath warm against my cheek. "Believe me, I'm not drunk."

"Now let me see how much you want this, princess."

I slide my hand under her shirt and brush two fingers over her wetness. Pulling my hand out, I hold them in front of her, rubbing my fingers between her slickness.

"Damn, Mia, you're dripping."

Her cheeks turn a darker shade of red. I cradle the back of her neck, bringing her lips to mine. Her taste, a sweet mix of wine and cotton candy, brings a smile from me mid-kiss. My hands make their way to her bare ass. I caress and gently squeeze them, savoring the reality of the very moment I've been dreaming about.

The room is quiet except for her sweet, occasional moans. Those moans that I've heard before from her room. Those moans I've wanted to jerk off to, too many times before.

She hesitates before carefully pulling down my boxers just enough to free me. Her eyes taking me in as she visibly swallows. "Is it supposed to be that big?"

The surprise and innocence in her question make me chuckle. *Who the hell has she been with before?* "If you're worried it's not gonna fit, it will." Reaching over my desk, I pull out a foil packet from the drawer. I tear open the wrapper with my teeth, rolling it down my length, ready for the moment I've been waiting for.

She has her legs straddling either side of me. Her arms wrap around my neck as she grinds against my big, hard cock, a soft moan escaping her lips.

She's dripping all over me, and I need to be inside her right now. "Mia," I growl, the word rumbling from deep within.

She shifts, lifting herself enough to give me space. Using one hand, I align myself at her entrance, ready for her.

Slowly, she lowers herself down. We both let out a sharp gasp at the connection. She's so freakin' tight. Her face scrunches a little as she stretches around me.

"Does it hurt?"

"A little." She nods.

"You're doing so good, taking me so well, princess." Like her pussy was made for my cock. With my hands gently on her waist, I help guide her down carefully, aware of every small reaction of hers. Her breath hitches.

Her slickness makes it easier for me to fit in.

"Oh, God," she moans once she settles, taking me all the way in. We stay like that for a few seconds, the feeling so intense I almost black out. I've imagined this moment so many times, but I never thought it would feel this good, and I haven't even fucked her yet.

The line between us blurs, and I'm completely lost in her. I know one taste wouldn't be enough. Now that I have, will I be able to let her go? But that's what we agreed on. We spend the summer enjoying each other. Then we'll go our separate ways, and no one gets hurt.

She rides me slowly, adjusting to the size. I capture her lips in mine, kissing her deeply. Trailing to her neck and collarbone.

My hand moves under her shirt; she's not wearing a bra. "Can I take it off?"

"Yes," she breathes out. Lifting her arms up, I pull the shirt over her head, revealing those beautiful tits. They're perfect, not too big, not too small. They fit perfectly in my hand. I love how her top is small, but her bottom is so thick and curvy.

She's so perfect.

I roll one of her nipples between my fingers.

"Oh," she cries out in response.

"You like that, don't you?" I smile at her.

"Yes," she gasps. I watch as they bounce every time she moves. I lean down and take one in my mouth, teasing it with my tongue as her hips move up and down. Her hands lay against my chest for support.

I can tell she's getting a little tired. So, I take over, sliding her hips up and down my length. She throws her head back, moaning with every thrust. Fuck! I've been with so many girls, but it never felt like this. The way her pussy clutches around my dick, drenching me in her wetness.

"You like how good my dick is making you feel?" Each word is followed by a deep thrust.

"Yes... Please don't stop."

Thrust.

"Never, not until you see the stars, baby."

"Oh, my God... Jake!"

I thrust in deeper, her moans getting louder. "That's it, let me hear you." I love hearing her falling apart for me.

She's close, a blazing heat of molten lava ready to burn us down.

"Hold on to me," I tell her as I let my hips do the rest of the work, thrusting into her. One hand rubs her clit while the other pinches her tit.

She lets out a whimper, and then another. Fuck, I love the way she sounds.

"Jake..." She clenches around my length. Her body trembles as waves of pleasure sweep through her, leaving her gasping for air, and she collapses onto my chest.

After two more deep and hard thrusts, my muscles tighten. "Fuck," I exhale, the world narrowing down to the raw intensity of my climax. My body becomes a volcano. A burst of pleasure and heat busting out of nowhere, pulsing through my veins as I empty into the condom. My nerves are on fire as I moan into her mouth.

"That was amazing." Her breath is warm against my neck.

I smile through her hair. "It was." I pull away to look through her eyes, watching her face for any regret. "Are you okay?"

"More than okay. I'm just thinking about how this is gonna be a fun summer." She gives me the most beautiful smile.

It's going to be an amazing summer indeed.

She gets off from being on top of me, and my softening length slips out of her. She walks toward the bathroom, my eyes following her naked body.

I didn't think I had a specific type, but God was I wrong. The attraction is undeniable, just looking at her gets me hard again.

I get up and follow her into the bathroom. She's sitting on the toilet. I discard the used condom, and catch her eyes lingering on me, where my shaft is hardening again. When her eyes meet mine, her face turns a darker shade of red.

Just a few minutes ago, she was bouncing on me and screaming my name. Now she's blushing shyly. Which makes me chuckle.

She rolls her eyes. "Are you just going to stand there? No privacy, huh?"

Privacy? I already saw everything. When I don't move, she grabs some toilet paper to wipe off before she flushes. She starts to walk away, but I grab her. Lifting her up and sitting her up on the sink.

"What?" Her eyebrows raise at my smile.

"You're just so adorable when you're shy."

"Well, I've never had anyone stand in front of me naked before...or been naked in front of anyone." She tries to look down, then she realizes she would be staring at my length again. She quickly shifts her gaze up.

"Are you saying that you're a virgin?" I should have asked because she's the tightest I've ever been with.

"No, but it's been a while. I only did it once, and it wasn't as good as this. He didn't even give me an orgasm. Not that I'm saying I've never had an orgasm. I've had plenty on my own." She stumbles over her words.

"Oh, I know you've had plenty on your own." My lip curls on one side.

Her eyes go wide, and her mouth forms a small 'o'. "Wait, what do you mean?" She tucks a curl behind her ear.

I lean closer. "I mean, those walls are thin, and you were not exactly quiet. Do you know how many times I wanted to jerk off to your sweet moans?"

"Oh, my God!" She covers her face.

I laugh at her embarrassment. "Did you ever think about me when you were playing with yourself?"

"Yes," she says, biting her lip.

The image of her legs spread out on her bed, her hands between her thighs as she thinks about me, makes me hard again. "Was it everything you imagined?"

"So much more," she breathes out.

I move between her legs. "You just boosted my ego, and with me, you won't have to worry about not getting an orgasm," I say, smirking at her. "I'll make sure of it, princess."

"We're being humble about it, aren't we?" She laughs, pushing against my chest, and I move backward. She hops off the sink, her naked butt bouncing as she walks out of the bathroom. I follow her and she grabs her shirt off the floor, sliding it over her head. I grab my shorts and slide them on.

"I'm grabbing a snack. You want something?" she asks me over her shoulders as she reaches for the door.

"No, you stay. I'll grab our snacks." I brace myself for her to argue with me.

"Okay." She smiles at me.

"Wait, that's it? No, 'I can get it myself.'" I act it out the way she would say it.

"Well, I think that's the least you can do after fucking my brains out," she says, whipping her hair over her shoulders and taking a seat on the couch.

I laugh to myself before I walk downstairs and make her pizza bagels, since she loved them so much. I use the air fryer this time. Adding them on a plate, I grab two beers and bring everything back to the room. She's sitting on the small couch with her legs tucked underneath, scrolling through her phone. She looks up when I sit next to her, placing the tray between us.

"You made pizza bagels?" Her eyes go wide, a huge smile on her face.

"I also got beers," I say, handing her one.

"So, how does this work?" she asks, finishing her bite. "Do I knock every time? Do I come to you, or do you come to me? Should I go back to my room? Or can I sleep in yours? Do we have a schedule?" She avoids looking at me, staring at her pizza like it's the most beautiful art she has ever seen.

I swallow my bite and take a sip of my beer, turning my body to face her. This is new to me, too. I've never shared a place with a girl, especially not the ones I hook up with. "Things will stay the way they are now. I have my room, and you have yours. We fuck whenever. You can come to me; I can come to you. It doesn't matter, and you don't have to knock."

"Okay." She adjusts her shirt, but I can still peek underneath. She looks behind me at the dark forest through the window. After a few seconds, she takes a big bite of her pizza and covers her mouth to chew. Then she grabs the beer and takes a sip, her nose scrunches at the bitter taste.

"Can we still hangout like buddies?" She places her beer on the tray as I place one arm on the top of the couch. "We can go kayaking, swimming. We can make one of those summer bucket lists. Only if that's okay with you." She trails off, pulling out a loose thread from the throw pillow next to her. "I'm fine staying here all day, every day, writing, reading, sleeping, and having sex." She glances up at me briefly before she looks down, and her shoulders slump.

I shift on the couch, watching her pull off the pepperoni from the bagel and pop it in her mouth. "We can hang out like buddies. You make a list of whatever you want to do."

"Okay, yay." She bounces a little, her face lights up like the early morning sun from the top of a mountain. "I'm going to make a list and put them in a jar."

Her joy is contagious, and I find myself smiling too.

"What's a food or snack combo that you like, but others might find disgusting?" She leans over with her elbow on her thigh, her hand cupping her cheek, and the other holds her pizza.

I rub my thumbs over my lips, aware of her watching the movement, wondering if I should indulge in her little game. I don't play 21 questions if that's what she's trying to do.

"You don't have to answer." She straightens herself up when I don't say anything. "I was just making conversation." She looks down, playing with her shirt.

"I eat pickles with peanut butter," I finally say.

She gasps, her face looking like the shock face emoji. "You should have told me that before we slept together." She shakes her head. "I don't think we can be friends." She sticks her tongue out in disgust.

I laugh at her dramatic reaction. "Don't knock it till you try it." I shift on my seat to face her better. "Besides, we don't need to be friends to have sex. You don't even need to like me."

"I don't know about that." She scrunches her nose.

"You're saying you wouldn't sleep with me if you knew?"

"Maybe." She adjusts her legs and her oversized shirt pulled up a little, giving me a peek of her pretty pussy.

"Such a pretty liar, aren't you? I bet you're wet again right now just thinking about it," I say in a gravelly growl. "The way my big cock stretched your tight, sweet pussy, and the way it hurts." She visibly swallows, her breathing shallow.

I pull back and adjust the tightening in my pants from thinking about her warm cunt. "Now that you know, you can call off the whole thing if you want," I call out her bluff. Her eyes widen, but she doesn't say anything.

"So, you don't have any weird food combo that you like?" I ignore the fact she didn't say anything about my statement.

She wouldn't call it off, would she?

She rubs her earlobe as if she's thinking or deciding if she even wants to tell me. "Hot Cheetos with cream cheese, and I love to add them to my popcorn."

"And you were judging me?" I laugh.

"Mine is not disgusting if you love hot Cheetos."

"Mine is not disgusting if you love pickles."

I'll eat pickles with anything. We both stare at each other and smile.

I look at the tray, which is now empty. I didn't realize we finished all of it. Grabbing my beer, I finish the last sip, and she does the same.

This was actually nice. We're kinda like roommates slash hopefully fuck buddies (unless she wants to crucify me for loving pickles), and maybe even friends. I grab her bottle and mine with the tray, putting them on my desk so I can take them downstairs.

She stands up, shuffling her feet as she stares at the ground. "Good night," she finally says, looking up at me. I step toward her, bringing our faces closer to each other.

"Good night," I whisper back.

Instead of walking away, she's looking at me with those eyes that look more like a midnight sky in the barely lit room. My hand wraps around her waist, pulling her closer. Her hands reach up to my chest, and she bites her lip. This is my cue.

Lifting her off the ground, she wraps her legs around my waist and her arms around my neck, her hand tangling in my hair. Parting my mouth, I take her bottom lip in mine. The one she loves to bite so much. I kiss them desperately, adding light pressure. I love the bitter taste of beer on her lips.

I carry her toward the bed and sit her down at the edge. Taking her shirt off, I take in the sight of her and her curves. "You're so sexy!" I say, rubbing my thumb across my lips, drooling like a teenager at how perfect she is.

She moves to the center of the bed, and I move on top of her, leaning down to press my lips to hers. I kiss her like I'm starving, my lips moving hungrily against hers. I like the taste of cotton candy mixed with the beer from her mouth, a combo I didn't know I needed until now.

She moves her hips, rubbing herself against my hardness. Someone is eager, isn't she?

"What does my princess want?" I kiss her neck.

"I'm not your princess," she pants, her words shaky and not at all convincing. "This is only a hookup, remember?"

I love that smart mouth of hers. "When you walked in here, you agreed to be mine for the summer." I kiss the top of her ear, and she lets out a small moan, her nails digging into my back. "Mine to please, however I want. That's the deal." I kiss the side of her mouth.

For the time we have together, I can pretend she's mine.

"Jake," she breathes out.

"What's the magic word when we need something?" I rub the sensitive bud of her nipples between my fingers. This is my time to tease her, after she implied, she wanted to cancel our whole agreement.

"Please." The word escapes with a moan.

"Please what?" I move my hands between her thighs, close to where she wants me, but not quite. She moves her hips up even more so she can rub herself against my fingers.

A frustrated growl escapes her lips, which makes me laugh. "Did you just growl at me, princess?" I'm going to fuck the sassiness out of her.

She rolls her eyes. "I want you inside me. Now."

"Such a bossy princess. Look at you so eager for my cock like I didn't just fuck you less than an hour ago." I pull my shorts down and kick them off my feet. Grabbing another condom from my desk,

I tear the package before pulling it on, and position myself at her entrance.

I enter her slowly, and even with the barrier between us, her warmth seeps into me. Feeling the way her body adjusts to my size, her nose wrinkling with the stretch. "Fuck, Mia, you're so freaking tight. How long has it been since you've been with someone before tonight?"

She raises her hand with all five fingers up.

"Five years?"

She nods her head.

Jesus Christ, she's practically a virgin. It makes sense now; she's never had a real man's dick before. I can't wait to stretch that sweet little pussy.

I continue to push in, inch by torturous inch. "Why five years?" I don't think I could ever go that long without sex.

Her face changes at my question, something like pain passing through her before she can recover. "I don't know. I guess I've never felt that attraction with someone, and I was always busy with school."

With a final push, I'm buried inside her again, her body taking me. Just as before, the wave of pleasure and emotions leave me breathless.

It's not supposed to feel that good, that intimate, everything fuses and intertwines in a way that is too intense to explain.

I pull out and thrust back again, moving my waist in a circular motion, finding that spot that always made them go crazy.

"Oh, my God! Do that again, please." She gasps, her eyes half closed, and her mouth slightly open.

"Such a good girl, begging for my cock." She clenches around me, getting wetter than before. Someone likes praises, I smile to myself at the realization. "There you go, Moonie." I repeat the movement over and over, grazing that sweet spot.

"Yesss, just like that, please." Her eyes roll back, her nails digging into my back.

"Do you still want to call this off?" I stop my movements, staring down at her.

"Why did you stop?" She pouts.

"Answer me, princess." I reach out and tease her sensitive nub.

"No, I don't want to." She purses her lips.

"You don't sound convincing." I move inside her slowly.

"I'm yours for the summer, yours to please however you want. Now please, fuck me." She rocks her hips, needing the pressure only I can give her.

I chuckle.

"You're so damn beautiful begging me like this," I say, increasing the pressure again.

She clenches around me.

"Rub your nipples for me." I watch as she rubs, pinching and pulling them slightly. My eyes devour the movement, intensifying the heat building inside me, as I thrust inside of her deep and hard.

She reaches to brush a strand of hair that falls over my face, clinging to my sweaty forehead, and she smiles at me. That smile is the sexiest thing I've ever seen. She is the sexiest thing I ever laid eyes on.

I pull out and plunge back in, now that she's so wet. It's easier for me to slide in. "Fuck, Moonie. You feel so fucking amazing." I drop my head to hers, grabbing her thick ass as I pound into her harder and faster. The sound of our bodies hitting each other, her whimpers, and my grunts fill the room.

My breathing grows heavier, and I can feel her tightening around my dick, her body on the edge of her climax.

"Jake..." Her words cut off as her hips arch off the bed. Her pussy clenches and unclenches around me, her body trembling.

My hip feels like it's moving on its own, desperate, as I chase my own climax. "Mia," I grunt, a gravelly sound. My body shakes as I thrust a couple of times, emptying myself into the condom. I collapse onto her, our breath heavy and mingling together as I try to recover my senses.

After a few more seconds, I roll off her and walk into the bathroom to discard the condom. What happens now? I don't cuddle after sex. They always leave unless we get too drunk and pass out. When I return to the room, she's turned to her side, her breathing even. She's fallen asleep. I could wake her up, so she can go back to her room, or I could let her sleep. She must be tired after the workout we just had.

Grabbing my shorts from the floor, I pull them on and head over to the bed. I gently pull the blanket over her body before climbing in next to her. After turning off the light on my side, leaving hers on, I cross my hands under my head and stare at the dark ceiling.

The bed shifts as her body weight moves onto me. She mumbles something before she rests her head on my chest, her arms encircling my waist, and her legs draping over my thighs.

Just like the night of the storm. There's no need to move her. She'll just move back, and it's not that bad.

"Good night, Mia," I whisper to her before my eyes grow heavy and I fall asleep.

The Forest
Summer 1921

For decades, seasons have come and gone, but the love between Ifunayla and Eadrick lingered like the initials carved into my oldest tree.

Standing with his friends, Eadrick's eyes found Ifunayla. They brightened, a response I had witnessed often. His friends, however, did not share his affection. "What is the negroe doing here?" One sneered, spitting the words like venom.

Her face tightened; eyes glistening with tears she would not let fall. She turned and fled, swift and graceful. Eadrick rounded on his friends. "Her name is Ifunayla. She is my friend." He then broke away, calling out, "Ifunayla, wait!" She had already disappeared into the woods.

He found her by my waterfall, a sanctuary for their shared moments and whispered secrets. She sat on a rock, shoulders slumped, lost in the water's cascade. He moved closer, cautiously. "Ifunayla, I did not—"

"You do not need to explain." She stood up to face him. "I know what your world thinks of me."

"They are wrong. They had no right." His voice was filled with regret and anger.

Her eyes clouded over. A cocktail of hurt and understanding. "Why do you care? We are from different worlds."

His hands cupped her face gently. "Because my world is not complete without you." His eyes met hers.

I felt her shiver, a vibration that echoed through my leaves. "You make it hard to stay away." She leaned into his touch at last.

"It is hard for me, too." He pulled her into a kiss that seemed to defy the worlds that tried to keep them apart.

As their lips met, my waterfall seemed to roar louder, as if in applause for the audacity of their love. It was a spark that felt like it could ignite me, and for a moment, it did. My leaves felt brighter, my roots more anchored, as if their love breathed life into me.

Though worlds apart, and despite society's harsh rules, here, beside my waterfall, they were simply two souls in love. And that is a story I would always nurture.

Chapter 21

Mia

"Embrace the pain. It'll help you push through," he says as we hike through the rugged mountain terrain.

The early morning sun is just beginning to rise, painting a soft golden hue that makes the dew on the leaves around us sparkle. This was his pick from our activity jar—each day, we draw an activity that one of us has written, and today is hiking.

Lucky me.

Trying to adopt his mindset, I focus on the burn in my legs, attempting to channel the pain into determination. But eventually, the pain wins and my legs buckle. I collapse onto a nearby rock, tears threatening to spill from the frustration and exhaustion. Jake is instantly at my side, his hand warm against my back. "Come on, we're almost there."

I shake my head. "It's too much."

His expression softens, his thumb gently brushing away a tear that has escaped. "Okay, don't cry. We're just a few more minutes from the top, I promise."

"You go ahead; I'll wait here." I cross my arms over my chest.

He grins, leaning closer. "How about this? I'll make it better once we get up there."

"Better how?" I pout.

"Remember how they make boo-boos better?"

"How?"

"By kissing it..." He lowers his voice to a whisper.

"You think kissing my legs will make it better?" I raise an eyebrow at him.

"I wasn't talking about just kissing your legs. I'm talking about making you feel good."

My pussy throbs when I understand what he meant. No one has ever kissed me down there before. Well, they never got the chance. I wonder how it will feel, his warm tongue kissing my pussy. Is it as good as Rylee said?

"I'll even give you a piggyback ride to the top," he adds, his eyes twinkling with mischief.

I laugh, the sound more genuine this time, despite the pain. "You can't possibly carry my big ass up there." I get up and stretch my legs.

"I can carry your thick ass anywhere," he boasts confidently, and his assurance makes me smile.

"Okay, I'll walk, but how about we play a game where we ask each other questions?" I know he hates it when we play the game of asking each other questions, but I need something to distract me from the ache in my legs. The rocky path and steep incline of the mountain trail is testing me more than I anticipated. *Embracing the pain* is not working.

"Sure, shoot," he says, his eyes scanning the path ahead as he adjusts his backpack.

"What is your favorite color?" I glance at him.

"Brown, like your eyes," he says. I turn to see a playful grin on his face.

"Stop being a flirt. There's no way brown is your favorite color." I shove him.

"Well it is." His grin widening.

I roll my eyes not believing him.

"And you?" he asks.

"Green, like your eyes." I stifle a smile.

He chuckles. "Myara, are you flirting with me?"

My full name rolls off his tongue like honey. I want to ask how he knows it, but I'm sure he just looked it up through the booking.

I laugh and wink at him.

"What's your favorite music genre, and artist?"

"That's two questions?"

"No, it's one question with two parts." I step over a large root that crosses our trail.

"Pop music, and I don't really have a favorite artist, but one that pops into my head right now is Benson Boone." He picks a stick and draws a circle on the ground. "What about you? Let me guess, Taylor Swift."

"No, I love Taylor Swift, but my favorite genre is R&B and my favorite artist is H.E.R. I think I might have a girl crush on her." I giggle.

He stops mid-step and laughs. My answers definitely caught his attention. "A girl crush, huh?"

"Hmmm." I nod, facing him.

He grabs his water bottle and takes a sip. My eyes follow the way he swallows, the water making its way down his throat. He passes the bottle to me to drink as if nothing. But again, we've tasted each other's spit. It shouldn't be a problem sharing a water bottle.

"What are the three things you can't live without?" I continue, wiping off a drop of water from my lips.

"Climbing, water, and sex." He answers without missing a beat, his gaze still on the trail.

I laugh at his answer. The sound echoes in the open air. "So, you can live without food, but not sex?"

"I could live off you. I bet you taste freaking amazing. I can't wait to find out." He winks at me.

"Oh, my God." I gasp and laugh, ignoring the slight tremble in my legs from both the climb and his comments. "I'm not food."

"That has yet to be determined." His laughter mingles with the rustle of leaves and the distant calls of bird's overhead.

"I'm done with you," I say, though my tone is more amused than annoyed.

"And you?" He turns to me, his step steady despite the uneven ground.

"Water, books, food," I list, sidestepping a puddle.

"No sex?" he teases, catching a low-hanging branch and holding it for me to pass.

"I have my fingers." I hold my fingers to him and step past a branch.

He stops and pulls me towards him, his hands firm on my waist. "Your fingers can't give you the orgasms that sex can, at least not the ones I can give you." His eyes lock onto mine, penetrating deep into my soul. The air I thought I could live without rushed out of my body.

His hand threads through my hair, and a smile plays on his lips before they crash into mine, hot and demanding. His mouth devours me, and I moan into the kiss. Then he pulls away, that knowing smile on his face. He steps to the side, releasing me. I stumble backward, trying to catch my breath, aware of the man who makes my heart race more than the climb.

"What's a secret you've never told anyone but want to share with me?" I ask after I compose myself, the cool mountain air brushing against my face.

He stops walking and takes a step away from me. I watch as he paces back and forth, running a hand through his hair. Whatever he's about to tell me must be big. He stops pacing, taking a deep breath before looking up at me. "I found my dad having sex with one of my friends," he murmurs against the backdrop of rustling leaves.

"Wait, what?" I thought it was something big, but not that.

"Well, she was more than a friend. We weren't officially together, but we had something." He kicks a small rock with his foot.

"You mean with Jessie?" I piece it together.

He nods, and a heavy sigh escapes him. "Yeah."

"I'm so sorry." I shift my weight from one foot to the other, looking down at the ground. "Is that—" I pause to clear my throat. "Is that why you don't do relationships?" I look up past his shoulder, not wanting to see the answer on his face.

He shakes his head, then nods, as if he's debating his true feelings. "No. Well, yes." He rubs the back of his neck. "I guess it's part of it. She's really the only girl I've cared about, even if I never admitted it."

His gaze drifts to the mountain trail ahead, avoiding my eyes.

"Despite what she might think, I was never with anyone else while we were together," he adds.

"But I thought you said you two weren't in a relationship?"

"Right, because I didn't want to label it. We weren't boyfriend and girlfriend. We were young, and I didn't want to hold her back or the other way around. After graduation, she moved to London." The words are heavy and raw.

"Oh, I see." *Kind of like us now.* The truth stings more than I let on.

"Maybe I wouldn't mind as much if it had been anyone else but my dad..." Anger simmering beneath his calm exterior.

"What did you do when you found out?" I ask softly.

"That was five years ago, and I told him I never wanted to see him again." His hands are shaking.

I reach for them, intertwining our fingers. He looks down at our joint hands, his thumbs brushing over my knuckles. "The worst part is they didn't stop seeing each other even after getting caught. Later, I found out he was financing her college in London with loans he took out against the hotel, and now we're deep in debt because of it." Each word is sharper than the last, as if saying it out loud brings back all the anger and hurt.

"I'm sorry," I say. My heart aches for him as if his pain is my own.

"Don't be." His jaw twitches, and he forces a smile that doesn't quite reach his eyes.

"Do Sarah and Alex know?"

"I never told them. Unless Jessie did." His eyes search mine, silently begging for something.

I step closer, closing the gap between us, and wrap my arms around his body, resting my head on his chest. I listen to the rapid beat of his heart.

He lets out a shaky breath. His chin rests on top of my head, and his arm tightens around me.

"What did she want last time at the bar?" I whisper against his chest.

He stiffens before responding, a hollow laugh escaping him. "She wanted to say she was sorry about my dad and that they were in love. She told me not talking to him really hurt him." His chest vibrates with a scoff.

"I hate this bitch." And I didn't realize I said that out loud until I heard him laughing. She ruined any chance I might have with him. Maybe if she didn't sleep with his dad, he might feel differently about relationships. Unless that's not the only reason why he doesn't do relationships.

He pulls away and stares at me, a line creasing between his eyebrows that I want to reach out and smooth it.

"What?" I ask when he continues his intense stares.

"Thank you. I wasn't planning on telling you any of this, but I'm glad I did." He looks directly into my eyes, unblinking. *Flirty* Jake makes me blush, but *serious* Jake makes me sweat. Causing moisture to build between my thighs like the morning dew on the fresh grass around us.

"You're welcome." I move my tingling toes in my sneakers, trying to ground myself.

"Look," he says with a catch in his breath, pointing behind me. I whirl around with wide eyes—it's just a few more steps to the top. "Come on." His excitement is infectious as he pulls me by my hand. We race the last few steps together, laughter bubbling up as we reach the summit.

Panting and laughing, we collapse side by side, the exertion giving way to exhilaration. Our laughter slowly dies down, and we sit up, taking in the panoramic view before us. The sunrise unfolds like a live painting, shades of orange and pink bleeding into the clear sky.

It's a moment of pure magic, the kind that makes you believe in a greater hand at work. I lean into him, feeling the rise and fall of his chest. "This is breathtaking," I breathe out.

"It is." He pulls me even closer, his arm wrapping around my shoulder, and his chest is firm against my back. Even though we've been hiking, he smells amazing, like pine needles and sun-warmed wood.

My heart beats a little faster, and I know I'm drawing too close to the flame. I want to lean in, to feel the burn, but the rational part of me knows this is supposed to be casual, uncomplicated. Yet here, in his arms, my heart doesn't get the memo.

Chapter 22

Jake

I am sitting on the ground with my knees bent and my head hanging between my legs. Tracing lazy circles with a stick as I think of my conversation with Mia.

There are a lot of things I keep to myself, stuff I don't even tell my best friends, but Mia has a way of pulling everything out of me. I want to bear my entire soul to her when she looks at me with those brown eyes.

I don't know how she does it. Maybe it's because we probably will never see each other again after this summer, or how it feels like I've known her forever.

Lifting my head up, she's leaning against the trees. Her knees are up, and her book is open on her lap. Our picnic is done, and now she's lost in her story.

Her bottom lip catches between her teeth, and I already know what kind of chapter she's reading. A slight smirk tugs at my lips. I promise to make her feel better after the hike, and this is the perfect time to fulfill my promise.

I approach her; she looks up and our eyes lock. She smiles shyly at me and bookmarks her page before closing it. "No, keep reading." I lower myself on the ground before her, the grass soft underneath me. Gently, I part her thighs open, as I rest between them on my stomach.

She hesitates for a moment, but as I carefully roll down her leggings and guide them off her legs, she reopens the book; her gaze flickering between the pages and me. "I promised to make it better, didn't I?" I ask with a playful raise of my eyes before I press a kiss on her inner thigh.

"Yes." She nods. Her gaze locks with mine, and her breath catches as I continue trailing kisses up her thigh.

"Is this better?" I breathe out against her skin.

"Yes," she sighs in the quiet between us.

My lips trace the path up her thighs, closer to where she craves them most. "I need you to read out loud, baby," I gaze up at her, "I want to make sure you're still reading."

Her pupils expand, swallowing the light, and darkening her gaze. "*...She couldn't breathe...as she felt the hard thickness of him inside her again.*" A soft moan escapes her as she clutches the edge of the book. The sight of her trying to focus on reading out loud while under the spell of my mouth has me unbearably hard, but I remind myself this is about her.

I slide her sexy black thong down and off her legs, revealing the sweetness I crave. She closes her thighs, and I look up at her. Her cheeks redden as she looks at me from under her lashes. "You haven't done this before, have you?"

She timidly shakes her head.

The fact that I'm the first to taste her sweet pussy makes me eager. "It's okay, princess. Trust me, you will love it."

She eases her thighs apart, and I stare at the prettiest sight I've ever seen. Nicely groomed, her pink slit glistens with arousal. I lean in, pressing a soft kiss to the nub, and inhale deeply. Her scent is intoxicating, sending my heartbeat into overdrive. "You smell amazing, baby." Sweet as a wildflower.

I slide my tongue up and down her clit, causing a small gasp to escape her lips. *That's some sweet pussy.*

With each swipe of my tongue, she struggles to concentrate on her reading, her breath catching in her throat. "Keep reading," I remind her, though I'm spellbound by the sight and taste of her.

"*...She...she arched...to meet his next thrust...*" Her voice breaks as I suck on her sensitive bud, drawing out gasps and muffled words. Her thighs tremble, and I can feel the tension building inside her.

The sweetness of her arousal deepens under the attentiveness of my tongue, and it ignites a fire inside me, almost overwhelming. Her fingers find their way into my hair, gripping slightly as her thighs part further, inviting me closer.

Pulling away, I roll onto my back and look up at her. She's staring at me, probably wondering why I stopped. "I need you to ride my face, princess," I say, and she lifts her eyebrows. "Come over here and squat on my face so I can devour that sweet pussy even more." I growl like a hungry man.

"My ass is too big," she says nervously.

"Baby, get your thick ass over my face now," I command.

She moves and straddles my face, the book still in her hands. Her thick ass covers my face. I run my tongue along her center to her clit, tasting the sweetest thing I've ever tasted in my life.

"Twerk on my face, princess." I say muffled, my face buried deep in her heat. Her hips grind and bounce on my mouth, her juices coat my tongue.

"Fuck, baby!" I slap one of her ass cheeks, and a cry of pleasure follows the sharp sound. I give her a slow, long stroke of my tongue, savoring her taste before sinking one finger deep inside her. Another stifled moan escapes her.

"*... She... she cried out...*" Her voice trembles as she continues to read. When I add another finger, she dissolves into a series of whimpers, her words a tangled mess of pleas and cries.

My fingers move faster, curling around the spot that I know so well. I continue to worship her with my tongue, sucking and curling around her clit. Then she goes quiet, as if her soul has left her body. The mountain seems to hold its breath in anticipation.

"Oh God, Jake." Her voice, raw and beautiful, cuts through the silence of the mountain. Her body trembles intensely against my mouth, her muscles clenching around my fingers. She grabs my shirt; her nails dig into my skin as she rides the waves.

I remove my finger before sliding her down so I can sit up. I turn her around to face me and she collapses into my chest, her body still shaking. A light sheen of sweat makes her skin glow in the filtered light through the trees.

Seeing her face flush with the bloom of her climax stirs something fierce in my chest. It's a twist and a roar that I can't quite tame or make sense of—a storm breaking inside me, wild and unbidden. A part of me wants to dive into that storm, to let it sweep me wherever it's heading, but I hold back. Instead, I let the beast snarl and pace within its cage.

As she comes back to earth, her eyes fluttering open, I can't help the smirk that plays on my lips. "Welcome back," I tease, and she lets out a breathy laugh, still recovering from the high.

"I love hiking," she says, laughter mingling with satisfaction in her voice. Her joy is contagious.

I join in the laughter, reaching for the baby wipes in my bag, cleaning her up gently. Her curious gaze meets mine, and I raise an eyebrow in response.

"Why do you have baby wipes?" She asks, that skeptical tilt to her voice that always gets me.

I shrug, playing it cool. "Picked them up a few days ago."

"Why?" she presses with that adorable frown.

"Because we're gonna need them. I plan on making you come to every place we go unless you're into the idea of being sticky all day."

Her gaze lingers on me, softening, a mix of emotions dancing there that I'm not ready to dissect just yet. I help her to her feet and gently guide her into her leggings.

"Ready to go down?" I gather our stuff and put it into my backpack. "Or do you need a few minutes?" I tease, "If we didn't have to walk back, I'd fuck you against the tree. But then I might have to carry you down ..." The image of her, pressed against the rough bark, is enticing. She tilts her head; that innocent yet undeniably sultry look she gives me, stirring a familiar desire deep within. I'm already thinking about the next time I can have her, feel her, taste her. It's like she's cast some spell on me; the more of her I get, the more I hunger for her.

"I thought you could carry my thick ass anywhere," she says, repeating my words back to me.

I close the gap between us. "Don't tempt me, princess." Her breath hitches, anticipation dancing in her eyes. My phone rings, breaking the moment. I sigh, reluctantly pulling away. "Hold that thought," I say, pressing the phone to my ear as I step back to take the call.

"Yes, Sergio?" My tone shifts to a serious one. If he's calling me, it means there's a problem.

"We have a situation. A pipe burst and flooded some rooms. We need to relocate some guests, and they're not happy."

"Fuck," I curse under my breath. "I'll be there in about two hours. But make sure you give the guests new rooms, even if they're booked, as long as they are vacant."

I hang up and turn to see Mia looking concerned: "Everything okay?"

"No, we need to go now. A pipe burst and we have angry guests," I explain quickly.

"I'm sorry," she says with genuine concern.

"It is what it is." I draw in a deep breath before releasing it. Everything just keeps getting worse; if it's not one thing, it's the other, maybe I should just sell it to the bank. My dad should be the one to deal with this shit, not me.

We make our way back down the trail, with Mia trying to keep up with me. Once we're in the car, I turn to her. "Is it okay if we drive straight there?"

She nods, her expression understanding.

Once we arrive at the hotel, I find a line of angry and frustrated customers waiting in the lobby. I approach Sergio, and he catches me up on the details.

"You can wait in my office while I take care of things here," I tell Mia. She doesn't have to deal with this.

"I want to help," she insists.

"I appreciate it, but you don't have to. This is my mess," I say, my tone a little firmer. I turn away, diving into the crowd of disgruntled guests.

Ignoring my protest, she stays next to me, offering reassuring smiles to everyone, even when I told her she doesn't have to. I know it's pointless to ask her to stop.

"Mia, seriously, I've got this," I whisper to her between guests, frustration creeping into my voice.

She turns to look at me. Her eyes narrow, and her lips press into a firm line before returning to the guests with a warm smile. I know not to say anything else. And to be honest, her presence is the only thing keeping me calm right now. Her smile eases both my nerves and the guests'. When she steps away to talk to Sergio, I miss her presence instantly.

After I'm done with the guests, I walk into my office. Mia's on the phone, her brows furrowed in concentration. I slump into my chair, running a hand through my hair, already mentally exhausted. I need to find a company as soon as possible to fix the pipe.

"I found a company that can fix the pipe tomorrow." Mia's voice breaks through my thoughts. I look up at her, puzzled. "I have their information right here with their estimate." She hands me the paper. "I already talked to them. You just need to confirm." Her eyes search mine.

"I didn't ask you to do that," I snap at her, the stress getting the better of me. She flinches but quickly recovers.

"I know, but I wanted to help."

"I'm sorry," I say, grabbing the paper from her, and then immediately call the company to confirm. As I speak, I watch her from the corner of my eye.

She's sitting on the couch, scrolling through her phone. She has her hair pulled into a ponytail and she looks a little exhausted, but she's still here. And she hasn't complained once.

I dig into my bag and grab a Snickers bar and give it to her while I wait for them to take me off hold. Memories of our first meeting at the gas station replay in mind. She immediately captivated me.

"Thank you," I tell her once I'm done with the call. "I really appreciate your help, even though you didn't have to."

She gives me a tired but warm smile. "You're welcome."

"Come on, let's go." I grab our stuff and head out of the office, Mia walking beside me.

We catch Sergio on the way out. "Go home Sergio." Today was a long day, but we handled everything.

"Okay, I'm leaving." His laugh follows me outside. The man is a workaholic.

"What do you want to eat?" I grab my keys from my pocket to unlock the Jeep.

"Mmm, how about Chinese food?" She rubs her eyes as I open the passenger door for her.

"Chinese food sounds great. Wanna place the order? There's a Chinese food spot on the way."

"Sure, what do you want?"

"Anything with noodles and some dumplings." My stomach growls at the thought.

"I'm gonna get some chicken fried rice, Tso's chicken, and spring rolls." She smiles at me.

"Do you want me to order it?" I glance at her when she doesn't make the call.

"I'm ordering it online."

"Why don't you call instead? It'll be faster." I put on my turning signal.

"I hate talking on the phone. Online is more convenient. It's all done, and the food will be ready in 15 mins." She adjusts in her seat.

I pull up to the restaurant and walk inside to grab our food while Mia waits in the car. I return with a big brown bag and place it in the back seat.

"We ordered too much." I say.

"Leftovers are the best." She yawns, leaning back into her seat.

We pull to the cabin, and I put the bag on the kitchen counter before we head upstairs to shower.

Once I'm done, and dress in some comfortable clothes, tank tops and shorts. I walk to Mia's room to see if she's done. She's lying on her bed with her legs hanging off the edge.

She hasn't even taken a shower yet. Something in my chest tightens at the sight.

"Mia, you need to take a shower." I gently shake her shoulder.

"Nooo," she moves up the bed and tries to snuggle into the blanket.

She must be tired; I should have made sure she took a shower before I did. But she can't sleep like this.

I walk into her bathroom and prepare a bath for her before returning to the bedroom. "Come on, let's go." I lift her into my arms, and her head rests against my shoulders. She's still groggy as I carry her to the bathroom.

Sleepy Mia is adorable.

I sit her on the sink, supporting her with my body. "Arms up," I say, and she lifts them as I pull her shirt over her head. Placing her down on her feet, I struggle to pull her leggings over her thick thighs. She kicks them off her feet.

I help her into the tub. She sighs, a small smile playing on her lips. I pull her curls up into a ponytail, my fingers brushing against her neck. Kneeling beside the tub, I grab the sponge and gently squeeze the water over her shoulders. Watching as it glistens on her skin. I pour her favorite jasmine soap into the sponge. It doesn't lather because she's sensitive to bubbles.

It glides gently across her skin. Her eyes close, and she relaxes under my touch.

Reaching under the water, I guide her hand between her thighs, cleaning it gently. A soft moan escapes her lips. "Eager, aren't we? Just making sure you're clean, baby."

Baby.

The word slips out so easily. I've called her baby before, but it feels more intimate. She's not exactly *my* baby. We're just hooking up.

Afterward, I help her out by wrapping her with a towel, patting her dry while she looks at me through her lashes, looking so innocent and sweet.

I've never done this before, taking care of a woman. Lately, I've been doing a lot of things I rarely do.

Back in the bedroom, I slip one of her oversized t-shirts over her head. The fabric drapes over her, and she looks up at me with a sleepy, grateful smile. "You would make the sweetest boyfriend."

That sentence breaks me a little. She deserves a sweet boyfriend, but I can't be that for her. Not now, maybe not ever. The walls I've built around my heart make it impossible to let anyone in, not even her. Love and relationships are too unpredictable and too messy.

"I'm just taking care of you."

I head downstairs to grab our food. When I came back into the room, she's already lying down, ready to fall back asleep.

"Come on, you've got to eat first. You haven't eaten all day." I place the food on the bed. Grabbing her hands and pull her up to sit.

"Open up." I bring the fork full of rice to her lips.

She opens her mouth to take it. She moans softly, chewing on the food while staring at me.

"Careful with those sounds Mia," I warn her.

She smiles deviously.

I take a few bites, switching between feeding her and eating some myself. I continue offering her more until she says she's full and ready to go back to sleep.

"Good night, douxy," she says with a sleepy smile. This is the second time she's called me douxy, and I wonder what it means.

"Good night, Mia," I grab our plates and the bag, bringing them downstairs. The rest of the food goes in the fridge, and the empty plates in the trash can.

I make my way upstairs, planning on going straight to my room, but my feet stop at her door. Most of the time we sleep in our own rooms, but right now I crave her presence.

Before I know what I'm doing, my feet carry me inside. I stand there and watch her like a creep. She's afraid of the dark, so her night lamp is still on. Her brown skin glows under the dimly lit room.

I take off my sandals and remove my shirt before climbing into the bed next to her. As if she knows I'm here, she moves closer to me in her sleep. Her head finds that perfect spot, and she lets out a small, contented sigh.

My arm tightens around her, and the sound of her breathing calms me. "Good night, Moonie," I whisper to her sleeping form.

She feels like mine, except she's not. She deserves more than I can give her. Someone who can love her without holding back, someone who can give her a future.

That's not me.

After everything that happens with my parents and Jessie, I'll never be ready to be in a relationship. I never want to be in that position to hurt her.

Chapter 23

Mia

My eyes flutter open to the soft light of the room. Checking my phone, it's only 4 a.m. and it's unsettlingly quiet, except for the gentle, even breaths Jake takes next to me. I watch him sleep; he's like the calm found in the eye of a storm.

How can he look so perfect? He doesn't even snore. Why doesn't he snore? I slide out of bed, snatch up the blanket, and quietly walk towards my desk.

I hate the fact that he does sweet things like last night. Instead of letting me sleep hungry and dirty, he gave me a bath and fed me. I'm grateful, and it was so thoughtful of him. I don't even know why I'm upset.

Then again, he says this is casual, no catching feelings, and goes ahead and does things like that. I don't know what kind of game he's playing.

Why is he even in my bed? I thought he doesn't cuddle after sex.

Sitting at my desk, I bang my head against my laptop before opening it. I try to focus on the blank screen in front of me, but it's hard when my mind is a tangled mess.

"Baby, why are you up so early?" His groggy sound startles me. I turn to see him sitting on the bed, bare chest, looking sexy even in the dimly lit room.

"I'm writing, and don't call me baby." The words escape me before I can stop them, and they're sharper than I intended.

He gets off the bed and moves to crouch in front of me. "Is everything okay?"

"Everything's fine," I say, avoiding his gaze.

"Why does it feel like you're mad at me?"

"I'm not mad."

"You sound mad, baby."

"Don't call me that," I snap at him.

"Why not?"

"Because I'm not your baby," I say, fighting back tears.

Stop crying for everything, I scold myself internally.

I know we're just two people hooking up, nothing more. "And why did you take care of me last night? You could have let me sleep hungry and probably a little stinky."

He reaches out, lifting my chin gently to meet his eyes. "Because I care about you, and you always smell good."

I pull away. "Well, you shouldn't."

Without another word, he stands, lifts me effortlessly, and I instinctively wrap my legs around his waist as he sits on the bed.

My body has a mind of its own always melting into him.

"Hey, look at me." He cups my face with both hands. His touch sends a thrill through my veins. "I know this is casual and just for the summer, but that doesn't mean I don't care about you." His voice strained. "I want to enjoy every moment we have left together, but not at the cost of hurting you. If this is too much, just tell me and we can stop." He pauses, panting as if the idea pains him.

He's so freaking perfect, except for one tiny little thing. He doesn't want more with me. And I have a feeling that I want everything with him.

"It's just that you confuse things sometimes." I trace lazy circles around his bare chest. He hardens beneath me.

"Confused how?" His hand rubs my shoulder.

"I've never hooked up with anyone before, but I don't think it is supposed to be like this." I know I'm not imagining the connection between us.

"You're right, it's not." He brushes away a few curls that fall around my face. "But it's different with you. You're not some random girl I met at the bar or the club. I treat you the same way I treat Sarah and Alex." He gently tucks a piece of hair behind my ear. I must look crazy, but the way he's looking at me makes me feel like I am the most beautiful woman he's ever seen.

I laugh. "Do you also fuck Sarah and Alex?"

"Minus the fucking and the orgasms." He laughs a little, but his eyes are still intense. He's waiting for my answer.

I should end it now. I'm aware of how it will end, but I can't bring myself to let go. Not when my body craves him, and his arms feel like home. I thought I was demisexual, but then he bumped into my life and woke up all my desires, all my wants, and all my cravings. I wasn't demisexual; I was Jake-sexual. It's like I was waiting for him all along. Even my boyfriend, who I thought I had feelings for, never made me feel like this.

I tighten my arms around his neck and pull him into a kiss, deciding to enjoy whatever time we have left, regardless of the consequences.

My fingers trace down his chest, his skin warm under my touch, and the steady pulse of his heartbeat thudding beneath my fingertips. With a swift motion, he rolls us over on the bed, folding me beneath him.

He pauses, his green eyes lingering on me with an intensity that seems to slow time. His fingers trace my face, as if he's memorizing every detail. He lowers his head and kisses my forehead, my eyes, cheeks, then my nose, which makes me giggle. His lips find mine again, kissing my laughter.

Lifting my shirt over my head, his hand glides along my body. He ignites a trail of goosebumps across my skin. His kisses trail slowly and deliberately, causing soft moans to escape my lips.

He pauses at each breast, gently drawing each nipple in his mouth, warm and inviting. Each pull sends a wave of pleasure that tightens my stomach and quickens my breaths.

His lips meet mine again, deep and soulful. My hands cradle his face, my thumbs gently stroking his cheek. I have to remind myself to breathe and remember this is just sex, even when each touch suggests that this is something deeper.

My heart doesn't listen.

Each touch, each kiss, is like the rain that falls to the thirsty ground of my soul, making new flowers of affection bloom in my chest.

He reaches for a condom, but I hold his hand, stopping him. "I want to feel all of you, and I'm on birth control, but only if you're okay with it," I whisper.

"I want to, and I've always used protection before," he reassures me.

"Okay," I breathe out, my heart fluttering with anticipation.

He positions himself at my entrance, his hands shaking as he slowly enters me. His gaze flickers, as if he's afraid of what he might find in my eyes, yet he holds it. They are widely unguarded and filled with emotions that make my breath hitch.

His breath is shaky, and his touch is featherlight, almost hesitant. No matter how much he stretches me, I'm still so fucking tight that it still takes him a few seconds to slide in. He softens my discomfort with kisses as he pushes in slowly, until he's all the way inside me, like he's the only one that belongs there.

It feels so much better with no barrier between us. "Hmm, it feels so good," I moan. I'm so lost in him, in us, that I might pass out.

"You're so wet for me, princess," he whispers in my ear. His grip tightens around me, his finger pressing into my skin as if he's afraid I might slip away. His gaze is searching, almost questioning the intensity of the moment.

He places his hand at my side, lifting himself into a push-up position. My legs are bent up and stretched out as he plunges into me.

"Yes, just like that, please." I reach out to grab his hips, my fingers digging into his ass, pulling him closer. I need every inch of him until he's balls-deep, stretching me.

"My greedy princess wants more, doesn't she?" His ass is tightening with every thrust.

I love it when he talks to me like that. Myself getting wetter than before. "Jake…" I grab the sheets on each side of the bed as flames run through my veins. As if I'm standing in the heat of a thousand suns, lighting up everything from the inside, touching every part of me.

"Yesss, yes," I whimper.

"That's it, come for me, princess," he whispers, his breath warm against my face.

It feels so intense, so overwhelmingly good, that tiny stars flash before my eyes. My soul momentarily leaves my body, transporting me to another world.

I cry out, my moans turning into a series of desperate, high-pitched sounds. "Jake, oh God, Jake!"

"I'm going to come, baby. Do you want me to come inside of you?"

I nod. "Yes, yes, please." My moans turn into soft, breathy cries. I try to open my eyes to look at him, but I can't—my vision's blurry.

He lets out a deep groan, his breath ragged against my face. The sound of his body hitting mine is enough to make me come again, a loud cry escaping my lips.

"Oh, fuck," he curses as his soul joins mine, and I swear we leave this world; for however long, I don't know. It's just our souls connecting together in a place of pure ecstasy as his liquid fills me up.

I don't know how long it takes for our souls to return to our bodies. My eyes open slowly, blinking a couple of times to adjust my vision. I didn't even know I was crying until his thumb wipes away the remaining tears. I don't know how much I cried out, but my throat feels dry.

We stare at each other as he lies flat on me, his arms wrapped around my shoulders. Our legs tangle together as he's still inside of me. He presses his lips to mine; our lips move slowly against each other. These are more than simple kisses—it seems as if our hearts, souls, and bodies are communicating, whispering words we don't dare to say out loud.

My heart, stubborn as deep-set roots, stretches towards the warmth he offers, soaking it up, growing despite my intentions to keep things casual.

Moving to lie next to me, he pulls me into his arms, holding me tightly against him, and quickly falls asleep. He didn't even bother to clean up.

A few minutes later, I untangle myself, careful not to wake him. I grab my shirt and put it on. Tiptoeing towards my desk, my legs still sticky.

I sit at my desk as the early morning light seeps through the glass windows, staring at the image of me and my mom on my laptop screen saver.

We took that picture last year, and now she's just gone.

I click on the window screen to open my document. I have a little over a month to finish this book, to prove to myself that I can do this. One thing I know for sure: I can't go back to medical school. I don't want to go back home, where my dad will remind me every day how I'm throwing my life away.

Maybe I'll visit my grandmother in Paris if the offer still stands. I know nothing about my mom's life there. Maybe learning that part of her story might help me find my own.

I know he's staring at me without even seeing him. I always know when he's looking at me. It's the way my heart beats a little faster, and the goosebumps on my arms. We are like protons and neutrons, pulling towards each other by nuclear force. "I thought you were sleeping," I say, trying to focus on my screen.

"I was, but I reached out for you, and you were gone."

It's impossible to keep my feelings at bay when he says things like this.

"I wanted to get some writing done."

"Anything for me to read?" He moves towards me and leans against the desk.

"I started a new story. Well, it's an old story I submitted to my school's story contest. It was a little over 10,000 words. I edited it and added about 10,000 more words this week. I figured if I want to get rid of my fears of not being a talented writer, I must start where everything falls apart."

"Can I take a peek?" he asks, looking at me with genuine interest.

"Um, sure. It's a little dark and spicy."

"I love dark and spicy," he chuckles.

"Okay, I'll send it to you."

"I can't wait to read it." He pulls me off the chair and into his chest, his embrace warm and comforting. "But right now, it's time for our morning walk."

"Don't you think we should shower first? We kind of smell like..."

He chuckles, sniffing me playfully. "You smell amazing."

Chapter 24

Mia

I love the sex. Okay, I more than love it. I am freaking obsessed with it. Those past few days, I've had enough sex and orgasms to last me a lifetime. From the kitchen to the couch, in the shower, and the jacuzzi.

We've made sure every inch of the cabin will need a deep cleaning before it's rented again. This man doesn't just please me; he seems to know every secret contour of my body. My toys stand no chance against him, and I doubt anyone else could ever compete.

Our bodies are perfect for each other, like they were made for each other.

When he said he was going to give me an orgasm everywhere we go, he meant it, and has been keeping that promise. We've done it at the waterfall plenty of times, in the restaurant bathroom, on the hood of his Jeep, and inside that little barn we found. I can even cross having sex in a library off my list. Not that I had a list.

What I love even more are those morning walks to the waterfall. It's become our routine; we always come here every morning before doing anything else.

Laying side by side on the cool, damp grass, our hands barely touch, we look through the break in the canopy where the morning sky blushes into shades of deep orange. I find myself captivated by the serene expression on his face, his jaw unclenched and a peace settling over his features that makes him look even more handsome.

"Stop staring at me," he teases without looking at me.

"I'm not staring."

He turns around and moves on top of me, his green eyes piercing.

"I wasn't," I stifle a laugh.

His fingers find my side, tickling me. "Admit it."

I gasp between laughs, my hands coming up to cover my face as an embarrassed snort slips out.

He pauses, watching me with an intensity that sends a warm flush across my cheeks. "What?" I ask, peeking through my fingers, my voice muffle behind my hands.

"I love your snort," he says.

"You're a weirdo. Who likes that awful sound?"

"I think it's adorable." He flashes me that boyish grin that I adore.

I roll him over and climb on top. He's still smiling, eyes twinkling mischievously. God, why is he so insanely beautiful? I hate how it makes my heart flutter like the leaves in the morning breeze.

"Race you down!" I get up and begin shedding my clothes to dive into the water first. But my shorts stubbornly cling to my hips, trapping me. By the time I wriggle free, he's already shed his clothes, sprinting past me with the grace of a deer. His laughter rings through the air, pulling my gaze to the muscular flex of his legs and the irresistible curve of his bare ass.

An exhilarated scream cuts through the air as he leaps into the water. I chase after him, my laughter mingling with the rustling trees.

"I'll never get tired of this!" I shout into the wind, the thrill of the chase igniting a wild joy in me. Despite the early hour, the water is always warm. We swim, chase, and splash before collapsing back onto the grass, breathless and grinning.

A shadow of guilt creeps over me, uninvited. I'm so happy, so carefree, and she's not here to share it. I shouldn't feel this good. My laughter fades, a tightness forming in my chest.

"What is it?" He props himself on one elbow, his gaze piercing, as if he can read the turmoil written across my face.

"It's just... I'm happy." I force a smile. The words are like a betrayal as they tumble out.

"I know, and I like seeing you happy." His hand reaches out, gently brushes a stray leaf from my hair, a tender touch that sends warmth cascading through me.

"But I shouldn't. She's gone, and this is usually our vacation, and I'm happy without her." The words are heavier than I intended.

"I'm sure your mom loved you so much, and she wouldn't want anything else than to see you happy. And that doesn't change the fact that you still love her," he reassures me as he pulls me closer. We meld into each other, arms and legs tangled as naturally as vines, with an ease that frightens.

His heartbeat against my ear is steady and comforting; he presses a soft kiss to my hairline, which send ripples of warmth down my spine. I repeat the mantra in my head: This is casual and fun, that's it.

I try to convince my heart to listen, but it's no use when his hug feels like home—when my skin gets all tingly from his touch, and his presence satisfies a hunger I didn't know I had.

With a sigh, I tighten my grip on him, craving the comfort that his body against mine brings. He responds by drawing me even closer, our bodies pressed so tightly that every breath he takes seems to fill the spaces between us.

"Are you ready to head back? We have our pottery class." His arms are still wrapped around me.

"Hmm," I whisper back, savoring his scent, the comforting warmth of his body. His hand drifts down to squeeze my ass playfully. "You're still holding me," I note, a smile tugging at the corners of my lips.

"Yes, and I'm not letting go until you're ready," he states, his fingers massaging gently, making it harder to leave. I could stay here forever, but the thought of pottery, molding clay with him, does sound fun.

"I'm ready." I reluctantly let go of his hold.

As I bend to grab our things, he gives my ass a playful smack. "Damn girl, your ass keeps getting bigger."

"It's because you keep feeding me," I laugh, the sound light and carefree as we start walking back.

"Wanna race back?" My feet thumping in the grass before he has time to answer. I reach the cabin before him, breathless and giggling. "I won!" I stick out my tongue playfully.

"I let you win, baby, so I could watch that ass bounce," he teases, smacking my ass again as he leans in to kiss my cheek, just as he opens the door.

I'm about to answer him when my phone rings.

"Bonjour, Grandma," I answer, walking through the kitchen and sliding the door open to step out back as Jake starts on his smoothie.

"Bonjour, ma chérie, comment vas-tu?" *Good morning, sweetheart. How are you?*

Her familiar greeting fills my ear. We've been talking more often lately, especially after a touching conversation about her regrets of not resolving her differences with my mom before she passed away.

"Life is too short," she'd said; apparently, they were estranged because my mom had fallen in love with my dad during a trip that was supposed to be a vacation and moved to the US to be with him.

"Ça va merci, et toi, ça va?" *I'm good, thanks. And you, how are you?* I stroll around the pool, the water shimmering crystal clear under the early morning sun.

"Ça va, Chérie. Have you thought about my offer?" She switches to English, her tone hopeful.

"Yes, and I think I might visit after the summer." I take a seat on one of the lounge chairs and tuck my legs underneath me.

"That is wonderful! Let me know the dates, and I'll take care of everything." She sounds excited.

We talk a little more before Jake walks outside with two glasses of shake, placing them on the table between us.

"Okay, bisous, talk to you soon."

"Bisous, ma Chérie."

The line goes silent.

Checking the time on my phone, it's already 8 a.m. and our pottery class is in an hour.

"Come on, we need to get ready, or we'll be late," I urge, quickly gulping down my shake as I head inside, Jake trailing close behind me. The temptation to join him in the shower flickers through my mind, but I dismiss the thought. Seeing him naked again would certainly sidetrack us further. I can't seem to get enough of him, but time is ticking.

After a quick shower, I slip into biker shorts and an oversized graphic shirt that says *I'm a sasshole*, pairing the outfit with my red Converse. I pull my hair back into a tight ponytail, keeping it simple but effective. A touch of light foundation finishes my casual, ready-for-the-day look. I grab an extra set of clothes, so we don't need to come back here to change after class.

Rushing downstairs, I find Jake casually leaning against the staircase, one foot against the bottom step, arms folded across his chest, looking like he's been waiting. He wears a pair of denim jeans and a gray t-shirt that shows off the contour of his muscle's underneath.

"How did you get ready so fast?" I raise an eyebrow.

He pushes off from the stairs with a chuckle. "I love the shirt." He points at my chest. "You have a thing for graphic t-shirts.

"I love to make a statement." I laugh, adjusting my bag over my shoulder. "Let's go." I walk past him as he follows me outside.

We pull into the pottery class parking lot at 8:55 a.m., right on time.

The small studio is cozy, filled with the earthy smell of clay and the gentle hum of spinning pottery wheels. We choose a wheel in the back, a quiet corner under a string of twinkling fairy lights. Jake sits behind me, his legs framing either side of mine, his presence a warm, reassuring comfort at my back.

He places his hands over mine, guiding them as we shape the wet clay. His touch is gentle yet firm, guiding my motions to center the clay that stubbornly wants to wobble off the wheel.

His lips brush gently against my neck, sending electric shivers through my body, molding my feelings and shaping them into something deeper.

"Stop, you're distracting me," I murmur, attempting to sound stern but failing miserably as a chuckle escapes me.

"Isn't this supposed to be fun?" His breath is warm against my skin. He gently nibbles the top of my ear, making my skin tingle.

I lean back slightly, his solid chest presses against my back, his heartbeat steady and comforting. "It is fun." I turn my head to meet his gaze, our faces inches apart. "But we're going to end up with something that looks like a pancake."

"Then it will be our baby pancake," he teases, capturing my lips in a soft, lingering kiss, not caring that there are other people watching us. His fingers skillfully push and pull at the clay, sending my thoughts to places they probably shouldn't wander. "Your fingers are really working the clay, huh?" I blurt out.

"I'm really good with my fingers," he whispers into my ear in a seductive rumble as he kisses my neck again. I can feel him hardening behind me.

"Oh my God, Jake," I laugh, "Are you...?"

"It's not my fault that you smell so fucking amazing and I'm touching you. I keep thinking about how much I want to mold your perfect body."

I can't help but laugh softly, shaking my head. "My body isn't clay," I protest, trying to appear serious, but my heart races with anticipation. I secretly look forward to his touch. He really does know how to mold my body under his fingers.

When the vase finally stands on its own, tall and oddly shaped, we both step back, hands smeared with clay, and our faces light up with satisfaction. Jake wraps his arms around me from behind, chin resting on my shoulder, as we admire our handiwork.

Despite the imperfections, or perhaps because of them, what we made feels uniquely ours—flawed, and all.

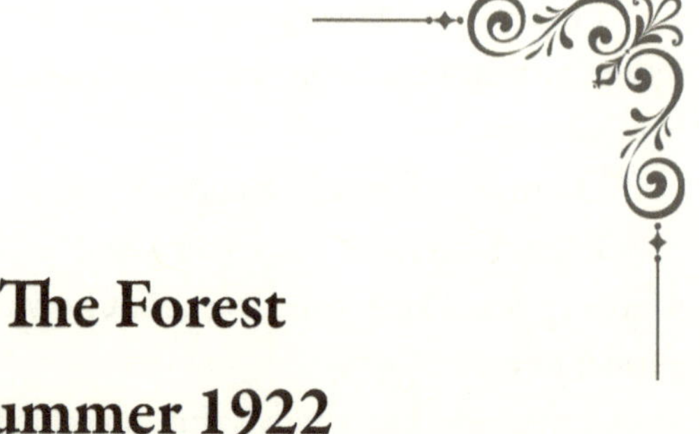

The Forest

Summer 1922

As Eadrick and Ifunayla swam in the waterfall, they discovered something extraordinary. Hidden within the rocks were emeralds, glowing with a gentle light.

Night after night, the moon's soft rays kissed the rocks of the waterfall. Its lights intertwined with the power of the moon worked its magic on the minerals, transforming them slowly and beautifully.

The waterfall, a silent witness to their pure and deep love, absorbed every tender glance and every shared kiss. This love, combined with the moon's light, infused the rocks and created the emeralds. A manifestation of their love, solidified within the earth.

They returned alone, and they each took a piece of the crystal.

Days later, they met again, their excitement filled the air. My leaves absorbed their joy, shining brighter than before.

"You seem really happy," he said, unable to hide his own grin.

"I've got you something." She bounced on her feet.

"Me too." His eyes sparkled with anticipation.

They hand the small bags to each other.

Their eyes widened as they opened it. They both took the matching necklace out of the bag.

"You made me a necklace." They said at the same time. Gently, they placed the necklace around each other's neck.

He pulled her toward him. Their forehead touched gently. "I love you," he whispered.

"I love you too," she said, bringing their lips together. Their kiss was a fusion of love.

Chapter 25

Jake

I need to get ready to head to the hotel and ensure everything is moving smoothly with the renovations. Instead, I am propped up on my elbow, watching her sleep.

Her curls spread across the pillow in a wild, beautiful disarray. Her long lashes cast tiny, perfect shadows on her cheeks. Those lips I enjoy kissing are slightly parted.

I could lay there and watch her for hours.

Eventually, I force myself out of bed and walk to the bathroom for a shower. Once I'm ready, I kiss her goodbye before heading out. I like the way she stirs and mumbles something.

I'm sitting in the office a few minutes later, poring over the budget. We didn't account for the broken pipe from a couple of weeks ago, plus we had to cancel some reservations to accommodate the guests—and we didn't plan for any of that in the budget. We're not even close to covering the loan payment for this month. My head rests in my hands as I stare at the spreadsheets. It's a disaster. I've already invested too much of my money and time.

A knock at the door pulls me away from the spreadsheet.

"Hey," Sarah peeks her head in.

"Hey." I walk up to her for a hug.

"How are you doing?"

"Not great. Nothing is turning out the way I wanted it to."

"It's going to be okay," she assures me, but her eyes don't hide her doubts. "So, I got your new website up and have a marketing plan for when the renovations are done." She opens her laptop before me, and her enthusiasm ignites optimism in me.

"This is amazing, thank you," I say, grateful for her help.

"I always got you." She takes the seat across from me.

I sense she wants to say more, so I lean back in my seat with my arms crossed over my chest.

"What is it?" I chuckle.

"Nothing, it's just... I really like Mia."

"She's easy to like." A smile curls on my face.

I can't help but think of how natural it is whenever I think of her.

"She seems to like you," she says, then pauses. "What's going on between you two?"

"What do you mean?"

"I see how you look at her with those goofy eyes and that idiot smile."

"What idiot smile?" Another involuntary smile makes its way onto my lips as I think about her sleeping face from this morning.

"That one." She laughs, pointing at my face.

"Nothing is happening; we're just two people enjoying the rest of summer together and having fun." I run a hand through my hair, waving off her observation. She's seeing things that are not there.

"What happens after that?" She crosses her legs.

"We go our separate ways."

"That's it?" She stands, facing me.

I shift uncomfortably in my chair; my throat tightens, making it hard to breathe. "Mia and I have been on the same page since the beginning," I sigh, the uncertainty of my words hanging heavy in the air.

"You're either more stupid than I thought or lying to yourself." She rolls a paper and throws it at my head.

"Ouch." I feign, even though it barely touches me.

"It's okay to feel, Jake, to want more." She stares at me as if trying to get me to confess something.

I laugh, a short burst lacking humor, and shake my head. "We're just enjoying the summer, that's all," I repeat, clinging to this narrative like a lifeline.

I avoid her gaze, focusing on anything but her too-knowing eyes. The patterns in the wood grain of the desk suddenly seem fascinating.

"Mia and I... we know what we're doing," I insist, more to convince myself than her.

"Ugh!" She sighs dramatically, moving towards me and I stand up to give her a hug. "I can't wait to tell you I told you so." She punches me before walking away and out of the room.

It's suddenly colder, and the quietness is more pronounced. I turn back to my computer screen, but the number blurs insignificantly. My thoughts drift involuntarily to Mia, her smile, her laughter, the way her eyes light up when she looks at me.

She occupies my mind. I miss her the second I leave the cabin. I could kiss her for hours. She makes me feel things; not even climbing can make me feel them. I hate that Sarah is right.

What the hell am I supposed to do in a couple of weeks when she leaves? I know it's the adrenaline talking. It will fade, like the buzz from a night out. Right now, I'm drunk off of her presence, but soon, I'll have to sober up.

I dread the inevitable hangover, the longing that'll ache like a migraine. And what, then, when I yearn for another drink or crave this feeling again? I can't go back to anything ordinary after savoring the finest whiskey.

She's not just any whiskey; she's the rare kind you come across once in a lifetime. Each aspect of her possesses a unique refinement that cannot be replicated.

The first sip that sparks the senses is her rich and warming laughter. Her kindness is the complex undertones that add depth and linger on the palate. Her spirit is bold and invigorating, like the fiery finish of a high-proof spirit that leaves you breathless yet wanting more.

Every moment with her deepens the flavor and enriches the experience, making it harder to settle for anything less.

I shake my head, diving into work, but the tightness in my neck remains, and a warmth spreads through me every time I think of her. Maybe we should give each other some space.

Just as I clicked the last form of submission and exhaled a sigh of relief, ready to leave, a notification blinked at the corner of my screen—an email that grabbed my attention with the urgency of a siren.

Opening it, I froze, the sender's name tightening a knot in my stomach.

Hi Jake,

I have tried to reach you, but you've blocked my number. I'm hesitant to address this in an email, but given our last conversation, I have no choice. You were pretty upset then; it didn't seem like the right moment to discuss this.

Before your dad passed away, he came to see you because he had something important to share—something he hoped would bring peace between you. Given the circumstances, he couldn't. He wanted you to meet someone very important: your little sister. She's one now; she was just a baby when your dad died, so she doesn't know him. I would really like for you to meet her. She has green eyes and blonde hair, much like you.

I want to say it again. Your dad loved you deeply; whatever happened was never about you. Sometimes, when we're young, we craft our own narratives. Your dad and I loved each other. When I started working at the hotel that summer, I didn't plan to fall in love with him, and he certainly didn't take advantage of me. I was 20 years old and fully aware of my feelings despite our age difference.

I've attached my address below if you want to meet your sister. I've also included my phone number if you'd prefer to start with a video chat.

Warm regards,

Jessie

My heart pounds in my chest as I try to process the words on the screen. A sister? My sister? A daughter between my dad and Jessie. Just thinking about it makes me sick. My hand's still holding the mouse, trembling. I let go, my fingers splayed out on the desk.

All the anger and resentment I'd felt before when I found Jessie in his office came crashing down, hot and seething. She thought that an email would fix everything, that I would forgive them now that our lives are more intertwined than ever.

But while there's a part of me that's curious about her, my sister, I can't ignore the complexity of the situation. I've always wanted a little sister, but not like this.

My elbow props on the desk, my head rests in my hands, and I let out a deep, shaky breath. The bile rises in my throat at the thought of my dad, and I swallow hard, trying to keep it down.

I drag the cursor to save the email into my important files instead of deleting it. Once I'm done, I slam the laptop shut harder than intended and push away from my desk, the chair scraping loudly against the floor. I stand abruptly, pacing the room before grabbing my phone and sending Alex a quick message to meet me at the climbing center. I need a climb to clear my head. My feet carry me out of the office, jaw clenched and fists tight by my sides.

Pulling up to the cabin, the music coming from upstairs catches my attention. I follow it until I find Mia standing in front of the mirror, lost in her dance.

She is wearing those booty shorts that drive me crazy, dancing to Lovin' On Me by Jack Harlow.

Her eyes catch mine, and her movements freeze.

"Jake, what are you doing here?" she squeals.

"Don't let me stop you." I walk to the closet to change and grab my climbing gear.

"How was your day?" She follows me.

I kicked off my shoes. "It was fine."

"Just fine?" She watches me as I remove my shirt, a frown forming on her face as she waits for my answers.

"Yep." I pull down my pants, leaving me only in my underwear.

"Did something happen?" Her eyes trace my body as she bites her bottom lip before looking up at me.

"I don't want to talk about it, and if you're looking for a quick fuck, I'm not in the mood." She flinches at my words, and I regret them as soon as they leave my mouth. But I can't take them back.

I pull my shirt over my head, and when I turn around, she's gone. I should go after her, but I can't. Not when there's a tornado brewing inside of me. I grab my stuff and head out.

Alex is already waiting for me, leaning against his car. He doesn't ask questions or make small talk. I guess he knows me well enough. We drive to the climbing center in silence.

At the climbing center, we set up everything before we start.

I've done this so many times that I can do it with my eyes closed. I begin with a slow pace; my hands and feet are moving instinctively. My hands know where to reach, and my feet know where to place. This usually helps me focus and block everything out to clear my mind, but it's not working today.

My mind drifts back to the email from Jessie, my dad's accident, and a little sister I never knew I had. Then, the hurt in Mia's eyes at my words. It's all too much.

I keep reaching, but my hand slips. I'm swinging out, then crashing against the wall.

"Shit, that hurts!" A sharp pain shoots through my arm. Alex tightens the rope and brings me down safely.

"You alright, man?" His brows furrowed together.

"Yeah." I wince as I cradle my arm.

"Do you need to see a doctor?" His eyes are wide.

"No, it's fine. I just need to put some ice on it."

Alex and I got into the car and drove back to the cabin. My arm hurts, but I prefer this pain over the tightness in my chest.

Pulling up to the cabin, heavy rain and strong winds greet us. Mia.

Alex drops me off, saying he has to go. I rush upstairs, ignoring the pain in my arm.

I find her sitting on the floor with her knees pulled up to her chest, rocking her body back and forth.

"Mia," I whisper softly.

She's staring out the window at the pouring rain and the angrily swaying trees.

"You, okay?" I approach her slowly, trying not to startle her.

She doesn't say anything, doesn't even bother to look at me.

I sit next to her, staring at the window as the incident that night plays in my mind. Turning my head to look at her, I notice her shoulders heaving.

"Mia, baby, look at me, please."

I gently grab her shoulders, turning her around, forgetting the pain in my arm. I grit my teeth, but it's nothing compared to the pressure in my chest when I see her red, teary eyes.

Fuck.

"I'm sorry about earlier. I didn't mean to talk to you like that." I look down, ashamed of myself. "I just had a lot on my mind."

She still doesn't say anything, her silence cutting deeper than any words could.

Releasing her shoulder, I hold onto my arm. "I received an email from Jessie, and apparently, I have a little sister." I pause, taking a deep breath. "It's my fault she's going to grow up without a dad."

She turns to face me, her eyes softening, pushing me to continue.

"That night, when my dad came to see me, he asked to stay over because of the storm, but I asked him to leave. I was so angry... If I had let him stay, he would still be here." Saying the ugly truth out loud, it's like ripping off a band-aid.

She sighs, moving closer to me. Her hand hesitantly reaches for my face. The gentle yet firm touch of hers ground me. Her presence soothes me, yet it makes me feel exposed. Does she know how much power she has over me? I crave control, but with her, I lose it all.

"You can't carry that guilt with you. You didn't know what was going to happen." She moved to sit on my lap, cupping my face with her hands. "It wasn't your fault." Her voice is still a little raw from crying, but here she is, comforting me even after I was a jerk to her.

I close my eyes, leaning into her touch. God, I needed this. For the first time in forever, I needed something more than climbing. I need her.

I tighten my arms around her waist, wincing at the pain.

"You, okay?" She pulls away to look at me.

"Yeah, I just hurt my arm from climbing."

"Let me see." She takes my arms in her hand. Her touch almost makes me forget about the pain as I look at her pretty face. Her cute nose crinkles slightly, and a soft frown forms between her thick eyebrows. Her full lips, which I love kissing so much, press into a thin line, the corners turning down as she examines my arm.

"Jake, it's swollen. We need to put ice on it." Her big brown eyes are wider. She starts to get up, but I pull her closer, not ready to let her go yet.

She seems to understand without me saying it, wrapping her arms around me, and I lay my head against her neck.

"I'm sorry," I whisper against her skin, pressing my lips into her neck. "I didn't mean to take it out on you." Closing my eyes, I inhale her scent. Her hair smells amazing, like sweet coconut and something else, like calm and fluffy clouds. Fluffy clouds? That doesn't even sound like me. I glide my left hand into her hair, and she arches her body closer to me.

One of her arms tightens around me, the other gently stroking the back of my head. "It's okay."

What is she doing to me? It's as if my heart is trying to whisper something, but the jumble of thoughts in my mind drowns it out.

"Come on, let's get some ice on your arm," she says, looking down at it with another frown.

"Do you care about me, princess?" I hold her down with one arm, trying to read her expression.

"Of course I do. We're... friends?" She looks down, playing with my shirt. I can hear the questioning in her voice.

What are we? I said I didn't want to hurt her, but it's inevitable now. Yet, I selfishly want to spend every last second we have left together.

"Yeah, friends with benefits." I lift her chin to look at me, bringing those big, beautiful eyes to mine. I didn't know brown eyes could be so captivating, so expressive, but I know she's sad just by looking at them.

I gently tuck her curls behind her ear, admiring her face. Her thick eyebrows, doe eyes, and the freckles you can only see when you are up close. It's crazy how much she's come to mean to me in such a short time, but I still can't give her everything she needs. I don't know how to, and I'll just end up hurting her more.

She was right, I'm a fucking asshole.

Chapter 26

Mia

Apparently, I'm a pantser, even a mood writer, if that's a thing. My attempt to outline my other book failed miserably, but this new story is flowing. Sitting at my favorite spot at Marie's café, the sunlight is just perfect. I'm trying to focus on the page in front of me, but my mind keeps drifting back to last night with Jake.

We curled up on the couch watching a movie. His head leaned against the armchair, mine nestled against his chest, listening to his heartbeat. His arms snug around my waist, and our legs tangled together. I was warm all over, and an odd giddy rush went through me. The musky scent of him mixed with lavender was overwhelming. I was aware as never before of the working of my flesh.

His finger traced lazy circles on my back, his touch sending tiny electric waves down my spine. His hand slipped between my thighs before he slid my panties aside and entered me slowly. My breath caught in my throat as he began his slow torturous pace that was unnerving and intoxicating.

His eyes remained fixed on the screen; the movie's dialogue mixed with our heavy breathing. "Keep your eyes on the screen, baby. You don't want to miss the movie," he whispered, a playful command that made it even more difficult to focus on anything but his slow and deep thrust.

I tried to focus on the images on the screen, but it was nearly impossible with the overwhelming sensations he stirred in me. A soft moan escaped him, mingling with mine, and barely audible over the sound of the TV. It felt so good, yet I needed more. I needed release. I squirmed, trying to adjust to find that sweet release, but his arms tightened around me, his grip firm, holding me exactly where he wanted.

"Please, I need more." The words slipped out as a plea.

"More what, princess?" His movements slow, tantalizingly grazing that perfect spot, pushing me closer to the edge, yet still so far from where I needed to be.

"Please, I need to cum." My words were desperate as the tension kept unbearably building within me.

He chuckled, a sound that was dark and smooth as velvet. "Since you asked so nicely, like a good girl." His soft growl filled the air.

He shifted, bending his legs up, moving faster, harder. My hand clung to his shoulder as he drove into me, sending shockwaves of pleasure through my body. My entire being tensed as an ecstasy surged like a supernova exploding within. I shattered into countless shimmering fragments, each wave of my climax scattering light across the dark canvas of my closed eyelids. The next thing I remembered was waking up this morning in my bed. I must have fallen asleep right after.

How can I go back to regular cuddling after last night? He is ruining me for anyone else. I shut my laptop, a little harder than intended. I can't write like this.

Marie comes over with a freshly baked cookie, placing it in front of me. "Looks like you need this," she says with a knowing smile. "Why are you attacking the poor device?"

"It's nothing," I sigh.

"Want to talk about it? I'm a good listener," she offers softly, taking the seat across from me.

Maybe talking will help. "I'm staying with this guy for the summer," I start. "It's been amazing. We've been enjoying each other's company, just like we agreed. Nothing serious."

Marie waits silently, giving me space to find the words. "It's just… We have less than two weeks left and I'm not ready for it to end. But it was clear from the beginning that it was just for the summer." My chest tightens with the reality that we have very little time left.

"Have you talked to him about how you feel?"

"No, and I don't think it would change anything. He doesn't do relationships, and I can't keep being casual with him once the summer ends."

I pause to watch a couple having coffee together.

"I want love, real relationships—the kind that makes your heartbeat wildly or fills your stomach with butterflies. But he doesn't." The words spilling out more freely now.

"I'm sorry, sweetheart," she says. "But sometimes talking can make a difference. It doesn't hurt to try."

She might be right, but I'm not ready to face that conversation yet. I don't want to risk the little time we have left.

"Thanks for listening, and for the cookie." I smiled at her.

"You're welcome, dear. It's my pleasure." She stands up to leave but then stops, turning around to look at me. "I almost forgot to give you this." She takes something out of her apron that looks like an old book. "It's an old journal. Remember the couple I mentioned? This is her journal. Maybe it will help with your mysterious waterfall."

I grab the journal from her. It's old and brown, with a worn cover. I stare at it as she walks away. Slowly, I open it, noticing the faded cursive handwriting inside. It's a bit hard to read, but I can make it out. I'm about to start reading when I receive a text message.

Jake: Hey, where are you? You've been gone all morning?

I read it with a wry smile tugging at my lips. Speaking of the sweet devil.

Mia: I'm at the cafe. I should be back soon.
Jake: Why didn't you wake me up before you left?
Mia: What, did you miss me or something?
Jake: I miss our morning sex. (winking emoji)
Of course, that's all he missed.

Instead of responding, I pack up my laptop and put the journal in my backpack and head back to the cabin. Pulling up, I notice Sarah and Alex's cars outside. I had almost forgotten they were coming over.

I step inside, and the house is eerily quiet. They must be in the back. I drop my bag on the kitchen island and follow their conversations coming from outside.

Peeking through the slide door, I see them lounging by the pool, which reflects the clear blue sky and the mountains behind them. "Are you and Mia a thing now?" Alex asks as he lounges comfortably with his hands under his head.

They haven't noticed me yet.

"Why is everyone suddenly so interested in me and Mia?" Jake sighs, his frustration audible. "I've already told Sarah—Mia and I are just enjoying the summer. That's it."

"So y'all just forget about each other in a couple of weeks like nothing happened?" Alex presses, not letting go.

"I... I don't know, maybe we can stay friends."

My heart sinks in my stomach at his words. It's the truth, but it still hurts. I turn to walk away, but Sarah notices me. "Hey, Mia, you're back."

"Hey, guys." I step out with a forced smile plastered on my face. Our eyes lock, his gaze piercing, searching for something in mine. I break away first, taking a seat next to Alex instead of him. I focus on the mountain view, finding some comfort in its steady presence.

"We have pizza, wings, and beers." Alex points out towards the table loaded with food. "Beers are in the fridge," he adds.

"I'll start with the beer." I get up to walk inside.

"Let me grab it for you," Jake offers quickly.

"It's okay. I need to change anyway. I'll grab it on my way back," I reply, brushing off his offer.

"I'll come with you." Sarah links her arms with mine, and we head upstairs to my room, closing the door behind us. She sits on the bed in her black one-piece bathing suit, which highlights her slim figure perfectly.

I open my drawer and pull out a yellow two-piece bikini. "You, okay?" Sarah asks from behind me.

"Yeah, I'm fine." I force a smile as I put on my bikini top.

Sarah watches me for a second in the mirror. "We're friends, right? I know we don't know each other that well, but I like you."

Smiling, I look at her reflection. "I like you too and yes, we're friends." I sigh as I adjust my bikini.

"So, talk to me. You don't look fine."

"I'm just not ready for the summer to end." The words spill out heavier than intended. Being here with Jake, he has a way of making me forget everything: my mom, my dad, and the freaking book I need to finish.

When I'm with him, everything else fades until there's nothing but him.

"Is it because of Jake?" Her eyes watch me closely in the mirror.

"Yes, and no," I admit, pulling my shorts over my bikini bottoms. "Being here has allowed me to escape everything else. Going back means facing all those issues again. And yes... I'm going to miss Jake."

How his smile brightens my darkest thoughts, how his touch seems to speak directly to my soul. I'm not ready to let go, not ready to return to a world where he isn't my every day. I push the feeling down, locking it away where it can't hurt me—for now.

"I see the way he looks at you. Even if he doesn't want to admit it, I know he has feelings for you, too."

"Jake doesn't do feelings. He made that clear." The idea of him having feelings for me is too dangerous to hope for.

"Men are stupid sometimes. Maybe you should talk to him and tell him how you feel." She's the second person today who has told me to talk to him. Maybe they're right, or maybe talking to him will only confirm what I already know. My mom always told me that men are simple creatures and if they want you, you'd never have to guess. If Jake wanted more with me, he would tell me.

I don't want to think about that right now. I just want to have a drink and have fun. "Come on, let's go have some fun." I tug Sarah's hand and pull her off the bed, eager to end this conversation. "Do we have something better than beer, possibly something that doesn't taste like goat piss?"

"Oh my God," Sarah burst out laughing, "how on earth would you know what that tastes like?"

"I imagine just like beer." We both laugh as we descend the stairs.

"Yes, we have whiskey," she says as we walk into the kitchen.

"Awesome!" I grin, opening the fridge, and looking for the passion fruit juice I bought last week. I take that out, and some ice from the dispenser while Sarah gets the glasses. And of course, we can't forget the whiskey. We head back outside to rejoin the guys, the late afternoon sun warming my skin.

His green eyes observe my approach, scanning me thoroughly, and making my steps clumsy. We settle everything down on the table as I mix the passion fruit with whiskey over ice.

Sarah hands a drink to Alex and I extend the other to Jake. Our fingers linger on the glass before I pull away. I watch as he takes a sip of his drink. "This is good. How'd you come up with the idea?" His eyebrows raise.

"It's my cousin's favorite." I smile, ignoring the flurry of bird wings flapping wildly in my stomach.

"It's good," he says before taking another sip. I sit on the lounge chair between Alex and Sarah.

After a few minutes, Jake jumps into the pool and Sarah joins him to see who's the fastest swimmer. Alex and I laugh as we watch them. Turning to Alex, I catch his gaze fixating on Sarah, a mix of longing and something deeper shadowing his features.

"How long have you been in love with her?" I whisper, nudging him with my elbow.

He flinches, clearly surprised, his gray eyes snapping to mine. "I don't know what you're talking about."

I tilt my head, raising my eyebrows.

"Is it that obvious?" he sighs, his shoulders sagging.

"To someone who is paying attention, yes."

"Since forever, I guess." His eyes find her like a magnet.

"You should tell her how you feel." I touch his arm.

He shakes his head. "And ruin our friendship? Besides, she has a boyfriend." His gaze drops to his hands as he fiddles with his drink. My eyes trace the detailed tattoo sleeve covering his arm. A compass rose that spread across the entire limb, with a delicate crown resting atop the compass.

"I still think you should," I insist, giving his arm a reassuring squeeze.

He chuckles, a bit ruefully, and looks up at me. "So, you told Jake that you're in love with him?"

I stiffen, my heart skipping a beat. "I'm not...in love with him," I say quickly, maybe a little too quickly, a flush creeping up my neck.

He stares at me with a knowing look.

"I'm not," I say, firmer this time, before standing up and brushing off the imaginary dust off my shorts.

I glance at the pool where Jake is already watching me. His eyes send electric waves straight to my chest, making my heart beats a little faster.

"I need another drink," I mutter, ignoring Alex's knowing eyes and Jake's intense stare. I make myself another drink, this time more whiskey than juice. Then another as the evening blurs into a dusky haze. I'm getting tipsy and the quiet is getting on my nerves.

Why is there no music?

I connect my phone to the surround sound system, and the first song that blasts through the speakers is *ICU* by Coco Jones. Maybe it's the whiskey making me bold, but I dance like nobody's watching. As I turn around, my eyes catch his, and he's watching. His gaze, hot like the sun at its zenith, scorches across the pool and lands squarely on me. Every moment we spent together, every touch, and every look, plays back in my mind like a movie. Something in the way he looks at me says he's right there with me, connected by an invisible string.

He pulls himself out of the pool, water droplets dripping off his body, each muscle defined and glistening under the moonlight. His approach is slow, deliberate, making every second stretch. He pulls me back against his chest, his body still damp.

"You know what you do to me when you move your body like that." His teeth catch the lobe of my ear. His breath, warm and intoxicating, mixing with the music, pulses through my veins, making my skin tingle with anticipation.

My hands rest on his arms, and his fingers interlace with mine. "Keep dancing," he whispers against my ear as Coco Jones continues to play through the speakers. His hand finds its way inside my pants, stroking me through my soaked bikini.

My fingers dig into his forearm, my breath hitching at the sensation. "What about Sarah and Alex?"

"They went to grab more food and drinks," he says. I hadn't even noticed them leave, but I wouldn't have been able to stop him even if they were still here. His touch strips away all my control; everything else fades, leaving only the sensation he provokes. My fingers clutch his bicep.

"Are you upset with me?" His finger continues to stroke me through the fabric.

"No," I exhale sharply, my body tensing and relaxing in waves under his skilled touch. My free hand clutches at his thigh, trying to anchor myself.

"You sure? Because you've been ignoring me," he observes, sliding two fingers inside, as if to underline his point.

My back arches, pressing closer into his embrace, our bodies hidden by the shadowy light. From a distance, it looks like we're still dancing. My hands grip his wrist, both pushing and pulling, unable to decide.

"I wasn't," I pant out as he thrusts deeper, my body grinding against his fingers as he hits just the right spot. My legs wobble with the building pressure, and I clutch at his arm for support.

"We got tacos and drinks," Alex announces, oblivious to the scene. I look up over Jake's shoulder, his back facing them as they walk towards us.

Jake quickly removes his fingers, stepping back as I pull away. I stagger slightly, still flushed from my release. He casually licks his fingers, savoring the taste, the sly grin on his face visible only to me in the dim light. My hands smooth down my hair and adjust my clothes, trying to compose myself, grateful for the shadows that hide my flushed face.

I laugh, a genuine burst of amusement that sets Alex off too. He doesn't know why I'm laughing, but it's contagious, and soon Sarah joins in, her laughter mingling with ours. I cover my mouth, trying to stifle the giggles, my shoulders shaking.

"What did I miss?" she asks through her giggles.

I shake my head, still smiling, feeling a mix of exhilaration and secrecy. "It's nothing."

Maybe it's the alcohol, the music, or that freaking orgasm, but whatever happens after this, I'll never forget this summer. It's been the best fucking summer of my life, even if I leave with a broken heart.

I was never the girl who just had fun, but I like this version of myself.

Chapter 27

Mia

I stand in front of the full-length mirror, staring at his reflection behind me. He's sitting at the edge of the bed, his gaze fixated on me as I step into my dress.

He suggested I wear something comfortable for the surprise he has for me, so I chose a white skater style mini dress. It's sleeveless, with a square neckline and a corset top that hugs my body. The skirt flares out at the thighs, short enough that bending over might reveal my white lace thong underneath.

He stands and approaches me slowly, his hands gently tightening the lace at my back. Our eyes meet in the mirror.

"You're exquisite." His words cascade over my skin, cool droplets of water thrilling me with anticipation.

He's wearing a white short-sleeve button up with the top buttons undone, revealing his collarbone. Khaki shorts and pairs with white Vans. He chuckles lightly as I pick up my pink converse. "No heels?" he grins at me.

"You said wear something comfortable," I remind him, smiling, excitement and nerves for the evening ahead mixing within me. And I hate heels.

"It's perfect," he assures me, guiding me down to sit on the bed. Kneeling before me, as he puts the shoes on my feet. His fingers brush my ankles, sending a pleasant shiver through me.

Once he finishes, he gets up, offers me his hand, and spins me around. "Fucking gorgeous," he breathes out, and I laugh to hide the flurry of butterflies in my stomach.

No, not butterflies, but something more fervent, like birds fluttering wildly in my chest.

"Thank you," I say. His hand is steady as he leads me out, though mine trembles as I think about the surprise awaiting us.

Once we're outside, he opens the passenger door for me. "Thank you," I say before he closes the door and joins me in the driver's seat. I try to ignore the way his muscles subtly flex as he shifts gears, not an easy task when I'm acutely aware of every movement he makes. My dress is pristine white, and I'm determined to keep it that way, so I turn my attention to the blur of trees lining the road. "Where are we going?" I ask, partly to distract myself from him.

His chuckle is light, teasing. "If I tell you, then it won't be a surprise," he says. "Just wait and see."

The anticipation builds as we drive along the scenic road, and my thoughts drift to the pottery making class we took last week, the memory a pleasant diversion.

"So, I've been talking with my grandmother," I begin, needing something to distract myself. "She's insisting I come visit her in Paris. She lives in a vineyard, and I think I might take her up on the offer once summer ends." Just mentioning the end of summer sends a pang through me, the realization of how much I'll miss moments like these. How much I will miss him.

"That sounds like a good idea," Jake says, glancing over at me briefly before his eyes return to the road. "You guys will have a chance to fix, or build, your relationship."

I nod, glancing at him. Looking for any clues that tell me he might change his mind about us, that he's going to miss me as much as I'm going to miss him.

"I realized, no matter how angry I was with my dad, and still am, I..." He sighs, his grip tightening on the steering wheel. "I wish I had tried to mend our relationship. But now, I'll never get that chance."

"I'm sorry," I say, placing my hand over his on the gearshift. My touch is light, hoping to offer some comfort, yet knowing full well the complexities of family and regret.

The crunch of gravel under the tires signals our turn off the main road onto a more secluded path, surrounded by a dense pine forest. The air turns cooler, filled with the scent of pine and probably nearby water. Which means his surprise involves the lake.

He parks and helps me out of the truck, leading me down a wood path, the sounds of water lapping at the docks. I'm greeted by the sight of a small yacht. "Is that for us?" I ask, wide-eyed.

"Yes," he chuckles, clearly amused by my surprised face. He steps in first, then holds out his hand for me to get in. He guides me to the deck where there's a picnic set up. I gasp and cover my mouth in awe.

A white fluffy blanket covers the deck, and pink, white, and beige pillows are scattered around. A vase of orange tulips sits in the middle with a gold bucket of two bottles of champagne and two glasses. The picnic spread includes a large pepperoni, sausage, and mushroom pizza. A tray of fruits with grapes, strawberries, and cantaloupe, alongside cheese and bread. Another tray offers a variety of sweets.

I watch him thank a woman who leaves the boat before he comes over to join me. She must have been the one to set everything up.

"This is... It's beautiful." The words catch in my throat. I've always wanted these intimate romantic dates, and thoughtfulness. Not the fancy restaurant. Even though this is not exactly a date, I love it. "You really didn't have to do all this. It's not like we're dating or anything."

"I know, but we've been having an amazing time together, and since our time together is almost over, I wanted to do something nice for you." He tucks a stray curl behind my ear, and I don't realize

I'm crying until he wipes a few tears from my face. I laugh, a light, nervous sound to mask the real reason behind my tears.

"Sorry, this is just so nice," I say between chuckles. "I guess I'm a bit of a crybaby."

"You're an adorable crybaby," he laughs.

We settle down on the plush blanket, ready to enjoy our evening together.

I grab a slice of pizza and take a small bite. My gaze travels to the cliffs where the sun begins to set.

"This is so beautiful. It's unlike anything I've seen." I say, eyes wide as I take in the view. The sky transitions from blue to a canvas of orange and pink. Their reflections simmer on the water's surface.

Turning, I find Jake's eyes already on me. "It is," he agrees, his eyes softening, and my stubborn heart swells just a bit more.

I snuggle closer to him as the air grows colder, my head resting on his shoulder. He drapes a blanket around us, our fingers intertwining naturally, as if they were always meant to fit together like this. Goosebumps form on my skin; not from the cool air, but from his touch.

I wish I could stay here like this forever.

We continue eating our pizza, and Jake pours me a glass of champagne. I take a sip and set it down as he starts to tease. "You owe me a secret from last time. I told you one, and you didn't tell me yours," he reminds me, his eyebrows raised expectantly.

"I don't know, I don't think I have any more secrets you don't already know," I hedge, trying to deflect. Except for the one where the person I'm falling in love with might never love me back.

"Come on, there must be something," he insists, his eyes locked on mine, not letting it go.

I pause, taking a deep breath to steady the nerves. "Well, it's not really a secret, but I've never really told anyone close to me... My first boyfriend in college cheated on me after taking my virginity, all on the same night. Apparently, it was just a bet to sleep with the new quiet freshman." I sit up, feeling uncomfortable as the words spill out, not even sure why I'm telling him this.

My best friend Rylee doesn't even know about this. It would be easy to pretend it's because we won't see each other after this summer, but it's something more. There's always been this connection between us that's hard to explain, like he knows me, and I know him.

"I was so naïve, thinking he actually liked me," I admit with a bitter laugh. "There hasn't been anyone else since then. I went on a couple of dates, but it seemed like they all just wanted one thing without bothering to really know me." I look down at my hands as a knot forms in my stomach. Why did I tell him that?

He turns to face me, his eyes tightening. "I'm so sorry," he says, and his brows furrow deeply. "People can be so cruel..."

He trails off, catching himself from saying more, his jaw clenching tightly.

"I want you to know I would never do that to you," he continues, reaching out to touch my arm. "I haven't been with anyone else since we agreed... And this is not just about the sex for me." He squeezes my hand.

"It's kinda about the sex, but at least you didn't pretend," I say, holding his gaze.

I know about his dad and Jessie, but that shou

ldn't be the only reason. I need to know why he won't even give us a chance. He insists this is casual, but treats it more like a relationship. He's been the perfect boyfriend.

"Can I ask why you hate relationships so much?" Besides what happened between his dad and Jessie.

He inhales, bringing his legs toward his chest. "Climbing has always been my thing. There's nothing like being hundreds of feet up, hanging by your fingers, relying on your strength and skills." He glances my way before turning his eyes to the dark mountains in front of us. "It gives me this high, this adrenaline that courses through my veins, this unbeatable feeling of conquering the world. Once I'm down, the thrill is gone, and I'm left craving more, looking for the next mountain to climb, the next peak to conquer." He pauses. "Relationships, love, however you want to call it, are much the same. It's just another adrenaline rush, promising this peak of happiness, but then it fades away. Just like the descent after a climb, leaving people chasing that initial high again somewhere else." I stay quiet, letting him finish while absorbing every single word. "In climbing, I'm in control. I can manage the risk carefully. But love... it's unpredictable, and someone always gets hurt."

I understand him completely, and everything makes sense. After everything that happened between his parents and Jessie, he's afraid of giving someone the power to hurt him. "Is that what you're afraid of? Getting hurt?"

He turns to face me. "I don't know. I guess I don't believe in *happily ever after*. And if there's no happily ever after, what's the whole point?"

"I understand your fear, but doesn't climbing come with its own risks?" My eyes lock on the side of his face. He's still staring at the dark water. "Despite the risk, the potential of falling and getting hurt, you climb anyway because of the journey, the entire experience, is worth it."

I reach for his hands, forcing him to look at me.

"You're right, love is a lot like climbing. Yes, there's the fear of falling, of getting hurt, but there's also the possibility of reaching new heights, of conquering a new peak."

I pause, taking a deep breath, begging myself not to cry.

"And perhaps the risk, the very chance of falling, is what makes the climb, love, so incredibly worthwhile. I really hope one day you meet that person worth falling for." The words squeeze my heart. I wish I could be that person for him.

"Mia, you're worth everything..." A slight tremor betrays his usually composed demeanor. "It's just, I can't give you more... I can't promise you more."

"I know what we agreed to. I just wish my heart would listen." The tears I'm trying so hard to hold back spill over. I turn away to hide them, but his hand pulls my chin towards him. He gently wipes them from my cheeks. His fingers linger on my skin.

"I'm sorry, Moonie. I never wanted to hurt you."

"I know." I sniff. "You're the most fearless person I know," I say, reaching up to brush a lock of blonde hair away from his face. My fingers trace his jaw, feeling the stubble beneath my touch. "But you're scared of love... Of what it means to really let someone in. To give them power to hurt you."

"I'm not scared. It's just the love that you believe in, the one you read in your books or the ones you write about. It doesn't exist."

"I'm not six years old, Jake... I know love isn't all sunshine and rainbows. And sometimes it requires work, patience, and it comes with the risk of getting hurt, but that's how it is for anything that is worth fighting for." I pause, thinking about my parents. "And maybe you're right, and it fades away, or people just don't put in the work. What happens if you buy a plant and just let it sit there? Eventually, it will die." I smile, thinking of my parents again.

"Even after years of marriage, my dad would bring my mom flowers, not because it's Valentine's Day or her birthday. Sometimes, I would find them just dancing in the living room, or he would cook for her." The memories bring more tears to my eyes. "He might not be the best dad, but he showed me what it means to love someone, care for them, show up for them. One day, I wish to find the same thing." He's watching me intensely as I continue. "It wasn't all rainbows. They argued, sometimes about me, or when my dad left his socks on the floor or didn't wipe the sink after using it. Even when they were mad at each other, they would still show each other love."

He looks away, pain etched deeply across his features. "That sounds nice and all, but I'm sorry...I—" His words trail off, incomplete.

"Let's not ruin tonight," I whisper, easing onto his lap, my hands wrapping gently around his neck. I lean in, my breath quickening as I inhale the blend of lake air and his subtle cologne. "Tonight, under the stars, I want to pretend you're mine."

He exhales, and his arms tighten around me. His gaze locks onto mine, the corner of his eyes soften with a look that stirs a warmth that spreads from my chest to the tips of my fingers.

"For tonight, I am."

Chapter 28

Jake

I sit on the queen-size bed in the yacht cabin, intently watching as she unzips her white dress and lets it fall to her feet, revealing her white thong and perfect curves. Next, she slides down her lace thong, stepping out of it along with her shoes. Standing in front of me, she looks utterly perfect; every detail sharpens my desire. Her nipples harden in anticipation of my touch.

She's the most beautiful woman I've ever seen. Her eyes, glossy and mirroring my desire, watch me as she slowly approaches. My gaze traces every curve, every subtle movement, marveling at how meticulously God has created her. If it weren't for the impatient swelling in my groin, I'd be content watching her for hours.

Once she's close enough, I pull her onto my lap, and she straddles me. My hands wrap tightly around her waist while hers cradles my face; her fingers stroke my cheeks, a gesture that touches a part of me I've kept hidden.

Rolling us over, her back meets the mattress. Her face never fails to mesmerize me, especially her eyes and those lips that I adore to kiss. I used to crave just the orgasm, but now, kissing her is a craving all on its own.

I kiss her cheeks, then the top of her eyelids, and she giggles when I kiss her nose, a sound that stirs something deep within me. Leaning down again, I kiss from her lips to her breasts, nibbling the soft tissue around her nipple, then rolling the bud with my tongue. I twist and suck on her nipple, eliciting a soft breathless "aah" from her lips before moving to the other.

My hand glides down her skin, igniting a trail of goosebumps. My kisses trail slowly and deliberately, coaxing soft moans from her. Her body is like a tree bending in a strong wind as it yields to my touch.

I travel back up to meet her lips again, taking my time, moving my tongue in sync with hers, sucking on her bottom lip and biting it gently.

Her hands reach around to rub my back, pulling me closer. The sex is the most amazing I've ever had, and we never seem to get enough of each other.

Her legs spread out, and I position myself at her entrance. She's so wet that I slide right in.

Her stare is deep and intent, leaving me breathless. The dim cabin lights make her face glow, and something about her gaze makes my stomach flutter. I move, each thrust slow and deep, reaching into the very core of her being. She grips my shoulders, her fingers digging into my skin, pulling me closer as if she can't get enough. I lift her legs over my shoulders, giving me deeper, more perfect access.

"Oh God, yes, right there, please," she moans.

"I know, baby, I know exactly how you want it." I continue my slow, torturous pace, not wanting this moment to end.

My fingers dig into the soft flesh of her perfect ass as she takes every thrust, as if it's the best she's ever had. I've learned every inch of her body these past few weeks, and I'm addicted to bringing her pleasure.

"Jake," she exhales my name. Her eyes glisten with unshed tears locked with mine. They look so innocent, framed by thick lashes that flutter. They soften around the corners.

"Yes, Mia." I roll my hips slowly, knowing she loves it.

Her eyes roll back, and the pupils disappear behind her lids, leaving the whites. She locks her legs tightly around my waist, her hands grabbing my ass with a desperate grip.

"Harder, please."

"Here you go, Moonie." I pound into her faster, deeper than I ever have before. I want all of her, every breath, every moan, every shudder.

My jaw clenches as the bed moves with each thrust, the sounds of our bodies coming together pushing me closer to the edge. A deep groan escapes me, my face contorting with the intensity of my release as I fill her completely.

Exhausted, I collapsed onto her, both of us riding the residual waves of our climax. She's a beautiful, crumpled mess beneath me.

Lying next to her, I pull her close so that her arm wraps comfortably around my waist. In moments like these, with her heartbeat steady against mine, the restless parts of me are calm in a way that nothing else has the power to do.

"I've decided I'm going to Paris to visit my grandma. I think it would be good to learn more about my mom and where she grew up." Her voice is a soft vibration against my skin. "I'll call her tomorrow. I know I still have one week left on my rental, but I might leave before that." She trails off a bit, as if she's still wrestling with the decision.

I gently roll her over to face me, needing to see her eyes, which shimmer with tears in the dim cabin light. My heart tightens at the sight. "You don't have to leave early, not if it's because of me. I can leave instead." My words are heavy, almost strangled by the lump in my throat.

"It's not because of you. It's my decision. Tonight, this entire summer, has been better than I ever imagined." She gives me a small smile. My heart twists at her effort to stay composed, and a wave of desperation surges within me. I want to ask her to stay, to not leave, to remain here with me. But I can't hold her back. Not when I don't know if I can give her what she deserves.

"I'll never forget our time together, not even the mornings you were an asshole and woke me up with your blender." She tries to laugh, the sound more like a sob, and my chest aches with the effort to keep myself together.

"I'm still an asshole." I smile to brighten the mood.

"No, you're not, and you never were," she says, her hand caressing my cheek, her touch so tender it almost breaks me.

My breath catches, my heart thuds painfully against my ribs, a visceral response to her closeness and the impending distance her departure will bring.

As I gaze into her eyes, my mind replays every moment of our summer, the laughter, the arguments, the wild moments. The realization that I won't wake up to her every day, won't be able to kiss her or laugh with her, squeezes my heart so tightly it feels like it might stop.

But I cherish every second we've had.

I lean in and kiss her slowly, letting my lips linger on hers, savoring her taste, committing this moment to memory. In this kiss, I pour everything I feel: desire, fear, gratitude. I could kiss her like this forever, but there's no such thing as forever. Everything fades eventually, but right here, right now, she is all that matters.

The Forest

Summer 1924

They lay together, the soft murmur of my waterfall enveloping them like a comforting shawl. A witness to the depth of their feelings. Ifunayla turned towards Eadrick, her eyes brimming with tears she fought hard to hold back. "I love you," she whispered, the sound nearly swallowed by the soothing backdrop of the waterfall.

His chest tightened as he looked into her eyes, so full of love and fear. Gently, he reached out to brush away a tear that had dared to escape, his touch tender against her skin. "And I love you, Ifu." His lips found her forehead in a kiss so soft it was like a sigh.

Pulling her closer, he enveloped her in his arms, her heart beating against his own, fast and fragile. Her sobs, barely audible, resonated deep within him, stirring a fierce protectiveness.

"What is wrong?" he asked, his brow furrowed with concern.

She curled into him, her body shrinking as she confessed her fears. "Time is running out for us. Your father will soon choose a bride for you, someone deemed suitable. Then you'll forget me," she said. Her shoulders trembled as she breathed in deeply, trying to compose herself.

He shook his head slowly, his fingers threading through her hair in a comforting gesture. "Your godmother spoke to you again, didn't she?" A growl of frustration lurked beneath the surface.

"Yes," she sighed, leaning into his touch, seeking solace in his closeness. "She said there's no room for love between our worlds and that I must leave, for both our sakes."

Tears welled up in his eyes, blurring his vision. He blinked them back, determined to stay strong for her. "You're the one I love, Ifunayla. There is no one else for me." His arms enveloped her more tightly. A fortress against their cruel fate.

Her heart fractured under the weight of their reality. "They'll never accept us, Eadrick. Our love is a dream caught between two worlds."

His heart ached to hear her so defeated. "I'm so sorry," he murmured, pulling her into a tight embrace, wishing he could shield her from all the pain and prejudice of their worlds.

As they clung to each other, the weight of their love pressing down on them, the waterfall continued its endless song—mourning for their sorrow and a whisper of timeless love.

Eadrick finally broke the silence, his voice a blend of hope and desperation. "Let's run away, Ifu. Let's find a place where we can be together, just us," he proposed, daring to dream of a different ending.

Overwhelmed by love, fear, and a desperate yearning for freedom, Ifunayla breathed out in agreement. "Okay, let's run away."

Their decision, bold and uncertain, hung in the air around them, filling the space with a mix of dread and anticipation, as they dared to dream of a world where their love could blossom.

But Fate had other plans.

Chapter 29

Mia

Soft lips press onto my forehead, pulling me out of sleep and spreading a smile across my face. Then comes another kiss on my nose, which always makes me giggle uncontrollably.

"Good morning, princess." His lips meet mine again. As he moves to hover above me, I open my eyes to stare into those green eyes that I love, and his smile that seems to thaw the chill of the morning air.

I reach up, my fingers combing through his tousled hair, tracing the familiar lines of his face down to the soft stubble on his chin. "Good morning."

I close my eyes as his kiss deepens, and the warmth of his touch completes me.

But when my eyes flutter opens again, they're greeted not by his gaze, but by the gentle morning light filtering through the cottage window.

It was just a dream.

I'm afraid I will never stop missing him, even though he's not mine to miss. Even though we're oceans apart, he's always here.

With a deep sigh, I push the blanket aside and muster the strength to start the day. I slide out of bed and pad across the cool stone floor to the double doors leading to the patio.

The vineyard stretches beautifully before me, rows upon rows of green vines undulating in the morning breeze. In the distance, rolling hills fade into the horizon, kissed by the golden morning sun. Stone pathways lead to my cottage covered in ivy.

I still can't believe that I'm here in France, in Les Collines d'Étoiles. A small vineyard town an hour away from Paris. My grandmother owns the vineyard which is half of the town.

It's been eight months now, but the beauty of it all still takes my breath away. When I first arrived here, I was lost, and a little confused. Although I knew what we agreed on, I stupidly hoped he would change his mind. At the airport, I waited for him to burst through the doors and confess his feelings for me like in the romance movies. But that didn't happen. Maybe it was for the best.

I'm glad I came here; I fell in love with the place. My grandmother was eager for me to stay at the Vineyard Real Estate, but I craved solitude to sort through my thoughts, to heal. So, I asked if I could stay in one of her cottages instead.

She agreed and even gave me a job managing the vineyard's blog page. It's been perfect, really. I get to share the magic of this place with others, connecting our visitors to the everyday beauty and charm of the vineyard. Plus, I get to write, which is something I have been doing more of lately. I've published a couple of novellas under a pen name, and the reviews have been good so far.

I spent most of my days wandering through the vineyards. At night, I love to cozy up with one of my mom's old journals and old drafts that my grandmother gave me. Some of them were a little cringe-y.

Growing up, her father didn't support her dream as a writer either. He wanted her to major in business so she could take over the family business. She still didn't give up on her passion and has touched so many readers with her stories.

She spent years writing and perfecting her craft, and one day I will be a best time seller too, and people will love my books because of the stories I can tell.

I take a deep breath, letting the crisp morning spring air fill my lungs now that the weather is getting warm again. After a few minutes, I walk back inside. The room has stone walls and a wooden ceiling, giving it a rustic charm that I love.

It's a two-story cottage with two bedrooms on the top floor, and an open space that includes the kitchen, dining room, and living room on the first floor.

I stay in the main bedroom, which is spacious yet cozy. It has a queen size wooden bed frame that faces the fireplace, perfect for colder nights. Next to my bed is my little reading nook, an armchair with a cozy blanket and a pillow. My bookshelf has a mix of books, both in English and French.

My favorite place to unwind before bed.

My desk is by the window, where I like to sit with a view of the vineyard as I do an hour-long writing sprint before starting my day.

So far, I've completed book one of my dark romance fantasy series with a splash of dystopian elements—the one about the underwater Gods. I've started querying, but nothing yet. Sometimes, the waiting is a heavy weight in my chest, but I'm not ready to give up. Even though most days it's hard to keep writing, I remind myself of my dream. I take deep breaths and picture a reader out there who is waiting to escape into my story, someone who will appreciate that I didn't give up.

I've started book two, I'm 20,000 words in, and ended my sprint today with 25,000 words total. I lean back in my chair, stretching my arms overhead, feeling a mix of relief and accomplishment. *Today is going to be a good day*, I say, smiling.

Pulling away from the chair, I make my way into the bathroom for a quick shower before I meet my grandmother for petit déjeuner. A white vintage tub, placed by the window, with the perfect view of nature outside. Although I love a good bath, most morning showers are quicker and more practical.

I step out of the shower. The tile is cool under my feet. Back in the room, I dress in denim pants, a short sleeve striped button-up shirt, and black loafers.

Ready to start the day.

Leaving the cottage, I take the familiar path through the field towards the main villa. I cherish the 10-minute walk, especially the mini garden waterfall. My grandfather, whom I never had the chance to meet, created this garden for my mother. He wanted her to understand that falling is a natural part of life.

He believed that falling, whether it's falling in love or facing setbacks, doesn't always have to hurt; sometimes it leads to new beginnings.

Standing there for a few moments, I watch the water tumble softly over rocks, letting the sound and sight wash over me. Now, I understand why my mom loved waterfalls so much.

With a deep breath, I resume my walk, the soft murmur of the waterfall fading behind me as the estate comes into view.

Stepping inside, the beauty still takes my breath away. The grand entryway opens into a spacious hall adorned with fine art and elegant furnishings that speak of history and grace.

I make my way to the familiar patio where my grandmother Elena is waiting. Now that the weather is nice and warm, she prefers to eat breakfast outside.

"Bonjour, Elena," I lean down to kiss both cheeks before taking the seat next to her. She prefers to be called Elena rather than Grandma.

"Bonjour, ma Chérie," her eyes light up. On the table, café au lait waits for me, and tea for Elena.

My eyes take in the sight in front of me. There are expansive vineyard fields, and tall trees that offer the perfect amount of shade. It's truly the best view here.

Before I came here, I wasn't sure what to expect, but her warmth and openness quickly made me feel at home. She reminds me a lot of my mom, except for her silver curly hair. Even in her late 60s, her energy is still infectious. Her brown skin glows in the morning light. I want to be like her when I'm older.

I think about the family history she's shared with me, especially about my mom. She was just 20 and on vacation when she met my dad. My grandfather, perhaps too rigid, gave her a harsh ultimatum: choose the man she loved and lose her family, or return home. Neither my mom nor my grandfather ever took the steps to heal their rift. Even after my grandfather passed away, they were too stubborn to fix their relationship.

"Luc is joining us for breakfast," she says, switching to English, breaking through my thoughts.

"Oh, that's nice," I tell her with a knowing smile. My grandmother introduced us. We've been friends. He's the only friend I have here.

Based on what my grandmother told me, their family goes way back. He's like the grandson she never had.

"Luc." A warm smile spreads across her lips.

My back is to the entrance, so I haven't seen him yet, but his voice, smooth and reassuring, fills the room as he greets her. "Bonjour, Elena," he says, planting a kiss on each of her cheeks.

Then he turns to me, his smile reaching his eyes. "Bonjour, ma belle," he leans down to kiss both of my cheeks and lingers just a moment too long.

His eyes catch mine as he takes the seat between my grandmother and me.

He's in his late twenties and handsome. His dark black hair, pulled into a ponytail, emphasizes the firm line of his jaw, softened by the carefully groomed beard that frames it. His brown skin contrasts with the crispness of his white shirt, and as he looks at me, there's a tenderness in his hazel eyes that seems to search for something.

I'm acutely aware of his appeal, and any girl would be easily smitten by him. My grandmother has been less than subtle in her matchmaking, but I've made it clear to him that I'm not looking for anything right now.

I'm content with the company, the conversation, and the stunning view that the morning has offered.

"So, I was thinking Luc could accompany you to scout the café location," my grandmother suggests casually, taking a sip of her tea. I had shared with her my vision of opening a bookstore café, capitalizing on the area's tourist foot traffic, and I truly believe it could thrive here.

"I don't want to impose." I give Elena a pointed look, not wanting her to push Luc into something out of obligation.

"I'm happy to assist." He looks up at me. His offer seems genuine, but I can't help feeling a bit of a burden.

"Are you sure? You probably have other things to take care of." I break a piece off my croissant.

"I'm never too busy for you."

"Thanks." I smile shyly, unsure how to handle the weight of his gaze.

"Isn't he amazing?" My grandmother's face lights up, her eyes darting between Luc and me, clearly pleased with herself.

I resist the urge to roll my eyes, not wanting to be rude to her not-so-subtle matchmaking.

We continue our petit déjeuner talking about business and how my blog has been drawing new visitors to the vineyard. Once breakfast is over, Luc and I get ready to leave to see the potential location for the bookstore cafe.

As we leave for the cafe, the anticipation builds with every street we pass until we finally arrive at the location. It's just as charming as I had pictured—tranquil and brimming with potential.

The building's facade, with its striking black accents set against the soft white of Parisian architecture, is a sight that steals my breath away.

I step inside; and take a moment to look around. I picture the shelves lined with books, cozy nooks filled with readers, the smell of coffee enveloping it all.

"It's perfect." My smile spreads uncontrollably.

"Great," the realtor says, a hint of a smile touching the corner of her lips as she senses my enthusiasm. "I'll get the paperwork ready for you."

"It's going to be amazing." Luc's excitement mirrors mine. In a spontaneous burst of joy, I reach out, wrapping my arms around his neck. His hands instinctively find my waist, holding me in a warm, solid embrace.

Pulling back, our eyes lock. There's a charged moment where the air seems to buzz with unspoken words and questions. "Sorry." I step back to put some space between us.

But Luc wasn't ready to let the moment pass. He pulls me back gently. "Luc, what are you doing?"

"I just thought maybe you changed your mind about us..." His sentence hangs in the air between us.

"I'm sorry." My heart sinks a bit, even as I struggle to maintain a boundary. "You're amazing, Luc. It's just... I can't. And I don't know when—or if—I'll ever be ready for something."

He watches me for a few seconds. "He did a number on you, didn't he?" Luc's smile is bittersweet as he looks at me with a softness that makes my chest tighten.

"Does this guy even know you're still hung up on him?" he asks, more into the nothingness than directly to me.

"It doesn't matter."

"It does matter." His gaze is tender. "Because he's in the way of any chance I might have with you."

"I'm sure you can have any woman you want," I chuckle. A feeble attempt to keep the mood light.

"Yes, but they aren't you," he admits with an intensity that causes my breath to hitch, laying bare the truth of his feelings.

"I'm sorry, Luc. If this is too uncomfortable for you, I'll give you space. I can talk to my grandmother." I look down, unable to meet his eyes.

"It's okay, Mia. I'd rather have you as a friend than not at all." His shoulders slump a little. "But hey, let's grab a bite to celebrate. It's almost lunchtime," he says, his smile returning, but I can see the effort behind it.

I nod, my smile forced as I follow him out of the building.

Every step is heavy as I think about Jake. Did I imagine the depth of what we had?

I've spent months caught in a half-dream, waiting for some grand gesture, some sign that he feels the same undeniable pull that I do. But if he did, if he truly felt it, why hasn't he come for me? Why hasn't he crossed oceans or at least sent more than just a casual message on holidays?

He's out there, probably living his life without a second thought of me, while I've been here, suspended in the half-light of what could have been, interpreting every word, every smile, as something more than it was.

I swallow hard, pushing back against the sting of tears, refusing to let them fall.

I have no time for wallowing.

There's a café to open and a book to get published. And maybe, with all that keeping me busy, I'll eventually stop thinking about him.

Chapter 30

Jake

My phone buzzes next to me, pulling me from my thoughts about Mia, thoughts that have been occupying most of my days.

Relief for the distraction, I answer and move toward the window. "Talk to me, Sergio." I press the phone to my ear, the cityscape below becoming a backdrop to our conversation. While I'm up here in Boston, Sergio's been my point man, keeping me in the loop on all the operations.

"Hey, Jake, I just wanted to give you some updates on the hotel expansion."

"What's happening?" A half-smile finds its way to my lips despite the tension I've felt all day. I might not have chosen hotel management as my dream career, but I've got a knack for it, especially when mixed with my marketing expertise.

About a year ago, our hotel was on the brink of collapsing. I rallied, brought in investors, and since then, business has been booming. We're on the verge of transforming from a simple hotel to a full-blown resort—a key player in hospitality.

"The expansion is moving early," he says, a bit of static cutting through his words.

I nod to myself, forgetting for a moment that Sergio can't see me. "That's great news. Just make sure the construction isn't too disruptive for our guests." My gaze drifts across the city as I imagine the future of the hotel.

"Will do. Oh, and we've had some inquiries about hosting events at the new conference center once it's finished." His enthusiasm nearly jumps through the phone.

The excitement is infectious, and I can't help but share in it. "Alright, let's tentatively schedule those and adjust if needed."

After we end the call, I put my phone down and stare at the ceiling, thinking about the past eight months. The hotel has been a welcomed distraction. It was hard staying at the cabin after she left, expecting to see her next to me when I woke up. Every corner of that place reminded me of her, her voice, her smell, her laughter. After getting everything settled at the hotel, I went back to Boston, but that didn't help.

I've thrown myself into work. The hotels, the brand collabs, the volunteering...they were meant to keep my mind occupied. No matter what I do, or how busy I get, she's always there.

My alarm goes off, breaking through my thoughts. I need to get ready for the brand photo shoot at the local indoor climbing center. We're promoting their latest climbing shoes.

As I pull up to the center, the professional team is already bustling around, setting everything for the shoot. After a quick briefing on the shot lists and the movements the photographer is looking for, I'm geared up and ready to go. My heart races as I approach the climbing wall.

I chalk up, my hands working automatically, patting and prepping as I assess the route ahead. Finding my initial grip, I start my ascent. The rough texture under my fingers and the familiar stretch of my muscles instantly reminds me why I love this sport. It's just me against the wall, where all other concerns seem to melt away.

"Good, good, hold that pose, Jake," the photographer calls out, snapping me back to the task at hand. I pause, maintaining my position, every muscle finely tuned and holding steady.

Climbing has always been my refuge. I revel in the control it offers, the way I can navigate risks on my own terms. Love is wild and unpredictable, revealing vulnerabilities and making leaving as easy as opening a door. Those thoughts often haunt me, lingering like unwelcome shadows.

Yet, as I cling to the wall, I realize climbing has taught me about more than just control. It's about embracing risks, about the calculated trust between me and the wall. There's a give and take here where you must sometimes risk falling to experience the thrill of the climb.

Maybe love is also about finding a balance between risk and trust. I've always kept everyone at arm's length, yet Mia found a way to slip through the cracks. Despite my efforts to move on, she still grips my heart with a hold I can't seem to break.

Pushing aside those thoughts, I try to concentrate on the wall, but memories of her keep playing in my mind.

And perhaps the risk, the very chance of falling, is what makes the climb, love, so incredibly worthwhile. I really hope one day you meet that person worth falling for.

Her words have been haunting me for the past few months.

I really want to be that person, worthy of her love, capable of loving her, but what if I can't? What if I end up hurting her even more?

I forced myself to focus back on the wall. The synergy between me and the team is palpable. We're creating art here—me with my climbs and them with their lenses. For a moment, I lose myself in the climb's physicality; the world narrowing down to the next hold, the next move. After reaching the top and satisfying the photographers, I lower myself down, still feeling the rush of adrenaline.

"You've made it look too easy, Jake!" One of the team members chuckles as she reviews her shots.

I wipe the sweat from my brow and offer a half-smile. "It's all about understanding your balance and knowing your strengths," I say, grabbing my water bottle and towel.

As the crew wraps up and the center clears out, I absentmindedly grab my phone and start scrolling to check if Mia has sent me a message. Nothing new, just the same old texts and social media notifications. My thumb hovers over the keypad; *I miss you,* I type, before deleting it. *Thinking of you,* I type again, and then delete it like always.

She probably doesn't even think about me.

I shove the phone back into my pocket.

Forcing the sinking feeling away, I gather my things and leave the climbing center. Focusing on the next part of my day. The sound of my own steps seems to mock the solitude I've crafted so carefully around me.

After wrapping up the photoshoot, I grab a quick lunch to refuel before my afternoon activities. I opt for something light, mindful of the active afternoon ahead. I open the Kindle app on my phone and find one of her novellas. She published them under a pen name, which she told me back at the cabin. I've read them many times but still love reading them. I especially enjoy the spicier scenes at night, imagining that we are the characters. Sometimes, though, I wonder if someone else inspired those scenes.

My next destination is the Peak Finders Club, an organization I founded to help young climbers. A place for them to learn technical skills, and the art of climbing.

It's there, among the eager faces of kids learning to climb, that I find a different joy. Watching their expressions transform from concentration to elation as they reach the top, I'm reminded of my passion for climbing—the blend of physical and mental challenges, the necessity for precision, and on-the-spot decisions. It's a love affair that's about more than conquering heights; it's about unlocking potential, something I aim to share with these kids most afternoons.

The laughter and chatter from the kids at the climbing club fade as I head home, a contrast to the silence awaiting me. The walls of my condo loom even before I get there, a dread in my gut at the thought of its emptiness.

I unlock it with a quick scan on my phone, stepping into the open floor plan. The kitchen's white marble countertops contrast with the black cabinets, and the expansive living room hosts a large dark gray sectional sofa, all oriented toward a 75-inch TV screen. The floor-to-ceiling glass windows frame the cityscape, a view I once thought was the epitome of a bachelor's dream. I thought that's what I wanted, but now I don't know anymore.

Everything just feels empty.

Something is missing.

Someone is missing.

Pouring a shot of whiskey from the bar, I head to the bedroom. The king-size bed is neat, untouched, and sterile. I let out a slow breath, imagining for a second that she's there, her laughter filling the room. I catch myself, closing my eyes to banish the vision, and my hand clenches around the glass.

In the shower, the warm water initially soothes me, washing away the physical traces of my day. I lean against the cool tiles and let the water run cold, not ready to face an empty bed.

The months have passed, and I waited for the adrenaline rush to fade, for the ache in my chest to subside, but it clings stubbornly, her memory as vivid as ever.

She's etched herself into my heart indelibly. I miss her—her smile, her laughter, the adorable way she would crinkle her nose when she gets frustrated, and yes, even her little snorts.

I was whole before her, or at least I thought I was. Now, it's as though she took a piece of me with her when she left.

Chapter 31

Mia

I stand in the middle of my nearly completed café, my gaze sweeping across the freshly painted walls. It's been a month since I signed the lease.

The past few weeks have been busy. Between choosing the perfect colors to designing the layout and figuring out how I want to set up the shelves. Picking out the perfect furniture that is comfy but fits the overall aesthetic.

Working on the menus was fun, especially coming up with the names for the drinks. I also reached out to potential authors to have their books stocked on the shelves.

A frown forms on my face as I realize the colors are all wrong. "That's not the pink I picked. I wanted pastel pink, not light pink," I utter as frustration bubbles inside of me. I chose pastel pink because it was my mom's favorite color. I wanted her to be part of this even if she's not here. I had spent days choosing just the right shades and coordinating the furniture to match a vision of pastel pinks and blues—soft, inviting hues—and they were now nowhere to be seen.

The disappointment is heavy, like a stone in my stomach, and tears burn at the back of my eyes. Everything was supposed to be perfect.

"Hey, hey, look at me," Luc says, turning me around to face him, his concern palpable. His brown eyes lock onto mine, his large hands gently grasping my shoulders. "It's going to be okay. I'll have them repaint it."

"But the soft opening is in a couple of weeks." My voice quivers with the fear that everything won't be ready in time.

"Don't worry, I'll make sure everything is ready, even if I have to repaint it all myself," he reassures me with a confidence that almost makes me believe him.

"But we can't start setting up the furniture until the walls are painted. They're supposed to be delivered tomorrow," I argue, breaking away from his hold and pacing around the room. My shoes click sharply against the hard floor. Tears threaten to spill, and I mentally plead with myself not to cry.

"It's okay, just breathe in and out." Luc guides me gently, trying to calm my frayed nerves. I repeat to myself that everything will be okay, but it doesn't quell the rising panic.

Deep breath with me, Jake's voice replays in my mind.

It always works, but right now, Luc is not helping.

My breaths come in short, shallow bursts, my chest tightening with each inhale.

I need him.

"It's just the café's soft opening is in a couple of weeks, and it's also my birthday. And my friends, my dad... They won't even be here." *Jake will not be here.* An embarrassing sob escapes me. I turn away, trying to hide my tears and breakdown.

I miss him so much.

I really wish he was here. Because I want to tell him all about it. In the little time we spent together last summer, he understood me and believed in me. I could text him, but when he tried to stay in contact, I couldn't. Because at some point, I would want to know if he's sleeping with someone else, and he wouldn't lie to me.

Luc turns me back around and pulls me into his chest, his embrace enveloping me in comfort and warmth. Although it is not the same, I surrender to the moment, allowing my tears to flow freely. Thank goodness he's wearing a black button-up that hides my make up stain.

"Maybe they're still mad at me for moving across the country," I mumble into his chest, the fabric muffling my words. My dad wasn't happy when I told him.

Mia, you can't just move to Paris, thinking that will fix everything. You're throwing away years of school and scholarships that so many people wished they had.

He pulls back slightly. His gaze is soft, understanding. "I don't think they're mad at you. They love you, so I don't think they would be mad at you for doing things that make you happy." He takes out a handkerchief and gently dries my tears.

"Great, now I've embarrassed myself in front of you." I chuckle nervously.

"You didn't embarrass yourself. You wear your emotions on your sleeve, and I like that about you," he says, lifting my chin gently.

"I probably look a mess." I pout.

"You're still pretty, even when you cry. Trust me, I've seen some ugly criers." His joke lightens the mood.

I let out a more genuine laugh this time, feeling lighter.

"Better now?" He looks down at me with a small smile.

I nod, grateful for his presence and support.

He then steps away to make a couple of calls. When he's finished, he turns back to me with a confident grin. "Everything is under control, okay? They will come back right now to repaint, and they will finish before the furniture delivery tomorrow.

"Thank you. I don't know what I'd do without you," I say, laughing from relief.

"I'm pretty awesome, aren't I?" He laughs, his humor infectious. "Let's wait for the crew so you can make sure they have the perfect color this time."

"Okay." I smile back at him, appreciating his understanding. A part of me wonders what life would have been like if I'd met Luc before Jake. I have this idea that everyone has their soulmate. I stupidly believe Jake is mine.

Maybe I could like Luc, or even love him, but not in the same way I feel about Jake. It's been a year, and my feelings haven't changed—it's like those resilient plants that thrive with little care, stubbornly hanging on.

Once the painting crew arrives, they apologize for the mix-up, pulling out the correct shade of pastel pink this time. "I know you think light pink is the same as pastel, but they have different undertones," I carefully explain, my tone firm yet polite, ensuring there's no confusion this time around.

Hours passed as they worked on the walls. Finally, they pack up and leave. It's Luc and I alone with the freshly painted walls. I can't help but grin, admiring the perfect shade of pastel pink.

"It's perfect." I twirl around. I step onto my tiptoes to plant a grateful kiss on Luc's cheek, but he turns just in time, and our lips meet unexpectedly.

The contact sends a warm rush through me, and he pulls me closer, deepening the kiss. Surprised, I push against his chest, stepping back. "Luc, I said I wasn't ready."

"I'm sorry," he steps back, "I didn't mean to..."

"Can we go home, please?" I'm physically and emotionally exhausted.

The ride home is quiet, filled with a tangible tension. I lean against the car window, the cool glass against my cheek providing a slight comfort. Luc's help today was invaluable, but his impulsive kiss has added layers of complexity I'm not ready to navigate. Watching the trees pass by, I'm reminded that while the walls of my café now reflect my dream, the walls around my heart remain cautiously guarded, still needing time to sort through the lingering feelings.

Pulling up to the cottage, he shifts the car into park, and we both sit in the quiet for a few moments as we avoid meeting each other's gaze.

"Thanks again for today," I finally say, breaking the silence. I keep my eyes fixed on the dashboard, not ready to confront the tension directly yet.

"Mia..."

"I really appreciate everything you've done for me. And I really enjoyed your company—as a friend." I emphasize the last word, turning to face him with a firm but gentle look. "I'm sorry if I've given you some kind of false hope. But if you can't respect my boundaries, maybe we need some space."

"You're right, and I'm sorry. I promise that won't happen again." His eyes meet mine, showing his sincerity. His response eases a bit of the tension, and I nod, accepting his apology.

I pause, taking a deep breath to gather my thoughts. "Okay, I appreciate it, and I'm sorry, too."

"You have nothing to be sorry about."

"Bye Luc." I reach for the door.

"Bye, Mia," he says, and I offer a small, tentative smile as I pull the door open and step out into the cool evening air.

I step inside the cottage, take off my shoes, and leave them by the door. My shoulders slump as I head toward the kitchen, where I quickly prepare a small cheese board. I carry it upstairs, my body craving a bath after everything that happened today.

The bath fills with warm water as I set up my tray with my cheese board and my iPad. Turning off the faucet, I shed off my clothes, sinking into the warm water. A sigh escapes as my muscles finally relax. I reach for my iPad and initiate a video call. Even though we're in different time zones, Rylee and Sarah are always up for a video chat.

Sarah's face appears on the screen, then Rylee's face pops up.

"Hey," I say softer than usual, a touch of fatigue bleeding through.

"Hey, you, okay?" Rylee leans in closer to her camera, her eyes narrowing slightly as if trying to read my expression more clearly across the screen.

"Nothing, I just had a long day." I keep my tone light. "They painted the wall the wrong color, and we had to repaint it, but everything is okay now."

They both listen quietly.

"Why do you still look sad?" Rylee asks.

I hesitate, caught between the desire to keep my emotions in check and the need to share. "It's nothing." I sigh.

Despite my resolve not to break down again, the look of genuine concern from my friends makes the barriers I've built crumble.

"The soft opening and my birthday are in less than a week, and you guys won't be here," I say with a pout, a lump forms in my throat as their faces stare back at me from their video square on the screen. I secretly hoped it was just a prank.

Rylee frowns. "I'm sorry. I really wish I could be there."

"Me too." Sarah's face scrunches up.

"It's okay." I stuck a strand of curls behind my ear. "So, what are your plans for the summer? Are you guys heading to the cabin?" I fix my attention on Sarah.

Sarah's lips press together as her eyes search mine. "I have other plans, so does Alex." Other plans that are more important than your friend's birthday and new business opening.

I roll my eyes when she purposely did not mention Jake.

"And Jake," I comment, my fingers absentmindedly tapping against my iPad.

"What about him?" She raises her eyebrows.

"Is he going to the cabin?" Heat rises to my cheeks.

"Why don't you ask him yourself instead of you guys putting me in the middle?" *A little harsh.*

I lean forward. "What do you mean, in the middle? Does he ask about me?"

Her smile turns knowing. "Maybe," she teases, giving nothing away.

"I don't care, anyway." My tone is sharper than intended.

"Okay." She lifts an eyebrow.

"I don't even think about him," I add quickly, forcing my hands to stop fidgeting and lay flat on my lap.

"So, are you seeing anyone? Any hot French guys catching your eye?" Rylee cuts in.

"No...not really. I should move on and forget about him, but I just can't. Then, Luc kissed me... And yes he's amazing, but I can't give him my heart when I don't have one to give. I left that piece of myself with Jake last summer." Saying it out loud, admitting these feelings to someone else, is both liberating and terrifying. It feels as if my heart has always belonged to him, even before we met. Like I've loved him before in another lifetime.

"Have you talked to Jake? Tell him how you feel?" Sarah asks, her tone serious yet supportive.

"What's the point? He had an entire year," I say, bitterness creeping into my voice. "I'm probably just a little splash in his memory."

The last time I heard from him was a Happy New Year's text message. Then I sent him a message on his birthday.

"But that's it. I'm moving on. No more wallowing. I was fine before him, and I will be fine without him, or any man, for that matter." I lift my chin upward. "The café and my book are my focus." The declaration is hollow, more like a wish than a potential reality.

Their faces soften. "We're here for you, no matter what," Rylee says reassuringly, comforting me through the screen with her words.

We talk a little more before we say our goodbyes.

I grab my phone and scroll through his messages and reread the ones l left unanswered. *Hi,* I type, then delete it. *I miss you,* another attempt, but delete it too, putting my phone back on the tray.

The tears have been holding back burn behind my eyes. I don't stop them as they make a path down my face. My body sinks deeper into the water, letting the ache in my heart consume me. Why can't I move on? It was one summer, and we weren't even a thing.

Maybe not all falls hurt, but this one definitely does.

Chapter 32

Jake

Stepping out of the shower, I pull on boxers and a tank top and sink into the chair by the bed. My hands run through my damp hair.

The city lights flicker and dance across the glass windows, but the spectacle holds no fascination for me tonight. I stare at the bed, too vast for a single occupant, and sigh.

My phone rings, piercing the silence. It's a group call with Sarah and Alex. I hesitate for a moment, caught between the desire for company and the inclination to wallow in solitude. I reach for the phone, preparing myself for their well-meaning chatter.

"You look awful," Sarah points out as soon as I appear on the screen.

I force a chuckle, rubbing the back of my neck. "Geez, thank you."

Her laughter is loud and unreserved. "Just admit you were wrong, and I was right." She leans into the camera, her eyebrows arching in playful challenge.

"What are you talking about?" I slouch back in my chair and pretend to be clueless.

Her smile softens as she tilts her head, her gaze knowing. "I told you had feelings for her, but you denied it."

"I just had a long day, that's all."

"She probably misses you too," she adds gently.

"Do you guys still talk?" The question escapes me before I can rein it in, revealing more interest than I intended.

"Yeah, we're friends, and I'm actually going to France for her surprise birthday party. I hate that she thinks no one is coming, and she's a little sad about it." Sarah says, and my heart skips a beat.

"Surprise birthday party?"

"Wait, you didn't know? Mia's grandmother invited us over, and she's paying for everything," she continues, and there's a pause as my silence fills the screen.

"Well, I didn't know." My gaze drifts away from the camera to hide the confusion and hurt that suddenly washes over me.

"You should come," Alex cuts in through the fog of my thoughts. "She would be happy to see you."

I shake my head and run my fingers through my hair. "I don't think that's a good idea. She probably doesn't want me there." My words catch in my throat.

I'm afraid of seeing her with someone else, or that she's moved on, and I haven't. What if she's happy without me? What if there's someone else now who can make her smile the way I once did? She deserves the world, and I was too stupid to see it. Instead, I offered her a summer fling.

"Plus, I'm busy with the hotel renovations. I don't have time for a vacation right now."

"Okay, I just hope you don't regret anything once she's moved on and is happy with someone else." Sarah raises her eyebrows.

"Does that mean she hasn't moved on? Does she ask about me?"

"I don't know, Jake. What don't you take your head out of your ass and find out?" she snaps. Sarah rarely gets mad, but when she does, it's both formidable and a bit terrifying. Alex is trying to stifle a laugh in the other square on the screen.

We all fall silent for a few minutes, each of us lost in our thoughts, before Alex tries to break the tension. "Since you guys' kind of know each other, any gift ideas of what to get her?"

"She loves crystals, and of course, books." I'm not even sure if he was asking me or Sarah. I reach out and rub the emerald necklace around my neck, which somehow makes me feel connected to her.

We continue the conversation for a few more minutes, and I can tell that Sarah's irritation hasn't fully subsided by how her eyes narrow and her mouth sets into a thin line.

Before hanging up she says, "I'll send you the information, just in case you grow a pair of balls and decide to come."

"I have balls," I mutter to myself as the screen goes dark.

I'm left sitting alone, the room suddenly too quiet. Her words linger like a challenge I'm not sure I'm ready to meet.

Standing up from the chair, I pace around the room. The city lights through the glass window do nothing to calm me. Is Sarah right? Do I still have a chance with her?

Walking into my closet, I throw on shorts and a shirt. My movements are quick and agitated. I head downstairs to the gym, unable to stand still. It's nearly 9 p.m. but sleep is impossible with all this pent-up energy.

In the locker room, I grab my boxing gloves and slam the door shut. They offer slight comfort as I slip them on. My breathing is heavy and uneven. I stride into the boxing room, body tense and ready to throw some punches.

I stand before the heavy bag, positioning myself, my fists ready. Each punch I throw lands with a thud, the bag absorbing the impact, swaying with each hit. It's been a whole year, and I've been with other women, but nothing compares to how it felt being with her.

Sweat pours down my face, each breath heavier than the last, as I confront the painful truth—she still owns my heart, body, and soul. After exhausting myself at the bag, I stumble into one of the gym showers, letting the cool water cascade over my muscles, numbing the physical and emotional ache for a moment.

Drying off, I change into fresh clothes from my bag and head back to my room. Once there, I strip down to my boxers, settling in to work on some posts for tomorrow.

As I sift through my emails, Jessie's name catches my eye—an email left untouched for a year. The unresolved feelings tighten in my chest. I know I need to reach out to her, but before I can, I need to talk to my mom. It's a conversation long overdue.

I hit the video call button, and my stomach knots with anticipation, tightening further when her face fills the screen.

"Jake, could this not have waited until tomorrow?" Her eyebrows pull together in a frown, her annoyance palpable even through the screen. I know it's late, but this couldn't wait.

I shake my head, my hands fidget on my lap. "No, Mom, it can't."

We've never really talked about what happened with her and my dad, why they split, and everything in between. There's a lot I need to understand.

I take a deep breath, steadying myself against the back of my chair. "So, what really happened between you and Dad?" I can blame the hotel and Jessie, but I have a feeling there's more to the story.

"Why now, Jake? After all these years." She sighed, her face softening a bit.

"I just... I need to understand." *Why did he stop loving me?* I rub the back of my neck.

Her eyes drift past the camera. "Your dad and I were high school sweethearts. I ended up pregnant, and our parents insisted we get married."

"Wait, but I thought you said you two eloped because you were in love?" My head flinches back.

She meets my gaze again, a trace of sadness in her eyes. "That was a story for the outside world. We did care for each other deeply, but it wasn't the passionate love we pretended it was. We stayed together for you, tried to make it work."

"Is that why you guys used to fight all the time? Because of me?" I rub my forehead.

"We were both struggling with our own issues, and we took them out on each other. He hated working at the hotel, and I hated feeling like I was stuck. Whenever he was home, we would always argue, so he started spending most of his time at the hotel."

"But that doesn't excuse the fact that you guys abandoned me. He would disappear for days, and when he was home, all you guys did was fight. Then you would hide yourself in your room." My voice catches as I let out years of pent-up anger and resentment.

I push away from my desk and stand up, pacing the room as I try to hold back the tide of emotions threatening to break free. I crack my fingers, my mind racing with memories I've locked away. The lonely nights I've cried myself to sleep. Or the ones where I hid in my closet, so I didn't have to hear them fighting again.

"I needed you," the words spill out with a slight tremor. "I needed both of you, and you weren't there." I lean closer to the screen, planting my fists on the desk. "Do you have any idea what that feels like? To be a kid and constantly wondering why my father stopped loving me. What the fuck did I do wrong?" My eyes lock on the screen, searching for some kind of explanation. Anything that would make this hurt any less. Her green eyes stare back at me, filled with unshed tears. But it did nothing to ease the pain in my chest. Because nothing can, I just have to learn to live with it.

She opens her mouth to speak, but I hold my hand to stop her. "Uncle Mark was a better father than Dad ever was. He was there for me when I needed him. Not you, not Dad. Him. If it weren't for Uncle Mark and my friends, I would be completely alone."

I really wish he was here. He died when I was sixteen and I mourned him for months.

I sit on the chair, crossing my arms over my chest. I didn't plan for this conversation to turn out the way it did, but I'm glad it did.

Her eyes shine with unshed tears. "I understand you're angry, and I'm so sorry. We were not the best parents, but your dad and I loved you very much. That never changed."

A sharp, almost bitter laugh escapes me. "You had some strange way of showing it. You don't hurt people you love and don't sleep with your son's girl if you love him." She doesn't flinch at my words. "You knew about Jessie, didn't you?"

"Yes." She rubs the bridge of her nose.

"Did you know they had a daughter?"

"Yes." She nods as pain crinkles in the corner of her eyes.

I tell her about the email Jessie sent me about a year ago, and how I never reached out to her.

"Jake, I'm not excusing your father's actions or what happened with Jessie. That was wrong on so many levels. How you handle this with Jessie and your half-sister is your choice."

"For years I've hated love, avoided it like a disease. I didn't want it knowing how easy someone could stop loving you, even your own father." My voice cracks, choked by the tears I'm trying so hard to hold back. "Then, there was Jessie. I really liked her. Maybe I could have loved her, but he took that chance away from me. My fucking father, and that hurt more than him neglecting me." A painful knot forms in my throat. Tears burn at the corner of my eyes, but I can't let them fall. I'm not that broken little boy anymore.

"Oh, Jake, I'm so sorry." She sighs deeply, her face softening as she looks at me through the screen. "Falling in love is exhilarating," she continues. There's a warmth in her eyes that I've missed. She leans closer, as if to emphasize her point. "Finding that person who makes you want to keep falling in love with them, to push through even when it gets tough. Eventually, that love will grow and mature into something truly beautiful." She pauses, her eyes pleading. "I'm so sorry we made you think it's something to avoid. You shouldn't deprive yourself of something so wonderful because of our mistakes."

"Sorry doesn't change the past." It doesn't change the fact that I did find the person I wanted to fall in love with, but I couldn't be the guy that she needed. The one that could love her completely.

She nods, her face crumpling. "I know I can't change the past, but I'm here now, and I want to make things right if you'll let me."

"I don't know, Mom." I turn away from the screen.

I still need time to process everything. Part of me wants to forgive her, but the little neglected boy inside of me is not ready to forgive her.

"I'm not asking you to forgive me right now. But I hope one day you'll let me try to fix this. Fix us." She pauses, her eyes searching mine, silently pleading for a chance. The silence stretches between us. Maybe one day I'll find it in myself to forgive her, but not today.

"Bye, Mom," I say, ending the call.

Sitting back in my chair, memories of the summer play in my head. The early mornings at the waterfall, the warm nights of her embrace, her smile, her laughter.

I had fallen in love with her every day that summer, and I could easily keep falling for her forever.

My mom was right about one thing. I shouldn't let their mistakes deprive me of the most exhilarating feelings I ever felt.

I miss her.

I love her.

I need her.

I just hope it's not too late.

Chapter 33

Mia

My eyes flutter open to a still dark room. I fumble for my phone on the nightstand to check the time, and it's only 4 a.m. A sigh escapes me. Why am I up this early?

Scrolling through my notifications, one message catches my attention. Happy birthday! I know you're still asleep, but I wanted to be the first one to say it.

I sit up quickly, my heart pounding against my chest as I stare at the screen. The message sends shivers skittering across my skin, as if someone dumped a bucket of ice-cold water on me. His name appears on the screen. Douxy. Even after a year I still haven't changed it. He doesn't even know I call him that.

It's just a *happy birthday and* doesn't mean anything. But there is no way I am going back to sleep now.

With a heavy sigh, I swing my legs off the bed and drag myself up, the cool air causing me to shiver as I snatch my robe and wrap it snug around my body. My feet pad softly against the cold floor as I descend the stairs; the quietness of the house amplifies my restless thoughts.

In the kitchen, I prepare a large cup of iced coffee. I'm going to need it.

Back at my desk, I lay the phone down next to my writing pad. I'm already up. I might as well be productive. It's another query, but it's my birthday, so why not send one more? This agent checks all my boxes. She's looking for new authors and is particularly interested in fantasy and paranormal romance novels.

After an hour of crafting what I hope is my best query letter, I steal glances at my phone as if it will tell me what to do with Jake's message. Ignoring it for now, I take a deep breath to steady my nerves, knowing I've done my best. With a final, hopeful look at the screen, I hit send.

Now comes the hardest part: the waiting, the silence, the possibility of rejection. My stomach twists at the thought, a constant reminder of how much I want this, and I bite my lip.

Desperate for a distraction, I grab my phone, seeking anything to take my mind off it. I mindlessly scrolled through Instagram, accidentally landing on Jake's page. My eyes are drawn to the latest posts about Peak Finders, the nonprofit he founded. It's a mentoring club for young climbers, focusing on techniques and safety, offering a variety of activities, all free.

There he is, smiling, holding a rope, surrounded by young climbers. My heart clenches as I watch the video of him teaching them a technique. The familiar timbre of his laugh in the clip sends a pang through me.

After a few minutes, I lock my phone and set it aside. I decide to draw myself a hot bath and keep my phone far from the edge of the tub, and out of reach.

I sink slowly into the water, letting it lap gently against my skin. I close my eyes and lean back in the tub, letting the heat melt away my stress. Just perfect.

As the water cools down, I notice the gentle rays of the early morning sun filtering through the window, highlighting the serene beauty of the greenery outside, setting the tone for the productive day that lies ahead.

Stepping out of the tub, I quickly wrap myself in a soft, plush towel. I walk into my closet to select my outfit. Light pink wide leg pants, white bodysuit, neutral blazer, and pair with pink shoes.

I do my hair before putting on my clothes. As I'm adjusting my blazer, my phone lights with another notification. It's from Luc.

Luc: Bonne fete, ma belle! I will pick you up to go to the café. See you in 30 mins.

Me: Thank you. See you soon.

Since the kiss last week, things between us have been surprisingly smooth, and I selfishly hope I don't lose him as a friend. He's the only friend I have here.

Setting my phone aside, I take a deep breath to steady myself and push aside any distractions. Today requires my undivided attention. Every detail of the café's soft opening must go perfectly.

True to his word, Luc arrives exactly thirty minutes later. The drive from the vineyard to downtown Les Collines d'Étoile—*Starry hills*, takes just a few minutes, but it feels like entering another world. As we leave the lush valley, the scenery shifts from the rolling hills, reaching up to the sky to the historical charm of the town.

My hand unconsciously reaches for my necklace, twisting it around my fingers.

"Everything is going to be amazing," Luc assures me as he notices my fidgeting.

I offer him a small, tentative smile, grateful yet still wrapped in a bundle of nerves.

Pulling up to the cafe, Luc hops out and comes around to help me from the car. It looks like we're the first ones here because the café is dark and quiet inside. But as we step inside, the lights suddenly flash on, and a chorus of "Surprise!" fills the room. I freeze in place, overwhelmed.

When I see my dad, Rylee, and Sarah in the crowd, my hands fly up to cover my face, barely holding back the tears. "You guys are here... How... You said you weren't coming."

My dad pulls me into a tight embrace, his arms wrapping around me securely, his scent enveloping me. "I thought you were mad at me for everything," I mumble into his shirt. "For not going back to medical school, and for coming here."

"Of course not, sweetheart. I know I've been hard on you. It's because I wanted what's best for you, and for you to be happy." He pulls back to look at me. "I'm sorry if I made you feel otherwise."

"I missed you, Dad." Although we have our differences, I love him.

"I missed you too, sweetheart," he says, his hand drawing circles on my back. "I knew about the letters. Your mom and I talked before she passed. Sometimes we just need a little push."

It takes me a moment to understand what he's trying to say. "So, you didn't want me to go back to medical school?"

"I wanted you to do what makes you happy. I know sometimes what I want might not be what you want."

I didn't know how much I wanted to hear that until now.

"Thank you, Papa. It means a lot." We hold each other for a few minutes before I pull away.

Next, I turn to Rylee and Sarah, and punch them playfully on the arm as they pull me into a sandwich hug that nearly lifts me off my feet. "Why did you guys let me think you weren't coming?" I shake my legs to keep myself from breaking into an ugly cry.

"Your grandmother wanted it to be a surprise," they say together as Rylee fans her face to fight back her tears.

"I've missed you guys so much." Although we video chat all the time, it's not the same thing as seeing them in person.

"You look so Parisian." Rylee giggles. "I love the look."

"You guys are so freaking gorgeous." I admire them from top to bottom. Rylee stands 5 feet 9 and looks even taller with those heels on. Her hair, perfectly straight and silky, falls beautifully over her shoulders. Under the gentle lighting, her dark skin looks flawless. She's stylishly dressed in a beige tank top matched with light purple high-waisted pants that crop neatly at her ankles. Beside her, Sarah rocks an olive-green jumpsuit. "I have the most gorgeous friends ever."

After a few minutes filled with emotional reunions and happy tears, I turn to my grandmother and plant a kiss on her cheek. "Thank you."

"You should thank Luc. It was his idea," she tells me, her eyes twinkling with mischief.

I turn to Luc and pull him into a grateful hug, about to express my thanks, when the door opens again. My breath whooshes out of my lungs as my eyes land on the new arrival—tall, blonde hair, green eyes, exuding a presence that immediately commands the room.

My stomach flips uncontrollably.

Flips after anxious flips.

I'm too young to die of a heart attack, right? And I can't die on my birthday, that would also make it my death date.

My throat tightens painfully, making swallowing difficult and speaking impossible. His green eyes are as intense as I remember whenever he would look at me. Penetrating deep in my soul, yet comforting.

I pull my arms away from Luc as he approaches. My heart thudding in my chest as if it's trying to leap out and bridge the gap between us.

He stops in front of me, and the room and everything else falls silent except for the sound of my heartbeat pounding loudly in my ears.

"Hi," he says with a nervous smile, a contrast to the confident demeanor I remember.

I stand there frozen, words failing me entirely.

"Hi, I'm Luc," he steps in, perhaps sensing my discomfort or breaking the thick tension. I had almost forgotten he was there, forgotten everything else existed except for the man in front of me.

I think I might need to see a doctor because my voice seems to have vanished. So, I do what any adult would do in such overwhelming situations, right? I walk out of the door, needing fresh air. It's too hot inside.

"Mia, wait! I'm sorry for showing up like this," Jake calls out after me, but I don't stop as I step onto the cobblestone. The early morning air is cool against my skin, and the sunlight filters through the leaves of the trees lining the street, painting patterns on the ground. Crossing the street, a cyclist whizzes by with a friendly nod, the bell on his bike jingling in the quiet morning.

I make my way to a small square with benches and a water fountain, desperate for space to breathe. The morning dew touches the cherubs and water lilies sculpted in the fountain.

He catches up, his footsteps quick and anxious. "Hey, talk to me," he says, his hand light on my arm, turning me to face him. I look down at where his fingers meet my skin, leaving an involuntary trail of goosebumps along my arm. When I look up, his green eyes, full of concern, hold mine, and my heart picks up its dangerous pace.

"Why are you here? Did my grandmother invite you? You didn't have to come." My eyes narrow as I cross my arm over my chest. Each word slices through the air with hurt rather than anger.

"I thought you'd be happy to see me. It's your big day, and your birthday..." His eyes scan my face.

"You didn't have to come. You could have stuck to the happy birthday text you sent me." I take a step back, distancing my body to shield myself from the impact of his presence. Waves of long-suppressed feelings come crashing down. Longing, confusion, resentment, and something more profound that I don't want to acknowledge right now.

"I wanted to come because I missed you." His hand reaches out as if to touch me, but stops inches away from my arm.

"You miss me?" My hands clench at my side. "What exactly did you miss? The adrenaline, the rush, or the sex?" The questions pour out bitterly and accusingly. I know I have no right to be angry when we both agreed to our summer fling, but he can't just show up out of nowhere.

"Mia, it's not... I... I missed you, all of you, but I can see now that you've moved on with someone else." His shoulders sag as if the weight of what he's saying is too much to bear.

"Move on?" The words escape me in a laugh, a brittle sound that barely covers the sting those words carry. "There was nothing to move on from. It was just summer fun." My words are sharper than I intended, and I forced the tears threatening to spill back into their ducts.

He steps closer, closing the distance between us. As he pulls me toward him, I'm enveloped in the familiar scent of lavender and a hint of forest after rainfall. It's a scent that brings back memories of long, carefree days and warm, entangled nights—memories I've tried to box away. For a second, I'm tempted to lean into that embrace, to let the comforting familiarity wash over me. "You know, it was more than that." His eyes pierce into mine, stirring feelings I'm trying to bury.

The proximity is too much, and the flood of memories is too intense. Maybe he wanted me, but not in the way I needed him to—fully, fearlessly. Maybe I wasn't worth that to him. My heart races, a painful lump form in my throat, and I forcibly pull away, needing to escape the magnetic pull of his presence.

"I can't do this right now. I need to get back to the café." Without giving him a chance to respond, I swiftly turn on my heel and walk away. I can't afford to get into this right now.

I fan my face with my hands, trying to dry the tears that have escaped. The cool morning air brushes against my skin, helping to clear the fog of emotions clouding my thoughts.

Standing outside the café, I pause for a moment to gather myself. With each deep breath that I take, my racing heart steadies, and the storm inside me calms. I straighten my blazer and lift my chin. Looking at the name of my cafe, *The Corner of Books and Coffee*, I muster the widest smile I can manage as I push open the doors. I can deal with my emotions about Jake later; right now, my focus must be on the opening.

Chapter 34

Jake

I watch her move around the room, laughing and engaging with everyone except me. Since she walked away from me at the square, it's as if I don't exist; I'm completely invisible and painfully ignored. I don't know what I expected by just showing up unannounced, but it was certainly not this.

The image of her arms wrapped around his waist, and the way her eyes narrowed when they met mine, still haunts me.

Each time that she smiles, my heart sinks a little lower. The memory of her words, "You shouldn't have come," and "There was nothing to move on from. We were just having fun, right?" reverberates through me like cold water. But I know the connection we felt wasn't just a fragment of my imagination.

Yet, seeing her now, it is as if no time has passed, except she is more beautiful than ever. Her curls frame her face beautifully. Her smile, bright and seemingly carefree, lights up her entire face, reaching those deep brown eyes that have always drawn me in—a gaze I find myself helplessly searching for, even now.

My heart races as if struck by lightning, surging painfully through my veins every time her eyes accidentally meet mine. Our hearts are still beating in sync despite the distance she puts between us. Every nerve of my body is acutely aware of her, as if my soul has always recognized hers.

I'm so absorbed in watching her, I barely hear Alex talking next to me. It feels distant, muffled by the thunderous beating of my heart.

"Are you even listening to me?" Alex's irritation snaps me back to reality, his tone sharp.

"You said something about the menu," I say, still caught in her orbit.

"I was saying I like the name of the drinks." He laughs, but his amusement doesn't reach me. I'm too ensnared by my turmoil.

"Yes, they're brilliant," I say, though my gaze drifts back to Mia, admiring her from afar yet aching from the proximity.

"So, what did you two talk about?" He leans in closer.

"Nothing, except that she's not happy to see me." The words are heavy with a mix of resignation and a lingering hope.

Alex frowns. "I'm guessing it didn't go well?"

Well, you'd guess right.

"I guess I'm a little too late." I sigh, the weight of my realization pressing down on my shoulders, bending me inward.

"What are you talking about?" Sarah, overhearing our exchange, interjects, her brow furrowed in confusion.

"Her and that French guy over there," I say, nodding subtly toward Luc as the green monster of jealousy claws its way into my tone.

"Luc? They're just friends." She chuckles, clearly seeing the jealousy written all over my face. Maybe they are just friends, but the way he watches her says more—at least to me. But maybe, just maybe, I still have a chance. If only I could find the right words, the right moment to show her that what we had was real and worth another shot.

Maybe this time, I won't let fear hold me back.

She is finally standing alone, absorbed in her phone. Maybe to avoid looking at me. The soft opening of her café is an amazing success, and I'm so proud of her.

People have been raving about the menu and the aesthetic of the place all morning. With most of the guests gone, and no sign of Mr. French, I seize the moment.

I make my way towards her. My heart's racing a mile per second, like driving in the fast lane. She's the only woman who makes me nervous by just being in the same room. I used to be good at hiding it, but right now it's a struggle. A lightning in my chest the closer I get.

"Hey." I clear my throat and wipe my sweaty palms on my pants

She looks up, a complex expression crosses her face. And my heart short circuits. She's so gorgeous. For a moment, her guard seems to drop, and the raw emotions I've always loved about her flicker across her features before she quickly masks them again.

"Before you say anything, I want to congratulate you. The place is amazing," I say, pausing as I notice her eyes soften just a touch. "I'm really proud of you." My heart swells with so much admiration. "I'm sorry for showing up like this and possibly running your big day."

She says nothing, and I'm about to turn away when her voice stops me. "You didn't ruin it, and… it was nice of you to come." Her words catch me off guard, and for a moment we simply hold each other's gaze.

An enthusiastic voice abruptly shattered our moment. "OMG girl, this has been amazing." A tall black woman approaches, her presence commanding. She eyes me skeptically.

"You must be Mr. Hot Asshole," she says, and I glance around, momentarily confused, before I realize she's talking to me.

"Wait, Mr. *What*?" I laugh, thrown off by the blunt words.

Mia's laughter hits me like a brick, and I can't move. I didn't realize how much I missed it until now. I don't know what is happening, but my stomach is doing many flips.

"I used to call you that," Mia says with a grin.

"I'll take Mr. Hot without the asshole." I laugh. "And you must be Rylee," I say, holding her stare and giving her a handshake.

Here comes Mr. French inserting himself into our interaction with an ease that grates on me. "Allons-y," he says, locking eyes with Mia, and I know just enough French to understand. "And do you girls need a ride?" He switches to English, turning his attention to Sarah and Rylee with a charming smile and his perfect accent. "Y'all staying at the vineyard, right?" he adds, folding his arms casually as he leans against the counter, looking relaxed and at home.

"Yes, we're staying at the cottage," Rylee says, her smile broad and unmistakably friendly as she looks up at him. A kind of smile that was absent when she looked at me earlier, and the difference stings more than I'd like to admit.

I watch the interaction, a tightness forming in my chest. Luc is undeniably good-looking, a fact that's clear to anyone with eyes, and yes, he's taller than me, and I'm 6 feet 2 inches. I cross my arms, looking cool and all, but I can feel my jaw clench.

It's annoying the way he stands there, confident and assured, and a part of me wants to find fault with him, to diminish his presence in any small way. It's clear he's inserted himself into Mia's life in ways I can no longer claim, and as much as I hate to admit it, his presence here is both wanted and welcomed by everyone but me.

"Where are you staying?" Sarah tilts her head to look at me.

"I booked a room at one of the boutique hotels nearby," I say, my gazes inadvertently following Luc as he stands a little too close to Mia for my liking.

"So, Mia's grandmother has a cottage reserved for us, all three of us." Alex points towards Rylee and Sarah. "Can I stay with you instead?" His eyes almost pleading. "Save me from this." He points between Sarah and Rylee.

"Sure, you can stay with me." I booked a suite and there's a separate pull-out bed. "I'll call an Uber."

We all walk outside, and Mia locks the door before they follow Luc to his car.

"After you," Luc says, opening the door for Mia, then for the girls.

"Merci," they say, giggling, like they have never seen a good-looking French man before. *For Godsake.* I resist the urge to roll my eyes, which reminds me of Mia of when she used to roll her eyes at me.

I loved that.

He pulls away, taking her with him. My eyes follow the car until it fades into the distance. The silence stretches between Alex and me as we wait for our ride.

"You're coming to her party later, right?" He breaks the silence while his eyes watch my reaction.

"I don't think she wants me there. Maybe it was a mistake coming here." The words taste bitter in my mouth as I shove my hands in my pockets. My gaze drops to the ground.

"So, you're just gonna give up?" He leans against the wall, crossing his foot over the other.

"I don't know, man. I had my chance and I think I ruined it." My chest tightens, making it difficult to breathe. I shuffle my feet and force air into my lungs. Every muscle in my body hurts.

"You don't know that." He pats my shoulder. "Talk to her, tell her how you feel. You're not the one to back down from a challenge, right?" He gives my shoulder a reassuring squeeze. "I think she's worth it, man."

His words bring back memories of my and Mia's last night together. *I hope you find someone worth falling for.* She did not know that she was and always has been that *someone* for me.

The driver pulls up, and we load bags into the back seat before climbing into the car. As we settle in, I pull out the necklace from inside my long sleeve shirt and rub it between my fingers thoughtfully.

Maybe there's still a chance for us.

Chapter 35

Mia

The short walk from my cottage to the villa seems longer than usual with those shoes. The click of my heels is louder than I'd like. I'm expecting a quiet, intimate dinner, just a simple chance to catch up.

As I get closer, the garden ahead is ablaze with twinkling fairy lights and shadows of people moving around. A soft groan escapes me, and my pace slows. I should have known better. My grandmother sees everything as an excuse to throw a party.

With a deep breath, I straighten up, adjust my black silk dress, and smooth a stray hair behind my ears as I prepare myself. Despite the initial disappointment, I let out a small chuckle. Leave it to my grandmother to turn a simple dinner into a gala.

Stepping into the garden, I immediately spot my friends sitting at one table, including Alex and Luc. Alex is sitting next to Sarah, and Luc is next to Rylee. At another, my dad is sitting with Elena and her friends. There's one person missing, maybe two.

"Here comes the birthday girl!" the DJ announces from his booth, breaking through my thoughts. Yes, she went all out. There's even a DJ. The party spills out onto the villa's large garden, and roughly fifty guests are mingling and laughing.

I force a smile and approach my group. Rylee catches me in a hug and spins me around. "Just gorgeous."

And of course, her words bring back memories of Jake.

Those flashbacks have been unstoppable since he showed up. Shaking off the memories, I focus on the surrounding faces, their smiles pulling me back to the present.

The party continues as they serve the entrées, meat, cheese trays, and, of course, wine. Next, they serve the main course, perfectly grilled steak with ratatouille. They refill our glasses with wine, and everyone is having a good time.

After the meal, the server rolls out a white table with my cake. It's shaped like a stack of books with a fondant of a mug of coffee on top. He places the candle inside the mug. The crowd gathers around to sing *Joyeux annivesaire*.

Once the singing dies down, he hands me the knife, and all eyes turn on me. This has been one of the best birthdays, but as I grasp the knife, a tightness forms in my chest, surprising me with its intensity.

I close my eyes for a moment, the air warm against my skin. Taking a deep breath, I lean forward, the candle's small flame flickering under my breath. I make another wish, knowing in my heart how improbable it is, but that's what wishes are for, aren't they? To dare to want something that seems so out of reach.

With one quick puff, the candle is out, and everyone claps around me. I cut the cake and take the first slice as the server diligently cuts the rest, handing pieces to the guests.

I return to my table, absentmindedly poking at my cake while Rylee dances with Luc, and Sarah laughs at something Alex says.

Seizing the moment of distraction, I slip away, drawn to the quieter part of the garden where the mini waterfall murmurs softly.

The farther I walk from the lights, the more striking the stars become—vivid and luminous against the dark sky. It's no wonder this place is called Les Collines d'Étoiles. Starry hills. The soft sound of the waterfall is soothing, a gentle whisper in the night.

"Hey, Mom," I whisper into the cool air, feeling the loneliness of her absence even more on my birthday. "I miss you. I really wish you were here." Despite keeping myself busy to avoid dwelling on her absence, the tears well up, burning the backs of my eyes. "I love you so much," I say quietly, wiping the tears as I settle onto a bench beside the waterfall.

"Hey," says a velvety voice from behind me, instantly recognizable. I turn to see Jake standing there, dressed in all white, a long-sleeve dress shirt with the top buttons undone, complementing his white pants. Under the moonlight, his blonde hair glows, and his green eyes seem to capture the very essence of the night itself.

My heart catches in my throat as I take in the sight of him.

He's gorgeous.

"Hey," I say, quickly drying my tears with the back of my hand. I can't take my eyes off him. He has a way of holding me captive with just one look.

"Do you mind if I sit?" He points toward the bench with a gentle smile.

I nod, scooting over to make room for him.

As he comes closer, I catch the scent of him, clean, and lavender, which mix well with the scent of the nearby grapevine.

He sits beside me, his gaze lingering on the waterfall. "Do you always find a waterfall wherever you go, or perhaps they find you?" He chuckles. Turning to face him, I catch his smile, lighting up his features, easing some of the tightness in my chest.

"I'll always find a waterfall wherever I go." My smile is genuine for the first time tonight. "I didn't think you'd come." I wanted him here, even if I didn't want to admit it. Having him at the cafe today was also comforting. I really needed him there.

"I didn't know if you wanted to see me, but I needed to see you." A small smile plays on his lip. "I got you something." He pulls out a small box from his pocket and hands it to me.

I hesitate before opening it, and inside, I find a rose quartz charm bracelet with charms in the shape of a book, an iced coffee, a tree, and an infinity symbol. Tiny diamonds glisten around the charms, catching the light from the waterfall.

"It's beautiful. You really didn't have to."

"I wanted to," he insists. He takes the bracelet from me and tightens it around my wrist, his fingers lightly grazing my skin. A shiver runs through me at his touch, my breath hitching slightly.

He stands up and offers his hand to me. "Dance with me," he says, a question and a command rolled into one.

Taking his hand, I meet his intense gaze, and my heart flutters wildly, like shooting stars streaking across the night sky.

He pulls me closer to him, his fingertip brushing the exposed skin at the small of my back. When he looks at me like that, I'm powerless to resist. A shiver of desires races through my body, from my core to the tip of my toes, settling a tingling warmth between my thighs.

My arms raise and loop around his neck. My body sinks into him as if coming home after being apart for so long. We sway together, the fading music from the party blending with the sound of the small waterfall, creating a world that is ours. The moment feels as natural as breathing.

"Can I ask you a question?" His breath is warm against my ear, traveling down my back. "Do you regret the time we spent together?"

"No," I exhale, my breath catching in the cool night air. I could never regret any second spent with him. "And you?" Knots tighten in my stomach, afraid of his answer.

"Never," he says with a conviction that causes my heart to flutter. "Do you remember what you said during our last night together? About finding someone worth falling for?"

"Yes." I nod, the memory stinging a little as we continue swaying lightly.

"I found her a long time ago, about a year ago, to be exact."

His eyes hold mine, and my heart picks up its speed as we sway together.

"I was scared that I wouldn't be able to give her all the love she deserves, scared I would end up hurting the both of us, and I messed up, big time."

My throat tightens as his words sink in, and I struggle to breathe.

"I would really like the chance to try again, and this time, I plan to fall for her." His gaze locks with mine, pleading.

I step back, removing my hands from his neck. An entire year of clinging to what could have been.

"You can't just show up and expect me to believe everything you say. I... I..."

I've already fallen for him once, and I wasn't even trying to. The terrifying part is, if I let myself fall completely and he doesn't catch me this time, I know I won't recover. I won't have anything left to come back to.

"Why now?" Months of waiting for him to say something like this, and now the reality feels both surreal and frightening.

"Because I've missed you," he says, looking into my eyes with a sincerity that is almost too intense. "God, I missed you so much."

The pain and relief in his voice are unmistakable. I want to say I missed you too, so, so much, but the words wouldn't come out. They're stuck in my throat.

"I missed your pretty face in the morning," he continues, and even though he's not touching me, I can feel the ghost of his touch. "Your smile, your voice, your laughter. I even missed you yelling at me." He chuckles, a bittersweet sound. "I've missed those quiet moments at the waterfall. They meant everything to me." He continues, his words swirling around me, making my heart race. A small involuntary sob escapes me.

He steps a little closer, and I hold my breath. His hand reaches out toward my face, his thumb tenderly wipes the tears from my cheek. My eyes close instinctively as a soft flutter tingle in my stomach.

"I'm sorry, princess." His forehead touches mine. I breathe him in, the smell of lavender and sandalwood. "I'm so sorry," he says again. I don't know what he's apologizing for, but it feels good to hear.

He brushes loose curls away from my face, and I shiver like a leaf in the wind. Opening my eyes, I'm met with his green eyes, glowing under the moonlight. He leans down, pressing his lip to mine, so light and soft. It feels like a feather blowing in the wind.

I step back, needing a moment to catch my breath and process everything. I turn my back to him, taking a deep breath, the cool air filling my lung.

Breathe, Mia.

"Mia." My name is like a siren on his tongue. "Please look at me."

I turn around to look at him and the longing and regret I see there are like magnets pulling me in.

"I have a proposition," he pauses, running his hand through his hair. "What if we try again this summer? But differently, no flings, no sex, just...dating, genuinely trying to connect. A chance for us to fall in love with each other. If, after that, you don't want this, I'll leave. No questions asked."

I study his face, struggling to connect this version of him with the man who used to avoid any kind of feelings and emotional connection. But he has never lied to me. He has always been brutally honest.

This is what I've always wanted. Someone who genuinely wants to get to know me for me, not just for my body. My heart wants to jump at the chance, but my mind remains cautious.

"Can I think about it?" I need time to sift through my tangled emotions, to protect the fragile parts of myself still mending from before.

"Of course, take all the time you need." His eyes meet mine with a look of understanding that melts some of the ice around my guarded heart.

"Thanks," I say, my smile small and tentative.

"Come on, let me walk you back. They're probably looking for the birthday girl." He extends his arm, and I wrap mine around his, noticing the firmness of his muscles beneath his shirt.

As we walk back, the lights and sounds of the party grow closer with each step. His presence next to me is comforting. No matter how long we've been apart, when we're together, he feels like home.

We're having a wine tasting brunch in the garden, the scenic mountain and the sprawling grapevines as our backdrop. They set our table under an oak tree, and its branch provides shade from the morning sun. Around the table, we have freshly baked bread, platters of cheese, salami, and, of course, wine.

It's me, Sarah, Rylee, and the guys, Alex and Luc. Jake isn't here. He probably wants to give me space to think about his offer.

I'm seated between Rylee and Sarah, while Alex and Luc are sitting across from us. Luc is chatting with Alex, but he glances often over our side. I can't quite tell if he's watching me, or Rylee.

Interesting.

"So, you were gone for a while last night?" Rylee raises an eyebrow suspiciously.

"Yeah, I needed a quiet time alone." I swirl the wine in my glass before taking a sip.

"Alone?" She presses for more.

"Jake showed up while I was there."

"And?" She leans closer, clearly not satisfied with my answer.

"We talked." I take a bite of the crusty bread beside my plate, buying myself some time.

"I'm gonna need more than that," she insists.

I chew slowly before swallowing. "Well, he wants to give us a real shot, dating and actually getting to know each other besides the sex."

"That's great," Sarah says, joining the conversation. "That's what you want, right?"

"Yes. I don't know." I fidget with my napkin. "He's never been in a relationship before, and thinks love is just a rush that will fade. What if this is just a thrill for him?" The last thing I want is to get my hopes up, only to have them shattered.

"I've known Jake for a long time, and he cares about you. I won't tell you what to do, but one thing you will never have to worry about is him lying to you. It will always be honest," Sarah reassures me.

I know she is right.

I sigh before downing the rest of my wine in one go instead of just taking a sip.

Even though the guys are engaged in their own conversation, I can tell they're eavesdropping. I want to ask Alex what he thinks, but I hesitate to put him in the middle of this.

After our brunch, I take out my phone and snap a few pictures for the vineyard blog. The sunlight creates a natural, vibrant backdrop.

"Who's ready for a tour by your one and only favorite tour guide?" I point at my chest and ask them to follow me. Sarah and Alex walk beside me. Rylee is trailing behind with Luc.

We continue our walk through the vineyard. The morning sun casts a playful shadow across neat rows of grapevines, each cluster of grapes almost ready for the August harvest.

I point at our oldest vines, which produce the deep complex flavors in our vintage wines. They've soaked up decades of sun and soil, enriching every bottle. During my stay here, I've learned a lot about the wine-making process.

Next, we make our way to the processing area. The sound of Rylee giggling behind me caught me off guard. *Rylee doesn't giggle.* Walking around, I show them the stainless steel and the rows of oak and barrels. The smell of fermenting grapes is thick in the air. "In these barrels, time does its finest work." I sweep my hand over the equipment.

Leaving the processing area, we climb to the highest point of the vineyard. The entire estate spread out below us, with a few charming cottages scattered along the way. The air is cooler, and the breeze carries a mixed fragrance of wildflowers from a nearby meadow and the rich smell of the grapevines.

"Incroyables n'est ce pas?" *It's incredible, isn't it?* Luc's eyes sweep the panoramic view. No matter how many times I've been up here, it always takes my breath away.

Everyone nods in agreement as we take a moment to soak in the view. The beauty of nature wraps around us. It's a moment that feels like a deep breath, soothing and serene.

This is exactly what I needed to clear up my head and stop overthinking. It took him a while, but he's here. It has to mean something.

Chapter 36

Jake

I sit in front of my computer, my eyes locked on the tiny human appearing on the screen. She really looks like me, with green eyes and long blonde hair that falls over her shoulders.

Jessie sits quietly behind her. I probably will never forget what happened, but Agatha, my little sister, shouldn't have to suffer for their mistakes.

"Hi," I say, my voice sounding unfamiliar even to my own ears, softer with more emotion than I anticipated. A surprising warmth spreads through my chest when her smile lights up the screen. "Do you know who I am?" I lean slightly forward, peering into the camera.

"Jake," she says in a voice as adorable as her smile, pure and melodic.

"That's right, I'm your big brother Jake," I say the words with a smile as I watch her bounce up and down on her mother's lap. The term brother feels real and significant for the first time since I've found out about her. I'm already in love with her.

After a few minutes, her attention drifts, and my story about me and my dad going camping doesn't seem interesting to her anymore. She runs off to play, throwing a "bye" over her shoulder that makes me laugh. Jessie and I exchange a few words before I end the call.

I lean back on the chair and rub my hands over my face. A small involuntary smile forms as I think about my sister, so adorable and innocent.

As the silence grows, my mind inevitably drifts to Mia like it always does. It's been two days since I laid everything on the line. Well, not everything, since I didn't tell her how utterly in love I am with her. The silence is deafening, yet hopeful. She hasn't said no, which means she's considering it.

Checking my phone, there are no messages from her. Alex is out with them, but I've chosen to stay behind, giving Mia the space she needs. I don't want to pressure her.

I need a shower to clear my head.

As I am stepping out of the shower, a knock at the door startles me. Alex has a spare key, and I didn't order room service.

I wrap a towel around my waist before stepping out of the bathroom. My hair is still damp from the shower.

The moment I open the door, I freeze. Mia stands there. Her eyes are wide, taking in my bare chest down to my biceps, and pausing at the tattoo on my arm. I got it a few months ago for my birthday. It's the first time she is seeing it and I wonder what she is thinking.

"Hi," I say, finally finding my voice. Does she even have the slightest idea how nervous she makes me? Maybe I'm good at hiding it.

"Hi," she says, her breathing shallow and quick.

I step aside to let her in, and my heart races with anticipation. "Give me a minute to put some clothes on." I rush back into the bathroom; the tiles cool under my bare feet. I throw on a pair of pants and a lightweight tank top before making my way back to the living area.

She's standing by the balcony, absorbed in the view of the mountains, where the sun begins its descent. Despite the breathtaking beauty of the scenery, it's her presence that truly captivates me. The subtle rise and fall of her shoulders with each breath, the gentle flutter of her hair in the evening breeze. She shines brighter than the sunset, her beauty is as radiant as the moon.

Sensing my presence, she slowly turns around, and our eyes lock as the silence stretches around us. "Water or wine?" I ask to break the ice.

"You got a tattoo."

Of course, that's the first thing, she blurts out.

It wasn't a question, but I answered with a soft "Yes."

"Can I?" she asks, not waiting for my permission as she steps closer, her gaze fixed on the ink that sleeves my arm. Her fingers trace the lines. She smells like wine and roses, an intoxicating combination. Her touch is feathering light, sending little flips through my heart, unsettling my composure.

"It's the waterfall," she says.

"Yes," I breathe out, struggling to focus on anything but the growing desire to feel the softness of her lips against mine. Damn it. The more I try not to think about it, the more it consumes my thoughts.

Get it together, Jake.

I thought my first tattoo would be a cliff or a peak, something related to climbing. But when I finally sat in the tattoo chair, my thoughts weren't on climbing. I couldn't stop thinking about her and the summer we spent together.

I thought of the waterfall—the place, the sound, the magic of it all... and us. And I knew then I wanted to carry a piece of that summer with me forever.

"Why?" she finally asks.

I turn to face her more directly. "It reminds me of you." I lock eyes with her. "You were right. Falling doesn't always have to hurt. With the right person, it's about surrendering to give up control."

Her fingers pause as she listens, and when our eyes meet, there's a noticeable softening around the edges of her gaze, the tension in her forehead easing as we connect. This connection, this falling with her. I'd choose it every day, especially when it gets rocky.

She paces before me, her arms folded across her chest, her movements betraying her anxiety. I can feel her fear, a mirror of my own.

"Mia," I call out gently, trying to catch her attention, but she keeps moving, wrapped up in her own turmoil.

Reaching out, I gently catch her wrist. Her pulse flutters like a caged bird against my fingers, though she doesn't immediately look up.

"Talk to me." I lift her chin so her eyes—vulnerable and brimming with unshed tears—meet mine.

"I'm scared," she whispers. She looks away briefly, gathers her courage, and then locks eyes with me again. "It all sounds so perfect, but you... You were the guy who avoided relationships, who never slept with the same girl twice to avoid any attachment."

Her words sting because they're true.

"Have I ever lied to you?" I ask quietly, needing her to see my sincerity.

She shakes her head, her curls brushing her cheeks.

"Meeting you... it changed all of that," I confess, my heart swelling as I hold her gaze. "I built walls around me for years, not wanting to hurt anyone, especially not you." The emotions threaten to overwhelm me, but I push through. "You've climbed over those walls, and there's something real between us I want to explore."

I let my words hang for a moment, my gaze searching hers for signs of acceptance.

"We're both scared," I continue, my voice steady despite the storm of feelings inside me. "I wouldn't do anything to hurt you, Mia. This...us...it's new for me, too. If I wasn't sure about my feelings,

I wouldn't be here." I take a moment, searching for the right words. "I want all of it with you—the attachment, the falling in love. " I trace my finger on the bridge of her nose, and she chuckles just like she used to. "I don't want to lose you because you mean everything to me."

"Okay," she says simply.

I smile. "I'm going to need a bit more than okay," I tease.

She tucks a stray curl behind her ear. "Let's try for the summer. Then, we can decide after if we want to do this long-term."

Joy and relief flood through me, lighting up every corner of my heart. This is my chance to make things right. To show her how much I adore her, and to really get to know her, and vice versa. It's an opportunity for us to open fully, no holding back.

A grin spreads across my face, so wide that it hurts. Without thinking, I lift her up and spin her around. Her laughter, light and infectious, fills the room.

"Put me down," she giggles, wriggling out of my arms. "You're squeezing me too hard. I need oxygen, you know." She laughs, pushing against my chest. I wait for her little snorts, and when it comes, my heart bursts with joy and love. *Oh God, I missed that laugh.*

I chuckle, my heart light, and place her back on the ground. "Sorry," I say, still smiling. I keep my hands around her waist, admiring her beautiful face up close. I look for the little freckles that are hidden behind her makeup.

"So, how are we going to do this?" Her brows furrow. "With me living here, and you in Boston."

"I'll rent a cottage for the summer; we can figure the rest out later."

She raises an eyebrow. "Or you can stay with me. I have a spare bedroom."

I hesitate, scratching the back of my head. "I don't think that's a good idea."

"Are you scared, Jacob Harrington?" Hearing my full name from her lips always sends shivers down my spine and straight to my shaft. She knows exactly what she's doing.

"I'm not scared." I try to sound confident. "But I think it's smarter if I rent a cottage." Being that close to her, and not being able to touch her, would only lead to disaster. And I know it was my idea, but I want to show her I adore all of her—mind, body, and soul.

"I meant what I said." I pull her closer. "I want to show that I care about all of you, your thoughts, your dreams, and your heart."

My forehead leans against hers, breathing her in like she's the very air I need. "Myara Cherie, would you like to go out with me sometimes?"

She pretends to think about it for a few seconds before nodding. "Yes, I'd like that."

I press my lips to hers, and the simple touch ignites a fire within my body. We stay like that for a few seconds, neither of us moves our lips. Pulling away, she grants me a beautiful smile, and my heart swells even further. I am completely and utterly enamored by this woman.

Chapter 37

Mia

The past two weeks have been insanely amazing since the café opened. We hosted the grand opening just three days after our successful soft opening.

Today is the busiest yet. It's been non-stop all morning, with more customers than we could have ever expected. I'm behind the counter with the baristas, but it's too much. Why did I think I could do this? I don't have enough staff. My breath grows heavier, and the familiar tightening in my chest returns.

Not again.

"Hey, you, okay?" Cyndie looks over at me, concern in her gray eyes. She has her pastel pink and blue hair pulled up into two buns.

I lean back against the wall. "Go, go help the customers. I'll be fine." I wave her off, but she hesitates before returning to the counter.

I try to breathe in and out, but everything blurs, and I slide down to the floor. "Hey, baby, I'm here." A warm voice reaches out to me. *I love that voice a lot.* For a second, I think it's my imagination. Strong arms grab my shoulders. "Breathe with me."

Inhale.

Exhale.

I follow his voice, slowly opening my eyes. There they are, those green eyes that always calm me.

They take me back to the forest. *Calm.*

The waterfall. *Soothing.*

"I'm here, baby girl. Are you okay?"

"Yeah, better now," I whisper, wrapping my arms around his neck. *Better now that you're here.*

"What happened?"

"It just got super busy, and I only have one barista. I should have hired more people. Maybe I can't do this."

"Hey, you're doing it. It's busy because people love the place. And you can always hire more people." He helps me up and wraps his arms around me.

"Thank you."

"Always."

"Cyndie, I need to go back to help Cyndie." I head back to the front, and Jake follows me, jumping in to help. Slowly, the line cuts in half, and the mid-morning rush winds down.

Now, the café has settled into a relaxed pace. A few guests linger over tea, and couples lounge upstairs in our cozy area. They recline on blankets and throw pillows, using iPads to place orders without leaving their snuggle nooks.

One customer in particular catches my eye. Jake has always been gorgeous, but now, with his tattoo sleeve showing under his black t-shirt, he's dangerously sexy.

His gaze follows me as I walk over, focusing intently on my face. Despite looking worn out from the day's chaos, he watches me as if I'm the most captivating sight in the room.

"Hi," I say, tucking a loose curl behind my ear.

"Hi." His grin is broad and warm, setting off a flutter in my chest.

"You know you didn't have to stay here all day. I'm fine."

"I know, but there's a girl here that I like."

"Is that so?" I smile at him timidly. He still makes me nervous. "Would you like something to drink?" I ask, attempting to sound composed.

"Un baiser volé," *a stolen kiss.* I'm pretty sure he's not asking for one of our teas.

Though we've gone on a couple dates, we haven't really kissed. I love the fact that we're taking things slow. I treasure our quiet walks by the garden and beside the mini waterfall, where the world seems to fall away, leaving just the two of us.

He's rented a cottage in my grandmother's vineyard, a choice that puts him tantalizingly close—just a short walk from my place. This proximity, combined with our promise to keep things slow, has only heightened the sense of anticipation that seems to crackle in the surrounding air.

"Can I steal the owner for the rest of the day?" His boyish grin has a way of melting my heart every time I see it.

"We're closing in 45 minutes."

"I'll wait," he says, leaning back in his chair. "Maybe I'll take a *baiser volé* tea in the meantime."

"Sure." I smile back at him. Though we rarely serve customers outside the designated snuggle nook upstairs, I make an exception for him—he's my special customer. After a few minutes, I return with his tea, but he's not at his table. He's in the book section. I set the tea down and head over to him.

"Since when do you read?" I ask quietly, though the cafe is nearly empty, just us and the staff preparing to close.

"Since I found someone important to me who is both a writer and a reader," he says, not looking up from the books, but I can hear the smile in his voice. "I was looking for one of those smutty books you love so much, but thought better of it."

"Who says I love smutty books?"

"Because every time I catch you reading, you're always biting your lips." The dark center of his eyes expands, devouring the green color around them. They lock onto my lips as if he's imagining the taste of them. I fight the urge to bite my lip as the sight of him consumes me.

"I'm opting for something fluffy instead." He picks up two copies of a romantic comedy.

"Can I pay for these?" He follows me to the register where Cyndie rings him up. He returns to his table, drinking his tea while we finish cleaning up.

Once we're done, the three of us head out, and I lock up the café.

"Walk or Uber?" he asks as I turn to face him. Despite feeling a bit tired, I love our long walks, especially here where the serene setting makes time fly.

"Walk, but you have to buy me an ice cream," I negotiate.

"Deal." He grins as we start our walk.

We stop at a small ice cream shop around the corner. I choose cappuccino flavor ice cream, and he goes for salted caramel. "You, owning a bookstore cafe is perfect. You love coffee and books almost as much as you love sleeping," he teases as we resume our walk.

I laugh, a sound light and freeing, unlike any I've made in months. My laughter fades as I notice a woman holding a little girl's hand as she bounces happily on her step. The sight brings back memories of afternoon walks to the park with my mom.

"So, how's it going with your books?" And then he stops walking when I don't immediately respond. "Come on," he says, guiding me to a nearby bench. "I know that look—talk to me." He has always had a way of reaching deep, pulling out my biggest fears and insecurities.

"It's just... I've been querying for almost six months now," I confess, the weight of my fears settling in, "and I still don't have an agent." Each denial is a heavy blow to my confidence. "I know I could just self-publish, but what if I can't get an agent because my writing isn't good enough? What if self-publishing changes nothing? What if people don't want to read my work?"

"Hey," he says, lifting my chin to meet his gaze. "Your writing is amazing. I've read some pieces you shared with me. You just haven't found the right person for your story yet. But you will." I want to believe him, to hold on to the hope he offers.

"Thanks," I smile, grateful for his support. He always knows how to make me feel better, and maybe he's right.

Then my thoughts scatter as I watch him lick his ice cream. I curse myself for suggesting ice cream, for watching him, for not being able to look away, and for imagining what else that tongue could be doing. He turns to look at me, and whatever he sees on my face makes him smirk.

"Patience, princess. I'll be enjoying something far sweeter soon." His words intensify the throbbing desire between my thighs. "It's leaking," he adds, snapping me back from my daze.

"Huh?" I say, confused, wondering how he could know—

"I'm talking about your ice cream," he clarifies with a chuckle, nodding toward my hand.

Oh, right—the ice cream. I look down to see it melting over my hand. *Get a grip, Mia.* I wrap my lips around it, gently sucking while maintaining eye contact with him. I let out a small moan as the cold sweetness hit my throat.

"You're very naughty, princess." The corners of his eyes crinkle, and his lips curve into a slow, teasing smile. The green of his eyes darken to a more intense shade, while his nostrils flare and his jaw tightens.

I finish my ice cream, licking the last traces off my fingers, aware of his eyes on me the whole time. Once done, I get on the bench, and he gets up to stand in front of me. "But you like naughty girls, don't you?"

"I like you," he says, smiling warmly. "I like you very much." He presses his lips to my forehead, making my body shiver. My body responds to everything he does.

I'm cheesing so hard my face hurts. "I like you too." My arms wrap around his neck. "Very much." He lifts me up and places me on my feet.

I more than like you very much.

We continue our walk to the vineyard. The crisp evening air carries the scent of grapes nearing harvest. "How's it going with the hotel?" I ask, eager to distract myself from the fluttering in my chest.

He takes a moment, enjoying his ice cream before answering. "It's going great." He pauses to take another bite. I catch myself staring a little too long. "We're almost done with the expansion and getting new reservations."

"That's amazing. I'm so proud of you," I say, warmth spreading through my words.

He stops mid-stride, his eyes widening momentarily as he processes my words.

"What?" I stop, turning around to look at him. My eyebrows shoot up as I try to figure out why he stops.

"Come here." He opens his arms. As I step into them, he wraps one arm around me while the other still holds his cone. People continue to stroll around us, probably wondering why we're standing in the middle of the cobblestone. He leans down, and whispers against my hair, "Thank you."

"You're too much." I laugh, but I can't ignore the butterfly wings that beat against the walls of my heart.

He pulls back slightly, looking down at me. "It might not seem like a big deal, but it means a lot to me."

"Well, you welcome," I say as we resume our walk toward the vineyard.

I stop when he heads toward his cottage instead. "Come on, baby, I promise to behave," he teases, holding out his hand with that boyish grin that always disarms me. Hesitating only a moment, I take his hand as we walk toward his cottage.

Inside, his cottage mirrors the layout of mine: an airy, open-plan living room flows into a small kitchen, with a balcony overlooking the vineyard.

"Make yourself comfortable. I'll be right back," he tells me before heading upstairs. When he returns, his presence commands the room. "Come on," he says, leading me upstairs.

To my surprise, he's prepared a bath with floating rose petals and flickering candles around the tub. "I also have fresh pajamas for you." He points to a neatly folded set on the chair next to the tub. My heart swells with affection. Every time I think I couldn't love him more; he does something incredibly thoughtful like this.

Now, I'm no longer scared of falling for him because when he looks at me, his eyes soften with tenderness, hinting that he's falling for me too. I want to confess how deeply I feel for him but hold back because I fear it might be too soon.

Instead, I lean against him, comforted by his presence. He wraps his arms around me, a secure embrace that makes the world outside melt away. I silently savor the warmth of his hug and the steady beat of his heart.

I love you.

"You've had a long day, so take your time, relax for a bit." He pulls away, his eyes cradle mine with a gentle caress. "I'll wait for you downstairs." He plants a soft kiss on my forehead before stepping out and closing the door behind him.

Alone, I undress, shedding my clothes along with my sticky underwear, and lower myself into the warm, lavender-scented water. And no bubbles. He remembered that I'm sensitive to bubbles.

I sink deeper into the bath, letting the fragrant steam envelop me as I close my eyes and let go of the day's tension.

After a few blissful minutes of soaking in the bath, I step out and find my favorite jasmine scented body lotion. He remembered my favorite lotion.

Drying off, I grab the pajamas off the chair. It's cute green shorts and a white top that says, *Do Not Wake Me Up Before 8 AM.* I laugh, remembering how he used to wake me up with his blender. I put on the set, and they fit perfectly. Also, they're unbelievably soft on my skin, it's fuzzy and feather like. Once dressed, I head downstairs but don't find him in the living room. Instead, I notice the light spilling in from the patio where he has set up a table with food, snacks, and the two books he bought earlier. He's laughing at something on his laptop, his face bright with a big smile. He's also wearing pajamas that match mine, with long green pants and a white tee.

"I got to go, I love you," he says into the laptop before hanging up.

I pause, processing the words I've never heard him say before; they stir a complex emotion in my chest that I can't quite name.

"How was your bath?" he asks as I approach the table. I choose the seat across from him instead of beside him. Part of me wants to ask who he was talking to, but I resist, not wanting to come off as jealous.

"What's with the frown?"

"Nothing." I look down at my hands.

"Come here," he says, his tone both serious and commanding.

I hesitantly move toward him, and as I do, he pulls me closer. His gaze is soft yet intense as he looks up at me from under his lashes.

"Let's try that again." He intertwines our fingers together.

"It's just you were talking to someone when I came out, and you hung up as soon as you saw me."

He chuckles softly, which deepens my frown—not the reaction I was hoping for.

"I hung up because I want to focus on you. I was talking to my sister." He rubs my knuckles, his eyes never leaving mine.

"Sister?"

"You probably don't remember, but I mentioned last year that I found out I have a little sister. She's two years old now."

He reminds me of how Jessie had emailed him about her, making me a bit foolish for my earlier suspicions. I want to know more, but I don't want to pressure him to talk about it.

"You're so adorable when you're jealous," he teases.

I'm about to deny it, but his lips meet mine before I can speak. Any thoughts of protest dissolve between our kisses, and I'm swept up in the moment, not sure I'm even breathing.

Chapter 38

Jake

The kiss is quick and sweet, but it's enough to leave me dizzy. Fearing I might lose control if we continue, I gently lift her up and set her beside me on the couch. She crosses her legs, and the intensity in her gaze tells me I'm not the only one affected by the kiss.

Needing a distraction, I turn my attention to the food. "I've got shrimp pasta and wine," I say. "And I thought maybe we could narrate the book I picked earlier. I'll read his point of view, and you can read hers."

"That sounds perfect." Grabbing her plates. "So, how do you feel about having to talk to Jessie?" She rolls her fork around her pasta.

"I'll never be okay with it. Even if I wasn't in love with her or we weren't an official couple, it doesn't change the fact she slept with my dad." The thought is still disturbing. "But Agatha shouldn't suffer from their mistakes. She's so sweet and adorable." A genuine smile spreads across my face at the thought of my little sister.

She nods, taking a sip of her wine. "And your dad. Have you forgiven him?"

"It's harder to hold a grudge against a dead man, but I've taken your advice and remember the good times that he loved me in his own fucked up way."

Talking about him doesn't feel as suffocating as before.

"You did it for you, not for him. You deserve to be happy, and holding a grudge can weigh you down." She places her hand over mine.

I've avoided love and relationships all my life, afraid of giving anyone the power to hurt me like he did. That if I let someone in, eventually they would realize I'm not worthy of love and stop loving me too. But looking at her now, I realize I would rather have my heart broken a thousand times than miss out on the chance to love her.

"You're right," I acknowledge with a half-smile.

"I am right," she laughs, twirling some spaghetti on her fork. After swallowing her bite and taking another sip of wine, she asks, "So, how's it going with Peak Finders?"

My smile widens involuntarily. "So, you've been keeping tabs on me?"

"No," she deflects, quickly shoveling another forkful of pasta into her mouth.

I stare at her for a few seconds with a knowing look. "It's doing great. I love teaching them."

"Do you miss them?" She asks, setting her wineglass down.

"I enjoy being around them, and yes, I miss them, but I'd rather be here with you than anywhere else," I tell her, catching her eyes as I speak. It's important to me she sees the sincerity in my gaze; I want her to know the truth in my words.

As we continue our conversation, my phone vibrates on the table, interrupting the moment. I set my plate aside and pick up my phone to check the notification. It's an email from Sergio, but I ignore it for now.

Out of the corner of my eye, I catch her trying to steal a shrimp from my plate. "You could have just asked instead of stealing my shrimp," I tease, chuckling. "I'll give you everything you want." I'd give her the moon if she asked, except she already is my moon. I pick the shrimps off my plate and add them to hers.

Once we finish eating, I grab our books, and she lays her head in my lap as we take turns reading.

"You know, if climbing or managing the hotel doesn't work out, you could be an audiobook narrator. Your voice is perfect," her words make me smile, though it's her voice that mesmerizes me. Everything about her does.

Finishing my chapter, I wait for her to continue, but she doesn't say anything.

"It's your turn, baby."

Glancing down, her eyes are closed, and her breathing is deep and even. The steady rise and fall of her chest sync with the calm night around us. Carefully, I brush a stray curl from her face, revealing her serene expression. God, I love her so much it hurts. Is it crazy to think I've loved her before in another life?

"I love you," I whisper, needing to say it before my heart explodes. She stirs slightly, as if she can hear me. "Come on, baby girl, let's get you to bed." I scoop her up, her head resting against my chest. Her body feels light and trusting as I carry her to the bedroom. Gently, I lay her down, pulling the covers up around her shoulders to ensure she's warm and snug.

I grab one of those bonnets she likes to wear when she sleeps, even if they always come off. Tucking her curls inside of it, I smile at how cute she looks. I'm about to go downstairs to sleep on the couch when her arm reaches out and stops me. "Please stay."

I hesitate before sliding into bed next to her. She buries her head in my chest, her warmth seeping into me. My arms wrap around her, pulling her closer. It's been a long time since I felt this content and complete.

"Good night, Moonie." I press a kiss to her forehead.

Chapter 39

Mia

A warmth kisses my face, like the sun on a clear day. It's like a dream I've had countless times before, as if someone is there kissing me, touching me.

My eyes slowly flutter open to the sight of deep green eyes tenderly observing me.

"Good morning, princess, did I wake you up?"

"Were you watching me sleep?" I rub my eyes as I adjust to the early morning light.

"You looked so beautiful and peaceful. It's hard not to watch." His lips curve into a tender smile.

I roll over and straddle him, his body hard and warm beneath me. My fingers tangle in his blonde tousled hair. I gently ruffle it as I lean down to kiss his neck. He shivers under my touch, his breath hitching.

"What are you doing, baby girl?" he says, his eyes never leaving mine.

"Nothing," I grin, my lips brushing against his skin.

"Douxy, you say *no sex,* but you didn't say *no kissing,*" I tease slowly, drawing out the words, watching the way his eyes darken even more.

"Douxy?" He raises an eyebrow. "That's french, right?"

"Yes, doux, it's French for sweet." I smile, biting lightly on his neck. He groans, a distinct sound that sends a thrill through me. "Hmmm," I moan, "so sweet."

I laugh as he rolls me over and pins me on the bed, his green eyes turning into a darker shade of hunter green. My laughter dies in my throat as his hardness pressing between my thighs, memories of early morning sex, middle-of-the-night sex, and the best orgasms I've ever had flood my mind. Desire shoots through me, and as always, it seems that he can read my thoughts.

He smirks and kisses my forehead before pulling away.

"I hate you," I grumble, throwing a pillow at his head.

"I hate you too, Moonie." He chuckles.

"Moonie?" I remember how he used to call me that back at the cabin, but I never asked him why. "Why do you call me Moonie?"

"You're like the moon," he begins. "You have phases, and each one is beautiful in its own way. Sometimes you're bright and full of light, and other times, you're mysterious and hidden. But no matter what phase you're in, I'm drawn to you and the light you bring to my life."

I take a moment to think about his words, a playful smirk forming. "Is that your way of saying I'm moody?" I pretend to be offended.

"That's what you got from that?" he teases, moving over to tickle me. "Maybe I should call you Moody."

"I was joking." I giggle, squirming under his touch. My laughs turn into embarrassing snorts as they always do around him. His eyes brighten as if it's the best sound he's ever heard. He never made me feel self-conscious about it. "This is the sweetest thing anyone has ever said to me." I look at him from under my lashes. "Thank you."

"I meant every word," he says as he leans in to kiss me again.

My phone rings, breaking the moment. I glance at the screen—it's my grandmother. I pick it up and bring it to my ear. "Bonjour, Elena," I say, listening to what she's saying.

"Perfect, à tout à l'heure."

"My grandmother invited us for breakfast," I tell Jake as I put the phone down.

"Is Luc going to be there?" His face turns into a frown.

"Yes, and what's with the face?" I tease when he doesn't laugh. I move closer. "Why do you have a problem with Luc?"

"Because" he hesitates, "I don't like him. With his perfect French accent, the guy is too perfect." His jaw tightens. "And don't forget he kissed you."

"It was one kiss, and he apologized for it. We're just friends now." I hop onto his back, looping my arms around his neck to kiss behind his ear. "You're my perfect guy, Douxy."

How can he not see that I'm utterly and completely in love with him? My heart belonged to him long before we met.

With one swift movement, he shifts me until I'm straddling him. When our eyes meet, my heart, my stomach, my whole body does all kinds of funny things. The look in his eyes is enough to make me melt.

"You're perfect," he says, tucking a few of my crazy curls behind my ears. Why does my bonnet always come off when I sleep? But I love the fact he started using a silk pillowcase without me even asking.

Oh, God, he is perfect.

"I've got to get ready," I blurt out when his intense gaze becomes too much.

"You can shower here, then we can go together, and I'll wait for you to get ready," he suggests.

"I don't think that's a good idea," I whisper. "You, me, naked in the same bathroom."

"I have self-control, baby. Do you?" He smiles knowingly. "You can use the tub and take a bath, and I'll use the shower."

"You know I can see you in the shower from the tub, right?"

"Yes, and?" He smiles again.

He wants to play—two can play this game, Jacob Harrington. Let me see that self-control, baby.

As always, he gets my bath ready for me, turning around to give me privacy as I slide into the warm water, even though he's seen every inch of me—even the little birthmark on my buttock.

Once I'm settled, he gets into the shower, keeping his back to me. I have a front-row seat to the best view of the world. My eyes trace the lines of his back, lingering on his firm ass. I love how it tightens when he's fucking me. Desire coils in my belly, and I need some relief. We agreed on no sex, but we said nothing about me pleasuring myself.

I slide my hand between my thighs and let out a small moan as my fingers find my swollen clit. He turns abruptly at the sound, his eyes widening through the fogged glass shower when he realizes what I'm doing. Now I have a clear view of his shaft, and I watch as it grows longer by the second. Fuck, I forgot how big he is.

The heat and desire radiating from him scorch my skin as my movements become more urgent and faster. Another moan escaped from me as I locked eyes with him. I'm almost there; Pleasure coiling in my stomach, ready to explode as I imagine his skillful tongue on me. The whole time, he just watches, his eyes dark and intense, not even touching himself. He watches as I turn into a beautiful mess in front of him.

Closing my eyes, I am consumed by the intense pleasure that courses through every inch of my being. When I open them, I find Jake standing in front of me. Water drips from his chiseled body, forming small puddles on the floor. My eyes trace down to where he's painfully hard, and I clench my legs under the water. Biting my lip, I realize I've never had the chance to taste him, but now I want to.

Just dating Mia. No sex, remember? That's what you always wanted.

I wonder if he'll stop me if I try.

He kneels beside the tub, gripping the edge so tightly his knuckles are white. His jaw clenches, and his green eyes, practically burning into me, darken.

"Do you have any idea what you're doing to me?" he growls, his breath hot against my ear.

A shiver runs down my spine at his proximity. "I guess I have some idea." I have the upper hand, and I know it.

He cups my cheek, his thumb brushing my lower lip. "You enjoy torturing me?" The question comes out rough with need, his eyes intense, yet teasing. "I could pull you out of the tub and fuck you against the sink, and you wouldn't stop me, would you?" His tone doesn't match the raw hunger in his eyes. "But I'm not going to do that." His eyes soften. "You just wait, Moonie. I'll show you self-control." His promise sends another wave of desire through me, making me ache for him even more.

He stands up, his eyes never leaving mine, and grabs a towel. The fabric rustles softly as he wraps it around his waist. The muscles in his arms and chest ripple with every movement, taking away my view, and I can't help the pout that forms on my lips. Who am I now? That's what a summer with him did to me.

He holds a towel for me as I step out of the tub, and I follow him to the bedroom, where he has my clothes washed and ready for me.

"Get dressed. We have breakfast to get to," he says, his brows furrowed, and there's a slight twitch in his jaw as if he's fighting to maintain control.

This game of self-control is just beginning, and I can't wait to see who breaks first.

After Putting on my olive-green jumpsuit, I grab my phone to check my email like always. There's a notification sitting at the top of my inbox. My heart pounds in my chest as I stare at it.

Could this be it? I try not to have my hopes up.

My thumb hovers over the email before opening it. Whatever the answer is, I'm ready to accept it. My eyes follow the line as my pulse quickens with each word. I re-read the last line over and over, my eyes and my mind trying to make sense of it.

I sit on the bed, my legs wobbly as I fight the tears burning in the back of my eyes. Jake rushes over and kneels in front of me, his hand on my knees. "Baby, are you okay?"

I shake my head, my breaths coming in sharp bursts.

"Mia, talk to me, please. What's wrong?" His hand squeezes my thigh gently, grounding me.

"I received an email."

"And?"

"I have an agent for my book series." Laughing and sobbing, tears spill over. "I emailed her about a month ago, and... this happened." I hand over my phone to him and wait for him to finish reading.

His face lights up with a smile as he puts the phone on the bed. He lifts me off the ground and spins me around. "Yes, I'm so proud of you." He laughs.

I giggle. "Thank you."

"You're going to be a published author, baby girl." He sets me down gently but keeps his arms around me.

"Well, let's not get ahead of ourselves. There's a lot that must happen before we get to that point." I know I need to be realistic and not set my expectations too high, but it's hard to hide my excitement. I've been waiting for this moment.

"You got this, okay?" His hands tenderly hold my face. The certainty touches the deepest corners of my soul.

"Okay," I say, wrapping my arms around him.

I have my bookstore, a chance to publish my book, and the love of my life.

Love of my life.

Chapter 40

Mia

The evening rush is in full swing. As the line grows, I step in to help and realize I'll need to hire more baristas soon. I've had interviews, and they're all amazing, but it's hard to pick just two.

While preparing a coffee, a customer calls for my attention. Suddenly, hot coffee splashes over my hand and shirt. I jump aside as the burning sensation hits.

"Mia, are you okay?" I hear Luc's voice as he rushes toward the back.

"Give me a minute," I tell Cyndie, my teeth clenched to contain the pain, as I rush toward the bathroom in the back. Luc follows closely behind.

In the bathroom, I immediately run my hands under the cold water, hissing softly as the chill hits my burning skin. The shock of the cold water offers some relief, and I glance down at my white shirt, now stained and sticking uncomfortably to my skin.

Luc, standing beside me, quickly removes his button-up shirt and hands it to me, standing there in his undershirt. He then turns his back to give me some privacy.

I struggle to undo my shirt, my hands trembling. Each touch sends a jolt of pain through my burned skin. My fingers fumble with the buttons. I only fasten two. The rest hang open because of the pain.

"I'm done."

Luc turns back around, his eyes immediately going to my red skin. His brows furrow in concentration, his jaw tight as he examines the angry red marks.

"It doesn't look too bad. Do you have a first aid kit?"

"Under the sink." I point with my free hand. He nods, retrieving the kit and quickly finding what he needs. "We need to get something on this to soothe the burn," he insists, his touch gentle but firm as he continues to hold my hands.

The bathroom door swings open again, and Jake walks in. His jaw tightens, and his eyes narrow as he scans the scene. "What's going on?" His eyes dart from my half-buttoned shirt to Luc.

"There was an accident, and I dropped coffee on myself. Luc lent me his shirt," I explain quickly.

Before I can react, Jake steps in front of me, pushing Luc aside. "Turn around, asshole," he snaps at him, unbuttoning Luc's shirt and thrusting it back at him.

"What are you doing?" Eyes wide with shock.

"My girlfriend is not wearing another guy's shirt, especially not some French assholes." He strips off his T-shirt and gently pulls it over my head, his touch gentle despite his harsh words.

"I'm not your girlfriend, and he was just trying to help. You're overreacting," I snap back, my hands trembling as I adjust his shirt over me.

"You're my everything, Moonie," he says, his tone softening, catching me off guard.

Did I really hear him right?

"It's okay," Luc says calmly, trying to defuse the situation. "I'll go help Cyndie." He steps out of the bathroom, leaving us in a tense silence.

Jake lifts me and sits me on the bathroom sink, his movements gentle as he applies some lotion to my burn. His eyebrows furrow in concern as he carefully wraps a bandage around the burn, his finger shaking. Then, he brings it to his lips and kisses it gently.

"Does it hurt?" The crease between his brow deepens, and his eyes narrow as they scan my face.

"A little."

I'm still upset with how he spoke to Luc when he was only trying to help, but his words replay in my mind: *You're my everything*. My anger cools down despite myself.

"You didn't have to talk to him like that." My words are sharp but shaky. "You owe him an apology."

"I don't owe him anything." He pulls away from me, running his hand through his hair. "The guy clearly still has feelings for you. Don't forget that he kissed you." He turns to face me, his skin flushed red with anger.

"We've talked about this. It was a mistake. He apologized and we've moved past it."

"It doesn't matter. I don't want you friends with him."

"You don't tell me who I can or cannot be friends with." I hop off the sink.

"Mia..."

"I'm going to check on Cyndie." I cut him off and storm out of the bathroom.

Back behind the counter, the evening rush has passed, leaving the café quiet with just a few lingering customers. The air is lighter, though a bit of tension still knots in my chest.

"You, okay?" Cyndie walks over to me, her eyes full of concern.

"Yeah, I'm okay, and I'm sorry for leaving you alone," I say, offering a small smile.

"Why are you apologizing? It was an emergency, and besides, Luc came to help." She gives my shoulder a reassuring squeeze.

"Merci," I turn to Luc with genuine gratitude in my eyes. He nods, a small smile playing on his lips. "And I definitely need to hire more employees."

From the corner of my eyes, I catch Jake walking towards me. His shoulders are tense. "I'm sorry about earlier," he says to Luc. "I overreacted."

Luc nods and says, "It's okay," in his French accent, his smile forgiving. "I get it."

He pulls off the counter and steps towards me. "I'm heading out. Take care of the burn, okay?" His brows furrow.

"Okay, and thanks again."

He stares at me for a few seconds longer before turning around and leave.

With Luc and Cyndie gone, it's just me and Jake left in the café. I try to clean up, awkwardly maneuvering with my left hand. Jake approaches me with a concerned look. "Sit down, baby. I'll get it," he whispers.

"I can manage," I insist, stubbornly.

He shakes his head, and before I know what's happening, he lifts me off the floor as if I weigh nothing. His muscular arm wraps around me, his intoxicating smell hitting my nose as he gently places me on the counter. He growls softly in my ear, "I don't care if you're mad at me. My job is to take care of you."

I pout, rolling my eyes. He's so hot when he does that, taking care of me, even when he knows I can do it myself (at least try to). Instead of resisting him, I cross my arms and watch him, doing my best to not bite down on my lip.

"I'm not even sure why you're mad at me. I apologized to him like you wanted," he adds.

"I'm mad because you don't trust me," I say, hurt lacing my words.

"You're wrong, baby. I trust you, but the woman that I love is not wearing another man's shirt. The only shirt you need to wear is mine." His words are firm, but there's a softness in his eyes.

It takes me a few seconds for his words to sink in, my heart fluttering into chaos. *The woman that I love;* I replay his words in my head.

He stares at me, realizing what he just admitted, his eyes widening.

"You love me?" My heart pounds in my chest.

He takes a deep breath, his gaze locking onto mine with a fierceness that sends electric waves through my body.

"Isn't it obvious? I've been trying to keep it to myself because we agreed to take things slow, but seeing you with him... It brought everything to the surface. I can't hide it anymore." He settles himself between my legs. His hand reaches up to brush a lock of hair behind my ear, causing a tingling sensation to spread through my belly. "I'm in love with you, Moonie." The raw honesty in his words fills the airl as if I could reach out and touch it.

Tears spring to my eyes, hot and insistent, and I try to blink them away. He looks alarmed.

"I..." Struggling to push through the tightness in my throat, I pause and draw a deep, steadying breath before reaching out to touch his face. My fingers tremble as they brush against his stubbled cheek, the slight abrasiveness grounding me. "I'm in love with you, you idiot," I confess with a shaky laugh, finally voicing the truth I've held back. "I've been waiting for you to say it first."

His face lights up with a smile that sends little flips through my stomach. I'm smiling so hard; I must look like the idiot.

"Can you say that again?" He leans in closer, his breath warm against my face.

"You idiot." I laugh.

"Not that part," he says, his gaze intensifying, locking onto mine.

I wrap my legs around his waist, pulling him closer. "I love you. I've been in love with you since last summer...but I thought you would never love me back." An involuntary sob breaks through. I didn't realize how much I've been wanting him to say it, and how much I wanted to let those words out, making them real.

"Moonie, I've been falling for you since the moment I met you. I was too stupid to see it. But now, I'm planning on falling for you forever." His hand slides into my hair before his lips find mine. This kiss is slow and deep. His tongue seeks mine, commanding and possessive. I wrap my legs around his waist, pulling him closer and gently tug at his hair. I want to get lost in him forever.

"We need to close the store," I mumble through the kiss.

"Hmmm," he groans as he continues kissing me. He lifts me off the counter while kisses trail down my neck.

I close my eyes as a moan escapes me. I wriggle out of his arms, and he gently sets me down.

"My shirt looks good on you. Do you know why?" He places a kiss on my forehead. "Because you're mine, baby." Another kiss lands on my nose. "Mine to love," a kiss on my cheek, "mine to adore, and mine to please." He growls at the last part.

His lips find mine again, and his hands squeeze my ass before giving me a playful slap as I walk behind the counter to grab my bag.

He's mine.

Chapter 41

Jake

Self-control is something I have mastered these past few weeks, and I should get a goddamn medal for it. I need to see a doctor just to make sure a guy can't die from lack of sex. I haven't even tried to relieve myself because, and this is going to sound stupid, I'm saving myself for her. There you have it.

Trust me, she hasn't made it easier, teasing me whenever she gets the chance. Walking around in those booty shorts that drive me crazy.

I've tried taking her out on dates as much as possible, not only because I love spending time with her and exploring the town. But because we needed to be somewhere in public where we had to keep our clothes on.

Besides that, everything has been perfect. Her café is doing amazing, and she's working on her book with her agent.

Standing outside her cottage, I wait for her to open the door. She walks out, wearing a short white dress that clings to her body in a way that should be illegal. I think tonight is where my self-control might fly out the window.

My eyes trace her body, starting from her legs and her gold high heels, lingering on her thick thighs. I take in her features, her dark red lipstick, her hair that is half up and half down, which gives me a better view of her beautiful face. Fuck, I just fall in love with her all over again, like I didn't just fall in love with her this morning when I found her dancing while cooking.

"Hi," she says with that sweet, shy smile, looking at me with her doe eyes.

"Hi." I grin like an idiot, my heart pounding in my chest. "You're stunningly gorgeous."

"Thanks," she says, flustered.

"Turn around, baby. Let me see that ass."

Her giggles fill the cool air as she twirls around. "Damn, you're so sexy." My teeth sink into my bottom lip, eyes roaming over her body. I'm this close to canceling the entire date and devouring her right there.

Taking a deep breath, I adjust my pants and ignore her knowing smile. "Are you ready?" I hold out my hand to her, and she places hers in mine. The scent of jasmine from her perfume mixes with the lingering smell of grapes, creating an intoxicating blend.

I lead her to the car and open the door for her. The drive to the restaurant is silent, but it's a beautiful and comfortable silence, filled with stolen glances and soft smiles.

That's what happens when you find your person. Sometimes we talk for hours and other times we just sit quietly, enjoying each other's company and still feel connected.

We pull up to the restaurant, and the valet takes our keys as we walk inside, my hand resting on her lower back. Her skin is warm beneath my palm.

"Reservation?"

"Yes, it's under Jacob Harrington." She nods and motions for us to follow her. She leads us to a secluded table set against an expansive window offering a panoramic view of the city, and the Eiffel tower. Then I pull out of her chair and help her sit comfortably before taking my seat.

The server comes over, and I order a red wine that she'll like.

"This is perfect," she says as the server leaves with our orders. My arm extends across the table, reaching for her hand, and giving it a gentle squeeze. "I wanted to make tonight special."

Even though we still have two weeks left, I can't bear to wait another day without making her officially my girlfriend.

"So, how's it going with the agent?" I ask as the server returns with our wine and fresh bread. He pours some into our glasses before walking away.

"It's going great. She's in New York, so I need to make sure our Zoom calls match our schedules," she says, taking a piece of bread and putting it into her mouth. She chews slowly before bringing the glass to her lips for a small sip.

"So, when's the release date, or..." I ask excitedly.

She chuckles. "We're not there yet. Right now, we're editing so we can start submitting my manuscript to publishers."

"Well, I can't wait. I'm so proud of you," I say, remembering when she was too afraid to even write. Now she's on her way to being a published author. I knew she would get there.

She blushes, looking down at her plate. "Thank you, again."

I lean in closer and smile at her. "You deserve it. You've worked so hard for this."

She tucks her curls behind her ears with a sweet smile.

"Can I ask you a question?" Her fingers nervously play with the edge of her napkin before she looks up at me.

Oh, no, I know that look.

"Of course, you can ask me anything."

"Have you been with anyone? You know, after us?" She looks down at her bread.

"Yes," I say, even though I wish the answer was different, but I would never lie to her.

I see the hurt cross her face before giving me a half-smile. "Oh."

She plays with her food, pushing it around her plate, pretending it doesn't bother her, but I know her better than that. Her shoulders slump, and she avoids my gaze.

"Princess, whatever you're thinking right now, please stop, okay?" When she doesn't look at me or say anything, I move my chair closer to her. Lifting her chin up to look at me, her skin soft and warm under my fingers. "I'm sorry, but it meant nothing. It was a mistake. I didn't even go through with it. I stopped because all could think about was you. I was just drunk, and stupid but that's not an excuse either."

"You don't have to explain yourself. It's not like we were a thing then," she says, her voice barely holding steady.

Wrong, baby.

"Moonie, you were and are my everything," I reach out for her shaky hands, and intertwine our fingers together. "Now talk to me, baby."

"I don't know why I'm upset," she admits. "It's just thinking about you kissing someone else the way you kissed me or making love to someone the way you made love to me... I mean, have sex... It kinda hurts because I didn't stop thinking about you even for a second when we were apart." Hearing the hurt in her voice stings, but I never want her to hold anything in.

"Princess, I could never kiss anyone the way I kiss you, and make love? I could never make love to anyone but you because I love you, and only you. Even when I was too stupid to admit it." This woman had my heart since the moment I met her, maybe even before then.

"I love you too." Her eyes glisten with unshed tears, and her smile is soft and genuine.

Just like that, I fell in love with her for the millionth time tonight.

"Why were you drunk?" she asks with a small, adorable pout.

I chuckle because the question was expected. "I missed you so much, and I couldn't stop thinking about you. So, I would drink, hoping it would help me forget. But no matter how hard I tried, moving on was impossible. I didn't want to, and I was angry at myself for letting you go. But I also knew I couldn't give you what you needed." I bring our intertwined hands to my lips and kiss her knuckles.

"I was scared of loving you because I thought that eventually you would realize I'm not worthy of your love and stop loving me." The last part slips out without thinking. Her eyes widen, softening with understanding.

"Baby, I could never stop loving you. I knew I was going to fall in love with you the moment you kissed me." Her fingers rub my stubble, and every nerve ending buzzes with energy. I close my eyes, savoring the contact. "But I was wrong because I'd already fallen for you. I don't know when it happened. It feels like it's been there all along."

Fuck, she always has a way of making me melt into a puddle. I had everything planned. They're supposed to bring a cake during dessert asking her to be my girlfriend, but I don't want to wait.

"This might sound cheesy, but will you be my girlfriend officially?"

She laughs; her eyes sparkling. "I didn't know people still ask but *yesss.*"

If it was up to me, I would ask her to marry me right now. But I want to enjoy every stage of our relationship with her.

We hold each other's gaze as the world seems to fade away around us. Our lips meet, leaving nothing but the softness of her lips, the floral scent of sweet roses and jasmine. Her tastes of wine and sin rolled into one, sweet and intoxicating. I can hear her heartbeat and feel the softness of her curls between my fingers.

"Jake," she moans into the kiss.

"Hmmm," I moan back, lost in the moment.

"We need to go now," she whispers, her breath warm against my lips.

Go where? I'm perfectly fine right here. She pulls away slightly, and that's when I remember we're still at the restaurant.

"Baby, we need to go now," she repeats, her brown eyes framed by thick eyelashes drawing me in, sparkling with a blazing fire.

I take some money out of my pocket and leave it on the table before we head out.

We stand, and I guide her out, my hand on the small of her back. The electric connection between us pulses down my arm, bolts of hot energy traveling all the way to my fingertips. The night air hits us as we step outside, but it does nothing to cool the fire burning between us. We hurry to the car, the anticipation building with every step. The city lights blur around us, and all I can think about is getting back to where we can be alone.

Once we're inside the car, she turns to me, her eyes smoldering. "Drive fast," she says, sliding her hand between her thighs.

"Baby, don't you dare," I warn, glancing over at her.

"Mmm," a soft moan escapes her lips, pulling out her fingers from under her dress. She holds them up to me, glistening with her arousal.

"Fuck Mia, you're killing me." I groan, my balls tingling, ready to explode.

We pull up to the driveway a few minutes later, and I'm quick to my feet, practically leaping out of the car. I hand the keys to the valet. "Wait, what are we doing here?" She raises an eyebrow.

"Well, when I planned our date, I also booked a room for the night just in case we didn't feel like driving the hour and a half back to the cottage." Thank God that I did. I wouldn't survive the drive back.

"Hmmm," she teases with a knowing look.

"Come on," I say, taking her hand as we step into the elevator, and as soon as the doors close, our mouths crash together again.

My hand slides to her waist, pulling her into me as my body burns with desire. Her hands tangle in my hair, tugging slightly, sending shivers down my spine.

The elevator dings, and the doors open to our floor. We stumble out, never breaking the kiss, and we practically fall inside, still entangled in each other. I move and sit her on the bed, laying her down in a swift motion. She rolls us over and sits on top of me.

My hands move to the hem of her dress, slowly pushing it up, but her hand reaches out to stop me. Pulling away from me with a sweet and devilish smile on her face.

Shit, I'm fucked.

"Mia?"

"Yes, is there something that you want, Douxy?" Her voice drips with teasing sweetness as she traces a finger down my chest. And I love it when she calls me like that.

"Yes, I need you." My body aching for her touch.

"Hmmm," she stares at me with a look I've never seen before. Her brown eyes are dark and full of promise.

"Do you think you deserve it?" She moves, and I reach out to grab her, but she stops me with a gentle touch.

"Not yet, baby." She draws out the words slowly, her breath hot against my skin.

Fuck, this is how I go.

"Have you been patient?" Her innocent look betrays the wicked glint in her eyes.

"Yes." My hands are trembling with the need to touch her.

"You've been such a good boy, haven't you?" she coos, running her hands up my chest and over my shoulders.

Fuck yes, I have been. Now I need to bury myself inside her, but my baby is taking control, and it's so hot I might just come from listening to her.

"Yes, I've been a very good boy." I grit my teeth, every word a struggle as I fight to stay in control. "Please, let me touch you."

"Not yet." She throws me a smirk, a fucking smirk.

"Please, baby, I need to touch you now." It's been too long.

"Patient, Douxy." Her sweet voice goes straight to my groin.

Patient? I've been very patient, okay?

I watch as she takes her sweet time unzipping her dress, her fingers moving slowly, deliberately. Meanwhile, I'm so hard that my dick is ready to burst through my pants. My heart races, and I clench my fists to keep from grabbing her, the anticipation driving me wild.

She lets the dress fall to the floor, and she's standing before me, bare and lethal. She steps out of the dress and turns her back to me.

"You got a tattoo?"

"Yes." She throws a look over her shoulder. "Want a closer look?"

She turns around and walks towards me. I remain still, devouring her with my eyes. Once she's close enough, she sits on my lap, dripping through the thin fabric of my pants. The smell of her arousal sends me into overdrive. She bends down, showing me the tiny tattoo on the small of her back. It's a little mountain peak.

My hands automatically move to touch it, tracing the delicate lines with my fingertips. "When did you get this?"

"After I left the cabin," she whispers. "I wanted something to remind me of you."

Her words hit me like a wave, my chest tightening and my heart pounding. I pull her closer, my lips finding the spot just below the tattoo, kissing it softly. She shivers under my touch, and her breath hitches.

"Baby." Emotion floods my heart while I whisper against her skin. My desire for her sizzles up my spine, and the string of my restraint that was holding me together... snaps. The need to possess her mind, her body. Every inch of her consumes me. "I love you so much. Please remember that, because playtime is over, baby girl." The need to be buried inside her slick heat pounds into me. "I'm not about to make love to you right now. This will not be slow or sweet," I growl, a raw whisper of need.

Her eyes lock with mine, burning with the same desperate hunger. "I don't want *slow* or *sweet*. I want you," she says, breathless, a seductive plea that trembles with urgency and desire.

"Get up," I command, and she complies. The sight of her sends a jolt of desire through me.

I pull down my pants to free myself, already hard with anticipation, a bead of pre-cum glistening at the tip. The air between us thickens with tension and want.

"Are you ready, princess?"

She flashes me a devilish smile, glancing down at my hard cock. "I want to try something." Her face transforms into an innocent, almost timid expression. "I've never gone down on you before, or anyone else actually, and I want to." She moves closer and kneels in front of me, staring at it for a few seconds.

"You don't have to do it. I can teach you later."

"I want to do it now. You've been such a good boy. Good boys deserve rewards. You've earned it." She smiles. The anticipation is killing me as I hold my breath, waiting for her next move.

She leans down and presses a soft kiss at the base, her hand holding my thighs. The softness of her breath is enough to make a moan escape my throat. I feel like a teenager getting his first blow job.

She licks up the length to the head, her tongue soft and warm. Fuck, I'm going to embarrass myself and come like a teenager. She swirls her tongue around the head, lifting her eyes to look at me—my fucking queen. I've gotten a blow job before, but it never felt like this.

She gags when she takes me into her mouth and pushes my dick into the back of her throat. Her face turns red and her eyes water, but she doesn't stop. She continues taking me deeper, her lips sliding down my length as she tries to breathe through her nose. The gagging sounds she makes are so freaking sexy. "You're doing so good, sucking my dick like a good girl."

She's sucking me with so much passion and skill, even though she's never done this before.

She's a natural, and I now know what heaven is like.

"Jesus, baby," I moan, my eyes rolling back as I grip the edge of the bed. She smiles at me, a sweet, proud smile. She's enjoying this. Some women give me oral because they feel like they have to, but I can tell she loves it. She wants to please me. Her determination and enthusiasm push me to the edge.

She pulls back for a moment; the tip pops out of her mouth with a wet sound. She lets out a breathy moan, saliva trailing down her chin onto my shaft. This is the most beautiful sight I've ever seen.

I look down, and she's using one hand to rub herself, her hips moving in small circles. As much as I want to come into her mouth, I want to come inside her sweet pussy even more.

"Get up and turn around." She gets up, her legs shaking a little, and turns around, her back facing me.

Holding her waist and carefully lowering her onto me. Her hands find my knees for balance as she sinks further down. She winces at the tightness, and we both moan as she adjusts, taking me all in. Once I'm fully inside her, where I belong, I pause, overwhelmed by the sensation. A feeling I've missed profoundly. In this moment, we're one, heart, body, and soul.

She leans into me, her curls brushing against my face, filling the air with the scent I love so much. Her hair always smells amazing. I brush them to one side, kissing her neck.

My hands grip her hips as she grinds against me. Picking up the pace, my movements become faster. Her moans, mix with my grunts, fill the room. She leans forward, her back arching beautifully as she bounces her thick sexy ass on my cock, pulling a deep, primal sound from my throat.

My eyes lock on the small tattoo on her lower back. So sexy! "Fuck, baby, I missed this," I groan, giving her ass a firm slap that draws a small, breathless "ah" of pleasure from her. "I fucking missed that ass and this pussy."

She adjusts her arms, shifting her weight, and the sensation intensifies, sending shivers up my spine. "God, you feel amazing." Her plump ass meets me with each descent, creating a delicious friction that has my head tipping back in bliss. "Fuck," I growl as she expertly manipulates every nerve ending. "You're so perfect. Fucking me so good."

She throws a look over her shoulder that's both innocent and devilish that makes me lose control all over again.

Grabbing her waist, I push her to her feet while still buried deep inside her. I guide us to the bed before pulling out. "Ass up." She obliges, her thick, sexy ass rising in the air, teasing me with the sight of her pretty pussy glistening with arousal. I slide back into her from behind, harder and deeper than before, losing myself completely in her as everything around me blurs.

Her moans intensify as I pound into her relentlessly. My hands roam to her breasts, which fit perfectly in my palms. I gently squeeze, feeling the warmth and softness, eliciting another sweet moan from her.

"Oh, yes, Jake," she breaths out.

She's close, I can feel it. A fire at the pit of her stomach, ready to burst out. Her body trembles beneath me, muscles tensing. I'm at the edge too, my control slipping, and I'm not even sure how I've lasted this long.

"I'm going to come inside you, baby. Do you want that?" My breath's hot against her ear.

"Please, I want you to," she exhales.

"I love it when you use the magic word, princess," I growl as I drive into her again, surrendering completely to the waves of my climax. My vision blurs, everything becoming dark and hazy. If I were to die right now, it would be the most exquisite way to go.

She clenches around me, her body shivering with her own orgasm, and I thrust into her a few more times, releasing every drop.

Gently, I pull out and turn her around to face me as we catch our breath. Her cheeks are flushed, her eyes half-lidded with satisfaction.

"You okay, princess?" I brush sweaty curls from her face, my fingers lingering on her warm skin, staring at the woman who has become the center of my universe from the moment I laid eyes on her.

"More than okay," she says with a smile on her lips. "Can we do it again?"

"Danm baby! You missed my dick that much, huh?" I chuckle.

She giggles. "You have no idea."

I move to lie on top of her, our bodies pressing close as our legs naturally entangle together. My arms wrap around her back while hers wraps around my neck. "With you, I could do this for hours," I bite the top of her ear, "and hours." I kiss the side of her neck before bringing my face back to hers. "Right now, I'm going to make love to you. Slow and sweet."

Lifting my hip slightly, I reach for my already hardening length. I position myself at her entrance, pushing in slowly until I'm fully inside of her. We stay like that, just breathing each other in.

"I love you so much," her voice breaks a little as she tries to blink back tears.

"What's wrong?" I search her teary eyes.

"Nothing... I just don't want to lose you ever again."

"Moonie." I grab her hand from my neck, bringing it to my heart. "My heart beats only for you. I'm not going anywhere."

I lean down, kissing the tears from her cheeks, tasting the saltiness. Next, I kiss her nose, which always makes her giggle. "I love you, baby, and I can't live without you. I tried, and it was the worst few months of my life." I move inside her slowly as her breathing grows heavier. My need for her is more vital than the need for air itself.

"Now the only tears I want to see is from how freaking good I fuck you, okay?" I whisper before pressing my lip to hers, kissing her smile.

She was right, falling doesn't have to hurt. It's exhilarating, and I'm happy to keep falling for her.

Epilogue

One year later

I walk into the room, she's sitting cross-legged on the bed, wearing an oversized shirt that says *moody AF.* Papers scatters around her. A chuckle escapes me as I lean against the door frame, watching her. The sunlight from the window glows in her hair. She looks up and smiles, and that smile always makes me fall in love with her all over again.

We're back at the cabin for the summer, wanting to spend some time in the place where we fell in love with each other. She needed the break.

The second book of her series is out in two weeks and the pre-orders have been amazing so far. The first book was an instant NYT Best Seller.

"What's all this?" I move closer, taking a seat at the edge of the bed.

"They're letters." She picks one and stares at it. "My mom wrote them before she died, and they've been guiding me." She pauses as her eyes scan the words. "Thanks to her support and her pushing me even when she wasn't here. Now I'm a published author."

"And an instant New York Times Best Seller," I add. "I'm sure she is very proud of you."

She nods and smiles. "Thank you."

"Can I read some of them?" I look at the box with the letters. Some of them are still unopened.

"Sure." She nods. I sift through them and spot an old journal, its leather cover worn.

"What's this?" I hold it out to her.

Her eyes narrow. "Oh my God, I forgot all about it. Do you remember the small café I used to go to down the main road, Marie's Café. The lady there, Marie, gave it to me." She stares at it. "I told her about the waterfall. She told me a story about a couple with a secret waterfall and said this was her journal."

"You still think the waterfall is kinda magical?" It's something I never told anyone because I like that we were the only ones who knew about it. Our secret place.

"How else would you explain why no one talked about it?"

I raise an eyebrow. "Have you read it yet?"

She shakes her head, her fingers brushing the journal spine.

"Well, let's read it." Scooting closer, I sit beside her with her body pressed against my chest. I wrap my arms around her waist, resting my chin on her shoulder as she opens her journal.

I met a boy by a stream named Eadrick. She begins. Strange—that's my great-great-grandfather's name, but hey, lots of people named Eadrick.

I continue to listen to her. For some weird reason, everything is so familiar, like old memories and dreams. The same way I felt when I met Mia. There's a pause as her eyes linger on the name at the end of the first entry. The person signed her name.

Ifu.

She stares at it as if she's remembering something. Turning to me, I stare back at her, the woman I love with all my heart and soul.

"What is it?"

"I don't know how to explain it. It felt like I was there while reading it."

My eyes widen because that's exactly how I feel.

"You know what's even weirder? Eadrick is my great-great-grandfather's name."

"That is weird." She frowns.

We dive back into the journal.

Our friendship grew over the years in secret because the Black maid's daughter couldn't be friends with the young master. According to my Godmother, my father was from France, but I never met him. As we grew older, I felt nervous around him, and he stared at me when he thought I wasn't looking.

I glance at Mia, seeing a smile spread across her face as she continues reading.

Then he told me he loved me. It scared me because I loved him, and I knew they would never allow us to be together.

The more she reads, the more lost we get in the story. At one point, it feels like I'm not listening anymore. I'm transported into the story, and I'm Eadrick.

My Godmother caught me coming from one of my meetings with Eadrick. She was so mad that she called me by my full name, Ifunayla.

Mia stops and freezes before turning to look at me.

"My great great-grandmother's name was Ifunayla."

My eyes fly open. This is just getting weirder by the second.

We continue reading as she talks about the waterfall and the necklaces they made for each other with emerald rocks from the waterfall. Mia stands up, looking at her necklace as she paces back and forth in front of me.

"You said your grandfather gave you your necklace, and it was from your great-great-grandfather Eadrick, right?"

I nod.

"And my mom gave me mine, but she said it belonged to her great-grandmother, Ifunayla." She rubs the necklace. "Which means it's the same necklace." She covers her mouth. "Oh my God, our great-grandparents knew each other, and they were in love."

She places her hands on her hips, deep in thought. "The waterfall, the necklaces—did they bring us together?" She halts as she seems to add things up in her mind. "Does that mean we're them and they're us? I mean, it makes sense." She paces again, biting into her finger. "They way we felt when we first met as if we already knew each other, and we're the only ones that knew about the waterfall."

Honestly, I don't know what to think. It's a lot to process. All I know is that the moment I met Mia, I felt there was something special about her.

"I don't know, baby." I get off the bed and pull her towards me. She raises her beautiful eyes to meet mine. My heart tightens at the sight of her. "I don't know what all this means—the necklace, the waterfall. All I know is I love you so much. And yet something in me recognized you the moment we met."

I rub her cheeks, her skin soft and warm under my fingertips.

"I've never loved anyone before you. Maybe it wasn't because of my dad and Jessie. Maybe it's because I already loved you in another lifetime." I've put up walls around my heart for so long, but with her, they crumble naturally. "I didn't believe in love or soulmates before, but I believe you're mine."

People always think just because you're soulmates, you get to spend every lifetime together. I don't believe that. There's no guarantee we'll be together in the next life. Some people can spend lifetimes without their soulmates, always missing that part of themselves.

"I believe you're my soulmate, too." Her eyes are filled with unshed tears.

I've been carrying this box in my pocket for months. I bought it the day after she agreed to give us another chance. Because I knew I didn't want to spend my life with anyone else but *her.*

"Baby, I don't want to spend another second in this lifetime without calling you, my *wife*." I inhale deeply, forcing myself to stay calm. My heart feels like it's beating out of my chest. "I let you go once, but I don't plan on letting you go ever again."

Lowering myself onto one knee, I pull out the box, showing the ring. It's a custom diamond ring with a moonstone—her birthstone, and a symbol of how she is my moon. My hands tremble as I hold it up to her.

"Every day, I find a million tiny reasons to love you, and I want to spend the rest of my life falling in love with you. Will you spend this lifetime with me?"

Tears cascade down her cheeks. Her body shakes as she kneels in front of me. "Yes, I want to spend this lifetime with you."

I take out the ring and slide it onto her finger, my hands still shaking. She looks at the ring, then cups my face with her hands, her eyes full of tears and love.

I close my eyes, leaning into her touch. Her hands are warm and soft, touching the deepest corner of my heart. I press my forehead against hers, breathing her in. "Je t'aime tellement, mon amour." *I love you so much, my love.*

"Je t'aime plus." *I love you more.* She wraps her arms around my neck, pulling me close. We hold each other tightly, our hearts pounding in unison, and I don't know I'm crying until her thumbs wipe the tears from my face.

Just like a waterfall, our love is a force of nature. It's powerful, unstoppable, and beautiful. No matter the obstacles, it will find a way to flow, always.

Notes from the Author

To my family, thank you for always supporting me, even when I disappeared into my writing world. Your love and encouragement mean more to me than words can express.

To my author besties @Akitasparkauthor, thank you for reading my drafts more times than I can count and for being there through every late-night rambling. I couldn't have done this without your constant feedback, laughter, and unwavering support. You're the best.

To my early readers and betas, your feedback meant a lot to me and gave me the confidence to bring this story into the world.

About the author

Smardline writes stories about love, soulmates, forced proximity, and a dash of magic. Born in the Caribbean, she currently lives in the US and has a deep love for waterfalls. She is excited to bring diverse and inclusive narratives to the romance genre, contributing to the growing community of Black authors.

More from Author!

if you love At the Waterfall you can read book two of the Soulmate Effect series Beneath the Sunshine here![1]

You can also read the first four chapters for free here.[2]

---

1. https://a.co/d/fKaz6AU

2.   https://open.substack.com/pub/smardlines/p/ready-to-fall-for-the-new-french?r=3mzit5&utm_campaign=post&utm_medium=web